WARRIOR OF THE WAY

WARRIOR OF THE WAY

Nathan Chandler

iUniverse®

WARRIOR OF THE WAY

Copyright © 2005, 2014 Nathan Chandler.

iUniverse books may be ordered through booksellers or by contacting:

iUniverse
1663 Liberty Drive
Bloomington, IN 47403
www.iuniverse.com
1-800-Authors (1-800-288-4677)

ISBN: 978-1-4917-2084-4 (sc)
ISBN: 978-1-4917-2086-8 (hc)
ISBN: 978-1-4917-2085-1 (e)

Library of Congress Control Number: 2014901313

Print information available on the last page.

iUniverse rev. date: 02/26/2015

For my four brothers:Matthew, Aaron, Andrew, and Quinton, who gave me friendship and encouragement, and my parents, Charles and Diann, who gave me love and showed me the true meaning of faith.

For years a people remained divided and slaughtered people related to them all. For so many years they could not be brothers, as they had been before. No man could explain the hatred that dwelt within. And now in the midst of so much hatred, true darkness is beginning to fall.

—Emperor Zolaio Pasha Navakari III,
last emperor of the Hebari

PROLOGUE

Outskirts of Kadisha: Mulamar Encampment

A strong breeze swept through the flaps of his pavilion as King Tashdar of the Mulamar sat on his short wooden stool, looking down at the low table before him. The table bore large maps of the surrounding area, which the king had studied intently for the past few weeks. It had seemed a lifetime ago to the young king when he had sat at a table like the one he sat at now. It had been in the jeweled palace of the Halor king among the presence of the Makar king and his counsel that they had met to discuss plans that would eventually topple the Hebari Empire. Never would the young king have imagined the miserable state that he sat in now during that time long ago when he and the other kings broke their tribes away from the empire and mobilized their armies together to attack the Naua, Yashani, and Sashramans who still sought to hold the empire together.

Now, however, the king sat alone, having aged considerably since that day. The young, dark brown flesh upon his face had grown hard with stubble, his youthful-looking, clean-shaven chin being replaced by a long, black beard. His long, black braids were now more ragged looking, serving as a good illustration for how the king felt in his body. Gone was the youthful strength and confidence. It had given refuge to various aches and pains along with a cautious demeanor, all to which the king had not given a sign of acquiescence. But that was what happened over the course of civil war; a man got his own hands bloodied no matter who he was, for civil war was a curse that touched everyone.

Another sudden wind pushed through the pavilion. The king would have ignored it along with the others, but this one pushed him from his stool and overturned the table. When the king arose, the wind had subsided, but he discovered that he was not alone. To his surprise stood a man in a black cloak that covered every part of him except his face. The man's face was young and dark, but also hard looking with bright eyes that appeared in the darkness of the night like bouncing balls of flame. His appearance made the king most uncomfortable as he demanded, "What are you doing in my pavilion?"

The man stared at him with an unconcerned, blank expression as he moved forward, drawing back his hood to reveal long, black hair that fell to his shoulders.

"Do you not know it means death to enter the king's pavilion unannounced? Guards!"

"I would not do that if I were you," the man said, speaking in a low, depressing voice that made him seem unnatural. The king called once more, shouting as loudly as he could, but no one came. His hand fell quickly to the hilt of the sword he wore, but there was something about the man before him that caused him to not feel inclined to draw his weapon.

"What are you? An assassin? For if you are, believe me when I say that I shall not fall easily!"

"I am not here to murder you, Tashdar," the voice droned on monotonously. "But you will fall if I merely wish it upon you."

"What is it you want?" asked the king, changing to a more neutral tone.

"To tell you something."

"What? Speak, stranger!"

"I want you to march your army toward the city as soon as possible and attack, and while your men attack the city; I ask that about sixty of your best warriors ride toward the plains near Kanai to intercept some escaping Sashramans and their Nashaliaa guard."

The king's temper quickly rose. "I do not know who you are, but I do not answer to anyone but myself! You will pay for ordering me like I was your dog!"

"Be still!" said the man as he raised his hand.

Just when the king had unsheathed his sword and started toward the stranger, he felt an invisible force keeping him planted where he was, able to move only his mouth.

"You are quite a repulsive man, King Tashdar. Your men have had their hearing dulled, and you are here alone with me, a man who can kill you without laying a hand upon you. Your supposed powers do not seem to exist in this situation, Tashdar."

A look of horror spread over the king's face as he felt his ears suddenly fall off when the man raised his hand in a clawing motion. Tashdar did not know if the pain he felt was a result of his fear or the result of losing both ears. Though not connected to both sides of his head, no blood followed, and Tashdar still found himself able to hear.

"Now, will you send your men out as I have requested?"

Tashdar, though dazed, tried to remain indignant as he refused an answer. At first, the man stared at him, his red eyes being the only brightness coming from his black face. Screams of pain escaped from Tashdar as he felt something like a sword being lunged into his midsection. However, when he looked down at his stomach, there was nothing, though he still felt as if a sword lay in his stomach at that moment. Sweat poured down his face as he stood doubled over in great pain, barely able to breathe, feeling as if life was slipping away from him.

"Shall we try again?" The man moved closer, crouching to look straight into the king's face, which was now twisted in agony.

"Now, what are you going to do?" The man waited patiently as the king summoned enough strength to respond. The man's eyes seemed to have a hypnotizing effect upon the king, for he felt as if his only option was to do as the man commanded.

"I will break camp and march on the city and send sixty of my best warriors toward Kanai to intercept the Sashramans and their Nashaliaa guard."

"And what will you do once you are in the city?"

"Slau-slaughter everything inside."

"I do think that we understand each other, Tashdar. Do not fail me, for I shall not be merciful if you do."

Within an instant, the man had disappeared, and the king dropped in relief as the pain in his stomach began to go away. Without hesitating, the king called forth his officers and had the order sent out to break camp.

Kadisha: The Final Moments

In the throne room of the emperor was the Nashaliaa guard who decided to remain with the quiet emperor. The air was tense with noise while siege weapons of the Mulamar tribe battered the city. What had once been a beautiful arched ceiling with images of the past emperors and their glory now bore glaring holes and cracks, courtesy of the Mulamar rebels and their king. Many parts of the walls had been blown out, and smoldering rock now littered the palace floor.

For the last few days, they had remained in that room, growing used to the loud thunder of the Mulamar siege weapons that rung out. Though the enemy tribes had not breached the walls, it felt as if they were already there. Screams and cries rung out all day and night. The emperor could not see their faces, but he knew his people were being killed.

For the last five days, the emperor had sat upon his throne of white stone, pensive and mournful. Emperor Zolaio had been mournful ever since Ozhalos, captain of the guard, had returned with news that the emperor's five eldest sons had been killed on the plains of Kanai

He had always expected that his older sons would live to reunite his falling house, but such ideas had seemed like folly at that moment. On that day, he had nearly begun to open his veins with a dagger, inviting death to consume him; however, he stopped at the sight of his wife, Januai, walking toward him, holding his two most recent sons, Miori and Keradi. In a sudden moment, hope had returned to him as he held them.

The emperor's eyes now looked up to see Ozhalos entering what was left of the throne room. Ozhalos was of a pale complexion like most Nashaliaa. He wore long golden locks which rested on his shoulders as did most among his tribe. The captain's white skin was soaked in sweat and dried bits of blood, bearing the obvious signs of war. "Are you prepared to depart?"

"Yes, my lord," Ozhalos answered in a faltering voice.

Instinctively, the emperor descended from his throne and went toward Ozhalos.

"I guess this is it, old friend," said Emperor Zolaio.

"I wish you would entrust someone else with this task," said Ozhalos, unable to contain his emotion as tears streamed down his face.

"What's this now? We went all through that!" said the emperor.

"You gave me your sons to keep them safe, and I got them all killed. Let me stay here, and you go. Let me die defending the palace as my oath requires. There is no guarantee I will be able to get your youngest sons away from here," Ozhalos pleaded.

"It is my place to die here; this is my city. And do not say we can't do this. We got my daughters away from here," the emperor asserted.

"Your daughters were already far enough away in different provinces, and we got to them in time. The Mulamar are all around this city, and the Halor and Makar control the countryside. I can't guarantee your sons will live. I promised to keep your five eldest safe, and they are dead. I obviously cannot keep my word to you. Please let me die here with you, my lord. Let your youngest die here in their mother's arms. It is better than at the hands of the Mulamar," Ozhalos said.

"I will not stand for that! My line will endure!"

"My lord, there is no way!" Ozhalos pleaded.

"There is a way! You must try!" shouted the emperor.

"My lord, you could negotiate. Tashdar, their leader, he might spare your children."

"You and I both know that Tashdar has sworn an oath to wipe my legacy from the face of this earth, starting with my wives and ending with my children. I cannot give him what he wants. You must try!"

"I will try."

In the hand of his friend, the emperor placed a gold amulet with a silver chain, which bore a red stone.

"Now go, Ozhalos. Things must end between us for now but we shall see each other again. If not in this life, then in the next."

The two men quickly locked into a brotherly embrace that neither wished to break.

"Travel well, Ozhalos!" said the emperor, looking into the captain's mournful blue eyes for the last time. Although he did not know what the future held, the emperor knew that he had said goodbye to his friend for the last time.

"Travel well, majesty!" said Ozhalos

Ozhalos stepped over the rubble and took his leave from the throne room, leaving the emperor solely in the company of his Nashaliaa guard. The emperor settled back into his once magnificent throne, now battered by rubble and ash. His mind went back to the holy city of Muzha where the oracle had made her final prophecy before the Halor razed the city. He remembered the priests gathered together in the Great Sanctuary about a young woman of a dark brown hue and green globes of light which were her eyes. They stood in silence as she had said these words, *"The House of Navakari shall not fall until the tenth of a dead line shall come. In his heart, he shall bear anger and know much sorrow. But when the time comes, he shall be tempered by the power of compassion. Great wars and great struggles shall come, but those who follow in the shadow of the righteous shall endure."* Though he had trusted the oracle many times as emperor, on the eve of his death and the certainty of his family's demise, her words rang hollow. Zolaio withdrew from his memories and looked to his guardsmen.

His Nashaliaa guard stood at the ready. The explosions were getting louder. Tashdar and his allies were close. Suddenly a loud boom invaded their hearing when another section of the ceiling split apart and crashed to the ground before the emperor.

The Hebari emperor chuckled to himself as his guardsmen looked on in concern. He had never realized just how finite things like a building were. The emperor let out a loud laugh as he remembered all the times his father admonished him for tracking dirt onto the once pristine marble floor. Nothing lasts forever.

Emperor Zolaio looked to the Nashaliaa guardsmen, most were young, very strong, and agile men, pale with gold and white hair like Ozhalos. It would be in their company that the last Hebari emperor would die. Zolaio did not fret, he had been in their company since he was a child and he trusted them as much and often times more than even his Hebari warriors.

Just then the loud booms from the enemy war machines had stopped. Leikos, the second in command looked over to the emperor.

"Majesty. I think this is it." he said more as a common reminder.

They could hear loud cries of men fighting advancing foes. Tashdar was almost close.

"Sounds like the guests are almost here." said Rehal, one of the guardsmen.

Zolaio stepped down from his throne and took off his crown. At first he thought about throwing it away, instead he placed it in the seat of his fathers. There the crown would rest one last time. The emperor released his blade from its sheath as he joined Leikos and the rest of the Nashaliaa who began to form up.

"What say you majesty? Do we negotiate?" said Leikos.

"Do Nashaliaa negotiate?" asked the emperor.

"We don't even have a word for it in our language, majesty."

"I guess that settles it." said Zolaio.

The sounds of war drew closer to the throne room. Destiny was at hand and Zolaio knew there would be no escape. Zolaio lifted his hand to wipe the sweat from his bronze face. He would not show signs of nervousness.

"Any regrets Leikos?" asked the Emperor.

"I was going take your gold and your daughter and set up my own kingdom. Shame that's not going to happen."

The two men looked at each other and laughed.

"The dreams we make . . . The dreams we make." muttered the emperor to himself.

Just then the wall exploded open and dozens of black bodies, which were the Mulamar and Halor warriors flooded into the throne room. Soon Zolaio caught sight of Tashdar's smiling face as he urged his men forward. Without hesitating the Nashaliaa and their Hebari emperor surged forward, blades bare to meet their foes.

Ozhalos managed to get through the enemy lines and deliver the two boys to Jadia and her husband, Daqyada, both former servants to the imperial palace. For the sake of their family, the memory of the imperial house would have to remain in the ruins of the palace among the fallen emperor and his men.

CHAPTER 1

This Life

Thirty Years Later
Southern Sashra: Farmland along the Aliso River

Though it was midafternoon, a steady breeze and storm clouds approaching from the south provided the coolness Miori Nuvahli had come to desire with planting season. After years of being a conscript in the wars against the northern tribes and seeing much of pain and suffering, Miori finally returned to the land he knew best, hoping to find some semblance of peace. For southern Sashra, peace had been difficult to achieve after the Great War.

After the emperor's death, all of the tribes split the empire into individual states for each tribe. Tribal chieftains became kings, and people who lived in the region that had once housed the imperial palace, Sashra, were made to suffer greatly. Miori remembered this time very well from when he was a child. He remembered Daqyada, his father, fighting off roving bands of Halor and Mulamar marauders from south of the border, while his mother, Jadia, hid them in the trees nearby.

Finally, all of the Sashraman clans came together and elected a leader to regain as much of the imperial lands as possible and keep the region safe from attack. They had chosen Saiyeri Junakten, a prominent general who had fought in the old imperial army. And Saiyeri did as they asked. He drove out the Halor and Mulamar bands and went north and pushed back the northern tribes before they attempted an invasion.

And so on the New Year, the clans gathered at Kadisha and tried to crown him emperor. However, Saiyeri, being a most humble man, refused. He felt unworthy of the title and worried that it would further complicate relationships with the other tribes. Nevertheless, the clans refused to accept his answer and continued to press him to accept. At long last, Saiyeri returned to them and said he would accept a title, but it would not be emperor. They eventually settled on an old title for former Sashraman chieftains, *malik*, which soon came to mean king.

Sashra had flourished under Malik Saiyeri, but those days had ended with his death ten years ago and the ascension of his son, Malik Nkwana. Under Malik Nkwana, taxes were high, and farmland could be seized without warning, both in order to pay for the lavishness of his palace and the foolishness of his foreign endeavors. There had been war after war with the Halor in the south. Thirty thousand warriors had been lost in the push to retake Ashul, losses the malik's father would have never accepted.

And it was under the malik that Miori had been sent north to fight the northern tribes in pointless engagements that endangered Sashra more than protected it. Northern tribes, most of them Baku, would launch devastating raids across the border. In certain pockets of Sashra, there were smaller bands of them roving the countryside and destroying villages and murdering the people. Still, the malik did nothing. To acknowledge them would be to prove his weakness and incompetence.

Still, Miori had survived the wars and finished his enlistment last year, and the only thing that occupied his mind was his family, especially his two youngest sons and his wife. Miori looked up toward his house in the west. In the distance, he could see his sons Pasha and Zailo playing some sort of game with one of the goats. His two eldest sons, Asdalaya and Malakim, had already grown into men and married. Though they had their own land, they still came by to help him with the planting and harvesting.

After a couple of more hours, Miori took a break. It was still cool outside yet his two eldest had not arrived to help. It had been an easy job when all of his boys were at home, but for one man, his wife, and two small boys, things tended to progress more slowly.

Inside the house, he found his wife, Larea, over the fire mount, fixing a hot stew made with lentils from the last harvest and rodent meat his sons had caught. After years in the army and seeing the glories of Kadisha where all warriors swore an oath to the malik, his quaint house seemed small in comparison.

It was a simple, white stone house with an open area where his family ate and his children played, and there were two smaller rooms, one where his children slept, and the other for him and his wife. The walls were smooth and bare, the floor was mostly rock and dirt, and there were no beautiful images or writings. Nevertheless, it had been all Miori needed upon his return.

"You got up before I could make you anything," said Larea, his wife, smiling yet scolding him, as was her way. Miori stopped for a moment to gaze upon her. In spite of the life they led, her dark brown complexion and bright smile never faded, and the globes of green light that were her eyes always welcomed him with love. In spite of the long months and years he had been away, she had never complained and never thought of leaving. Women like her were rare, and when Miori returned for good, he swore an oath to make it all up to her and be the husband she deserved.

"What?" she asked, noticing he was staring at her.

Saying nothing, he reached out to her and kissed her with all the passion he could muster.

"You and our children . . . you mean everything to me," he said as he held her.

"As you do to us," she said, kissing his beard, which she liked to do.

"Here," Larea said, handing him a bowl of stew.

"Thank you. Did Asdalaya and Malakim say when they would get here?" Miori asked as he sat on a cushion beside the low table where they ate.

"They said sometime this afternoon," Larea answered.

"I wanted to get it all done before the rains came," said Miori.

"You do know they are married and have children of their own?" Larea asked while carrying two more bowls to the table.

"Yes, I know. It's just strange not having them here every day," said Miori.

"You have to let go sometime. They say it's harder for us women, but sometimes I think it's really harder for you men," said Larea.

"I won't lie. It can be," Miori replied.

"You'll always have me. That has to count for something," Larea said, placing her hand on Miori's shoulder.

"You know it does," said Miori, kissing her hand.

"And these two . . . Pasha, Zailo!" Larea called out to their two youngest.

Within moments, quickly moving feet rushed through the doorway. Miori looked over to see his two youngest sons, Pasha and Zailo. They had been conceived at a late age and had been difficult for Larea to bear. Nevertheless, as Miori looked at Zailo, who was thirteen, and Pasha, who was seven, he knew the trouble had been worth it.

Zailo was very dark like his father, with light brown eyes and a small but muscular frame and curly hair. As for Pasha, his complexion was black like his father, but he bore a skinny frame and had green eyes like his mother. His hair was long and thick like hers, and his face constantly bore a joyful expression, as did his mother's.

"Come now and eat. The food is ready," Larea said, directing them to their bowls on the table.

The boys tore ravenously into the stew meat and drank the broth like it was water.

"Slowly now. Slowly," Larea cautioned.

Larea took a place beside Miori and joined them.

"Father?" said Zailo.

"Yes, Zailo."

"Why don't we go fishing like we used to?" asked Zailo.

"I love going to the river," said Pasha excitedly.

Miori smiled.

"Like I told you, son, around here a man has to farm as well as fish in order to feed his family. We'll go again soon once planting is over."

"Will you need me to help again this year?" asked Zailo.

"Possibly. Asdalaya and Malakim will be coming to help, but I'm going to start needing you boys to step up," said Miori.

"Can I help?" Pasha asked.

"Maybe next year, Pasha. Right now I need you to keep helping your mother with the goats."

"That reminds me. It will be your birthday soon, Pasha. What shall we get you?" said Larea.

"How about letting us build a raft so we can race the other boys down the river," Zailo said, putting his arm around Pasha, smiling.

"That would be great!" said Pasha.

"I think not," said Miori.

There was a knock at the door, and Miori's two eldest sons, Asdalaya and Malakim, entered.

"Asdalaya, Malakim!" Pasha and Zailo cried out as they ran into their older brothers' arms.

"Daiyu, look at you two. You seem bigger each time I see you," said Asdalaya, embracing Pasha.

"What have you two been doing?" Malakim asked Zailo.

"Mainly looking after goats. Father says I can help him this year with the planting again."

"Good. You can help us when we're out there."

"Mother, Father," said Asdalaya, embracing his mother.

"How are things?" Larea asked her oldest.

"Well, you know, always work. Amaria has her hands full with the children and now another on the way . . . I don't know. She seems more nervous than before," Asdalaya responded.

"I'll have to go see her and do what I can to help," said Larea.

"With two boys and a husband, she hardly has any women to talk to. I think she'd really like that," said Asdalaya.

"Well, let's go," said Miori, standing up and reaching for his tools.

"Oh, Father is already ready," Asdalaya said smiling.

"Is that midday meal you're eating there?" inquired Malakim, looking back and forth between his impatient father and the alluring food.

"Hurry up and grab a bowl and eat it on the way. The rains will be here soon. Zailo, you and Pasha will have to help your mother herd the goats back into their pens," said Miori, stepping out.

Pasha ran, excitedly whooping and hollering along with Zailo while they chased down grazing goats and herded them back toward their pens. After turning the herd in the right direction, Pasha joined his mother, who led them from the front while Zailo stayed in the rear.

"I think they know my voice now!" said Pasha, leaping to his mother's side.

"Well, they should by now, considering all the times you and Zailo have chased them," Larea replied.

"Mother, why doesn't Father let me help in the fields? I know other boys my age who do," said Pasha.

"Well, your father is different, my love. It's very hard to do, and you have to be very strong," said Larea.

Pasha's face dropped.

"Don't worry about it, my love. He'll ask you eventually. Besides, you're a great help to me." Larea tried to sound reassuring, but she knew by his face he longed to be with his father and his older brothers.

"Your father will be going to the city soon to sell some of the goat's milk. I'm sure you could be a great help to him," said Larea.

"Do you think he'll let me?" Pasha asked, unable to hide his rising excitement.

"If I ask him, he will. He's even said he might go by the stables to look at some horses. You'd like that, wouldn't you, Pasha?"

Pasha vigorously nodded his assent.

Larea turned to check on Zailo. Her eyes locked onto twelve riders in the distance. At first she thought they might be Sashraman, but the closer they came, she realized they were not Sashramans. Looking around at her children and the approaching riders, Larea could feel something bad was about to happen.

"Zailo, run to get your father!" she shouted.

"Mother, what is going on?" asked Zailo, coming closer.

"Go get your father now! Don't argue. Hurry!"

Saying nothing, Zailo ran toward the fields where Miori and his brothers were working.

"Miori! Miori!" Larea shouted, but she knew he couldn't hear her.

"Mother, what is going on?" Pasha asked, tugging her dress.

"We've got to go, Pasha," she said.

The riders had sped up and were riding at full speed toward them. Though they were still far, Larea soon began to distinguish that they were Baku. In their hands were massive spears adorned with animal furs and large shields made of iron.

"Run, Pasha! Get to the house!" Larea shouted. They began running together as the riders got closer.

"Mother, I'm scared. What's happening?" Pasha cried.

Saying nothing, Larea took him in her arms and continued sprinting for the house. The sound of their hooves pounded in her ears as she ran. Going down a large hill, she was getting closer to the house, but the noises from the horses only grew louder. She knew they were close. The goats ran amok in all directions. Larea turned around and saw the riders in their clearest form.

On their bodies the Baku riders wore thick triple-stranded leather armor with iron strips, and on their pale brown faces, a yearning for blood. Along with massive spears, they bore bows as well. Larea knew they couldn't outrun them together. They would be on them soon if she did not act.

She stopped and put Pasha down.

"Listen, my love, I need you to keep running. Run as fast as you can to the house."

"What about you, Mother? What about you?"

"I'll be there soon, my love," she said, kissing him repeatedly.

"I'm scared, Mother. I don't want to go alone. I don't want to!" Pasha wailed uncontrollably.

"Listen to me. I need you to go now, Pasha. Please do that for me. Now go!" she said, breaking from his embrace.

"Mother!" Pasha wailed.

"Go!" Larea shouted, pushing him from her. Pasha fell to the ground sobbing.

In the distance, she could see Miori and her sons running toward them, armed with swords and a bow. Nevertheless, the men of the north had almost reached them.

"Run! Go to your father!" she said.

"Mother!" Pasha cried.

"I love you, Pasha." Saying no more, Larea took her staff and ran toward the riders.

"Pasha!" Zailo called.

Pasha looked up to see his father and his brothers coming for him.

"Father!" he cried, running toward them.

But his father was not calling out for him.

"Larea! Larea!" shouted Miori.

Pasha looked back for his mother. In the distance, he could see her beating back the riders with her stick. His mother fought bravely. She had knocked two of the riders from their mounts, stopping the group's advance. Soon the group converged on her. Pasha's breaths stopped coming, and his insides turned as he saw his mother fall under a slashing wave of swords.

"No!" shouted Miori.

"Mother! Mother!" Pasha cried.

His mother's lifeless body slumped to the ground, and the riders continued toward them.

"Mother!" Pasha fell to the ground in sobs.

His father and brothers soon reached him.

"Pasha, come on," said Pasha's brother Asdalaya as he took him in his arms.

"Father! Father!" Pasha desperately wanted his father to hold him. Instead, Miori continued sprinting toward the attackers, sword ready, Malakim behind him.

"Zailo. Get Pasha somewhere safe. Hide along the river until we return."

"Asdalaya, please," said Zailo fearfully.

"Please don't leave me, Asdalaya!" Pasha buried his head into his older brother's chest.

"Here. Take him!" Asdalaya said, loosening his grip on Pasha and pushing him toward Zailo.

"Asdalaya, please!" Pasha screamed.

"You're in charge now, Zailo. Get him somewhere safe! Do as I say!" Saying no more, Asdalaya took off after his father and Malakim.

Soon the air was filled with the noise of clanging metal and the cries of death.

"Come on, Pasha, let's go!" said Zailo.

The brothers sprinted as fast as they could toward the river in the east. Neither looked back while their father and brothers fought the enemy. In what felt like hours, they finally came within sight of the river. Zailo led Pasha down a sloping bank into the shallow water.

When their feet hit the rushing water, Zailo stopped. Fear coursed through his body. He didn't know what to do. Soon his ears caught the sound of approaching hooves; the riders were still coming.

"What do we do, Zailo?" asked Pasha, unable to contain his anxiety.

"I don't know," said Zailo.

"Zailo," Pasha pleaded.

"I don't know!" he shouted. "Daiyu, please show me a way," he begged, looking toward the skies.

The riders were getting closer. Zailo knew they didn't have much time. Just then, Zailo noticed the tree hanging from the tip of the high banks on the river's other side.

"Come on!"

Within moments, they had reached the other side and climbed up the banks to reach the tree. The inside of it was hollow, and the boys went inside. Zailo knew that it would not be enough to protect them. The dirt beneath them was soft and parted easily. Without hesitating, Zailo began to dig.

"Come on! Dig!" he shouted to Pasha. Pasha got down to help.

It was not long before they had made a good sized hole. But at that moment, they could hear the riders and their horses splashing in the river. They were close.

"Get in." Zailo took a piece of a hollowed out branch and gave it to Pasha. "Put this in your mouth." Doing as his brother said, Pasha got into the hole.

Pasha nearly screamed when Zailo began to cover him back up. Zailo quickly placed a hand on his mouth.

"Listen to me, Pasha!" he said, whispering. "They're close. This is the only way. I'll hide you here and lead them off and come back for you."

"Please, Zailo, don't leave me," Pasha cried.

"Asdalaya told me to keep you safe, and that is what I'm going to do. I promise I won't be gone long. Now get in!"

"I'm scared, Zailo," Pasha pleaded.

"I know, Pasha. I know. I'm right here with you, and I'm going to come back for you, and we're going to go to Uncle Keradi for help. I promise."

"Zailo, please, I'm so scared," Pasha whimpered.

"Pasha, please, I'll be back. Whatever you do, don't move. Don't make any noise."

Eventually, Zailo managed to get Pasha back into the hole. Moving quickly, he covered him up with dirt and put branches and leaves on top. Using the hollowed-out stick to breathe, Pasha did as his brother said and didn't move, even as Zailo left. Little did he know that his brother would soon break his promise.

Pasha remained in the hole for two days before coming out; his uncle Keradi found him and took him back to his house. It was there Pasha found his father badly wounded and barely clinging to life. He hoped against hope that his mother and three brothers were all right, but his hopes were crushed when his uncle took him to the back of his home where four bodies were being prepared for burial.

CHAPTER 2

Deeds

Fourteen Years Later
Oslaqdom: Palace of the Baku King

In the palace of King Vladshak, heavily armored Baku swordsmen stood rigidly at their posts in the royal courtyard. Torchlights flickered about from the nearby gates and various places within the courtyard itself that led to the Great Hall.

Storm clouds were gathering overhead, but the warriors remained still. There were at least twenty of them keeping watch from all sides of the courtyard while ten kept watch in the towers overhead. In spite of their silence, the Baku warriors grew ever more restless. Their silver armor and long shield were flexible and useful in combat, but the armor weighed them down uncomfortably as they stood still.

Huwran, who was the head Tashik officer, longed for the dawn to come, which was when they would be relieved. The one thing a Baku warrior hated most was standing still. Nevertheless, he was glad to be with his men after losing so many fighting the Sashramans at the border; he did not wish to lose any more.

He heard the sound of chains and gears moving to open the courtyard gate. No one was allowed to come through the gate at night. Something felt wrong.

"Stand ready!" Huwran ordered.

In moments, they came together in a line with their swords drawn. Tekan and Elos were their bowmen; both stood ready with their bows carefully aimed at the gates.

"State the watchword and live! Do it not, you die!" Huwran shouted.

"Shakaina, brother, Shakaina. Huwran, it's me, Arzim."

"Come forward!" Huwran ordered.

A warrior in thick armored plates bearing the jeweled sword of an officer came forward. Huwran quickly recognized Arzim, whose long, wavy, black locks and pale features were not covered with a helmet.

"Hold," ordered Huwran as he went toward Arzim.

"Are you crazy, Arzim? In the name of the gods, what are you doing? You know the gates are to remain closed, and no one is to pass. I should kill you where you stand! Do you know how much trouble I can get into for this? Who let you in?" Huwran demanded angrily.

"Calm down, Huwran. You know I wouldn't come through here if it were not important. I have important news for the king. It cannot wait," said Arzim.

"No one sees the king after dark, Arzim. You know this!" Huwran shouted.

"Brother, this cannot wait. I have news from General Wanar at the southern border."

"You have to go through Hekar, then through Shanak, and then through me if you have such news," said Huwran, becoming more wary of Arzim's story.

"I cannot follow normal procedure. This news is for the king's ear alone. And you will be the one who suffers if you delay me any longer."

Huwran took note of Arzim's right hand; it was twitching toward something on his leg and away from his sword.

"You know procedure. Why are you so eager to see the king? I don't believe you have any such message. Stand ready," Huwran said quickly when Arzim's hand took hold of something.

Suddenly two daggers flew from Arzim's right hand into two of Huwran's men. Before Huwran could react, all of the torches were snuffed out, and Arzim disappeared into the shadows.

"Fan out! Fan out!" Huwran shouted, but his words were cut off as invisible arrows whistled through the night. He knew his orders were not heard as he listened to steel tips tearing into his men's flesh.

Huwran raised his shield above his head and retreated toward the palace doors.

"To arms! To arms! The king is in danger!"

His cries were immediately silenced when a quickly moving spear swept his feet from under him. Huwran recovered quickly and lifted his shield while several warriors attacked him. He rolled back and came up swinging his sword wildly. However, his eyes saw nothing, and his blade caught nothing.

"Come out, you cowards! Where are you, Arzim, you coward!" Huwran shouted.

In the end, he said no more when a metal bolt tore into his throat. He fell to his knees as he felt his life leaving him. Just then, his eyes caught sight of Arzim standing before him.

"First rule of war, brother: never give up your position," said Arzim coldly.

"Trai-i-tt," Huwran struggled to say, with blood dribbling from his neck.

"What is that, brother? What are you trying to say?" asked Arzim, bringing his ear closer in mockery.

"Trai-tor," Huwran finally managed to get out.

"Traitor!" Arzim said, laughing.

Without warning, he slashed his blade into Huwran's neck. The head fell off with ease.

"There's no such thing, brother," he said, wiping his blade.

Soon, General Ivadar and his men joined with Arzim, and together they stormed the palace. Within an hour, all of the guards were dead, and they gathered in the throne room with the king as prisoner.

Inside, the throne room was dark, with the only occupants being the king and his family along with their captors.

"Is he coming?" Arzim asked the general.

"He'll be here," the general answered.

"A detachment from the palace usually reports to the garrison commander by now," Arzim said anxiously.

"Have patience, brother," the general cautioned.

"Arzim! Ivadar!" cried the bound king while his family wept behind him. "Why are you doing this? You're better than this! I am your king!"

Arzim and Ivadar ignored him, but the king persisted.

"Release me! Tell me what you want, and I'll make it so!" the king begged.

Ivadar never liked the king. He was nothing of the warrior his father had been. His father would have never begged for his life, and he would have never fallen for such a trap. Ivadar doubted whether there was anything left of the old king in his son.

"You know what you'll be if you kill me? Traitors! Ivadar, you served my father! Why?" the king continued to shout.

"I served a true warrior and great king. You are just a whimpering child. You are nothing to me!" said the general in a cold manner.

"Please let him go! Please!" pleaded the king's wife.

One of the warriors guarding her struck her with his iron-studded glove. The queen fell back silent, with blood trickling from her head.

"Do not strike her! Do not touch her, you son of a whore! I'll kill you! I swear I'll kill you all!" the king shouted as his skin turned blood red.

Arzim seized the king and cuffed him across his face before placing his dagger's cold blade against the king's neck.

"You were born with the body of a man. The least you could do is die like one!" said Arzim.

"That is enough!" shouted a thunderous voice that filled every corner of the chamber.

A tall man with red eyes and a black complexion entered the room, followed by ten warriors in black robes with their faces covered. He proceeded down the path to the king's throne and stopped before the Baku king.

"You!" King Vladshak said, shaking with anger. "I took you into my home and treated you as a brother, gave you land, women, and prominence! Then you curse me and curse my family! And now you have poisoned my men against me!"

"There is no poison they do not make themselves," said the red-eyed man.

"Why are you doing this? What do you want?" demanded the king.

"What do I want? What I want, Highness, is continuity. You've served your purpose. Now it's time to die!"

A hidden dagger plunged into King Vladshak's stomach, and the king felt nothing but punishing agony as his life left him.

"Your story has ended. Mine shall endure!" Saying no more, the warrior sat down upon the Baku king's throne while the former king collapsed and began to bleed out.

The warriors in black went to the king's family; undeterred by their screams, the warriors put a permanent end to King Vladshak's line.

"You did well," said the red-eyed warrior to Ivadar.

The general nodded.

"And you as well," he said to Arzim.

"Those who stand beside me will gain more than wealth and power. They will gain power over their destinies. That king over there was weak. He would have had peace with your enemies, the southern tribes. But I say true peace only comes through absolute dominance," said the red-eyed warrior.

"Things that I believe as well. We will make a great future here in the north and in many other countries," said General Ivadar.

"There is no future with me that will not be great," said the red-eyed warrior. "And you," he said to one of the warriors in black.

The face of a lovely honey colored woman was revealed as her hood was drawn back.

"Helomar of the south, you shall be the tip of my spear, which I shall plunge into every corner of this earth."

She bowed reverently as a crooked smile filled her face.

CHAPTER 3

Away from Home

Year 1150, Six Years Later
Plains of Northern Sashra

Storm clouds quickly gathered over the plains of northern Sashra, delivering a fertile torrent of rainwater for the ground below. Still, nothing could save the black earth of the Sashraman plains, its long, green grass dead, and the ground blackened by the fires of war. Before, lush green grass and fertile earth had supplied farmers with abounding crops and thatching for the roofs of their huts where they and their families lived a simple way of life. Rolling hills, fertile land, and an open sky had made the plains country a good place to raise crops and a family. All of that changed when the wars came.

Instead of crops and families, there were only the fifty Sashraman warriors trekking through the expanse. Pasha was reminded of the changed reality each moment his mount struggled for balance as the blackened earth turned to mud and slick.

The wars with the Baku and the other northern tribes had started twenty years prior, after a one hundred year lull, and since then, things had only grown worse. When the Hebari Empire splintered into different tribes and kingdoms fifty years ago, the northern tribes had taken it as a sign of weakness. After thirty years, they decided the time was right to attack. And it was for that reason Pasha found himself there twenty years later.

He had grown from a young boy to a man, being both tall and very dark, with the same sharp features as his father. On his face he wore a slight beard that helped to hide a long battle scar. Nevertheless, his eyes were the same green globes of light he had inherited from his mother.

Pasha remembered how she had wanted him to be a learned man. She labored for hours, teaching him to read and write, trying in earnest to prepare him for study under a scribe. However, the death of his mother had brought on a different kind of understanding. It meant nothing to be learned if you were not strong.

Pasha's father had barely survived the massacre, but instead of raising him properly, for much of his childhood, Miori immersed himself in war and drink. Miori did not succeed in keeping his final and only son away from the warrior's life.

Ever since joining the army at sixteen, Pasha had served in the western campaigns under Malik Juktan, son of Malik Nkwana. A friendship grew between Pasha and the young malik, so much so that the malik had made him captain of the guard in Kadisha. Though he served honorably, Pasha did not care for splendid cities, fine clothes, and rich food. He was a warrior, and war was his place.

Raindrops pounded his armor relentlessly while he led his men on patrol. His mount, Daimon, stepped slowly but surely through the mud and slick, blackening his marvelous white legs.

Pasha looked over to Abayomi, who rode beside him. Abayomi was very black, with a permanent scowl etched over his dark face. The two of them had joined the army at the same time and served in many campaigns together. After being released from service in the malik's guard, Pasha specifically requested for Abayomi to accompany him to his new post in the north.

The young commander did not know if his friend approved of being summoned to the northern plains to patrol and chase after Baku marauders. Although only two years older, Abayomi possessed wisdom seldom found in younger men, which was something Pasha needed.

Pasha, Abayomi, and his third officer, Leyos, rode at the head of fifty men. Each day, they did nothing but patrol until they came within range of the Sashraman garrison along the northern pass. Upon arriving, they would turn back and head southwest where they would circle back toward their garrison in the east, just outside the city of Kirara.

They did this ritual in anticipation of a coming strike by the north. Although the north had not attacked in eight years, all Sashramans knew it was not due to a sudden love of peace.

Pasha looked over to Leyos, who had taken off his helmet to let the rain run through his long, wavy brown locks. Although, most Sashramans tended to be brown complexioned to very black, Leyos bore a very light complexion and skin that reddened during heat of battle and turned pale during the cold. His mother had been a Lakina woman while his father had been a Nashaliaa warrior who served in the imperial army.

Ever since Pasha had met the young warrior, he had found him an easygoing spirit saturated in mirth, always sparing with recklessness and never lacking in compassion. At times, Pasha had wished for him to be more solemn and disciplined. Nevertheless, Pasha had seen his skill in a fight and the power of his personable nature to ease anxiety and inspire confidence where there was only fear.

"We're going to get a good soaking today," said Abayomi, noting the rain.

"It'll be good for your old tired bones," said Pasha as he moved ahead of him, watching the horizon.

Rain and dark clouds drastically reduced visibility. They would have to be even more vigilant.

"Tired? Yes. Old? No. Especially considering my bones are about as old as yours," Abayomi said.

"Really? Sometimes you make me forget," Pasha replied in the sarcastic manner his friend had become used to.

"What's rain like where you're from, sir?" Leyos asked Pasha.

"Harder. A lot harder," Pasha replied, still searching the dark horizon.

"In Alansu, it tends to be like this . . . except salty," Leyos said in the matter of fact way he liked to speak, which always elicited bewildered looks.

"What? In the west, you spend time tasting the rain?" Abayomi said in an unbelieving manner.

"Alansu Province is near the sea. Besides, it's just something you notice, you know," Leyos answered.

"No, I don't know," said Abayomi.

Pasha suddenly stopped. The rain had nearly hidden it, but in the east he could see a grouping of large stones that had been disturbed in order to make an unmistakable barrier for an encampment.

"What do you see?" Abayomi said in a low voice.

"In the east," Pasha said, nodding his head toward the distant rocks.

The Sashramans made their way toward the encampment, finding it deserted. Besides the rocks, there was very little evidence that it had been a campsite. Azia, Pasha's rank master, dismounted to examine the ground.

Azia quickly found slight depressions where the ground had been disturbed. Pasha moved forward when he saw Azia stoop down to retrieve something from the earth.

"At least ten men slept here. Perhaps more," said Azia.

"What are those?" asked Pasha, pointing to Azia's hand.

"Threads, more than likely fur threads from a blanket. It's amazing the rain hasn't washed them away. The nights get real cold here." Suddenly Azia dropped the threads and rushed further east, following the ground. Pasha followed him.

The commander soon saw what had seized his rank master's attention, very slight marks cut into the ground heading in an easterly direction.

"They're tracks, aren't they?" asked Pasha.

"Yes. Looks like they tried to cover them up and let the rain do the rest. They're hard to see if you're not looking for them, but they're there. These people don't want to be found," Azia concluded, looking back at Pasha.

"What do you think?" Pasha asked Abayomi.

"It can't be sheepherders. There's no grass for them to feed their stock," Abayomi answered.

"Leyos?" said Pasha to his other officer.

"It was obviously a large group. Only a large group up to no good would bother hiding their trail up here," Leyos replied.

"Agreed. Azia."

"Sir," said Pasha's rank master.

"You take the lead," Pasha ordered.

"Yes, sir."

Rain and a growing wind struck hard against a lone Sashraman caravan as it made its way across the plains. Thirty Sashraman warriors rode in a box formation around one lone carriage flying the standards of the malik. At the front sat one of the malik's servants, driving the horses that were pulling the carriage. Behind him were two of the malik's guardsmen. All three wore scarves about their faces to protect against the biting wind and hard rain.

Inside the sole compartment, Malik Juktan was immersed in correspondence from the *alcaldes* of various cities. Many were complaints, reports on trading disputes, and tax duties gathered.

The malik's father, Malik Nkwana, had taken a Lakina woman as his wife, Juktan's mother. Instead of a black complexion like that of his wife, Calisha, Malik Juktan bore a bronze complexion with remarkably smooth features, which were typical of Lakina people. Still, he wore the same warrior locks as did most of his men.

Across from him sat his captain of the guard, Rakimo. Rakimo was very black and deceptively strong, which his skinny frame hid well. Juktan had been reluctant to find another captain after Commander Nuvahli had left his charge for a post in the north. Nevertheless, Rakimo had fit in well, took charge, and proved an effective leader to his guardsmen.

The malik and his men were returning from Kirara, where he had honored an aging general who had fought alongside his grandfather, Malik Saiyeri.

In the aftermath of the Great War, Sashra was nearly destroyed. Belligerent tribes had tried to divide the land among them after the emperor's defeat. However, none saw the coming of Saiyeri, who forced out the rival tribes and established a kingdom for the Sashraman tribe. Juktan was fourth in the new line of maliks his grandfather had established, being preceded by his older brother and his father. Neither had ruled well. Juktan swore daily to strive toward his grandfather's example and not toward that of lesser men.

Several rolls of thunder exploded overhead, making a terrifying sound across the northern plains.

"Sounds like it's getting stronger," said Rakimo.

Juktan nodded. "No doubt it will delay our progress," he said.

"Hopefully not too much. The men can handle a bit of bad weather," Rakimo said reassuringly.

Juktan smiled. He knew the captain was proud of his men and confident in their strength.

"The sound of the wind and rain reminds me of a lion hunt I went on. Commander Nuvahli and me. We were in the thicket in the Casala jungle; wind was slamming into us from every direction, kicking up dirt and tree limbs. And there was the lion walking through like it was nothing. I remember a tree falling, and my leg was trapped beneath it. Commander Nuvahli saw the lion coming for me, but he was too far away. The beast came up to me and put its legs onto the trunk that was holding me down. And he just sat there pushing the tree trunk down harder onto me. The beast just stood there looking at me with its eyes, as if to tell me something. As if to tell me that in spite of my weaponry and tracking knowledge, I was still the weaker one and it the stronger."

"You've never told me this story. What happened then?"

"The lion ran off into the thicket. By then, Pasha reached me and pulled the trunk from over me, and we headed back to our camp where more warriors and physicians were gathered . . . I remember how I was so confident that I could do this and win my prize. For so long, my mentors taught me to control every situation and not let fate dictate the terms of my life. But at that moment, I had no control. I was completely in the hands of Daiyu and my fathers."

"What happened then?" Rakimo inquired.

"I recovered, and we went back into the jungle and found the thing and killed it. I encrusted the hilt of my sword with its teeth," Juktan said, lifting his sword from his sheath for Rakimo to see.

"That's very intricate," said Rakimo, examining the blade's hilt.

"It reminds me every day that fate is cruel, which is why you have to fight it each and every day."

"Are you eager to get back to the palace, Malik?" Rakimo asked, handing the blade back.

"Except to see my wife, not really. Being surrounded by squabbling chiefs and clansmen is not my idea of a good time."

"Nor mine," said Rakimo.

Juktan laughed as he put down the letters to look at his captain. "You have far greater wisdom than I give you credit for, Rakimo."

Suddenly the carriage came to an abrupt stop, sending Juktan flying into the floor.

"Malik," said Rakimo as he helped Juktan to his feet.

"What happened?" asked Juktan.

"We've stopped," Rakimo answered.

Juktan immediately opened the door of the carriage to find his warriors gathered about in a box formation. Outside it was pitch black while hard rain and biting wind assaulted them from all sides. His warriors and his officers remained still.

"Rank Master Cheo," he called out to one of his officers.

"Malik," Cheo answered with a slight bow from his mount.

"What is going on?" Juktan demanded.

"We're being followed, Malik. It may be an ambush. You should stay within the carriage until we—"

The rank master did not finish his words as a dark arrow punched through his throat.

Juktan immediately leapt back into the carriage with Rakimo crashing beside him.

The rank master crashed into the ground, gasping for air that would not come. Within seconds, he was dead.

"That's an ambush all right," said Rakimo, drawing his sword and pulling the malik back. Dozens more arrows soared through the night and found their mounted targets easily. Juktan watched as more of his warriors fell from their horses, dead.

"Where are they coming from?" shouted Amran, one of Juktan's officers.

"Dismount, you fools! Dismount!" shouted Rakimo while he drew his shield before him and leapt to the ground.

The rest of the warriors immediately raised their shields and leapt from their horses.

"Amran! Form a line on me! Form a line on me!" Rakimo ordered.

Amran nodded, shouting orders for the men to form up.

The Sashramans' effort to stand in a line fell apart quickly under the constant hail of invisible missiles. Arrows punched through many of the warriors' legs and backs before they could regroup.

The three warriors on the carriage tried to return fire with their own bows, but they were quickly put down.

Rakimo mustered what warriors he could to form a shield wall around the carriage.

"You are warriors of Sashra! In the name of Daiyu and our fallen brothers, protect the malik!" Rakimo shouted to rally the men.

The shield wall stopped enemy arrows from reaching them or the malik. Soon, the fire stopped. However, both Rakimo and Juktan knew it was not over.

It had been five years since Juktan had done battle. Nevertheless, the malik drew his blade and readied himself.

Loud cries came over the howling wind, soon followed by the outlines of more than fifty mounted warriors charging toward them. Their pale complexions and silver armor became more visible as they came closer. The men of the north drew long straight swords, letting off a deafening roar as they bore down on the Sashramans.

Juktan stood ready, but when he looked at Rakimo, they both knew victory was unlikely.

"Stand ready," cautioned Rakimo.

Juktan knew his men would not break, but he could feel the anxiety building within them.

"Bare your spears!" shouted Rakimo to the men with spears.

Baku cries filled their ears like a raging drum, bringing only greater terror to their thoughts.

"Look! Over there!" shouted Amran.

Juktan turned to look toward the northeast where the warrior was pointing.

Riding hard toward them was a long streak of blue, headed by Sashraman warriors.

"Daiyu be praised! They're with us!" shouted Rakimo as the blue streak slammed into the oncoming northern force.

Mud and water flew high into the air while the two forces clashed. Pasha and Rakimo grouped together, spearing as many northerners as possible. Azia led the main body of the force pushing forward against the northern force. Leyos hurled two of his many spears before drawing his long, curved sword. Before he could react, several northern blades had cut down his mount at the neck, sending him flying into the mud below.

Pasha and Rakimo converged quickly, blocking the northern warriors as they sought Leyos's life. Soon Pasha's spear broke off into a Baku body, forcing him to draw his sword. Daimon, Pasha's mount, kicked out his legs, forcing many riders from their mounts.

The northern warriors' attention was diverted once more when Juktan and his men hit the enemy on their right flank. Pasha and his men picked up the momentum and began slashing their way through the northerners. This time, their enemies began to give way.

Pasha's men hurled their spears at the northern warriors, trying to ride Juktan's men down, each spear hammered into their foes allowing the Sashramans to push forward.

About a dozen Baku tried to fall back and use their bows, but the Sashramans quickly closed the gap. Soon the entire northern force was beginning to splinter, and it was not long before a retreat was sounded.

Shouts of victory filled the plains while the men gathered around the malik, who had stood with them in the fight.

Pasha and his men dismounted and proceeded toward the malik.

"Talk about just in time," Juktan said, embracing him.

"Malik," Pasha said, bowing his head.

"How did you know?" Juktan asked.

"We were following their trail, and we came upon you here," Pasha answered.

"We weren't sure what we were following until we saw the men of the north," Abayomi added.

"Praise Daiyu you found us," said Rakimo, coming to stand by the malik.

Juktan then turned to his men.

"Long life to our brother Pasha Nuvahli and his men, without whom our victory would not have been certain!"

The malik's few remaining warriors let out loud cheers for Pasha and his men. Heavy rain did little to lessen their spirits. From the mouth of death, they had escaped once more.

"Just like the Sadras campaign," said Juktan as he began walking back to his carriage. Rakimo and Amran followed him closely while the rest of the men tended to the dead.

Pasha walked alongside him.

"Hopelessly outnumbered and little chance of living through it, yet somehow we kept going," said Juktan.

"It was your strength that gave us strength then, Malik, and that gives us strength now," Pasha replied.

Juktan wiped his bloody cheek with the sleeve of his drenched robes.

"It does me good to see you. How long has it been?" said Juktan.

"A little over a year, Malik," Pasha said.

"Feels longer. You know, my wife is with child?" said Juktan.

"Yes, I heard," Pasha answered.

"My coming son nearly lost his father today," said Juktan.

"But he didn't, Malik, and that is all that matters," Pasha said strongly.

Juktan let out a heavy grunt as he climbed into the carriage.

"Are you all right, Malik?" asked Pasha, standing outside.

"Yes, I'm fine. Still it makes you think . . . makes you think about what you leave behind," said Juktan.

Pasha felt a strong pang in his stomach as he thought about Hadassah, his wife. It had been many days since he had seen her.

CHAPTER 4

Adjustments

She drew her breaths slowly while bringing down the long stick to pound the grain before her. The long hours of threshing grain had left an intense pain between her throbbing shoulder blades. There was no help that day. Mizram, her husband's cousin, would be helping his own family tend to their fields. Though not much would get done that day, Hadassah could not idle. Eventually though she took a respite from her labor and went to the house to rest.

The sun shone brightly even though it was still early. But she no longer cared. Her days were nothing more than work and quiet hours to herself. She sat on the grass before her home and lay back to look upon the sky, letting the sun warm her bare brown feet.

Suddenly the air shifted and carried a strange sound to her along the wind. Not knowing why, she rose and looked to the south. Hadassah felt her insides twisting and turning painfully when a figure on a familiar white horse rose from the horizon. In her mind, she questioned if it was real.

After what seemed like hours, her eyes clearly made out the features of her husband on his horse. A sudden weakness came upon her as Pasha waved to her. Her eyes swelled with tears, and she remained still. At that moment, she did not know what to do. Without warning, she fell to the ground while her husband approached.

Pasha leapt from Daimon's back and ran toward where Hadassah sat. It surprised and pleased him how little she had changed over time. Her honey-colored face was still lovely and shone like gold from behind her piercing bronze and green eyes. When he had left, her hair had flowed freely from her head. Now it was arranged in neat rows of tight black braids. The muscle about her arms and legs was thicker than before, obvious signs that she had dedicated herself to laboring in the fields since his departure.

Though her face seemed to still be full of the same spirit and life he remembered, he noted something new about her. She was older, and the years seemed to have taken something from her. Pasha was unsure if it was merely a couple years of her youth or something else. He sat before her, unable to think of any words of meaning. His eyes fell to the ground. Looking upon her tears was too painful.

"Hadassah, I . . ."

Saying nothing, she fell into his arms and halted his feeble words. He wiped her tears from her lovely face as she kissed his hands and pressed them to her face. They held each other tightly for a long while, wishing to savor every moment of their reunion. After long moments, they both rose and went hand in hand toward the house.

"You have done a lot. I didn't think you would ever make that garden grow," he said, gesturing to the small patch of earth on the south side of the house. "It is quite lovely," he said, kissing her hand.

"Thank you. When you use your time wisely, you can surprise even yourself."

She went on before him while he leashed Daimon to a post. For a moment. he looked around to what he could see of the fields in the west. Harvest time had come and gone, yet not even half of their yield had been tended to. Even from that distance, Pasha could see some of it was rotting. There was much that needed to be done. He turned and went inside.

Hadassah had removed a platter from the fire mount, and taking a knife, she cut its contents into many pieces.

"Are you hungry? I have some bread."

"Yes, that's fine," said Pasha.

He came beside her while she tended the food.

"A shame you didn't get here earlier. Your aunt sent over some delicious goat cheese. I'll have to ask her to send more. Water?"

Pasha nodded.

She made her way to the far corner of the room to the water pitcher, drawing water with a small clay cup, which she handed him.

The water was cool and refreshing. Nevertheless, eating and drinking were not important to Pasha at this moment. He put the cup and bread aside, taking his wife's hand once more. His lips went forward and embraced hers, which eagerly awaited his touch.

Her tongue struggled to utter the mind's thoughts when she looked at him.

"The first few days, I could not do anything, because all I could think of was where you were and what you were doing. Then your father came."

Pasha felt sickly at the mention of his father, guiltily remembering that he deliberately had not sent him a single message or dwelt his thoughts long upon him during his posting. There was much he wished had not happened.

"What happened?" he asked.

"He kept me company, got me back on my feet, back to work. He told me not to worry. He said, 'My son loves you, and wherever he is, I am sure he is thinking of you this moment.'"

"There was not a day that passed when I didn't," said Pasha

"Why did you have to go, Pasha? Why couldn't you stay with me?"

He kissed her cheeks to stop the tears from marring her lovely face.

"You know why I had to go. The harvest was so poor, and the storms were getting bad; we wouldn't have survived the winter."

"But what are we going to do, Pasha? I cannot live any life having you here and there for small moments of time. Nor can any children."

"Hadassah . . ."

"I cannot do it alone, Pasha. Two years apart, two hardly together! You can't build a family on that!" said Hadassah through tear-stained eyes.

"I don't know what you want me to do. Farming around here can be unpredictable. I cannot risk you or any children starving. We barely have a chance out here with the fat merchants dividing everything up and raising prices. The service is all there is, and the service is what I know."

"We could go to the western provinces. My uncle could get us a good piece of land."

"These are our problems, Hadassah, no one else's. And I certainly won't run to your family when things get a bit difficult," said Pasha, immediately wishing he had not said it.

"All I know is that I didn't marry you just to keep your house!" she shouted.

With that, she left his embrace and went silently into the second room. Pasha grew angrier at himself each moment. After all he had been through, he was not going to return to his wife with angry words. Drawing a long breath, he followed her path.

He found her looking out of the open window from the bed.

"I know it has been hard, all of this. I wish I could give you better. As Daiyu is my witness, I would do anything to do so."

She turned and looked back at him.

"The malik came here, visited me. Before he left, he told me that he was always there to help his friends and allies if they would only ask. I love you, Pasha, and I would have no other man but you. But you have many faults, including being too timid to do right by yourself. You have a friend who cares about you and who is powerful and in a position to help you."

"I will not use the malik's favor to advance myself," said Pasha.

"Do not use it for yourself then. Use it for us and the life we are missing together. That is what you do with the favor of a malik. There is nothing dishonorable about it. He could find you a long-term posting or even reinstate you in the guard. I don't ask much of you, Pasha. All I have ever wanted from you was a husband and a family. I know you can give me that."

He paused, considering all she had said.

"Come here," he finally said.

She came to him and took his opened palm.

"Nothing is more important to me than our happiness. I will do right by you. I promise."

They drew in the life of each other as their lips met and locked tightly.

"When was the last time you smiled?" Pasha asked.

"I don't know," said Hadassah, trying to clear her face.

"It seems there are many things that need to be taken care of," said Pasha, smiling.

Her face brightened up as Pasha took her in a tight embrace. No more words needed to be spoken as their forgotten passion overwhelmed them.

A Month Later

"I cannot believe that you forgot how to put one of these on," Hadassah said, pretending to be annoyed while she tightened the last fold of her husband's turban with a small bone needle.

Pasha had not worn the traditional white prayer turban for two years. Finding time for prayers at Kirara and on patrol had been difficult.

"It has been awhile," he replied, watching his wife smooth out his long, white tunic. Pasha remembered that before it had annoyed him the way Hadassah would fuss over the way he looked. But at that moment, he watched, pleasantly realizing he was truly at home.

The first few weeks had been difficult at times. Most of Pasha's days were spent tending the fields. And at night, Pasha worked to rekindle the intimate bond between him and Hadassah. Though she welcomed this, at times Pasha was at a loss around her. She was tender and easygoing like before, but a layer of hardness dwelt around her.

That day was an especially important day because it would be the first time he had seen his father since his return. Though his father resided only six miles from them, Pasha had not seen him. He told himself it was because of work, but in reality, he feared how a meeting between them might end. Still, Hadassah had convinced him it was time.

Outside the house, he called Daimon to him; the two of them had been close since childhood. Pasha seldom thought of him as a horse but more of a companion. Daimon was a fine white Miza, a former possession of Asdalaya, his eldest brother. Every time Pasha climbed onto Daimon's back, he thought of Asdalaya and all the brothers he had lost.

"Oh, Daimon, just as beautiful as ever," said Hadassah, stroking his neck.

"Do you want me to be with you when you meet your father?" she asked.

"I can handle my affairs," said Pasha, looking away.

"Can you? You seem . . . Let's go," she said, quickly changing the subject, which Pasha had always appreciated about her.

Hadassah held out her hand, smiling, prompting Pasha to quickly jump upon Daimon's back and reach down to pull her up. She grabbed his shoulders for support to balance herself upon the horse's back.

Drawing in the reins slightly to the right, and commanding Daimon with a nudge from his heel, they started north in the direction of the temple at the base of the mountains.

"Do you remember when we used to go riding, Pasha, just you and me?" asked Hadassah.

"Yes, I remember," said Pasha.

"When you left, I think that was what I missed the most," Hadassah said into his ear.

"Seriously, the riding!" Pasha laughed.

"What?" she asked, seeming bewildered.

"It's just, I always thought you hated it," said Pasha.

"No, I . . . Why would you think that?"

"Because you were always complaining about horse smells and washing your clothes immediately after we got back," said Pasha.

"Oh no, I loved it each time! It was always peaceful just to sit here and listen to you talk and try to impress me with your singing." She lingered on the last phrase with a stifled laugh.

"I thought I did impress you," said Pasha.

She smiled. "Pasha, the only thing that kept me riding with you was the fact that you didn't do it every day and never for a long time," said Hadassah.

"You're a wonderful woman, Hadassah, but you obviously have no ear for music," said Pasha.

"Really!" Hadassah said, exploding with laughter. "You sounded like a lost dog all alone in the middle of a desert—because no one wants to listen to him!"

"Let's see how funny it is when you have to walk home." Pasha nudged back into her like he was going to knock her off.

"I'm sorry, Pasha, I'm sorry." Though he did not turn to look at her, he already knew that she wore no sign of sincerity upon her face.

"You're a wonderful rider, my love, but you do not have the voice of angels," said Hadassah, playfully kissing the back of his neck.

"Laugh and doubt me if you want, but I have put whole companies of men to sleep with my voice. Wherever I was posted, my voice was known well throughout this land," said Pasha.

"No. No, my husband, I do not think so. Do you not remember that my father nearly had you beaten out of his house, and almost the entire province, because he mistook you for a drunken fool when you sang for me one time?" said Hadassah.

"Well, your father's wit did not always bear a sharpened edge in such matters."

"Curious! He said the same about you," said Hadassah, laughing.

Pasha said no more, listening to her laugh quietly as she pressed herself tightly upon his back, wrapping her hands around his waist.

"It's been too long since I held you like this," she said.

Pasha grasped one of the hands that had crept about his waist, bringing it up to his lips.

"I'm not going anywhere," he said.

It was not long before they came within sight of the temple. Hadassah drew her hands back quickly and brought her robes tightly to her.

The great doors to the gray and white stone temple were wide open. At each door stood members of the priesthood, greeting people and blessing them while they entered.

Pasha and his wife removed their shoes in reverence before entering the great sanctuary. The throng of people quickly reminded Pasha of just how crowded a temple could be during the prayer hour.

There was hardly any part of the floor not covered by cushions, pillows, and rugs for the faithful to sit upon during the shazhia's teaching. Hadassah soon departed for the left end of the sanctuary, occupied solely by the women and young children. The men took up the rest of the space.

Though so many bodies crammed closely together would have made the room into a sweltering oven; this was avoided due to the large open windows and the numerous priests bearing stiff palm branches to fan air upon the worshippers.

Pasha settled himself at the rear of the room, leaning back on the hard wall next to the entrance. At that moment, the prayer hour had not yet struck, leaving time for the men to meet and talk with friends or take a few moments of quiet meditation. A familiar face dropped into a place beside Pasha.

"Still skulking in the back, cousin?"

"Mizram!" Pasha laughed, embracing his cousin.

Pasha had seen his cousin two weeks before for the first time in two and a half years. He had been greatly surprised by how much he had changed. When he left, his cousin had been a skinny, awkward, tall, dark boy with black hair cropped down quite shortly. Now upon his return, he found a tall, well-built man, with long, black locks reaching to his shoulders and eyes full of warmth and confidence.

"I was wondering how long it would be till you came," said Mizram.

"I do honor to Daiyu each day, cousin, in spite of how occupied I have been," said Pasha.

"Right," said Mizram, pretending to believe him. Both men smiled. "So what are your plans today? My father and mother would be pleased if you came by today. My sisters especially miss you. Why, I don't know," he said, adding a jest.

"I won't be going by today. I have other plans right now," said Pasha. He looked anxiously to the front of the sanctuary.

"He'll be most glad to see you," said Mizram.

"What?" said Pasha, taken aback.

"My uncle, your father, has been concerned about you, Pasha. He has missed you terribly, more than you know. You should go to him. He's right over there."

Mizram pointed to the far right corner of the sanctuary, a couple of rows in the middle where the dark, wizened face of Pasha's father was very visible. In spite of two years, he had not changed much, except for two or three new scars on his neck.

"Four months ago when he was at my father's house, he talked about you nonstop," said Mizram. "He just wants his son back."

The prayer hour struck, and all rose to watch the shazhia approach the head of the sanctuary. Two priests who were his personal students followed the shazhia while he made his approach. He stood out greatly among the congregants, being adorned in a red tunic, black robes, white trousers, and a red turban upon his head.

He stopped before all of them and began the slow chant to prayer in the Hebari tongue, and then repeated it into the common tongues of Sashra. At the end of the chanting, the shazhia led them in prayer.

Every man but the shazhia dropped to his knees and began the sacred oration. On his knees, Pasha recited it, silencing himself whenever he stumbled on certain parts.

"I pray blessings for my family that they grow well and strong, pray for my wife that she be given wisdom and strength. Pray for my father that in old age he will cling to you, the father of all mercy, pray for my brother that his love for you never wane, pray for my sister that her devotion remains the same. Pray for my mother that her wisdom and love never fails."

The final part was continued by the men.

"And pray for me, the warrior in whose heart burns the righteous flame; steady my hand as I strike down your enemies who would curse your holy name. Pray for me when I am young that I stay righteous and pure, pray for me when I am old and gone that in peace I see your righteous face. Praise be to Daiyu, lord of the heavens and earth."

And the last line they all repeated three times before falling into silence before the shazhia. The men sat back in their original positions when the shazhia began to speak, his powerful voice reaching out to every corner of the room.

"Daiyu is the word, and we are his children. But like all children, many have fallen into darkness. Yet our father stays his hand, for he sees the faithful gather to exalt his holy name. Beware the servants of the evil one who seeks to seize the crown of evil and build his throne upon the earth. It is due to the acts of the believers that the dark banner of the evil one has not prevailed against us.

"We must be the light in a world of darkness, my brothers. Our lives must show it, and our minds must know it. The great battle is coming, a battle when the faithful must make themselves known and stand firm."

Pasha could feel the warmth of the holy writings of the Cofra ease his mind and bring peace to his heart. However, this feeling was briefly interrupted when he felt eyes upon him. He looked to the side of the sanctuary where the women sat.

At first there was nothing, and then he saw him. A man with burning red eyes, and long, black hair stood next to Hadassah. His words echoed in Pasha's ear.

"Remember, *hajarra*. We are one, never apart, always together," he said.

"Hadassah!" Pasha jumped back as the man disappeared. None had noticed him or heard his voice but Pasha. Who was this tormentor who invaded his mind and denied him peace? His body shook with fear as he looked toward Hadassah, who looked briefly back to him.

"Are you all right, Pasha?" whispered Mizram.

Only his cousin and several men at the rear had noticed something amiss. Deciding it was better not to speak, Pasha remained silent, returning only a brief nod. He had seen the stranger for many years, and as far as he knew, only he could see him. Never had he appeared anywhere near his family. Often it was the unexplainable things that drove Pasha to prayer.

Pasha tried to rid himself of concern by reminding himself that none of it was real and could harm no one. Still, at times, Pasha felt there was more to the visions than could be explained. Nevertheless, he discussed it with no one. He did not know how to explain what he did not understand.

Not wanting to dwell upon it anymore, he buried his head into his arms and tried to lose himself in quiet meditation while the shazhia began the conclusion of his sermon.

Outside of the temple, Pasha sat at the pool of reflection with Mizram to wait for Hadassah. He did not see his father anywhere. Possibly he missed him on the way out, and he was already gone. No matter, he would see him later.

"I wonder what she is doing in there," murmured Pasha.

"Probably interceding for your immortal soul. Daiyu knows you need help." Mizram smiled as he said this.

"Well you're certainly no help. What are you doing here anyway? Don't you have to get back to your family?"

"I thought I would stay with you for a while. I have a feeling something special is going to happen today."

"How do you know that?"

"Oh just trust me, Pasha. It's going to happen any moment now."

The doors opened again, and Pasha felt a sharp pang in his stomach as he saw his wife coming from the temple, arm in arm with his father. He stood and came to them, standing uneasily before his father.

"Father," Pasha said.

"My son," said Miori.

"I don't know what to say," Pasha said, unable to meet his father's gaze.

"Don't say anything. Just come here," said Miori.

Both men embraced tightly. Everything that had been said before seemed irrelevant.

"I didn't want what I said to be the last thing I ever said to you," said Pasha.

"I know, son. Your mother always said that we men of Nuvahli were always quicker with words than common sense."

Pasha laughed. "And like always, she was right."

"Yes, she was. Ever since you were young, I wanted you to have the best. And now you and my daughter shall soon have an abundance of it."

"What do you mean? Hadassah?"

She looked deeply into his eyes and took his hands into her own.

"My husband, I am with child."

The words came into Pasha's mind, but he was unsure how to translate them. "You're what?"

"I am going to have a child," said Hadassah.

"My child," Pasha said without thinking.

"No, you fool," she said, kissing his cheek. "Our child. Are you not pleased?"

A great wave of excitement came over Pasha as he considered it all. He forgot his earlier fears and felt only happiness.

"There is nothing you can do that displeases me," said Pasha.

She smiled, kissing his hand once more.

"The two of you make an old man very happy," said Pasha's father, Miori.

CHAPTER 5

The Visitations

Eventually as the summer grew hotter, Pasha's aunt came to live with them. She was Pasha's only close woman relative experienced in such matters as childbirth. In the coming days, she would be there to help Hadassah through the transition to becoming a mother. Soon his aunt's daughters came to help prepare the house and help Pasha with any remaining work he had in the fields.

Then on the last day of that week after returning from Kadisha to secure his posting there, Pasha came home to find Hadassah in the final actions of childbirth. He sat in the darkest corner of their bedchambers in silence, watching as she heaved and pushed painfully. His aunt occasionally came to wipe the sweat from her face with a clean rag. For the most part, his aunt said nothing. She merely waited as the natural progression of events took place. Pasha sat on the cold, hard ground, praying silently as he observed the most dangerous stage in the life of a woman.

He thought of his own mother. She had gone through childbirth four times and endured the most painful sensations a woman could endure. It made Pasha wonder what made women celebrate it—desire it so much when it was so painful and often deadly.

Pasha turned his head away as his aunt opened Hadassah's legs more and began urging her to push. Moments later, a loud scream ensued and died down under the loud cries of new life.

Covering Hadassah back up quickly after loosening the child from her, his aunt wrapped the child delicately and placed the newborn on a bed of cushions beside their bed. Still feeling shaken, Pasha came to her side.

"I didn't think you were going to make it over there," she said, sounding quite tired yet still managing a smile.

Pasha could think of nothing to say.

"You should not underestimate my capabilities."

"I suppose so, my love."

Quite abruptly, her speech stopped, and she fell back into the bed unconscious.

"Hadassah! Hadassah!" Pasha shook her, but there was very little response.

He looked to the end of the bed where she had been covered with a large blanket. Lifting one end of it back, he gasped at the sight of the bloodied rags.

"Aunt, look! Why is there so much blood? Will she . . ."

She came to him quickly once she had registered what happened. Moving quickly, she bound several rags together and used them to stop the bleeding. She then turned to her worried nephew.

"Pasha, Pasha, be quiet, listen to me. It's all right. In every birth, there is a little blood. She is just tired."

"How can you be sure?"

"Trust me, nephew. She will be fine. Just let her rest for a while."

"Are your certain?"

"I have been through this many times, Pasha. Almost every woman loses consciousness the first time, but there is nothing wrong."

She knew that her words had brought no comfort to her nephew, for he always troubled himself greatly over his wife.

"Take that sad look from your eyes. Here!" She bent over to scoop the babe into her arms.

"It's a boy. Here, Pasha, hold your son."

There were no words Pasha could use to describe the feeling as he held his own blood within his arms for the first time. Though he bore a small frame, his head was large and well rounded, his curled hair and complexion dark like his father. His crying stopped quite quickly as he peered up at Pasha.

"He knows that you're his father," said his aunt as she tended to Hadassah.

"Yes, he does," Pasha said softly to himself. Slowly he came back to Hadassah's bedside, and going down to his knees, he held the child up toward the heavens.

"Daiyu, lord of us all, you have brought to us a gift beyond measure. Bless this child whom I dedicate to you. Guide his path . . ."

"And keep him in the light when he faces adversity." Pasha smiled joyfully as Hadassah raised her hand and placed it upon the child's head.

Carefully, Pasha placed him into the arms of his mother as he placed many tender kisses upon her lips.

"All right, Pasha. All right. I just needed a little sleep. Ah, look at him," she said as she softly pushed him away.

"He seems confused, scared almost."

"You were too when you were this young," said his aunt.

"We never decided upon a name," said Pasha to Hadassah.

"Don't worry. I have the perfect name for him."

"Don't I get a say in the matter?"

"Maybe next time, my husband, but I really want our child to have this name. We will call him Kamili."

Pasha smiled, bearing himself in silence. Though he had many ideas, plans for the child and his name, he would not go against Hadassah's wishes. It was common in Sashra for women to give the children their life names, or how they would be called on a daily basis, a tradition that Pasha decided was not worth breaking.

"All right, you two. Pasha, go to your father and the rest of the men."

"But, Aunt—"

"She needs her rest, and so does the child. Go on, Pasha. She will be fine now."

Pasha stood after kissing her once more. "I'll see you later."

Though tired, Pasha had never seen Hadassah look so happy and fulfilled as she did at that moment. As he left her, a wave of pride shot through him as he fully realized that he was now a father and he had a son.

Outside, all of the men stood upon seeing Pasha.

"Well?" asked Mizram as his father and Pasha's father stood.

"It's a boy."

"Daiyu be praised!"

"Daiyu be praised!" said the rest of the men as each embraced Pasha.

Feeling even more tired at that moment, Pasha sat upon one of the many cushions around the low table, where the men joined him.

"What does he look like?" began Mizram.

"What does it matter, Mizram," began Pasha's father. "A healthy boy has come to life this day. That is reason enough for celebration."

"Father, was it like this when Asdalaya was born?"

At first Pasha cursed himself for asking that question, noting the pained look in his father's eyes and the forced silence of Keradi and Mizram at that moment. Though it had been many years, neither of them had found any way to talk about the tragedy they had experienced together. Nevertheless, his father smiled and looked at his son thoughtfully.

"The day your brother was born was when I truly began to believe in the divine purpose of Daiyu. It was during a great winter rainstorm; the rains were heavy, and some of our land had been flooded. Inside, your mother was having difficulty giving birth to Asdalaya. Moment by moment, things got worse. Your brother came out the wrong way. So your grandmother had to help pull him out with her hands, which in turn broke Asdalaya's arm. Asdalaya was quite sickly at the start, and it did not seem that he would live long. But I had never been so scared as when your mother started bleeding, and we could not stop it. She and your brother started to slip away quickly. For three days, they were at death's door, but then I prayed to Daiyu. I said that if my destiny would be to experience the pain of the loss of a wife and child, then I would openly accept that. But whether or not it was my destiny, I begged that he end your mother and brother's trial immediately. Within an hour, your mother's bleeding stopped, and within a week, Asdalaya was well again."

"It must have been terrifying to go through that again."

"Not particularly. After Asdalaya, I truly accepted that your mother was like a treasure. No matter how careful you are with it, it will eventually leave you, or you it, and that the point of it is to truly appreciate the joy it brings while you have it. As you must do, my son. No matter how much you love them and how much you protect them, you must always be prepared to lose them, for nothing is certain, my son, nor permanent."

"I shall remember your words always, Father."

"Well who is this!" came Keradi as Pasha's aunt came to them bearing Pasha's son.

"Look well, Miori. You're an old man now."

"It matters not. I feel as rich as a king."

"Why does he have so much hair?" asked Mizram, seeming both awestruck and perplexed by the significance of a newborn child.

"All Sashramans are born with a full set of hair, as yours will be as soon as you stop dragging your feet and get to your duties," said Pasha's father.

Mizram tilted little Kamili's head to see his face more clearly.

"Careful with his head," said Mizram's mother in rebuke. "And don't crowd him so. It will be a miracle if he survives a week with you as company."

"Now you have seen him. He needs to rest."

"Come now, good woman," said Keradi to his wife. "Let us hold him awhile."

"Not now, Keradi," she said, pulling the babe away from Keradi, who had just made a face, prompting the babe to cry only more and hide its face beneath the wrap in which Pasha's aunt held him.

She began to turn back to the other room where Pasha's wife still lay in her bed.

"Oh, nephew," she said, turning back to Pasha. "Will you put him through the holy ceremony?"

"I hadn't thought of it," Pasha answered.

"This is a special child, nephew, the first. You should do honor to Daiyu for this mighty blessing."

"I will, aunt. I will."

CHAPTER 6

A Different Life

Though he had planned to wait a bit longer, four weeks after the child's birth, Pasha decided to go forward and start the posting in Kadisha that the malik had offered.

Being at home for so many days had felt strange to Pasha. No longer would he be called to far flung places and placed into constant danger. From that point on, he would be like the other fathers in Nuva Province. At times, he wondered if he could come back to a life that he left years before; however, he needed only to look to his wife and child to reassure himself that he had done the right thing.

Ever since the child's birth, Pasha's troubled dreams began to fade. Hadassah had changed as well; to Pasha, it had been for the better. Though she labored more to care for their son, her mouth was constantly curved into a smile, and her demeanor easygoing and brimming with joy each moment as she held her child. Though he had not expected it, little Kamili only seemed to be bringing Pasha and his wife closer.

The day of Pasha's departure came, and both he and Hadassah, who stood holding Kamili, found themselves once more along the path before their house. Daimon stood nearby to carry Pasha away once more, as he had so many times before. This time, things were a bit different. There were no tears in their eyes, none of the pain many departures can cause a man's family, for on the day Pasha would be leaving, he would return by nightfall. No longer did he wear his armor or spears, only a simple shirt of mail above his blue tunic and a sword for defending himself. Looking at her husband at that moment, Hadassah thought to herself how much more she preferred things that way.

"Well?" Pasha asked, truthfully not knowing how to say goodbye to his wife again, for they had grown tired of that word.

"You look good. You should make the malik proud."

"I hope I do. Are you still going to the river with the girls?" he said, referring to his cousins.

"Yes."

"And Mizram."

"He will accompany us, my husband. Do not waste time worrying over us; everything will be fine. A baby needs to breathe and see as do we, Pasha. Now I thought you had to go."

"You be careful; the birth can still affect you in some way."

"I appreciate your concern, but I know better than you what I can take. Now get going."

With no more words, he mounted Daimon, whose sharpened hooves cut apart the soft dirt, taking them along their short journey south.

Mizram and his sisters arrived shortly after to walk with Hadassah to the river in the east.

"Cousin Hadassah," her husband's cousins said in unison as they charged toward her and little Kamili.

"Oh Caldaia, Alsaya, and Aria, it's so good to see you." She kissed all of them as they clambered around to see Kamili.

"Is that him!" Aria said in amazement.

"Yes, it's him; this is Kamili."

"Why is he so small?" asked Aria.

"That's the way most babies are born, Aria, but he'll get as big as all three of you within no time."

"He looks a lot like cousin Pasha," said Caldaia.

"No, his nose isn't big enough. I think he looks more like Hadassah," said Alsaya, starting a friendly argument among them.

"Hello, Mizram," Hadassah said as Mizram came closer.

"Hadassah," he said, nodding.

"Can I hold him, cousin Hadassah? Mother showed me how to hold a baby," said Caldaia.

"She showed me too," rebuked Aria.

"But I can do it better, and I'm older," said Alsaya.

"Not now, girls," said Hadassah to quiet them down before they truly began to argue.

"Let's wait until we get to the river, and then you can all hold him. And we'd better go if we want to catch all of this beautiful sunlight."

"Please, cousin Hadassah!" pleaded Aria.

"When we get to the river, Aria. Why don't you girls go on ahead and show me how you're going to dance at Kamili's ceremony."

"All right. Caldaia, Alsaya, cousin Hadassah wants to see us dance."

Slowly they began toward the east. The little girls ran and twirled everywhere, making sure Mizram and Hadassah could see them clearly.

"I'm surprised your father spared you from work today," said Hadassah, trying to start a conversation with her husband's cousin.

"There was not much to be done. Besides, he knew Pasha would be going into the city today and would want someone to see to you and the baby."

"He doesn't like to leave me alone, bless him. Pasha trusts you a lot, doesn't he, Mizram?"

"I suppose he does. Ever since he lost his other brothers and his mother, I suppose we sort of bonded like brothers do. Why do you ask?"

"He just seems to depend upon you a lot." She paused before speaking again. "So what about you, Mizram? What interesting tales have been woven in your life?"

He laughed. "No tales as of yet, just those little ones and how crazy they make our mother at times," he said, gesturing toward his sisters.

She smiled. "Is it not about time you went out on your own, Mizram? I know that you tire of being here season after season."

Mizram lowered his head slightly. "I have wanted to see new things and perhaps find a woman, hopefully one as lovely as you."

Hadassah laughed and returned an appreciative smile. "Ever since I met you, you have grown from a most kind boy to a good man. I know you shall find someone special."

"Thank you. May I ask you a question?"

"Of course."

"Was it hard for you to leave your home and your parents?"

Hadassah drew in a deep breath. She looked ahead to the girls, who were farther in front of them, picking flowers.

"It was a bit hard leaving home, because I never expected to go very far from it. At the time, I had been promised to a boy who eventually grew and entered the priesthood in our province. My father was proud of the match, for the boy came from a good family, and he was on his way to becoming a shazhia.

"I think my father really liked the idea that any of his future grandsons would be able to bring my family's blood into the priesthood. However, a year and half before we were to wed, this young warrior from the east came to my home to help my father fight the Sadras uprising, which had spread throughout my home province.

"He came every week with his superior, Captain Cheokto, to meet with my father. Before then, I had only seen my intended once. But when I saw your cousin, I was so taken by him nobody else seemed to matter. My father never approved our marriage, but eventually he allowed it."

Mizram laughed lightly. "I never thought Pasha had very much charm to begin with. I wouldn't have blamed you if you had started to hate him all the days he left you."

"It doesn't matter. He's here now, and things are going right again."

"So how did Pasha convince your father to let him have you?"

"My intended was killed by Sadras raiders a month before we were to wed. In compensation, my father made Pasha carry out several duties for his house. I don't know everything he made him do, but eventually Pasha came to me, took me to a priest, and we wed."

"I am glad he eventually got you from your father. All of the girls love you dearly."

"And I them."

"Have your parents come to accept your marriage to my cousin and your living so far from home?"

"I like to think they did before their time came."

"I'm sorry."

"Don't be."

"No, I am. I should never have asked that."

"It's all right, Mizram. I needed to talk about them. So tell me, Mizram, are you going to take a trade or continue farming like your father?"

"I have been thinking about going to Ashul Province or somewhere and apprenticing myself to a sword smith."

"That's quite far, isn't it?"

"Not too far, only about a week on horse. I can already work metal; Father taught me a lot of what I know already. It's possible I could stay here and join the blacksmiths guild in Kadisha. But in Ashul, the opportunities are even greater. Ashuli smiths repair and rebuild all the damaged arms for the fortress at Haluda, so they never have trouble finding work."

"I hope that one day you can make these aspirations into a reality. I'm sure Pasha can give you gold to make the trip when you're ready."

"I wouldn't feel comfortable asking cousin Pasha for gold."

"Nonsense. Pasha cares a lot about you, Mizram. You're family, and we want to help."

"We're here!" shouted Aria as they came to a blanket of open trees surrounding a riverbed.

Her little cousins' voices were filled with glee and excitement as they splashed around in the water. Mizram, who pretended to be a water monster, disappeared beneath the water and grabbed the girls from behind. It was a simple game that they enjoyed immensely. Her son rested peacefully on the riverbank, watched closely by Pasha's father, who joined them.

Although they were really supposed to harvest some of the green plants that grew in the river's rich black soil, going to the river had always been a time for companionship and relaxation. Hadassah had also thought it would be nice for the girls to see their new cousin, whom they showered with kisses as they held him.

Finally growing tired, she came from the water to sit with her father-in-law and the child.

"Mizram, control your sisters. They are going to get Kamili wet," she shouted to Mizram as water flew in her child's direction.

"Sorry, cousin Hadassah," all the girls said in unison.

"It's all right. Go back to what you were doing."

"In just a little while, he will be just as rowdy and full of life as those three," Miori said, greeting her with a smile.

"Well if I have learned one thing from your son, it's how to handle rowdy boys. I'm still unsure about girls though."

"Yes, Pasha was that way when he was younger. So, Kamili it is."

"Kamili Miori Okala Nuvahli in honor of my husband's father."

"This is a big step for you and my son."

"Yes, Father, it is."

Miori did not hide his satisfaction with her calling him father. Ever since her own father's death, he had tried to be as much of a father to her as he could.

"This child will test the strength of your union as will those soon to follow. You will be forced to sacrifice much for this child, but then you will realize just what a great blessing the child truly is."

"My mother told me that when I conceived my first child, my husband's manner toward me would change."

"All things change. But I know my son, and he loves you. Things will change, but the love between you will only grow stronger, as long as you make time for what is important."

"Thank you, Father," she said, taking his hand and kissing it. "I shall remember your words."

"I have never said this before, but I am honored to have you as a daughter."

"Thank you."

"I never noticed how much good wood grew around here," he said, taking out a knife, looking around at the trees that surrounded the riverbank. "I think I feel like fishing," said Miori.

"I'll be back soon."

With that, he rose and made his way through the thicket of trees to the river.

"Hadassah, you want to go look at the caves downstream?" called out Caldaia as she and the other girls emerged from the river.

"Come on, cousin Hadassah! It will be a lot of fun!" they pleaded.

"No, not now. Kamili needs some rest. Go on without me. Be sure to go with them, Mizram."

"Are you sure you will be all right? Where is my uncle?"

"He just went to cut some wood down the path. He will be back soon."

"If you are sure?"

"I am sure, Mizram."

"All right, girls, if you want to go, let's get this over with."

Being led away by the loud cheers of excited young children, Mizram disappeared behind a rocky hill along the bank as they headed downstream.

Just then, the babe awoke and resumed his crying.

"No, no, no. Quiet, little one, it's all right," she said as she took him into her arms.

"You're all right, you're all right." She began to remember a melody her mother once sang to her as a child.

"You're all right, precious one. Nothing will harm you. Sleep peacefully now, precious one. Know that I am beside you, precious one. Dream of me as I love you in my arms."

"As always, a lovely melody," came a strange voice from behind.

When she rose with Kamili clutched in her arms, she found herself standing before a figure in black, a mask covering the face. Surrounding her were nine more, all wearing black robes and masks.

"It's a strange what things you remember after so long, a mother's lullaby, a sister who wronged you," said the figure, beginning to pace around Hadassah.

"Who are you?" she said as she grew more terrified by the strangers surrounding her and her son.

Lifting her right hand to her face and loosening the veil, a young, hardened, yet still lovely face was revealed, being close in detail to Hadassah's. "It does me good to see you, Hadassah."

"Helomar. What are you doing here?"

"What am I doing here? No, no, sister. What are you doing here?"

Her hand extended forward, and Hadassah fell to her knees, feeling a large weight upon her. Without warning, her arms were pried open by invisible hands.

"With a child, such a lovely child that you do not deserve," she said contemptuously as she held her nephew.

"What is this, Helomar? What have you turned into? Please give me my son! Give him back to me!"

Helomar's palm opened once more, and Hadassah felt her body rooted to the earth. "It's time to pay for the life you stole from me!"

"Helomar, please! I swear I knew nothing of Jezareel's death. I had nothing to do with it!" Hadassah's face became inundated with wells of tears and fear as she kept her eyes fixed upon her son.

"You lie."

"Pasha swore to me that he did not kill Jezareel."

"His honor is dung beneath my feet. I could see the blood on his clean hands as he pressed them all over you."

"What do you want from me, Helomar? Whatever this is, please leave my son out of it!"

"I am sorry, sister, but little Kamili here is a big part of this."

Her eyes widened with terror as the sister she once loved drew a knife from her robes.

"Miori, Miori, Miori! Mizram!" she cried out as tears streamed down her face. She turned to run, but the rest of the strangers in black closed in to cut her off.

Without saying anything, Helomar went to a nearby rock and laid Kamili down. Hadassah rushed toward him frantically but did not get far, as Helomar drew a long dagger. Without hesitating, she moved forward and plunged the dagger into her sister's flesh.

Hadassah cried out while pain and weakness overwhelmed her. Breathing became harder as she collapsed into the earth. When she touched her side, all to be found was a pool of her blood.

The new mother looked up at her sister. Helomar stood over her, holding Kamili once more. Her child's wailing filled her ears as his small eyes saw his mother on the ground covered in blood.

Helomar started to rock him and croon him to try to calm him. The child's crying continued to fill the trees around them.

Helomar looked down at Hadassah once more. Both sisters stared at each other in silence. Darkness began to cloud Hadassah's sight, but her eyes saw clearly as a small tear fell onto Helomar's cheek.

Her once proud face was now one of sadness and remorse.

"I'm sorry it had to come to this. Farewell, Hadassah." She then turned to one of the others. "Arzim, let's go."

The stranger nodded, and along with his fellows, they disappeared into the trees.

"Helomar! Helomar!" Hadassah shouted as her sister began to walk away into the trees, clutching Kamili tightly in her arms.

In spite of her shouts, Helomar did not turn back. When she had disappeared, Hadassah cried out for Miori and Mizram. Still, she knew it would be a long while before her cries were heard.

CHAPTER 7
Tests and Trials

The work turned out much easier than Pasha imagined, still it lacked the excitement of his previous profession. Mostly all he did was make his rounds along the southeastern gate where all trade goods were to be given a thorough inspection after tariffs had been paid. After the inspection of every merchant group, he would go to the marketplace to keep an eye on the merchants while they sold their wares. His day ended when the market traffic died down to more tolerable levels.

Overhead, the sun was waning yet still bright as Pasha passed through one of the last northern outposts on the road home. He stopped as he looked to the west. By now, Hadassah, Mizram, and the girls would be finishing their task at the river. Pasha decided he would meet her on her way home; she would like that. Leading Daimon off the path, he rode into the vast plain of grass. He rode at full speed, desiring to learn of his wife's day and to tell her of his. Upon spotting the long wall of trees at the end of the plain, he went down the hills toward them.

A strange sight met his eye as he proceeded down the hill. As he got closer, he made out the figures of his father and his three little cousins walking very fast in his direction.

Pasha went to meet them, worried by the sight of his father's naked blade. The closer he got, he discerned another figure being carried on Miori's back.

Miori suddenly fell to the ground without warning. Mizram quickly slid from his back and collapsed alongside him. The girls wept fearfully for their uncle and brother as they remained on the ground and did not get up.

Pasha leapt from Daimon and ran to them.

"Father! Father!" Pasha shouted.

Miori rose back up, gasping for air. "Son! Son!" he said wearily.

Pasha looked at his drawn sword and then checked him for wounds. "Are you hurt?"

"What?" said Miori, not understanding.

"Are you hurt! Speak to me, Father!"

"No. Just been running. I'm all right though. See to Mizram; he's in bad shape."

Pasha went to Mizram. When he came upon his cousin, it was as if a knife had hollowed out his insides. Hastily made bandages barely covered the open gash where a sword blade had slashed him.

"Mizram! Mizram!"

His cousin's head moved about aimlessly as he tried to take in air. Fatigue had settled in every corner of his body. Pasha helped him when he tried to sit up. "Mizram."

"Pasha," he said in a tired whisper.

"What happened? I need to know what happened."

Mizram gasped and began to breathe rapidly. Every breath was becoming a difficulty for him. His cousin began wheezing and coughing when he tried to speak. Soon his body was rocking back and forth uncontrollably. Pasha put his hands on the wound and steadied him.

"I got you. I got you," said Pasha.

"Pasha . . . Pasha," said Mizram.

"I'm here. Mizram, what happened? Where is Hadassah?"

"She . . . gone."

"Gone? What do you mean she's gone? What about Kamili? What about my son!" said Pasha. His heart pounded in his chest, and a frantic heat filled his flesh.

"She's gone, Pasha. I try to . . . try to stop them . . . black rider . . . too many."

Mizram's words stopped, and his head fell back into Pasha's shoulder. Feeling the breath escaping his cousin's nostrils, Pasha knew he was still alive, though quite weak.

"He's going to get worse," said Miori, who had finally come to his feet.

But Pasha did not hear him. Inside, he felt hollow and cold. Though he tried to think of what to do next, all of his thoughts were immediately consumed by fear. Looking down at Mizram, he remembered that fateful day as a boy living along the Aliso River. It seemed that the nightmares of the past had come to haunt him once more.

"Pasha, we need to move. Get him to the house."

"What of Hadassah?"

Miori lowered his head. "I don't know, son."

"What do you mean you don't know!" Pasha shouted as he leapt and seized his father by the neck of his tunic. "You were supposed to be watching her!"

"I was watching her, Pasha. I left her for a moment because I did not think this would happen."

"You know what happened to us before! How could you be so foolish?"

"Pasha, please."

Pasha released his father and drew his sword. Confusion and fear clouded his steps as he paced about, trying to decide what to do.

"What if it was brigands, Father, or slavers! Daiyu knows what they'll do to her. And Kamili!" Suddenly a torrent of tears swept over Pasha. "Where is she? Where is my son? How could this happen?" Pasha said as fear and dread continued to overwhelm him.

"Pasha, take it out on me if you need to. But do it later. We need to get Mizram back to the house and get your uncle. And then we can go look for her . . . Pasha, son! Mizram is going to die if we do not help him!"

Pasha turned to look at his father.

"I need you to trust me, son. Now more than ever. Come help me."

Pasha nodded and helped put Mizram onto Daimon's back. They went toward home in silence. Aria and Caldaia clung tightly to Miori while he led Daimon, who carried Mizram. Pasha walked ahead of them, holding Alsaya in his arms.

Soon they had crossed through the hills and came within sight of the house. But when they looked in the distance, their eyes beheld a lone figure walking in a crooked manner. It did not take long for Pasha to realize it was Hadassah.

He set Alsaya down and sprinted toward her.

"Hadassah! Hadassah!" he shouted as he ran toward her.

She stopped and turned once he was within a few dozen paces of her.

"Hadassah!" said Pasha. He stopped within ten paces of her, relieved to see her alive.

But when Hadassah looked back at him, he saw the same weariness and confusion he had seen in Mizram's face. Her hair was crumpled and strewn in all different directions, and hanging from it were bits of dirt and leaves. And her disheveled face was scratched and marked with cuts.

His wife's hands clutched her side and stomach. In her hands, she held bloody rags, but within moments, Pasha realized that they were Kamili's baby clothes.

"Hadassah?"

She began moving toward him. "Pasha. I'm sorry. I'm sorry." Suddenly she stopped, and her hands fell to her side, giving Pasha a thorough view of the massive stab wounds that had ripped open her flesh.

"No!" he shouted as his wife collapsed to the ground. "No, no, no, no!" he pleaded as he cradled her head within his arms and pressed her tightly to him.

"Pasha," she called out to him.

Pasha pressed his hands against the wounds. "Father!" he shouted.

Miori was already sprinting down toward them, leaving the girls to stay with Mizram.

"Oh no!" were the only words Miori could utter when he saw Hadassah.

"We've got to do something, Father. We've got to."

But Miori did not move. The entire ground around them was coated in his daughter-in-law's blood. She was barely conscious as Pasha held her.

"What are you doing? Come on!" Pasha shouted angrily.

Miori came down beside her and peeled off his tunic. Together they wrapped it about her. The bleeding slowed, but Miori knew they could not stop it.

"Pasha, I . . ."

"Pasha," came Hadassah's voice once more. Her eyes opened again and focused intensely upon her husband.

"I'm here, Hadassah. I'm here."

"I'm sorry, my love. I'm sorry I couldn't be stronger."

"This is not your fault, Hadassah. And you're going to be all right, you hear me?"

"She took him."

"Who was it? Where is Kamili?"

Suddenly her voice grew weaker, and Pasha could see she was slipping away. Pasha shook her as his fears grew. "You cannot leave me, Hadassah. You cannot. There is too much, too much to do, too much to see."

"My . . . Lomar . . . she's still . . . she's still . . . husband . . . love of my heart . . . Kamili . . . Kamili . . . Kami . . ."

No more words came from his lovely wife as she closed her eyes and the last bit of life left her. Pasha hardly heard the cries of his three cousins as they cried out for woman they had come to love as a sister. At that moment, everything seemed dark and sickening.

"Son. I'm sorry. I'm so sorry," said Miori.

He stood to meet the girls as they came down the hill toward them. Pasha felt nothing but emptiness when he looked down at her. Even in death, her beauty haunted him as it had in life.

When he looked up to the heavens, he found no answer for the madness that had befallen him once more. Perhaps there were no answers, he thought to himself.

Remembering the sword beside him, he reached out to grab it. No longer caring, he slowly positioned the point of the blade below his heart.

He did not hear the cries of his cousins as they saw what he was doing. But he was quickly stopped when his father struck him hard in the head and pinned him to the ground, knocking his sword away from him. Pasha struggled as he held him. His face twisted into uncontrollable sobs and he cried out, "No! Let me go! Let me go! Hadassah! No, Hadassah! Why? Why?"

His cries rang like a mighty horn throughout the night. All of Sashra would know that Pasha Nuvahli mourned that night.

Long wails of mourning went throughout the plains for seven days as the family of Hadassah and Pasha came to mourn the passing of one they had loved so well. For six days, they mourned, and on the seventh day when she was buried, all of her family and many of the house of Nuvahli came to say one final farewell, all but the man with whom she had shared her heart.

To their relief, Mizram pulled through and managed to tell them of the black riders and their leader who was a woman. Though Malik Juktan sent his captain, Rakimo, along with more than fifty warriors to track down them down, in the end their efforts had been fruitless.

The riders had been tracked to the farthest northern provinces, but from there, they disappeared. Garrison commanders along the border pass were duly notified, but Pasha had begun to realize that the woman who may have played some part in his wife's death and taken his son would not be found.

Bearing knowledge of past dreams that may have prevented this was like a silent torture upon Pasha's mind. Yet even in grief, he could not mention them, though he desperately needed for someone to take the responsibility for Hadassah's death.

It was on the fifth day that Pasha left the grieving families and disappeared. After the sixth day, no one went to search for him, for they knew of the battle raging inside of him.

He had gone to the temple to think. Although the time of prayer had passed earlier that day, the doors to the temple remained open. Before the prayer altar, which stood in front of the shazhia's speaking platform, was Pasha on both knees, a mourning basin beside him.

With tears streaming down his face, he looked up to the large meditation window behind the shazhia's platform as he dipped his hands in the cool water and washed his face.

"My mother, my brothers, my wife! What have I done to deserve this? Why do you treat me so?" he shouted.

"That's always been our question ever since the time of birth."

Pasha turned to the sight of his father coming slowly toward him. "How did you know where to find me?"

"After I lost your mother and your brothers, I tried to hide myself in the temple," he said as he knelt beside him.

"She's gone, Father, just like Mother!"

"Yes, my son, she is gone for now, but she is not lost. I grieved myself into a frenzy after your mother and brothers were killed. I left you with your uncle because I was too afraid to raise you. I wanted to do what you attempted days ago, and one time I nearly did."

"What happened?"

"I felt arms, soft arms wrapping around me, and though I saw nothing, I heard your mother whispering into my ear. She whispered four words. 'Not yet, my love.' It was then that I realized that nothing could truly take away a woman like your mother, and so I took heart and gathered up the courage to live again."

"And that is how you went on?"

"Yes, it is. Oh, my son, you have lost far more than I wished you to. But we are mortal; we live today as if tomorrow may never come. That was how you loved Hadassah, and that is how you must go on. But take heart, for you shall see her again, as you will see your mother and your brothers."

"See her again? The shazhia is not quite sure that she was attacked. Some like him say that she died by her own hand and is therefore subject to damnation. Do not give me anymore of this worthless religion and this worthless god!"

"You do not really believe that do you, son? Do not curse Daiyu in your anger. There is a plan and a purpose for all he allows to happen and does not allow."

"I know not what to believe, Father . . . I had a son! A beautiful child. I know not where he is, whether he is alive. I am his father, but I cannot find him! All I know is that I am alone, and your god does not comfort me."

Pasha said, stressing each word angrily, "Pasha, please. You are angry and confused. That is understandable. But your family has not forgotten about you. Daiyu has not forgotten about you. His plan may not yet be clear, but believe me, Pasha, there is still a purpose for your life as there was for Hadassah's."

"No, old man! There is no purpose! There is no Daiyu! Do you expect me to pray or live my life in his service? I have been doing it all of my life! As my reward, he takes away my mother and my brothers. And now my wife! Daiyu is no more than a curse!"

"Do I mean nothing then, Pasha? Do your cousins, your uncle, and your aunt mean nothing?"

Pasha paused and breathed heavily before speaking again.

"I feel like that little boy I knew years ago. Scared."

"I know, Pasha. I know."

Within three months, the whole of Sashra was in fear once more as a secret Baku and Jakshima army emerged from the refuge of the northern wilderness. They moved quickly against the city of Cafura and the other Sashraman northern provinces. Soon, an even larger force of northern tribes descended upon the tumultuous northern pass.

As events unfolded and nights of unceasing dreams and visions consumed the malik of Sashra, he knew it was time to call his servant and friend to him. Though it took many days, the malik eventually found Pasha, who had disappeared after the funeral for his wife. The malik summoned him immediately to his palace.

In the comforting solitude of his chambers, the young malik collected his thoughts. Sharp pains swept through his head, making the weight of his crown almost unbearable. Still, this pain would be nothing compared to the pain and confusion he would inflict upon the man, the friend he had summoned that day.

The door opened quickly. As the malik turned, Rakimo entered, saluting him and shutting the door behind him.

"He is here," he said softly.

"Very well." He sighed, drawing deep breaths.

"Show him in," the malik commanded.

"Sire, are you . . ."

"Rakimo, not again. Show in my friend."

"Yes, sire."

Rakimo returned to the doors of the throne room, opening them to let in the malik's guest.

His friend seemed different as he walked through the door of the splendid hall for the first time in many months. It was as if he carried the weight of all the years on his shoulders, a burden impossible to lay down.

"Glory to Juktan most high Malik of Sashra, beloved servant of the most high God. May Daiyu forever keep him and his house." His voice, though respectful, was quavering, having lost its once profound confidence.

As Malik Juktan looked to his friend, he beheld a near stranger. "You may go, Rakimo." Once his captain had gone, the king descended from his seat of power, going to his friend as he stood rigidly in place. "You have been gone a long time," he said as they embraced.

"I needed time," said Pasha in a low voice.

"I know," said Juktan as he led Pasha to the center of the room. "I am so sorry for your loss, my friend. It is unjust that one who has given so much must suffer such agony."

Pasha lowered his head as if in acknowledgment, but his tone was direct as he changed the subject. "You have been looking for me for quite awhile and in many places."

"I need you, Pasha. What I am about to ask you is more than a malik asks of his men, but I ask that you listen to my words before deciding anything."

Pasha drew a hesitant breath.

"First, you should see this."

Going back to his gilded seat of power, the malik reached down beside it and withdrew a piece of parchment. It was very old and rough, Pasha noted as it was handed to him.

"What does it say?" he asked.

"Oh sorry. I forgot," said the king, taking back the parchment.

Pasha hated dealing with things he did not understand, most of all the strange marks on parchment that were supposed to be language.

"During the Great War, the emperor and his family perished with him. However, not all were killed, as many believe. One of the emperor's wives, Januai, gave birth to two boys within three years before the Mulamar invaded Sashra. This is an account of a servant woman who served the emperor's wives, including Januai. In it she tells of how the two young princes were smuggled out of the city by a Nashaliaa guardsman called Ozhalos. She recalls how the warrior against all odds managed to deliver the two boys to her and her husband. They were given the children to raise in secret until one day when the name of Navakari could be proclaimed once more. The name of this servant woman was Jadia, and her husband was Daqyada."

"That account is truly incredible, my king, but I know not what it has to do with me, nor do I believe any of it is true," said Pasha as he tried to sound indifferent.

"Why is that, Pasha?" asked Juktan.

"Everyone knows that the emperor and all of his family were slaughtered by the Mulamar during the invasion. What does this have to do with me?"

The king shifted his weight uncomfortably as he began to take slow steps toward Pasha.

"It has everything to do with you. I saw your face as I said the names. You recognize the names of your grandfather and grandmother. The names of the two princes were Keradi and Miori, Miori and Keradi, your father and your uncle."

"My family has nothing to do with this, because they were not there."

"I know you recognize the names: Daqyada was your grandfather."

"It is a very common name," Pasha said.

"I am sorry, Pasha, but that is no coincidence. This letter was written by your grandmother three years before she died. The babes she spoke of are your father and uncle."

"Stop it."

"Your real grandfather is the emperor of the south. You are of the royal family."

"Stop it! I do not know what this is, but you most clearly have gotten your facts wrong, sire. We have had nothing to do with the imperial family!"

"In the aftermath of the siege, the bodies of the princes were never found. You know as well as I do that there is no history of your grandparents' family along the Aliso River where you grew up."

"They returned to the Aliso after living north," Pasha countered.

"If so, why is there no record of them?"

"You can't have a record for everything!"

"I know, but there are records that your grandmother was born in the emperor's house and grew up as a servant there. There are records that she married a merchant called Daqyada who came from a prosperous family. Nuvahli used to be a prosperous house until the war. After the war, they fell into destitution. Why did your grandfather not tell you that part of your history? I have seen old records that survived the siege; one of them was a record of all the servants who served the emperor's house. Your grandmother's name is in that record. To the Nuvahli you may have been born, my friend, but Navakari is your true blood."

"That is a lie! I will hear no more!" Pasha shouted. Though he was testing tense waters, Pasha felt no reluctance as he began to walk from the malik's presence.

"Why do you think they killed your mother and your brothers?"

He stopped, turning swiftly in anger. "What did you say?"

"They were not killed by random Baku marauders, Pasha."

"Do not presume to tell me that. They were Baku!"

"They were more than that. The men who slew your family were bought off by a fearful, selfish tyrant of a man with no compassion left in him. He feared the prophecy and the coming of the one warrior the oracle spoke of."

"Prophecy?"

"Every Sashraman knows of the prophecy, Pasha. The oracle spoke of a dark day when the kingdom Daiyu gave to the descendants of Navakari his servant would break apart in strife.

"All of this has happened, Pasha. *The House of Navakari shall not fall until the tenth of a dead line shall come. In his heart, he shall bear anger and know much sorrow. But when the time comes, he shall be tempered by the power of compassion. Great wars and great struggles shall come, but those who follow in the shadow of the righteous shall endure.*"

"Your family was killed because of these words."

"I am Pasha Miori Okala Nuvahli, son of a farmer and warrior, from a long line of farmers and warriors. These words mean nothing to me!"

"Your family has been hiding from this truth for half a century. Do not try to discard the words as meaningless, for they are not!"

"My life is real. It is my own."

"The man who had your mother and brothers killed was my father."

Pasha nearly stopped breathing, choking on air. His fists became weighted down with anger and struck the malik's face. Juktan fell to his knees, clutching his face.

"Tell me it is not true. Tell me you did not know about it!"

"Do not act as if it is hard to consider. You know what my father was like; all of Sashra does. All that concerned him was holding onto the throne that my family has held ever since the end of the Great War. Yes, Pasha, I knew, but I was too young to do anything about it. I saw him sending messengers late in the night to whomever he planned it with. I saw the gold he gave to his assassins. I listened to him boast when he heard that your home had been destroyed. I did not realize until I read this account left by your grandmother that it was your family that my father sought to destroy."

Pasha stumbled, falling to his back as a violent fit of tears and anger overwhelmed him.

"The band of marauders who murdered your family was the only Baku band to go so far south during the Border Raids and commit successful raids; it was because my father paid them and cleared the way for them."

"Why would he have done this to us? My brothers were no threat! My mother was no threat!"

"He came after all of your brothers so that none of you could rise and take Sashra from him. The red-eyed general whom they call Rashtak has taken the throne of the Baku king and imposed his dominion over the Jakshima tribe. There are over fifty thousand northern warriors at the border pass, and their numbers continue to grow, while there are more than twenty thousand already in our lands attacking Cafura.

"What I ask of you, Pasha, is to go to the king of the Halor and petition him to bring the other tribes together into a pact with us that we may defeat our enemies before it is too late. I assure you, I would never lie to you, my friend."

"I cannot accept that, Malik. My life is not a lie; it cannot be."

Pasha turned back for the doors, resolving to not stop as the malik spoke once more.

"Think on this, Pasha. Your wife was killed because someone is still trying to get to you and destroy you. Why do you think they took your son? They are still out there, Pasha."

Saying no more, Pasha continued for the doors and left the malik's presence.

Though he rejected much of the malik's words, Pasha could not put them from his mind. He considered what the malik had proposed for many days.

CHAPTER 8

A Troubled King

Again the awareness of another presence robbed Hanasa of a once peaceful sleep. Hanasa, though lean and near middle age, bore adequate muscle and nimbleness about his tall, black body. Unlike most men of the south, he wore his hair short and cropped down to the scalp.

He rose carefully from his bed so as not to wake his two sleeping wives. Hanasa moved quickly and stole away into the darkness as he had done more than ten nights prior. Leaving his bedchambers, he moved quietly so as not to arouse the attention of the guards who stood at the far end of the stone corridor.

Going up the hall, Hanasa went through the oval shaped marble doorway and started up the plain stone steps in his nightclothes. Eventually he came to the roof of the palace, paying no mind to the cold night breeze.

All was as it had been before; the night was cold, the sky full of stars, and the whispering of many voices carried along the wind.

At the far end of the roof was a black shape beside an old tower looking out upon the city of the Halor king. Hanasa went toward the figure in black and stopped within eight paces.

She continued her gaze upon city, letting the strong wind catch her robes and her hair, yet the veil that covered her face remained.

"You still gaze at my city, strange woman. Tell me, does the view improve each night you call me here from my sleep?"

She remained silent, which always angered Hanasa. He had tried once to get his guards to apprehend her, but each time, she disappeared. Besides the door he had come through, there was only a long drop onto the solid stone of the courtyard below.

Who she was, he did not know. Who she said she was, he could not believe.

"Though you see as I do, Hanasa, the debauchery, heresy, and the blasphemy, you still see through the eyes of the unworthy below us."

"If I am unworthy, why don't you leave me and disturb the sleep of some other miserable soul?"

"Whether I go or not, you shall know no more until you pay heed to the words of the heavens and act now. Act now for the salvation of your people and the tribes of the one."

"Again you speak about the salvation of my people like you know us. Our salvation came years ago when we broke from the empire and our tribe became one again. Now you come again another night to tell me to cast my lot in with my enemy and bind the fate of my people with theirs."

"You know who I am, Hanasa. Your people once knew me when they were one and along the right path, loved and received by the heavens. Now they are broken, and they have forgotten."

"If you truly were who you say you are, and Daiyu truly spoke through you, he would not tell me to throw away years of peace, tranquility, and progress to fight the war of the very enemy who would enslave us once more. The emperor is dead, the empire is dead! I will not lower myself before Malik Juktan, nor his harlot, or any assassin he sends to my city!"

"You will see in time, Hanasa, High King of the Halor, that the warrior who comes does so with the righteous fire of Daiyu. The blood of Navakari, his servant, must be respected if your city is to last another fifty years and regain Daiyu's favor."

"Daiyu's favor has not been lost. We gained it in the battlefields, bleeding our enemies until they fell. The emperor's seed was cut. I will not send Halor warriors to fight for our enemies in a war that is not theirs. Be warned, woman! This is the last time you disturb my sleep. I give you an opportunity to warn your assassin. For the moment he steps into my city, he is dead."

The king turned to go back to the steps, followed by the woman's unwavering voice.

"As you so desire, Hanasa; this shall indeed be the last time I come to you. But know this. The blade that cuts down the son of my lord's servant Navakari shall be turned upon the heads of your children."

The king spun back toward her in fury, grinding his teeth as he reached for a stone brick.

"I beg of you, do not turn a blind eye to the danger ahead of you. You will be remembered as either a great king or a fool whose memory shall be washed away as the many sands by the sea."

She was gone before Hanasa could reach her, leaving him alone and free to return to his sleep. But Hanasa knew as he considered her words that he would not sleep until the matter of this man who came bearing the face and sign of the emperor was resolved.

The pain that a lack of sleep brought nagged at King Hanasa the next day as he sat upon his seat in his great hall, oblivious even to the monotony of the chief scribe's voice as he delivered news, concerns, and pleas from the various provinces. King Hanasa's hall was not the same in magnificence to the old emperor's in Kadisha, but the simple red stone walls, finely polished wooden floor, and the open windows suited the king well enough.

Four days of worry, anger, and anxiety toward the tidings that would be brought by the unwelcome guest had kept the king most occupied. The man would arrive any day now, and in spite of his careful preparation, the king still feared the veiled woman's words. The first time she had come to him, he had sensed a presence around her that he could only describe as unnatural.

Though he tried to convince himself that she was either a witch, a ghost, or an assassin, nothing could assuage his fear that she truly was the oracle, returning to man after more than fifty years. She had spoken Hanasa's very thoughts as though she were reading a piece of parchment.

Nevertheless, he did not know how she could expect him to toss aside the legacy of poverty and violence left to his people by the empire. The empire had left his people weak, poor, and allowed the Sashramans and Yashani to maintain dominance over them. He knew from his history, the words of his father, and great kings like Tashdar the Magnificent, that the Great War was just. Yet this woman spoke a certain truth to his ear, one that was difficult to ignore.

The king rubbed his temple vigorously as tense thoughts seemed to burn themselves into his head. His eyes opened widely when he saw a tall, black warrior in bright silver armor staring at him. His dark face and brown eyes seemed to pierce into Hanasa.

Hanasa stood and went toward the warrior, wondering in his mind how he got into his throne chamber. The king winced and felt a quavering fear needle itself to the bottom of his stomach as Hadda, his captain of the guard, walked straight through the stranger, who continued to glare at the king.

"Sire, the men are in position," he said quietly, noting the many stares upon them as the king pointed to an empty space.

At first, Hanasa could barely speak.

"Who are you?" he demanded.

The warrior did not answer.

"I have not seen you before. Go now I say before I have you executed for insulting me with your presence."

"Sire?" said Hadda uneasily.

"Seize him, Hadda. Throw his body into the streets."

"Seize who, sire?"

"Him! The warrior in silver armor! Disarm him!"

"Majesty, please." The captain came closer to the king, gesturing him to lower his hand, as people began looking on with most confounded expressions.

"Do not touch me, Hadda! Do you disobey my orders?"

"High King, I know not of whom you speak. If I could see this warrior, I would most gladly carry out the order."

It pained Hanasa to continue to look at the warrior who stood rigidly in place, seeming to not breathe or bear any discomfort.

"Seize the warrior in silver armor or your head shall fall quickly from your shoulders!"

"Sire, there is no warrior in silver armor."

"You take me for a fool, Hadda. He is standing right behind you, right before me and my throne."

"Sire, please, there is no one there."

The scribe finally stopped his news delivery and turned to address the king.

"Perhaps His Highness if fatigued from the heat. It may be fitting for us to continue at another time when he has fully gathered strength."

"Do not mock me, you old fool. He is there, right in . . ." When the king looked around, he found no sign of warrior in silver armor.

"My lord!" Hadda said, steadying the king as he suddenly stumbled.

Hanasa ignored him as the doors were thrown open and a servant entered quickly, prostrating himself before the king.

"He is here, is he not?" said the king more to himself than to the servant.

"My lord, a Sashraman bearing the standard of Malik Juktan of Sashra seeks an audience with His Majesty. He wishes to deliver the respects and message of the Sashraman king."

"My lord, you are not well. Allow me to dispatch the Sashraman so that he does not offend you," spoke Hadda.

No matter how he denied it, he knew a force was manifesting its will in Hanasa's palace that day.

"No, No!" he said aloud to himself. "We did not give so much blood just to run back into the arms of deception of the Sashramans. Daiyu gave us victory. Daiyu stands beside us now."

"My lord," spoke Hadda as he knelt before the king. "Do not allow yourself to become vexed by the lies of your enemy. Command me, and he shall breathe no more."

Composing himself, Hanasa turned away from them and slowly took his seat upon his throne. The Halor king could not shame his father by giving up all the family stood for and had taught him; he would not dishonor his family.

"Hadda, tell your men to stand ready. Show the Sashraman in."

"Would it not be better that we dealt with him elsewhere, my king, rather than in the magnificence of your court?" Hadda inquired, still worried by the king's actions and his demeanor.

"Show him in!" ordered Hanasa.

Hanasa raised his voice, and the air of command that it carried moved the servant quickly to the door. He hesitated as Hadda stood and looked to his men. With a quick hand signal, they fell into a tight oval formation about the king, weapon hands ready for bloodletting. The doors came open quickly to admit the unwelcome visitor.

Anxiety gripped Pasha like a hawk's talons as he stood in the corridor of white stone. Every other moment, the Halor guards threw him looks of silent disgust as they stood at the entrance to the king's hall.

Pasha knew not what would befall him inside. His treatment ever since his arrival in Halor land was all the evidence he needed to know that he would have to be on guard while among the Halor tribe. Pasha looked to the tall Halor to his left who held his sword. Silently he wished he could feel the hilt in his hands.

Fortunately, they had not discovered the small dagger wrapped in tight cloth around his ankle; it was not a common practice to search so low. The guards were probably so hateful of Sashramans they desired to touch him as little as possible.

His thoughts shifted to the Halor king. He knew not how he could convince a man who was more an enemy to join a cause and believe in something that he himself did not.

Pasha remembered how the malik had told him before he left that no man would impede his journey. Juktan had said this with such outrageous finality that Pasha could not believe it; it was all he could think of as the doors to the king's hall finally opened.

All were silent as Pasha entered the room, bowing in a polite manner. Pasha noted an air of contempt from the servant who admitted him. Sitting before the king on both sides of a narrow path leading up to his throne were men and women, possibly there to entertain one of the king's moods.

Coming forward, he saw his death awaiting him inside the oval shaped formation of well-built Halor warriors standing around their king. His end was near.

His eyes came up to meet the king's as he stopped within the center of the formation, barely eight paces from the king.

King Hanasa's face was blank, yet Pasha sensed the same kind of anxiety about him as he had felt the moment he entered the palace. Pasha touched the silver amulet of his family, passed down to his father and now to Pasha.

Whoever his ancestors were, Pasha prayed for their strength as he bowed low before the king.

It surprised him that he had risen with his head still intact. Still, danger dwelt all around him. The one who stood at the right side of the king's throne bore the same blank look as the rest of his guards, but his impatience showed as he continually tapped the hilt of his sword.

Finally Pasha tried to speak, but he was cut off by the king before his tongue could create a word.

"I know why you are here, Sashraman. Your king sends you to beg for my help in cleaning up Sashra's mess, as if I am one of his noble, bastard sons that he can summon at his will."

The warriors about him laughed as the king delivered his insult.

"My lord, if I may. In spite of what you may know of my malik and think of him, he bears only respect for the king of the Halor."

"And well he should, for he knows full well my power is great and my people unconquerable. Shame that boy king of yours cannot say the same for his pitiful province!"

"My lord is right; your power is great, and my malik knows this. He asks that both of our tribes put aside our differences. Lastly Malik, Juktan asks that you call the other tribes together in order to help us defeat the men of the north."

"Tell me. What makes your king dare assume that I would send my warriors to fight Sashraman enemies or that any other tribe would do the same? Any warrior of mine who goes to Sashra will go only to conquer."

His men warriors pounded their spears on the ground in agreement.

"You will have nothing to conquer, Majesty, once the Baku and their allies have wasted our lands and come for yours."

"You sound as if I should fear this little invasion. Well, have your king know that I do not fear my own shadow, nor do I castrate myself from my honor as he obviously has! I do not fear your king's warnings nor his threats or even you. Your king actually believed that I would listen to you because you wear that amulet and claim to be of the line of the emperor! He is more foolish than I imagined."

Pasha's insides burned with anger as the Halor king continued to speak offense toward Malik Juktan.

"Oh yes, I know of the prophecy and of you, Sashraman. You would try to rob me of my kingdom with your lies and clever deception!"

"Under the emperor, sire, the northern tribes never managed to penetrate the northern pass because we were united. Right now there are not just a few hundred of them at our gates but thousands upon thousands. And though you may not see it, they're coming for all of us, not just Sashramans.

"Even after the Great War, we have kept your lands safe from the growing arm of the northern kings. It is by the blood of Sashramans that the men of the north do not meet you in your own lands at this moment. All we ask is that you, all of you, our Halor brothers, come along with the other tribes under the mantle of brotherhood, a mantle that our ancestors maintained for more than a thousand years!"

"The mantle of slavery. That is what you mean, Pasha, son of Miori."

His muscles tensed as he heard the Halor king say his name.

"Do you know what you represent? Centuries of oppression and neglect, caused by your family. Tell me the truth. You desire to reclaim your birthright, do you not? Juktan, the boy has fallen under your influence, and now you reach out for the rest of the tribes. Or do you even believe you are who the prophecy says you are."

"It is difficult to accept, but I cannot deny who I am no matter how I try. Just as you cannot deny this vital fact: as long as the tribes stray apart and war on one another, the south will never be strong again. The kingdoms of the north and across the southern seas will come and overwhelm us. You know the prophecy, these days were foretold. All I seek is an understanding!"

"During the war, whole battalions of imperial warriors could not halt the resolve of my family and those of the other kings, Daiyu stood by us as he stands by us now. We are free, and we are strong, too strong to fall prey to your foolish words.

"I am glad of one thing though. That boy king did send you to me. Your malik will see once I have sent him back your head, that I am not someone to be fooled with."

Hanasa sat back contently while his men slammed Pasha into the hard stone floor. But as Hanasa signaled Hadda, the man in silver reappeared directly behind Pasha.

"I know not what sorcery you bring, but you shall not defy me. Kill him!"

Hadda's eyes lit up with quiet joy as he signaled the men. However, that joy ended quickly and turned to confusion as the men's swords would not release from their sheaths.

"What are you waiting for? Kill him!"

In spite of the order, his warriors' swords would not budge as they pulled against them with all of their strength. The people who sat watching this stood with great curiosity and fear at what they were seeing. Hanasa glared at the silent man in silver with hatred and fear as he shouted at Hadda, "What are they doing? Cut off the Sashraman's head!"

But even Hadda could not loosen his sword as he came toward Pasha. Quickly he went from man to man, tugging on their swords, releasing the blade locks on their sheaths, but they were fixed like stone inside.

"My lord, the blades will not draw. They are stuck."

"That is absurd! Kill him or you shall join him!"

Hadda seized a bow from one of the men who stood along the wall to the king's right, but the bowstring broke the moment the arrow touched it.

"My lord, this is sorcery of some sort. Our weapons will not touch him."

The king's subjects murmured amongst themselves, moving back to opposite sides of the Sashramans, to the walls, distancing themselves from the supposed sorcerer.

Looking at the Sashraman and the warrior in silver standing by him inflamed the king's anger.

"Get the warrior in silver. He is doing this. He is the witch. Kill him now!"

"My lord, there is no one in silver armor."

"You will not supplant me! My will shall not bend!"

With a feeling of relief, the king drew his small ceremonial dagger from the sash on his robes and ran to strike Pasha. Happily, he managed to thrust his blade into the Sashraman's neck and throat. After a few moments though, he realized that the dagger drew no blood, nor had it broken the skin.

Angrily, he lunged toward the warrior in silver, but his arm succumbed to a heaviness that forced the blade from his hand onto the ground.

"This is impossible. What evil is this!"

"Only the evil of your heart, Hanasa."

The king turned and became light in the head as the woman in black sat upon his throne.

"I have told you before, Hanasa, the will of Daiyu resides in the continuation of his servant Pasha's life. Today you have committed a great sin, Hanasa. You have defied the will of Daiyu before his servant Maikael and allowed your senseless hatred to overwhelm you. Mercy has been shown to you this day, but it shall not be shown again if you do not accept what must come now for your people.

"In five days, his life shall be in your hands. If you take it, your children shall never again wake from their sleep. If you still continue to resist, the Halor tribe will be destroyed. You know the truth, Hanasa, the truth that your mother raised you with. Do not turn your back upon it."

"My lord, he is a witch. We must take you from his presence," spoke Hadda.

"Let me cast him from a high tower! Not even a witch could survive that!"

"No."

"My lord?"

"The heavens have cast their lot against me in this matter. I cannot resist. Take him away."

The men at first were reluctant to touch Pasha, but they moved past this fear, desiring to leave him in a prison rather than among them. With hurried strength, they lifted him to his feet and led him toward the door. As they did this, the woman in black and the warrior in silver disappeared, leaving Hanasa before a stunned, murmuring crowd trying to understand what they had just seen.

"Scribe!"

"Yes, my lord," responded the old man as he moved forward.

"Prepare your parchment and return in an hour with a messenger. Hadda!"

"Lord," he said, standing smartly at attention.

"Get these people out of my sight!"

"Yes, Highness."

"And, Hadda," continued Hanasa.

"Sire!"

"Triple the guard around my wives and children until I say otherwise."

"Yes, my lord."

CHAPTER 9

The Messenger

Pasha crashed into the unforgiving stone floor as the guards threw him out of the throne room. His first attempt to resist was met by a strong blow to his throat. The impact was too much and caused Pasha to fall back and curl up while they kicked his stomach. A blow to his head robbed him of all strength and left him open for more abuse.

Looking up at the guards through his bloodied eyes, he expected more. Instead, two of the men grabbed him by each arm and began dragging him down the opposite end of the corridor from where he had entered. Already his arms felt like snapping twigs and his knees like soft meat being cut into many pieces. The guard who held his right arm continued to crack at his head with a thick piece of dried cowhide.

It seemed clear they were tired of dragging him. With that in mind, Pasha resigned himself to an uncooperative posture. Though he was too weak to fight, he would not allow them to take him to his death easily. Pasha began to look around the long corridor. At the end he could see three more men in different robes, all armed. Pasha could not accept that they were his execution party. Hanasa had to be more cautious than to simply murder a messenger of the Sashraman king, he thought to himself.

Pasha flew into the air and then felt more of his head tear open as it was ripped by the stone beneath him. He knew he was at the end of the corridor, but how he would meet his last moments, he could not decide.

Instinctively he curled up into a tight ball as they flayed him with the ends of their spears. Not one of the men held back as they tore Pasha's skin apart. One pegged his head with the dull spear end, forcing Pasha to open up his body to them once more.

The last blow to his head was so intense Pasha nearly lost consciousness. He knew as the blows kept coming that they were about to kill him. His vision began to fail him along with his other senses. One more blow came, and all was black. Pasha's body moved no more.

"Is he dead?" asked one of the guards.

"We haven't gone far enough to kill him. These Sashramans tend to bleed easily. Throw him out!"

Quickly they opened the door behind them and tossed Pasha into the room's embracing darkness.

The place bore a foul stench that, like the darkness, seemed to cling to every part of the room. Inside, the Sashraman lay with others like him. Beside him were piles of the troublemakers, the shameless, and fearless whose quick tongues, failing virtue, and offensive nature had resulted in their numerous broken bodies, those whose names had forever been erased by the shroud of darkness.

Still, they had been left with constant company. Each day, their little rodent friends came to call upon them. Most came from the damp, open walls, invisible to all with living eyes. Happily, they arrived like friends invited to a celebration, ready to join in the festivities, ready to feed upon the abundance of rotting flesh.

When they moved to the newly arrived Sashraman, they huddled in delight. Moving carefully, they drank in his warm blood and body's juices. However, as their teeth sank into his sensitive parts, they awakened the nearly faded life within him, causing them to attack more ferociously. He was a good feast, and they would not let him go so easily. But eventually they broke off and fled as a stranger approached and drew them off with flame in his hand, something they had learned long ago to fear.

Pasha's eyes opened with blood inside of them and blurred vision. Eventually his eyes fell upon a red light in front of him. Two servants lifted Pasha and took him to the wall near the door. They propped him up against the wall and began to clean his wounds with strange potions with offensive odors.

The man of Sashra looked down in quiet terror. His black body was covered in purple bruises, welts, and long gashes. All of the fingers on his right hand had been broken, and his entire left side was riddled with the punctures of many small teeth that had cut away much skin.

Pasha did his best not to move any part of his body. Despite his efforts, his head was like a battered boat in the middle of a tempest at sea. His eyes eventually began to focus and looked out in disgust at the place where he had been left to die.

It was like an enormous stone box that had been filled with bodies left to rot. The liquid and dampness that he felt upon his hands was the blood and fluids of the men who had expired long ago. Though he lowered his eyes, he could not block the half-eaten corpses, spiked heads, and the remains of disemboweled men from his mind.

"What is this barbarity?"

The servants ignored his words, continuing their work.

The words had been painful to release, for he still felt the many blows the guards had inflicted upon his throat.

"It is what happens in a world where we must be as fierce as lions in order to survive."

Pasha quickly recognized the voice of King Hanasa. He looked to his right as the man came toward him.

"I should have known to expect this from the Halor. Your people hunger for blood. It makes sense that a place like this is where you keep your stores."

"I see my men broke your body but left your tongue. You should be grateful to them for that."

"Yes, I believe so. Most boys possess the strength to draw a sword from its sheath, but I suppose your men were just too worn out."

The king came closer and pulled Pasha's face directly toward him.

"Are you a sorcerer of some kind?"

Pasha did not answer.

"Who was the woman in black? The warrior in silver armor whom none could see?"

"They are obviously signs of a mind that has succumbed to the madness in Halor blood."

Hanasa suddenly released his dagger and dug the blade's dull end into Pasha's tender throat.

"I saw the warrior in armor cause all of my men to be unable to draw their swords against you. It is obvious that he protects you."

"If this supposed . . ." Pasha coughed hard, sprinkling the ground with blood. "If this supposed warrior was protecting me, more than likely I would not look like this right now," Pasha said through heavy, gasping breaths.

"You just want me to kill you, is that it?" Hanasa flipped the blade and pointed the sharp end toward Pasha's exposed, throbbing throat. "I see men like you all the time, warriors who do not fear offending even a king. But let me tell you a little secret. In the end, we are all afraid. You will tell me everything of this sorcery and how to combat it. The woman and the warrior, tell me who they are."

"I think you already know, King Hanasa of the Halor. They are a sign, a sign that you need to rethink your response to the message I gave you. Before I left, my malik told me it was written that no evil would touch me while I was in your house."

"So it is Juktan who has cursed me."

"The only curse is that of ignorance and violence, which you have shielded yourself with ever since my arrival."

"It is not as simple as you might believe, Sashraman. Do you know what you would represent if I acknowledged you and your message?"

"I am not the emperor, and I shall never wear his crown."

"Many would not see it that way! The prophecy has plagued the minds of our priests ever since the emperor's death and the death of his family. Some say that since the emperor's family was dead, the warrior would come from among one of us. Others say the oracle's prophecy is not to be trusted. But now you are here. After what I have seen today, I cannot deny that a great power resides around you. Your very presence is an affront to all of the Halor who died to free us from the empire!"

"There is something else. There must be. Something about this woman and this warrior gives you a greater reason to fear them. If not, I would not be alive right now."

"The woman in black has come to me every fourth night past twilight. She would tell me to prepare for the path I must follow. Eventually, she told me of you. I did not believe her at first, but soon reports began to come in, and everything was falling into place as she said. The woman told me that if I took my dagger," Pasha's throat throbbed once more, and he began to sweat as the cold blade pressed down into his throat, "and put it to your throat like this and ended this before it has a chance to begin . . . She said if I did this, none of my children or my wives would survive the night."

"You must be asking yourself, *Is this man worth it?*"

"You do not scare me! My family is under triple guard, and you are under my hand!"

"You do seem in control. But as a man who has seen equally strange things in his own lifetime, I caution you. Never underestimate what you do not fully understand. I am ready."

The king began to respect the selfless nature of the man whose life lay between his hand and dagger. A heavy silence filled the room as Hanasa considered what he was about to do.

Pasha took deep breaths, knowing it was over.

King Hanasa stood and went toward the door, stopping to speak to one of his servants.

"Wash his body and tend to him. Give him a bed where my physicians can see him."

Dismissing their bows of obedience, Hanasa left Pasha once again in the hungering darkness.

At first, his healing was slow. For many days, he had been unable to sit up, let alone walk. Pasha slept for days and was awoken solely by the physician who came to change his bandages and tend to his wounds.

The man who seemed to be charged with his care was an older Halor man called Yaradai. Like most Halor, he was very black, and his face did not hold back his disgust towards Sashramans or Pasha in general. Every day he came, he would rub some sort of salve or potion along Pasha's opened flesh. Though Pasha assumed it was something to help close the gashes, every night his flesh would open and bleed, making him weaker the next day. It was as if the old man was trying to keep him bedridden.

Pasha began to doubt that, however, when he awoke one day with enough strength to sit up. Sliding back, he laid his back against the wall. Stretching out his arms and pushing hard onto the stone beneath him, he pushed himself up.

In spite of reaching his feet for the first time, his legs failed him, and he crashed to the ground. Pasha rolled onto his back, content to stay there as he began to sweat profusely, and his breathing became ragged.

Nevertheless, all that his mind dwelt on was his mission and whether or not it would be successful. Not knowing disturbed Pasha greatly.

Again he cursed his weakness, beating the ground beside him, scraping the skin on his hand. Pasha's distraught mind did not allow him to hear the sound of another entering the room.

"You must think me a fool if you think I am going to clean that too."

Pasha looked up to see Yaradai coming slowly toward him, his look of disgust and irritation unchanged.

"Scum, Sashraman, you bleed like a gutted pig!"

He bent his knees deeply to wrap his arms around Pasha and lift him to his feet.

"I don't know what you're doing on the ground. You can walk now. I have more important things to do than look after you."

Stepping back, he let Pasha balance himself, holding out an arm for support.

"Really, I don't see what the king wants with you anyway. When I was young, we killed Sashramans on sight! Now I am expected to bandage and heal them. There's something good to be said about the old days."

"I never asked for your help, old man!"

"You had best be grateful for it, *bushim*. One more session with Naylok and Kishei, and I would be burning your wretched corpse instead of wasting my skills on you."

Pasha's head was swimming. His insides burned and felt constricted. He could not stand to be on his feet much longer.

The old man thought differently as he pushed Pasha forward. Immediately Pasha fell onto his knees.

"Walk, bushim! Walk!"

"I cannot."

"I am wasting no more time on you. Now walk!"

He bent forward to pull Pasha up.

"Leave me be, old man!" said Pasha, trying to push away his hands.

"I'll leave you be when I decide to."

"I said leave me be!" Pasha pushed harder, trying to direct a quick blow to the man's face, but that only caused him more pain.

Yaradai caught his slowly moving fist and threw it back to the ground. He kicked Pasha, though not as hard as the ones who had beaten Pasha before. Nevertheless, the all too familiar pain shot through Pasha's insides like a flaming arrow.

"Daiyu damn you, you worthless bushim! You either walk or I will send you back to Naylok."

"You must be a fool if you think that you scare me. Halor bastard!"

Yaradai responded quickly with a thick strap of dried goat hide that he struck Pasha's head with. He continued by striking Pasha's hands repeatedly.

"Get up or you will never use those hands again!"

Pasha could feel the embedded pieces of metal and glass tearing away the skin. Already his hands were covered in blood; his right hand's fingers were not completely healed. Yaradai seemed to remember this; he paused in order to draw a thin stick from his robes. Using the stick, he continued to beat Pasha's hands without mercy. Pasha began to cough, his throbbing body continued to weaken, and the pain continued.

With one final effort, Pasha pressed his palms to the stone and pushed up as hard as he could. Yaradai did not stop until he finally came to his knees and raised himself up.

"Good, bushim. Now walk!"

Dreading even more pain, Pasha moved his right leg forward, and his left soon followed. In spite of his dizziness and difficulty breathing, he began to follow Yaradai who was leading him to the open, oval shaped doorway. Drawing back the overhanging cloth, Yaradai stepped out from the room into the long corridor.

Pasha paused. He was in a completely different part of the palace. The stone around him was white but not finely cut as that in the hall that led to the king's chambers. Cut into the opposite wall was a small circular chamber that held what appeared to be small animals, sealed inside by thick reinforced cedar bars.

Moving closer, Pasha saw they were in fact men curled into tight balls, their knees coming to their mouths for lack of space. All were like filthy balls of dark flesh. Many cried out to Yaradai for mercy, and others for food. Pasha noted one who tore at the bars so furiously with his few teeth that his mouth was nothing but blood. The moans and groans echoed through the open hall like a death cry Pasha had heard many times in battle.

"Move!" Yaradai prodded him with the stick.

"What is this place!" Pasha whispered more to himself. Yaradai ignored him, stepping sideways to avoid a mound of excrement.

"Animals! Daiyu curse all of you!" His thick spittle sprayed the different cells, an obvious sign of his contempt for them.

Being able to focus more, Pasha could see that the corridor led to the outside. Yaradai was leading him to what appeared to be an open garden where a figure stood waiting.

Coming into the light for the first time in weeks overwhelmed Pasha; he lost all balance and fell forward. Yaradai came down hard with his stick, causing Pasha to cry out, but he could not stand again.

"Bushim dog!"

"That will do, Yaradai," King Hanasa spoke softly. "Let him rest."

"Yes, my lord."

"That will be all."

Once Yaradai had left, Hanasa wrapped arms around Pasha's waist and brought him to several cushions that sat by a well.

"I hope you can see why this idea of an alliance is impractical," said the king as he wrapped Pasha in a bright new robe. "Little has changed since the war. Especially for men like Yaradai."

"Where I come from, a man has too much respect to lock another away in tiny cracks in a wall!"

"What do you mean? Oh, you have seen my enemies. Do you not do the same to your enemies in Sashra? Does your king not have a place like this?"

"In Sashra, we kill our enemies and let their souls rest in peace, not beat them from men into quivering children like you Halor."

"You are quite right, my friend; we are quite different. Nevertheless, you still believe that our peoples have a future together. How can you expect our people to rise from the war and become the people of the south? The Hebari spirit the stories speak of is dead. You obviously must expect a miracle or something."

"If it is our destiny."

"Destiny! Hah! Tell me, after what you have been through, can you really believe that! Can you believe that more than fifty years can be erased, and we can go on and become friends?"

"I do not pretend to know, King Hanasa, but my path has led me here."

"Well I do not, Sashraman. The prophecy says that the evil one comes upon us again with a massive army to destroy the faith of the people. There is only one person who has been called that in our history. You know of whom I speak."

"Janaha the witch king."

"Who lived nearly one thousand years ago! Are you telling me that we have to come to your aid to help defeat someone who has been dust for centuries!"

"His body was never found after the Battle of the Mahara Fields."

"So what, you believe that a one-thousand-year-old man is leading the men of the north?"

"I don't know."

"Do you believe any of this, Sashraman?"

"I haven't the luxury of beliefs anymore, not since . . ."

"Not since what?"

"It does not concern you!" Pasha turned his head as small tears came to his face. For so long he had tried to not think on his wife or son, but he was weak, too weak to fight.

"I used to believe that I was always in the right. That Daiyu smiled down upon me and my work and upon my family. Ever since you came though, all is different. You must think me a heartless man, Sashraman. Like you, I have many defenses."

"We are nothing alike."

"Says the man who continues to say that we are all alike, we are one people. I know now that there is a better way, better than all of this. I pray that I can find it with you, Sashraman, for our people."

"Then you will acknowledge my malik's message."

"I will do all that I can so as not to upset the wrath of that woman in black and her silver armored warrior. Whether the other tribes wish to follow or not, I will send warriors to Sashra, but rest assured of one thing, Sashraman. I do not trust you, nor do I trust your king, but I hope that if we go to war together, a bridge of trust can be built."

"Perhaps it will be built between our people, but never between you and me."

"I understand. I will have the servants bring you some food."

Pasha fell onto his back. Though exhausted with pain, he gazed upon the sunlit sky, content that no more pain would come that day to his body.

Hanasa walked around him, looking down upon his body.

"Daiyu be merciful! My men sure do their work well."

"Granted."

"I shall pray for your recovery. Yaradai shall tend to you no more. You can stay here awhile if you wish."

Pasha ignored the king, who left him alone upon the sweet grass beneath the warmth of the sun.

CHAPTER 10

The Council

Within weeks of receiving King Hanasa's messengers, the kings of the other tribes responded. Their response came in the form of their presence rather than that of runners.

More than three weeks after sending his initial message, King Hanasa and Pasha rode out to meet the other kings on a plain just outside of the Halor city. During the passing weeks, the Halor king's demeanor had changed toward Pasha, being one of patience and understanding. Nevertheless, Pasha felt no trust.

They gathered with the kings below a white tent to hold council. The kings sat upon low stools surrounding a low table. All about them were their warriors and diplomats.

"Never before would I have imagined you playing host to a Sashraman, Hanasa," said King Uznaya of the Makar.

"Things have changed, my friend," said Hanasa.

"Yes, they have. For the first time in years, you want us to make Sashraman problems our own," said King Manyar of the Mulamar.

"I would not call this a Sashraman problem, but one facing all of us," countered King Volero of the Yashani. "Have you not heard the reports coming from the north of this massive army gathered there? An army of a size we have not seen for nearly a century," the Yashani king said forcefully.

"We gave up concerning ourselves over such things years ago," said the Mulamar king.

"Then why are you here?" said Masala, the Naua king.

"You keep bringing up things that happened fifty years ago while letting your hatred of Sashramans blind you. If you didn't think this northern army was a threat, you wouldn't have travelled so far just to lob insults."

Pasha then stood and went before the kings to speak. Although he did not know what he would say, as Malik Juktan's representative, he knew he had to speak.

"My lords," he said in acknowledgment while searching for the right words to say. "I know that things in the past . . . sins of the past have divided us in many ways. But I believe that at the core of our being, we have something in common—this sense of being Hebari, that the south is our home. The Great War was bloody, and there were many wrongs done, on all sides."

"Especially one in particular," interrupted the Mulamar king.

"Yes. I know! The empire favored the Sashramans for many years above all of you. And I know that at times emperors asserted control with an iron grip. But that score is settled. It is settled, and it is buried. Do not try raise it again, especially in light of the danger we face," said Pasha

"What is it you're getting at, Sashraman?" asked the Makar king.

"That we go north to the besieged city of Cafura. And when we get there, we say to our enemies that we are Hebari people, and the south is our home. If we don't send that message, then what good are we? Malik Juktan is not reaching out to you as a Sashraman king but as a Hebari man asking his Hebari brothers for help."

Knowing nothing else to say, Pasha stepped back and took his place beside King Hanasa.

"Tell your malik that the Yashani will be there," said King Volero.

"Thank you, my lord," Pasha said, bowing his head toward the Yashani king.

"So shall the Naua. We have trade agreements with the northern cities. We would hate for our investments to be lost," said the Naua king.

"Thank you, my lord," Pasha said, bowing again.

"Mulamar do not do anything for free. Especially where Sashramans are concerned. There are nine cities in Baku southern provinces. We want raiding rights and control of all their goods and treasures," demanded the Mulamar king.

"That goes for us as well," said the Makar king.

Although Pasha knew Sashra could never tolerate a Mulamar presence in the north, he had to compromise.

"You will be allowed raiding parties of no more than five hundred men. And your movements will be closely watched from our northern border. You will be expected to withdraw within two months after your raiding is done. That is nonnegotiable," Pasha said, firmly expecting rejection.

"I will assemble my generals," the Mulamar king finally said.

"Then let us make it a true and honest pact," said King Hanasa, lifting a chalice filled with goat's milk. Drawing a dagger, the king sliced open his hand and let droplets of blood mix with the milk.

As the chalice was passed around, each king drew his own dagger and did the same. It finally came to Pasha. He knew the ritual demanded that all make the blood oath, so after drawing his dagger, Pasha's blood flowed into the chalice.

It then came back to King Hanasa, who drank from the chalice and sent it back around to the other kings. When the chalice came back, and Pasha had drunk from it, the pact was established.

The kings soon gathered with their entourages and left, leaving their generals, with whom Pasha and King Hanasa had counsel for many hours.

CHAPTER 11

The Beginning

Central Sashra

Pasha gasped as he awoke, struggling for air as he tried to steer his mind from the terrible images that had just visited his thoughts. The sight of Hadassah, deep within her own blood, and his frantic search for their stolen son were not things a man could easily forget.

Every night, his heart and body burned with the longing to feel Hadassah's warmth and to hear their son at the foot of the bed.

Though he had believed the malik when he had said it was possible that he may find his son somewhere in the north, Pasha knew it was unlikely. Such knowledge was cold and discomforting, but Pasha knew he had to accept it. It had been far too long to cling onto to any foolish hope.

Far into Sashra's eastern plains, the tall green gave way to a long chain of foreign men who pushed deeper into Sashra's most fertile lands. Flying tall and proud were the banners of each tribe, a strange sight in the kingdom, one that had only been witnessed before in much darker times. At times, villagers and farmers would journey out just to see their new allies. Pasha did not condemn their fear and concern, for he felt much of it himself.

He rode at the head of the formation, which was all cavalry, mostly Halor. A dozen paces back were the missile contingent, archers, and slingers. They were followed closely by the infantry, mostly made up of spearmen bearing heavy shields, along with small groups of swordsmen.

Yashani and Makar tribesmen took up the rear, protecting the long supply train. Ever since leaving the city of King Hanasa, Pasha had been frequently shrouded by the presence of the muscular, black, red-robed Halor. King Hanasa had taken no chances following the end of negotiations at his palace.

Twelve days after crossing into Sashra, they had reached the heart of the eastern central provinces, Kirara being only a day away by horse. In compliance with Malik Juktan's orders, Pasha assumed the rank of *kaudi*, or captain, and would soon take charge of the Sashraman army at Cafura once they arrived.

Upon the eighth day, the army had passed the fortress at Haluda, receiving the last few of the fort's garrison, about two hundred Sashraman warriors. They rode under the charge of a commander called Nalar, whom Pasha found most capable.

Nalar was very black like most Sashramans, but his eyes were of a strange yellow color, which Pasha had heard was the result of eating too much raw meat. Still, he decided not to ask if that was the case. Being slightly older, Nalar possessed a wealth of necessary wisdom. He tended to be quiet and reserved, but in spite of those traits, Pasha found him to be of a generous and caring nature toward the warriors he commanded.

Hakan, his subordinate, seemed his opposite in many ways. His complexion was very light and reddish His mother had been a Lakina trader and his father of Hebari and Nashaliaa blood. He wore a bald head instead of the traditional warrior's locks. At times, he seemed rash and had little restraint. Nevertheless, he fought well and knew how to lead men. Though doubting at times, Pasha resigned himself to Nalar's faith in his men.

Mulamar warriors were very black and stocky, favoring nimble, double-bladed spears and round wooden shields that bore thick iron plates at the center.

Among the Makar, their warriors tended to be of a black or bronze complexion with very long curly hair. They complemented their arms with long, straight swords, a weapon first brought by invading Lakina armies long ago.

Still, the Makar did not march as well as the Mulamar. Among their tribe, formation was not as important as strength and agility. Orderliness seemed to be more appreciated among the Yashani and Naua. Their tribes still bore the old imperial warrior mindset when training their warriors. They all wore orange and black robes beneath their armor, with intricate patterns that were typical of their tribes. Most Yashani had a very light complexion after years of mixing with the paler toned Lakina and Nashaliaa tribes. Most Naua tended to be honey colored, but among them were many who were of a black complexion.

Armor varied among them, and most of the tribes did not armor themselves as heavily as Sashramans. For most of the tribes, a body plate was more than sufficient. Few except for the Sashramans and Yashani wore helmets.

The day grew hotter. Sashra's sun showed them no mercy while they marched through the grassy plains.

"A lot like home," commented King Hanasa as he rode alongside Pasha.

"The heat usually gets very bad during the spring here," Pasha replied.

"Yes, ours as well. Does your northern army still have a presence here? I understood we would be coming upon an outpost very soon," the king said.

"We should come across it any day now. I doubt the enemy has gotten this far south," Pasha answered.

"We should be cautious about assumptions. Often the enemy does not act accordingly," Hanasa warned.

"I do not need you to tell me that," Pasha snapped.

Hanasa quickly changed the subject. "What are they like, these men of the north?"

"You have met them before," said Pasha.

"Yes, but never in battle."

"You shall see soon enough, sire."

"I understand that you have quite a lot of experience with them," said the Halor king.

"I have some, yes," Pasha answered, while inside he grew more uncomfortable with the conversation.

Even though he and the Halor king had somewhat resolved some of their differences, it was hard for Pasha to trust him. The fact that the man had almost tortured him to death did little to bridge the gap of trust between them.

"Did you always know that you were the warrior spoken of in the prophecy?"

"I see no reason to continue this subject!" Pasha urged Daimon further up the line, but the king stayed with him.

"Do you not feel that Daiyu bears some great purpose for you?"

"I know not what you saw, Hanasa, in your palace during your twilight hours. But there is nothing holy or promised about my existence or purpose," Pasha answered angrily.

"You put it so simply, but you have visions as well. Don't you? I hear you when you fall asleep in your saddle. If you do not believe in your purpose, then how are your men to follow you?" Hanasa demanded.

"Do not try to understand me. I have no patience for it," said Pasha.

Pasha's head moved right as dark shapes appeared along the northeast, coming toward them.

General Shabaz of the Mulamar was already riding east toward them with a group of archers. When Pasha got closer, he saw that there were hundreds if not thousands of Sashramans coming toward them. Shabaz gestured to his archer, who quickly prepared their bows for their deadly work.

"Shabaz, stop! Can you not see they're just people!"

"Do not order me, Sashraman!"

His men's bows quickly rose to the air. Pasha rode into them to make them part their line.

"What is wrong with you! They're just farmers with their families!"

"Families that need food, Sashraman, and water. There is nothing innocent about that mob that approaches."

"They are not even armed!"

"Do not interfere, Sashraman!"

Pasha moved with Daimon towards Shabaz, his hand resting on his sword. "You will not cut them down in front of me like sheep."

Shabaz smiled wildly and his men eased down their weapons. Shabaz turned and rode back to the main body of the army. Pasha moved back as well to regroup with the rest of the force. Soon the main army came to a halt and turned to face the oncoming wave of people.

The fact that they were running told one clear fact; the enemy was close.

Their cries and screams wrenched the silence of the plains from around them. Pasha could feel the sense of terror that enveloped them as it enveloped him also. There was no doubt that they were extremely frightened, but he could not accept that they were coming to loot their caravan.

Pasha and the Sashramans grouped with Shabaz and the other generals, along with King Hanasa, who stood near the center of the line before the cavalry, the infantry standing ready behind them.

"Have you seen the northern tribes yet?" asked Hanasa.

"Not yet," answered General Tayla.

"They're out there," said Shabaz to the Halor king. "The question is what to do about these Sashramans here?" He said gesturing towards the oncoming wave of people.

"What do you suggest?" asked King Hanasa.

"This is what we do. Keep your infantries at the ready while your horsemen maintain a good flanking position around them in case they attack us."

"Attack?" said Pasha. "Shabaz, they are frightened and running for their lives."

"Yes, which means they will not be thinking clearly."

"They are trying to get away from the violence, Shabaz, not start it over again."

"I have seen thousands throw themselves into the sea because one decided to. Your people are no different!"

"You will only frighten them by having the cavalry flank them."

"I will protect my men, Sashraman! They're almost upon us. Tell the archers to stand ready!" he said to his subordinate.

"Shabaz!"

"That does not look like a mob that wants to talk!"

"Pasha, he is right!" said King Hanasa. "The mob is out of control."

The Halor and Mulamar cavalry began to move up the right and left flank toward the oncoming swarm.

Moving down the line, Pasha called as many Sashramans as he could toward him, and together they raced toward the oncoming Sashramans.

"Don't get in my firing line, Sashraman!" called Shabaz. "Don't think I won't!"

Pasha ignored him as he concentrated fully on the crowd before him. The distance was closing rapidly between them and his men. Still, Pasha was unsure of what to do. They were only several dozen paces in front of the other tribes' cavalry; whatever he did would have to be done quickly.

Motioning to Nalar, the Sashramans split into two groups. Nalar took fifty men down the middle of the crowd while Pasha's group covered the right and left flanks. Using the blunt ends of their spears, Nalar's group struck down at both sides of the crowd. The people's cries grew louder as Nalar's men circled within them, causing them to slow.

Pasha could now see them fully for the first time. Most of their eyes were red, and their faces riddled with cuts and bruises. But on many, the captain saw bright red boils that seemed all too familiar. They were weak and clawed out toward the Sashraman, crying for help and food. Within moments, Pasha's men had them completely stopped, but they continued to press forward against them, crying out for food and water.

"Where do you come from?" Pasha shouted above their cries. "Silence!"

They did not listen, and he did not have enough men to control them.

"Get out of the way! They're coming!" they cried.

"The one with the red eyes seeks our blood!"

Pasha looked down upon the old man who had said this.

"Who? Of whom do you speak?"

"Let us go! They're coming!"

The younger men took up the earth and began to hurl it at Pasha and his men, the people's cries now deafening their ears.

"Calm yourselves! We will protect you!"

"No one can stop the master of hell and fire! No one can resist his will! He will break our bones and gnaw on the flesh of our children for a thousand years!" said the old man.

"Of whom do you speak!"

"Sir! I know these signs. They have the plague!" shouted Hakan.

Pasha noticed again the boils, the weakness, the foul smell among them. "Do not let them touch you! Cover your faces! Follow me!" he ordered his men.

Using his spear's blunt end, Pasha tried to beat back the many hands that were reaching out toward him and Daimon. Daimon, along with many of the horses, was about to go berserk. The people suddenly became violent. Men pounced upon his men, dragging them from their horses and beating them. They left them on the ground as their women, using knives and their hands, cut apart their flesh.

Having no other choice, Pasha plunged his spear into one of them and drew his sword and began to cut down all who stood in his path. Once they had freed themselves from the swelling mass of bodies, they rode back toward the main army.

Pasha was stunned as the slowly advancing cavalries of the other tribes veered off in opposite directions back toward the main army. His stomach dropped when he realized what was going on.

"Veer off! Veer off!" he shouted to Nalar, who relayed the orders. They spread out from the crowd and rode far right just upon coming within range of the Halor and Mulamar archers. A swarm of arrows flew straight into the heart of the mob, punching deep holes into each target. This only terrified the people more and did little to slow them down.

Signaling his men, the Halor king's best horse archers broke formation and rode in a flanking position toward the crowd. Circling them on both sides, they rained death upon them without mercy.

"No!" shouted Pasha as he rode, unable to tear his eyes from the sight of the Halor horse archers firing repeatedly into his people.

"This cannot be! This cannot be!" Pasha stopped and violently pulled Daimon's reins back toward the crowd.

Nalar rode into him to force his horse away from the fray. "There is nothing you can do for them! They will kill you!"

"Get out of my way, Nalar!"

Nalar ignored Pasha and drove his mount into him. Daimon reared up and threw out his hooves toward the opposing horse. Pasha fell from his back into the freshly dug up earth. The captain drew his sword immediately when he rose and ran toward the Halor horse archers who were bringing their deadly work to a close.

The people had stopped advancing and remained clustered together, begging the Halor for mercy. But none came as the horsemen, with their turbans tied down across their faces, came closer and began to spear the ones who were left, most of them being women.

Pasha was so overwhelmed with anger he did not note Nalar who was following him on foot. Taking careful steps, he pounced on Pasha and knocked his sword away from him. Before he could do anything, Nalar had wrapped his arms and legs about Pasha from behind, pinning him to the ground.

"You bastard, let me go!" said Pasha.

"They have plague, sir. There is no hope for them now!" shouted Nalar as he pleaded with Pasha.

"No!"

"Listen to me, Pasha!" demanded Nalar.

"No!"

"Listen to me! It's over for them! There's nothing we can do!"

Pasha fought to get upright, but Nalar kept him pinned down.

As he heard the last arrow fly, Nalar slackened his grip to let Pasha sit up.

"It could not be helped, sir," said Nalar. In that moment, Pasha succumbed to a violent fit of sadness and rage.

"Do you hear me?" Nalar asked as Pasha struggled against him.

"Get off of me!" Pasha shouted at Nalar, who tried to pull him away.

"Come now, Pasha, it's over. Let it go!" Nalar pleaded.

"I said get off of me!" With all of his strength, Pasha rammed his knee into the exposed part of Nalar's body. Seeing his opportunity, Pasha threw Nalar from him and escaped his hold.

The plains seemed darker than before, the soft grass swaying slowly while it sang a song for the dead. Pasha sprinted as fast as he was able toward the mound of dead flesh awaiting him.

"Kaudi, no!" called Nalar.

In silence, the Halor and Mulamar archers circled the bodies on their horses, unsure of what to do next. All of them had tied long scarves around their mouths and sheathed their hands with their riding gauntlets. An opening was made in their circle around the bodies for Pasha, who quickly found himself among the piles of dead.

Again an opening was made as King Hanasa and the generals came through, all with scarves covering their mouths and heavy gauntlets sheathing their hands.

Pasha's anger flared when his eyes caught sight of a young Halor warrior kicking the remains of a young boy to the side in order to make a path for his king.

"You murderers!" Pasha shouted. His mind was so fraught with anger his thoughts did not come clearly; all he could think of was hurting those men who had done this.

"You murdering Mulamar, Halor bushim!" Crouching down suddenly, he took up piles of earth and hurled them at King Hanasa and the generals.

Hanasa's horse archers reacted quickly. Several moved between Pasha and the king, bows drawn and notched.

"So that is what you want, is it? Go on shoot then!" Pasha said in challenge to one of the horsemen. "Come on! I know that's why you're here, why you're really here! Surely you can hit one Sashraman who is not even moving! I know you want more! More of our blood! Take it if you can, you wretched, gutless dogs!"

"Nuvahli, stop this at once!" ordered King Hanasa.

Pasha began to tear off his armor plate that covered his body. "Feast on my blood if you dare! Bushim cowards!"

From the corner of his eye, Pasha noted the young mounted Halor warrior whom he had thrown most of his words of abuse. Within seconds, the anger upon the warrior's face had flowed into action when he released the arrow from his tightly drawn bow.

His aim was not precise and direct. The missile came at an angle and punched a hole into Pasha's left shoulder where it became lodged in his flesh.

Nalar had finally reached them and quickly jumped in front of Pasha, his sword high as he stood over his captain.

"Weapons down! Weapons down! Veer out now!" the king said, his loud voice fighting to drown out all around him. His men responded and moved back.

Nalar cradled Pasha's head in his arms while he inspected the wound. Pasha's breathing was ragged as pain burned through his body.

After several moments, Pasha realized he was on the ground, with Nalar bent over the wicked gash in his flesh.

"It's all right, Nalar. I'm all right," Pasha said, trying to bat away his hands.

His entire left side protested painfully as he tried to use it.

"Don't do that, you fool! Let it be or it will go in deeper!" said Nalar as he poked around the wound.

"How bad is it?" asked King Hanasa, coming over to them.

"It's hard to tell. The arrowhead went through, but he might lose a lot of blood if I break it apart and pull it out."

"My physicians will attend to him."

"No!" said Pasha, pointing toward Hanasa.

"Not one of your filthy dogs will touch me."

"Like it or not, they may be able to help you!" said Hanasa.

"I said they will not touch me!"

"Sir, please," said Nalar.

"Only a physician can deal with this!"

"I am perfectly willing to offer the services of my physicians."

King Hanasa shot a dangerous look at General Ishok of the Yashani, who came closer to Pasha.

Pasha said nothing, but his silence seemed to signal assent.

"What were you thinking, eh?" King Hanasa shouted. "Do you have a death wish? Is that it, Sashraman?"

"Only for one!" Pasha answered.

"We did what had to be done!" King Hanasa shouted.

"I think we had better take him," said General Ishok.

"Yes," said Hanasa. "Get him out of here."

Clustering all around him, the Sashramans put Pasha on a horse. Nalar led the reins and followed General Ishok back to the supply train.

"It seems the men of the north have shown us they're clever as well as deceitful," said General Shabaz to the Halor king.

Hanasa did not like talking to the Mulamar general. He moved out from among the bodies, but Shabaz followed him closely.

All seemed on the verge of collapse before their mission had even started. Hanasa could see the coldness and lack of emotion in the eyes of the Mulamar general and his warriors when they looked upon the dead Sashraman.

Hanasa had believed that he could maintain enough influence over his tribe's old allies to keep them in line while in Sashra. This plan had almost unraveled. The only way to keep former enemies from killing one another was to give them a common enemy. The Halor king hoped they would see combat soon.

"These Sashramans are quite an emotional lot, aren't they?" said Shabaz.

"They have a great love for life," Hanasa said flatly.

"And a great aversion to reality," pressed Shabaz.

"They begged us to come here, to help them drive out the men of the north. Yet when it comes to sacrifice and hardship, they still don't seem to understand. They don't seem to know how to anticipate it and be ready."

"I don't think even you could have anticipated this, Shabaz, nor I for that matter," the king said, turning his eyes toward the northeast.

"Have the scouts seen any movement?" Hanasa asked, changing the subject.

"Yes, about four hundred of them, mostly Baku and Jakshima tribesmen. They were angling further south for a while, but after what happened today, they're going back north," Shabaz answered.

"I suppose from now on we can expect regular visits from them. They may try to avoid a direct fight," said Hanasa.

"Yes, they'll send skirmishers and try to push us toward trees or a rocky valley where they can set up an ambush and slow us down. I have Makar scouts circling north and south for us as we speak. Wherever they are, we should have some general idea," said Shabaz.

"Perhaps," Hanasa replied.

"More than likely the Baku brought the plague with them from the north. Disease is rampant in those lands . . . The bodies are going to need to be burned," said the Mulamar general.

Hanasa turned to face Shabaz.

"It is forbidden to turn the remains of a believer into ash," the Halor king said forcefully.

"Believers or not, sire, they have plague. I will not risk the lives of my men. It will spread fast like the last one if we don't take action," Shabaz insisted.

"We'll bury them, deep in the ground," said Hanasa.

"No matter how much earth you use to cover up poison, the poison remains," Shabaz said firmly.

"And what about your men? What if some have been exposed? What about the Sashramans? Should we burn them too?" demanded Hanasa.

"If need be. I won't let this come to Mulamar land."

"Give the ground time to breathe again," said the Halor king.

"We cannot wait!" Shabaz shouted.

"We will wait!" Hanasa shouted back at him.

"What is it about them that makes you castrate yourself from the ideals your father fought for?" Shabaz said angrily.

"As always, you make a great noise, but you say nothing," Hanasa said.

Shabaz turned to the other direction, sensing that it was time for him to leave.

Near the end of their lines where the supply train stood, the Sashramans congregated around the Yashani physician's makeshift tent. It brought no comfort to Pasha as he thrashed about on the grass, his face flooded by a river of sweat. Though the armor had been removed along with his heavy tunic, Pasha still felt afire beneath the unmerciful sun.

His mind dwelt solely on the plague-ridden people crying out for mercy. He tried to rise, but Nalar held him down.

"No! No! We must get after them before they get away! Unhand me, Nalar!" Pasha demanded.

"You must be quiet!" said Sajal, the Yashani physician attending him. "You'll only make it worse!" He warned.

"Sir, please!" Nalar pleaded.

"How could it come to this, Nalar? How could it!" Pasha shouted.

"I don't know, sir, but you'll be no good if you do not let the man see to you."

"And what are all of you doing here!" Pasha tossed his head around, looking at all of his men who stood staring down at him. "Do you like this? Why are you not out there tracking the enemy?"

"Captain Nuvahli," said Sajal, pushing down Pasha's head and turning it toward him. "You need to calm down," he said firmly.

"Get your hands off me!" Pasha spat in the Yashani's face, cursing him as he did so.

Sajal wiped his face before looking up to Nalar. "I cannot stop the bleeding until he calms down and stops moving that arrow."

"And what do you expect us to do?" he said, looking at Hakan, who drew a blank expression.

"He wants to fight," Nalar continued. "Not lay on his back."

"I'll kill you all! Traitors!" Pasha shouted in delirious repetition as his vision began to blur.

"That arrow should not be moved at all. It will tear more flesh and make him bleed out."

"Well you explain it to him!" Nalar shouted impatiently.

Saying nothing, the physician released Pasha's shoulders and went to a wood box containing his tools.

"What are you doing?" said Nalar, growing irritated as Pasha continued to struggle.

Sajal did not answer.

"Sir, please," he pleaded again. "Let him see to you."

"I will not let the pride of Yashani whores poison me with his touch!" Pasha ranted.

Sajal came back to Pasha's side again. Without warning, he seized Pasha's head and struck him, his fist reinforced with a thick leather gauntlet.

Pasha fell back half unconscious.

Sajal worked quickly as Pasha stared back at them partially conscious and blurry eyed.

"What kind of physician carries one of those?" asked Hakan.

"A good one," said Sajal.

"Will he be all right?" asked Nalar.

"Uh . . . yes . . . yes, he'll be fine," he answered without looking at him.

"I can't tell you how much your words comfort me," said Nalar sarcastically.

Sajal eventually broke the arrow and cut out as much of the arrowhead as possible. Nevertheless, small bits remained inside the wound. In order to stop infection, the physician used a fire treatment, which also served to stop the bleeding.

Eventually, Pasha regained consciousness, and against Nalar's wishes, he gathered the men to go track the enemy.

In a sudden burst of speed and determination, the Sashramans rode northwest. They picked up the trail easily. The Baku obviously saw no reason to ride further spread out or in opposite directions to confuse any potential trackers. Pasha cursed their arrogance and resolved to kill every one of them.

As they went further north, the greenness of the plains began to slowly disappear, replaced by rock and burned hills. Seeing a smoldering village in the east, Pasha and his men could sense they were close to the Baku lines.

Pasha cursed the warrior who had shot him, and his men for having wasted so much time. They would probably never find them and would be forced to turn back. Just then, Nalar rode ahead of them.

"There!" he shouted, pointing. "In the east!"

Then Pasha saw it, about fifty fires stacked high with blazes that could be seen for miles. Such foolishness was the way of the men of the north. Night was almost upon them as they pursued the light to its source.

"Bows!" Pasha shouted.

Following the order quickly, all of the Sashramans with bows drew them as those without them fell back to the rear.

Though the pain had been unbearable during most of the ride, it began to ease the closer they got to the Baku camp. There were no trees or hills to provide cover, making it an easy place to attack.

The pain was gone as Pasha made out figures of half-awake Baku running around in search of their weapons. Several arrows flew toward them, but they were poorly aimed. Once the enemy was within range, not one target escaped their aim.

Sashraman horses trampled the wine-sodden warriors that had not yet awakened. The stinging force of their bowstrings was pleasant to the Sashramans while they brought down their targets and those in the rear cut down any survivors.

Nalar took twenty men and circled the camp, firing at anything that moved. There were more of them than Pasha had imagined, but they had been caught in their lazy moments of idleness, an act for which there would be no mercy.

A group of twenty confronted Pasha and his group, but their horses tore through them with ease. Pasha drew his sword quickly when twelve men with spears almost caught him by surprise. He blocked their fierce blows with equal ferocity and swung down low so as to catch as many unguarded throats as possible.

Suddenly a bright flame hurled toward him. Daimon came to his hind legs in sudden fright as the fire bit into his neck. Pasha fell from his back. Unable to find his sword, he took up a spear and came at them before they could spear Daimon as he ran wild through the camp. Four came at him at once, but they were quickly surprised by his strange movements as he jabbed with both ends of the spear and blocked their blows.

He got into a low stance, his spear above his head, the point coming down at an angle. When they lunged, he blocked them all at once. He made his feet and legs fluid, never keeping one stance. The men of the north returned his cries with curses in their own language, spitting at him while they lunged for him again.

Pasha blocked most of their blows with the spearhead and spun quickly out of their reach. He leapt forward to crack the skin off the face of one of them with the dull end of his spear.

The man fell, making the mistake of grabbing his face. Pasha flipped his spear over to its pointed end and tore apart his enemy's throat. Seeing their fallen fellow, they fell back quickly and hurled their spears at Pasha.

He fell to the ground while swinging his spear up in a fanning motion to block theirs. Screaming their hatred of him, they came back at him with axes and a sword. Pasha went even lower, watching his head as he fanned his spear left and right to block them.

When he turned, he felt his left leg fall out from beneath him. But his attacker was met with a spear in his chest as Pasha dropped to his knees and drove the spearhead toward the man behind him.

The final two dropped quickly when Nalar noted Pasha's situation. Short work was made of the rest of them as death rained down upon the men of the north from the shadows of the night. Pasha and his men rode down all who fled. Before long, that sandy plain of Sashra was still once more.

The Sashraman captain stood in awe and deep respect of his men's work. Much of the campground was littered with the corpses of Baku. There had been at least a hundred of them for sure, but they were unprepared. Thus they had fallen as sheep rather than men.

Immediately the pain came back, tearing at Pasha's insides with greater intensity than before, bringing the captain to his knees.

"Sir!" Nalar came over to him quickly, seeing him on the ground.

Pasha came to his feet again, ashamed of his weakness.

"I am all right, just tired, quite tired."

"It was a mistake agreeing to this!"

Hakan called for Nalar, and he left Pasha for a moment.

"Sir, I think you should see this!" he called out to Pasha from one of the Baku tents.

"What is it?" Pasha asked as he joined him.

Nalar threw open one of the tent flaps, gesturing for Pasha to enter. Inside, it was dark, the only light being two torches held by two of his men inside.

The air bore a strange odor, not yet foul, but quite unpleasant. As he came closer, his ears picked up the sound of whimpers and fearful whispering. The light then fell on ten Sashramans women and two young girls, all dressed in a sensual manner.

His stomach turned as his eyes came across the boils and open skin along their midriffs. The women grasped one another tightly, looking down as Pasha's eyes passed over them. The pain in his body was nothing compared to the pain he felt in his heart as he considered what must be done.

"All of them?" he said to Nalar.

"Yes, sir, even the children."

Putting a scarf over his mouth, he came closer to them, only prompting more fearful cries and tears from the children and the women who seemed to be their mothers.

Pasha came down into a crouching position as he observed them. They had taut black skin and were quite lovely in spite of their blemishes. Most likely they had been quite popular among the men of the north. The girls looked thirteen, perhaps fourteen, not much older than his cousins back home.

"How did this happen?"

At first they were too frightened to answer him. Then one of the women, who was unmistakably the mother of the whimpering child she held in her arms, answered. She was barely able to hold Pasha's gaze when she did. "They came out of nowhere, my husband and I along with our chi . . ." She stopped, trying her best to muffle more cries. "We were out in the fields, my husband was teaching my sons to ride, then . . . They came from nowhere, they burned our village . . ."

Pasha lowered his head. His mind went back to the smoldering village in the distance.

"They killed him and my two boys. I wanted to die! I wanted them to kill us both! But they took me and my daughter and turned us into this. Now we are sick, and things grow on our skin. My daughter has one of them growing inside of her, as do I."

"Why did you not fight?" asked Hakan.

"Don't you think I tried! Don't you think I wanted to die? You men! You cannot understand."

"A true woman of Daiyu would have killed herself and her children before letting bushim northerners turn you both into this!" Hakan said flatly.

Pasha turned, surprised to hear these words coming from him.

"I lost both of my sons and my husband. All of the men who should have avenged our honor are dead," she said, directing her words to Pasha, pleading with her eyes.

"My child deserves life. I deserve life! Yet you judge me now because I . . . because we dared fight for the right to live! Do not talk to me of Daiyu! We did not leave him. He left us!"

"Careful, woman," said Hakan.

"Do not tell me to be careful! You don't tell me anything. Who are you to say these things to me! Where were you?" Her voice trembled with anger. "Where were those noble Sashraman warriors who are charged with protecting the honor of women?" Her mocking tone only incensed Hakan even more.

"Do not test me, woman! Or I swear . . ." he shouted, moving toward her.

"Hakan! *Azhera!*" Pasha ordered in Lakina.

Saying nothing, he stepped back slowly into the darkness and left the tent. The woman's fierce gaze followed him until he had gone.

Pasha searched his mind for some source of wisdom imparted to him from long years of soldiery.

"Good, sir, please! My girl is innocent!" she begged, holding her daughter even tighter.

"No, she isn't," said Pasha.

"What kind of man are you to blame this dishonor upon us? Please, be merciful!"

Pasha's insides burned even hotter while he considered what he must do.

"Nalar!"

"Sir!" Nalar sounded off.

"Bring blankets!"

Within moments, Nalar had brought heavy woolen blankets that the once living Baku and Jakshima had used. Pasha took them and tossed them to the women.

"Cover your daughters from head to foot in these so that no skin is exposed."

The wailing became more furious while the women pried their little girls from their arms. They kissed them and hugged them repeatedly as they covered them with the blankets.

Rising from his haunches, Pasha held out his heavily gloved hands to the girls.

At first the girls clung to their mothers and refused to move. But eventually the mothers pried them apart and sent them forward. With their heads low, they inched forward to Pasha, who grabbed their hands gently.

Using a dagger, he cut three holes into the blankets so that they could see and breathe more easily. The girls were silent as the cries of their mothers filled the air.

"Nalar, my horse. Tell the men to make way."

Nalar went out first. The orders were relayed quickly, and within moments, he returned to the tent to hold the flap open for Pasha and the two girls who held each of his hands.

As he passed Nalar, he turned to speak to him. "Be quick."

"Yes, Kaudi." He nodded, fully understanding the grave nature of the order.

Outside, all of the mounted Sashramans stood back in a line a good distance from Pasha and the girls as they moved. Daimon stood at the center of camp waiting. After helping to mount both of the girls on Daimon's back, Pasha mounted and began to ride south.

While riding, he could not stop thinking of their mothers. He knew their pain. In many ways, losing both Hadassah and Kamili had changed him, turned him bitter and at times confused.

In spite of the revenge they had exacted upon the men of the north, their enemies had destroyed the girls and their mothers forever. It was not wise to take them with him, he knew that. Plague carriers would have to be killed wherever they went, no matter their age or if they were man, woman, or child.

One of the mothers had spoken of how Daiyu had abandoned them. When Pasha saw things like he had seen that day, he could not argue. The whole world was coming undone, but the heavens did nothing to save man from peril.

Perhaps therein was the error in thinking; perhaps man could not count on the heavens to solve his every problem, as the Shazhias taught in the temples.

The rest of the Sashraman horseman rode behind him at a fair distance, Hakan at the head of them. If he did not kill the girls, the plague would spread. Still, there was no way to be sure. More than likely, it had already spread throughout much of northern Sashra.

He stopped once they had reached the plains again.

Once they touched the ground, the girls began to cry. Still, they did not run. Their end was coming. They both knew it.

"Quiet!" Pasha said, becoming irritated.

"Are they coming with us?" asked one of the taller girls from beneath her blanket.

Pasha reached out to them and removed the blankets from their pretty young faces, which seemed to have aged twelve years that night. It made him sick to observe the contrast between their lovely faces and the open skin and boils on their arms and legs.

"What are your names?" Pasha asked.

At first they did not answer.

"Speak!" Pasha ordered.

"Tarah," answered the taller one whose mother had addressed Pasha.

"And you?"

"Haleah," she said, whimpering.

"Tarah. Your mother called me a good sir. But she was wrong. I am not good. Your mothers are dead. I did not stay my hand. I did what I had to."

Fierce tears seized them when Pasha confirmed what they had feared.

"I am not going to explain my actions to you, nor ask your pardon. The men of the north destroyed what was good about your mothers and turned them into weapons. Such weapons would have killed thousands more of our people if I had not ended their lives. We live in evil times now; love, respect, and honor don't mean what they used to. But perhaps that will change.

"There is a legend of an ancient river in the River Lands to the east. It is said that a boy stricken with leprosy was visited by the oracle in his home. She told him to go east and not stop until he reached a land abounding with water and light.

"He walked for two years until he was nearly dead. Then one day he fell unconscious onto an embankment along the River Shauli. His body rolled down into the water, and he stayed there for seven days. And then on the seventh day, he awoke, and his leprosy had gone. Still, it's just a legend. One of those foolish things . . ."

Reaching to his left, Pasha drew one of his daggers and brandished it before the two girls. Their weeping began to grow into shrieks of terror as their eyes stayed fixed upon Pasha, fearfully awaiting his next move.

He looked back to his men who had formed a line more than fifteen paces behind them. They all bore the same expressionless gaze; none blinked nor twitched a muscle. Their unhesitant and silent agreement with their captain only made Pasha more uneasy as he stood before them all holding his dagger.

Slowly he stepped forward, sending the girls into furious whimpers and cries.

Just as he lowered the dagger to a striking angle, his eyes became fixed upon figures moving in the grass further to the south of them. The Sashraman captain's stomach dropped when he discerned familiar faces. Running back and forth in the tall grass were two children, two boys, one older, one younger, in white tunics and blue pants. Their eyes were full of joy as they wrestled and jumped about.

Without warning, they stopped their play and turned. Pasha felt numb and hollow at the sight of them. The younger boy was black and plain in the face, like he was, wearing short twisted hair. In the taller boy, however, he saw the unmistakable softness and serenity of Hadassah's face, with eyes that seemed to be globes of light within the darkness. He seemed sure of himself and proud, like she had been. The vision ended as quickly as it had come. Pasha became lightheaded and staggered to the ground. Feelings of sickness only worsened inside of him.

Pasha looked down upon the girls whose cries had not ceased. The captain felt the stares of his men upon his back, still waiting for him to carry out the deed.

"Look at me," Pasha said to the girls in a low voice.

Though they were overwhelmed with fear, they obeyed him.

"I don't know what spirits do their work upon me this night. But I will not become like my enemies. If I ever see you two again, by this knife," he said, raising it to their eye level, "I will end both of you! Now go!"

At first they were too scared to move, for they suspected it was a trick. When they saw Pasha sheath his knife and return to mount Daimon, they took the chance he had given them.

The Sashraman line shifted uneasily when the two girls turned and began to run as fast as they could for the east.

"Kaudi, what are you doing?" called out Hakan. "They'll carry the plague even further into Sashra!"

"This is what the men of the north want of us, Hakan, cutting down our own. They're just children."

"And more children, more men, more women will die if they are allowed to live!"

"If you're so afraid, go then. Ride them down!"

Hakan's face twisted into silence as Pasha spoke.

"Go on, ride them down! Ride down children of your own kind! What? No takers! Any of you?"

The men shifted uncomfortably in the line, and none spoke while Pasha challenged them. No matter the circumstances, Sashraman warriors were not trained to kill children, for such was forbidden of them by Nateo and The Way.

"I'm tired of this! Let's ride!"

Saying nothing, they all fell in behind Pasha's mount and began to ride further into the south.

Upon their return, the hour of the dead had come. Pasha had half expected to find the other tribes already moved on further north. Upon their return, they were still there, waiting for something. Some slept, and others sat around low burning fires amusing their fellows with vulgar tales that were unfit to be spoken.

Pasha found himself distracted by the sight of King Hanasa and his warriors unceremoniously tossing Sashraman bodies into a ditch. He rode quickly in King Hanasa's direction.

Yet the closer he came, the more his fear began to subside as he saw no sign of torches or wood. His eyes quickly came upon the dozens of freshly dug mass graves.

He stopped at a short distance from the king and dismounted, and leading Daimon by the reins, he came to the Halor king's side. To Pasha's surprise, they were also joined by two Sashraman priests, dressed in white, going from opposite sides of the grave, blessing the bodies.

"Three hundred men, one hundred twenty women, forty-five children," the king said, drawing a heavy breath. "Barely a few weeks into this war, and Maikael is already exacting a heavy price against us."

"The keeper of the dead did not fill their flesh with arrows," said Pasha, unwilling to let go of his anger.

"I know you do not trust me, Captain, but I did not come this far north to kill women and children," said Hanasa.

"It's funny how well men do the things that they did not mean to do," Pasha countered.

The king said nothing. Pasha was not done.

"I am surprised you even got one of your men to touch a Sashraman corpse. You must have eased their dishonor handsomely with coin from your purse."

The king laughed, though he was not amused. "My men do this because it is shameful to leave the bodies of the vanquished uncovered."

"Shame your father did not do the same the last time your people were here."

"You're just not going to give me a chance, are you? I bring my army, help bring the other tribes into this fight. But that's not enough for you, is it?"

Both men looked at each other, mistrust and dislike seeming to fill the air between them.

The king spoke again. "They wanted to burn them." He gestured toward the area where warriors from the other tribes were gathered. "But I thought that I could use this as a small gesture of trust between you and me."

Pasha said nothing. His head turned to look down upon the graves before them.

"Maybe not. From what I have seen, Daiyu's good fortune seems to have been well spent in you."

"What are you coming to, Hanasa, or do you try to kill me with the senselessness of your words?" Pasha replied angrily.

"You say my men do this now because of extra coin. But no coin will build a bridge of respect and trust. If we cannot come together, the pact will not last a week when we reach Cafura. It will not last because you cannot put aside this stubbornness all you Sashramans carry," said the Halor king, gazing directly into Pasha's eyes.

"It keeps us safe . . . and aware," said Pasha.

"The way men trust depends heavily upon the amount of respect between their leaders," Hanasa responded.

Growing irritated with the conversation, Pasha turned to leave.

"Shabaz," said the king.

Pasha stopped.

"I trust the Mulamar king. But I do not trust Shabaz You should watch your back.," Hanasa warned.

CHAPTER 12

Kaudi

Pasha and his men tore through the high grass of the jungle with streaks of coming daylight illuminating their paths. The Sashramans stepped quickly yet carefully so as not to give off too much noise.

They had discovered signs of wagons and half-used supplies five days before, clear signs that they were coming close to the main northern force. The men of the south had stopped at the mouth of the Huyundi jungle after running into several *kads* of enemy skirmishers. Pasha and his men had gone out to range their distance from the enemy lines.

The jungle echoed with the cries of its native inhabitants. Their ears were filled with cracking sounds, chirping from animals and insects they could not see. Each of their movements was closely watched by the monkeys and other creatures that dwelt in the trees. But the Sashramans ignored it all. Their ears searched only for the sound of those who did not belong there.

Fifty men had come with Pasha, all of them spread out in a long line. As for the rest of his fellow tribesmen, he had left them under the charge of Hakan, while Nalar stayed with him. After what Hanasa had told him about Shabaz, Pasha decided it would not be wise to leave the main force without a significant Sashraman presence.

At times, he did not know what to do about the state of the pact. Mistrust still lingered among them and showed no sign of abating. Juktan had said that he would bring unity among the tribes. Still, he was just a man. They would soon regret placing all of their hope in him. Pasha could feel it.

He moved more toward the center of the line, moving in behind Nalar. Of all the places to walk through, the jungle was one of the most dangerous. In spite of its striking beauty, the rustle of trees and leaves betrayed the presence of sinister beasts or at times men, waiting for the moment to strike.

Pasha took some comfort in their dark blue and orange tunics and robes over their armor, which blended in well with their surroundings. But nothing was ever certain.

Nalar suddenly stopped and dropped to a knee, holding up a closed fist. They all stopped and did as he had done, weapon hands shaking with anticipation.

"Steady, boys," he said quietly. His eyes fell into rigid observation of a tight grouping of trees before them. Nothing could be seen within them but a foreboding darkness.

Pasha moved up beside him.

"What do you see?" he asked.

But Nalar did not have to answer his query as the dawn sliced through the thicket. Its rays quickly bounced back as it came across a shiny metal surface. At that moment, they could all see the bright silver armor of their foes.

"Trees!" Pasha said in a high whisper.

His men responded quickly, all of them falling back to the nearest tree. Pasha quickly disappeared into the tall grass at the base of a thick palm tree. Until they were sure of how many there were, caution would be their code.

His eyes came upon a thick line of proud northern warriors who seemed to be parading more than marching.

Pasha slowed his breathing as he stared upon the line snaking its way from the trees into the part of the jungle they now occupied. At first it seemed his worst fears were coming true after he counted the seventieth man, but then the line cut off, and no more came. It was a scouting party.

Drawing in a deep breath, the captain considered his options. He could let them go through and let the other tribes take care of them, but they were probably on their way to a raid. If they turned right and went straight west, they would completely miss the other tribes who waited at the jungle's entrance to the south.

In spite of being unable to see his men, Pasha could feel them. The captain felt their need for blood, their thirst for vengeance. Today they would not be denied.

Moving cautiously, Pasha leapt from his perch, shield before him as he ran forward and hurled his spear into the bulging line of silver-plated men. His men followed suit, and within moments, a flurry of spears and arrows punched into the necks and chests of the unwary line of northern warriors.

Blood had been spilled; the time for killing had come. Pasha dived back behind the tree as the northerners raised their shields into position to cover their archers who fired into the trees. Their commanders shouted hurried orders in the Baku tongue. Moving quickly, the men of the north fell into the grass as well. The shield bearers formed an outer shield wall. Inside of the wall, northern archers held their bows ready.

They were smarter than Pasha had hoped. If they tried to pursue the Sashramans into the thicket, none of them would come out of it alive. Still they could not sit there forever.

Catching sight of Nalar, who stood on the other side of the northerners with most of the men, Pasha began to move in a circle around the enemy force. He stayed low within the grass, giving their impulsive archers no good fix upon him.

Some of his men fired randomly into the enemy, distracting them as Pasha moved toward Nalar's position. He fell beside Nalar and ten of his men crouched behind a thick olive tree.

"This appears a bit more difficult than we thought, Kaudi," Nalar said.

"Must you say the obvious so much, Nalar?" Pasha replied.

He looked out at the Baku, who still showed no sign of breaking out of their formation.

"We need to try something else or the men will just be wasting arrows," Nalar said in the same tone.

"Agreed. This lot seems a lot more cautious than I'm used to," said Pasha.

The captain looked toward the formation and the men around them. "Anyone hit?" he asked.

"Don't know. I haven't had much time to do a head count, you know," said Nalar sarcastically.

"How many bows?" Pasha demanded.

"At least twenty."

"Good."

"What are you thinking of, sir?" Nalar inquired.

"You up for a bit of danger?"

"Well I don't have anything better to do than get killed," said Nalar.

"Follow me."

Pasha stood, hugging the tree with his back as he did so. He looked down into the eager faces of his men.

"Yuwatu," he said to one of the rank masters sitting on his haunches among other the bowmen.

"Sir," he said attentively.

"Spread the word. Keep firing into them. Aim low toward their feet until they expose themselves. Don't stop until you see them break formation."

"Yes, sir."

"Nalar," he said, prompting him to follow him.

Though attempting to stay low, Pasha kept looking up for the perfect spot. Eventually he came to a high, slightly inclined palm tree. There were no lower branches to latch onto, but it would have to do.

Saying nothing to Nalar, he slung his shield across his back and wrapped his hands around the base of the tree. With a deep breath, he leapt and dug his feet into the solid wood, using his hands to hold himself in place.

Without hesitating, he lifted himself up, hand over hand, right foot before left. To his amazement, he ascended with great ease. Nalar followed him closely, mirroring his every move.

Though they made a great amount of noise, it was masked by the many Sashraman arrows crashing into Baku bodies and metal.

Pasha stopped on a long tree limb just short of the top of the tree where the wood was beginning to thin. He looked down upon the Baku, invisible to them as they dodged and blocked Sashraman arrows. They were exactly above them at exactly the angle Pasha knew he would need.

"All right, so why did we climb into an archer position if we don't have any bows?" Nalar wondered aloud.

"We won't need them."

"Then what are we here for? To gaze upon the magnificence of Baku defenses?"

Pasha drew his sword without answering.

"I get the feeling that when I said danger, you did not take me seriously."

Nalar's face immediately caved into worry and anxiety when he understood what Pasha was about to do.

"No . . . You're crazy! I'm not doing that," he said while shaking his head.

"I'll see you in the middle, brother," Pasha said with a smile.

"Sir!"

Pasha leapt from the tree and fell quickly toward the Baku formation below. Though he was not sure if he would live from the fall, it mattered not to him.

The moment the Baku looked up, it was too late. Their armor was strong, but it did not help the northern warriors when the captain crashed into them.

Pasha's entire body cried out in pain; fortunately his enemy's body broke most of the fall. He could not feel his left arm or shoulder, but he ignored it as the other Baku closed in. Another Baku soon fell under the force of Nalar's quickly descending body. Rolling off his first kill, Pasha quickly drew out his blade and turned to face the others.

In their eyes, he could see their fear and apprehension as the formation was undone before them. All the Baku came to their feet and turned to engage the two who had entered their wall.

In spite of the pain, Pasha pulled his shield quickly from his back, blocking the first of many blows. The Sashramans swung their swords wildly around them, their shields following. Pasha sidestepped two and bashed three more with his shield, enabling him to meet Nalar in the center.

Both Sashramans came back to back and used their shields for both protection and round clubs to fight off their enemies. As five came at Pasha, he sidestepped to Nalar's right, his shield finding two exposed faces, which he quickly tore apart.

Nalar blocked three blows, and dodging a fourth, he cut down an exposed neck and pushed himself into the remaining four. Pasha felt a strong push force them apart. The moment he turned, he watched in concern as a wicked northern blade tore into Nalar's side.

"No!" he shouted.

Mustering all the strength he could, he pushed back into the Baku, cutting down as many as he could. He fell forward as he dodged one's blow, bringing him to the ground with a swift kick he cut out his throat.

Nalar was staggering, struggling to block their blows and stay up. Pasha jumped with all his might and knocked down the two closest to making a killing blow.

Finally, their relief came when Baku began to drop like flies, freshly fired arrows jutted out of their finely polished armor.

Yuwatu and the rest of the men finally began to close in, firing arrows and hurling spears into the quickly disintegrating Baku lines. Pasha stayed close to Nalar, who could barely stand, as the Baku sent blow after blow. Two Baku jumped into them, pushing Nalar to the ground.

Pasha blocked their blows, bashing one in the head with his shield. The captain seized his head to throw him back, and he was quickly dispatched by another Sashraman. He dropped his shoulder toward the other one and with the aid of his shield threw him over his back. Pasha immediately jumped on top of him to thrust his sword into the Baku's heaving chest. His foe expired quickly.

With his shield, he blocked another who came at him with an ax, but his arm cried out in pain from the stinging slash of a loosely swinging blade that pierced his shoulder. But by that time, Yuwatu had reached them and swiftly ran the Baku through. Pasha was beginning to see more of his men while the Baku who were left began to cluster together again to make the shield wall.

Still, it was over for them. The Sashramans peppered them with arrows and in unison broke into them as bodies began to fall out of the line. Alongside his men, Pasha hacked down the rest of the Baku. Five of them attempted to run and disappear in the grass, but the Sashramans immediately ran them down.

They closed in on the remaining three who refused to surrender. Two of his men who came at them fell quickly. Pasha and Yuwatu then rushed them. Every one of Pasha's blows were blocked as he engaged the one in silver armor with plumes in his helmet, a sign that he was one of the officers. The officer seemed more disciplined in his sword learning.

He let Pasha do all the attacking, blocking his every move carefully as he slightly moved back. Pasha lunged toward his left side, which seemed open. Instead he was kicked in the back when the officer sidestepped, spun about, and came at Pasha from behind. Leaping to his feet, he pushed his shield out in front of him.

The officer took hold of the shield and tried to pull it away while he came at Pasha with his blade. But Pasha read him in time and delivered a sharp kick to his chest. The kick dazed him, and he crashed into the ground.

Without hesitating, Pasha slid in behind. The captain immediately grabbed the Baku's helmeted head and exposed his neck. In an instant, Pasha's blade came down and tore out the cords of life from the Baku officer's throat.

He looked up, ready for more Baku to pounce upon him, but none came. Yuwatu and his men had finished the other two. All was still at that moment. Even the jungle had ceased making noise.

"Yuwatu." Pasha nodded toward him.

"Sir," said Yuwatu.

"Are you all right?" Pasha asked.

"Yes, sir, thank you."

Pasha looked back to Nalar, who had finally come to his feet, though in intense agony.

"Nalar," he said, going to him. "Are you all right?"

"It's nothing, sir. It will heal."

"Are you sure? You should head back to the rear."

"Please, sir. I'm all right."

"No, you're wounded. You'll slow us down," Pasha tried to say as gently as possible.

"Kaudi . . ."

"Please, my brother, see that our dead make it back," Pasha insisted.

"All right," Nalar finally agreed.

Though crestfallen, Nalar did not argue while he limped away.

"As for the rest of you," Pasha said to the rest of his men.

At first the words did not come as he looked upon how many of the original fifty were gone. Only about twenty-seven remained standing. He did not know yet how many were wounded. But that would have to wait.

"Five of you stay and see to the dead and wounded. Make your way back to the rear. Yuwatu."

"Sir."

"You're with me."

Five Sashramans immediately stepped out of the group as Pasha and the rest began to head deeper into the jungle.

After a couple of hours, the Sashramans found themselves at the edge of the jungles and within sight of the village of Haretii, five miles from Cafura. The Sashramans came in close as they approached the village, Pasha at the head of them.

He held his sword low and his shield high after passing the first house. Haretii was like many Sashraman villages, the typical cubed stone houses built in a circle around the home of the grijo, the elder and keeper of the village history.

Being close to Cafura, a village like Haretii would have been expected to be bustling with life and people. But Pasha and his men saw and heard nothing while they went down the village road. They began to search the houses, but in each one they passed, there was nothing.

"Kaudi!"

Pasha came outside of one of the houses upon hearing Yuwatu call him. He did not see him, so he followed the dirt path farther into the village where the voice seemed to have come from.

"Yuwatu?"

Pasha stopped when he passed a house and was hit by strange odor. Not foul, but not pleasant. He rushed forward, fearing the worst as he closed in on the village center. There before the *grijo*'s house he found Yuwatu and the others, just steps away from a floating sea of death.

Floating in midair were the people of the village. Men, women, and children all cut and gashed open, with many of their torn limbs wandering aimlessly in the air, levitated by some unknown force. Pasha had never seen anything like it. Looking closely at their bodies, he saw the boils and gashes that must have been there before.

"They had plague. Yet someone came here and did this," Pasha said.

Yuwatu fell to his knees, and others soon followed.

"Daiyu, lord of mercy. Save these people from this evil."

"If only he could," Pasha said, not caring whether or not his men heard him. "Cover your faces!" Pasha ordered.

All the men took off their turbans or tore off a part of their tunics and wrapped them about their faces.

"This is dark magic. We should not be here!" Yuwatu began to shout out.

"Be calm!" Pasha warned.

"It's dark magic. We should not be here!"

Pasha grabbed Yuwatu, shaking him to his feet. "Get a grip of yourself, man!"

"Who could do something like this?" said another.

"I don't know!" Pasha shouted, looking to each of his men.

Fear wrote itself upon their faces while they instinctively distanced themselves from the floating corpses.

"I do not know where this comes from. But we shall be of no use against it if we lose ourselves to it and run in fear. We are warriors of Sashra. Nothing shall break our will."

"Kaudi, Kaudi," called one of his men from behind the grijo's house.

"What is it?" he asked.

"The grijo. He's still alive! Come, come."

They rushed to the back of the house where three of his men were crouched over an old man whose head had been propped up with a rolled up tunic.

The grijo was a very dark man with a bald head. His tunic had been removed, revealing a frightening crescent-shaped gash in his side. Though awake, he did not seem lucid. His breathing was ragged, and his eyes could barely focus.

"Grijo, Grijo," Pasha called out to him.

The old man's eyes began searching for the source of the voice calling for him, and they fell upon Pasha. His face bore the weariness of a slow death, and unlike the rest of his village, he bore no sign of the plague.

"He doesn't have much more time left, sir," warned one of the warriors beside the grijo.

"Grijo. Who did this?" Pasha asked anxiously.

"He-her and . . ." His throat spurted up fresh spittle and blood. One of Pasha's men wiped the grijo's mouth with a torn off piece of cloth.

"Her?" Pasha asked, urging him to continue. "Who was she? How many were there? Did she have anyone with her?"

"Boy . . ." He fell to the side as he was taken over by a violent fit of wheezing and coughing.

"A boy?" Pasha asked, pressing him for an answer. He crouched down and came closer to the grijo. The warriors beside the old man gently put him onto his back again. However, the ancient storyteller was beginning to hack up heavy amounts of blood.

"What were they doing? This woman and boy? What did they do?"

"Bad . . . bad magic . . . I nev . . . never saw someone . . . so beautiful . . . so evil . . ."

The captain grew more concerned when the old man's eyes began to roll aimlessly in his head.

"Sir, he's going," one of his men warned.

"No. No. Not yet," he said, shaking the old man by the shoulder. "Grijo. Stay with me!" Pasha said, shaking him harder.

The old man came back suddenly, his eyes fixed upon Pasha.

"Grijo. The boy. What did he look like?"

Looking deep into Pasha's eyes, he fought to raise himself up. Pasha held him while he spoke.

"Like . . . you." And that was all he said as his eyes went white and his body crumpled like loose rocks.

"He's dead, Kaudi," said the warrior attending him. With his hands, he closed the grijo's eyes forever.

The captain fell to his knees, overwhelmed by the anguish within his heart. Pasha did not know what to make of what the grijo had said. So long he had taken his son for gone, forever. But now a dying old man he had never met was telling him differently. Still, Kamili would still be barely a babe. The grijo had called him a boy. Pasha did not know what to think.

Pain that Pasha thought he had buried now coursed through every part of his body. For so much time, he had longed for hope, yet when it came to him, he dared not reach for it. The captain feared it would take him and rip him apart. He had already been torn and crushed too many times . . .

Within an instant, he found himself back there on that fateful night. Hadassah lying in his arms breathing her last words. Even at that moment, he was still angry with her, angry that she had left him to deal with the pain of her absence and that of their son. At that moment, Pasha remembered. Lomar. She had said something about Lomar. Now Pasha understood.

"Helomar," he said angrily. That was the name Hadassah used to call her sister, Asah being Helomar's name for her.

Everything made sense now. She was the mysterious woman that had disappeared that fateful night. The sister of Pasha's wife was so like her in so many ways. Though beautiful and bearing the same mannerisms of her sister, she had always been different.

Helomar had an element about her that was darker, perhaps the most striking difference between her and her sister. Unlike Hadassah, Helomar could be as cold as the winter's rains and as venomous as the most deadly viper.

Years ago in the west, she loved a man called Jezareel. Along with being a slaver, Pasha had come to learn that he practiced dark magic. These revelations along with strong pressure from Hadassah's father led to the encounter where Pasha had been forced to kill him.

Then he remembered, Helomar had promised vengeance upon him and all he loved. He had not thought much of it after she had disappeared and was considered dead. But now, in the manner of the most deceptive tempest, she had returned on a cloud of darkness to exact the price of vengeance upon those who had wronged her.

"Kaudi."

Pasha looked up to Yuwatu, who had called out to him.

"What is it, sir?" Yuwatu asked in concern.

"Um . . . I . . . after so long . . ." Pasha barely knew what to say. So much had happened, and now more had been revealed. Still his burdens were his to bear alone. The Sashraman captain rose. "We should leave this place."

"*Sim*, Kaudi," said Yuwatu in agreement. "But, sir?"

"Yes?" said Pasha.

Pasha knew what he was about to ask, but he did not want to answer.

"What about them?" Yuwatu's head arched back toward the stream of floating death before the grijo's house.

The captain lowered his head; he could not look in their direction.

"Dark magic or no, it's not right. They're Sashramans, sir," he said to Pasha.

"We'll get them on our way back. Right now we need to move," Pasha ordered.

CHAPTER 13

The Fight

The once still clearing had now erupted into flame and the terrifying sounds of war as missiles tore into the walls of Cafura. All along the walls, Cafura's defenders scurried to their positions. Though determined, the city's finest archers tried in vain to mark their targets that stood behind a thick barrier, still out of range.

The fever was high that night. Baku and Jakshima infantry beat their spears and shields together while they waited anxiously for a breach. In unison, the men of the north made the frightening song of war, singing verses of contempt for the defenders that night.

Pasha ran as low as he could, leading Daimon by the reins. In the northwest, the Sashramans tore through the hills and tall grass like mice. Being only two miles from the enemy encampment, they had to be vigilant; there were ample patrols moving around that night. As an added precaution, they had muzzled the horses with tightly bound cloth. The captain hoped they would not be discovered before they reached their position.

Pasha's blood raced when one of the men and his horse skidded while they moved down a steep hill into a small creek bed. However, the man's fellows caught him before he fell. All that time, Pasha had been concerned about northern patrols. At the moment, he spotted one, further along in a patch of hills that overlooked the city of Cafura and the clearing where the enemy continued the siege, exactly where they needed to be.

His men dropped the moment the captain raised his arm. Even though it appeared the Baku had not heard them, he could take no chances.

"Sir," whispered Hakan as he and Yuwatu fell beside Pasha.

The captain looked upon his officers, lamenting Nalar's absence. His wounds had been too severe for Sajal to put him back in the field. No matter, Pasha acknowledged. They would press on.

"Go and—"

He cut off his words quickly when the Baku speech from above them grew louder. The captain made out four Baku warriors moving about the edge of the hills. Pasha realized the moment had come.

"Go!" he hissed.

Lifting his spear smoothly and unhurriedly, he pressed it tightly to his lightly armored body as he led a group of ten up the hill while Hakan led another. Pasha left Daimon with his men. Like a cat on all fours, he balanced himself with his free hand during his ascent.

Their enemies had astute ears. They rose from the tall grass on the hilltop. Instead of just four, Pasha's men discovered twelve northern warriors, who pounced upon them with all haste once they caught sight of them.

Dodging a sweeping Baku blade, Pasha gutted his first kill with his spear and drew his sword to meet the next. For a moment, they locked blades. The captain pushed him back with all of his strength. The warrior leaped forward, banging into Pasha's chest with his shield. Temporarily dazed, he stumbled back.

Pasha lifted his blade to block his enemy just as the Baku came in for a killing stroke. However, the warrior was strong. Locking Pasha's blade with his own, he used his feet to sweep Pasha's own from under him.

Coming to his knees, the captain rolled sideways, narrowly avoiding a kick to his face. At that moment, the Sashraman warrior had not recovered his balance. The Baku jump-kicked sideways, slamming his heavily booted foot into Pasha's helmet.

He found himself suddenly blinded as the helmet turned backward on his head. Rolling two more times, Pasha peeled it off of him. The warrior advanced on him, sweeping the ground in search of his lightly armored stomach.

Having no time to think, Pasha threw his head and entire body forward. Using his hands, he flipped his body forward and rose into the air with all his power as his feet locked into the Baku's chest. The warrior collapsed onto his back. Losing no time, Pasha dug his knee into the warrior's heaving chest and slit his throat.

Pasha rolled off of him quickly and ran another one through as the Baku warrior and a fellow attempted to corner Hakan. Hakan made short work of the other when his fellow fell. The night around them steadily grew calmer. Pasha watched as Yuwatu and the rest of his men surrounded the four who were left.

Yuwatu brought down two in moments. The rank master bashed one's head in with a shield and pushed him back. Yuwatu then jumped into him with a hard kick and sent him to the ground. The Sashraman used a spear to crush his face into a bloody mess of bones and flesh once he fell to the ground. In a flurry of spears and the crashing of shields against flesh and metal, the Sashramans finished off the rest of the Baku patrol.

Arzim sat mounted along with General Ivadar at the rear along the offensive line. The Sashramans inside the city had stopped fighting back, and their machines tore through the walls with ease. Tonight would be the night it all ended. Arzim thought of what he would do once they took the city.

Just then, his eyes caught unknown flickers of light to the west. They had patrols in that area, but they were ordered not to give up their position.

"General. Something's wrong," Arzim said, pointing west.

"That's not us!" said General Ivadar. "Get word to the left flank to set up a defensive line."

"Here they come!" said Arzim.

"Incoming! All ranks pull left! All ranks pull left!" shouted the general.

His cries went unheard under the swarm of arrows. The northern siege machines stopped, and the entire offensive line halted. Confusion and chaos took over the left flank as the flames from the arrows ignited their flesh and the ground beneath them.

"Set up a firing line! Set up a firing line!" shouted Arzim.

But few in their midst heard their orders. Just then, black riders in red shot out from the jungle trees toward the men of the north.

"Those aren't ours either. Arzim!" said the general, drawing his sword.

Arzim nodded in understanding. He and the remaining cavalry chased after the general toward the center.

From the east, the Halor horsemen tore out of the darkness toward the northern end of the barricades, directly in front of the city. At their head rode King Hanasa, whose heavily armored men wasted no time in peppering the barricades with rapidly flying Halor arrows.

Though the Jakshima archers at the northern end sent arrows back at the Halor, Hanasa's men stopped them cold with their shields. In the night, his men rode so fast that the Baku gathered on the outer left flanks could not come together to stop them. All that stood in their way were ridden down. Before the men of the north could respond, the Halor had disappeared into the night and were making their way back toward the jungle.

In spite of the heightened tension among their enemies, they still did not break their formation behind their barricades. Still, Pasha could sense their growing apprehension of the darkness around them and what would come next. He could not let them have even a moment to consider what to do.

"Hakan!" he called out in a loud voice, for it no longer mattered if he was heard. "Let's go! Let's go!" Within moments, Hakan's entire kad spilled over the hill down upon the enemy's left flank.

Though the men of the north were a bit more prepared, Hakan's kad's arrows tore through them easily as they tried to form up to stop them. The Sashraman horseman broke through their formation before it could form, planting their arrows deep into enemy barricade.

"Sir," said Yuwatu. "What kept our people from shooting at the Halor when they passed in front of the gates?"

"Did you not see the banners they were flying?"

"The white banners?" asked Yuwatu.

"Seven white banners with blue streaks. No Sashraman commander may fire upon a force as long as it carries those banners. We'll be carrying them too when we advance upon the city."

"I see," said Yuwatu.

"Oh this is bad," said Pasha, looking down upon the fight below.

Ivadar and the entire Baku right flank surged forward while the left closed in. Dozens of Sashraman warriors were trampled and cut down beneath Arzim's horse. The enemy attacked them with many spears, but Arzim and his fellows pushed back with heavy infantry behind the cavalry.

Arzim's sword swung to block the many spears coming at him. He kicked back the Sashramans trying to dismount him while driving his blade into them. In spite of the enemy's best efforts, the men of the north were gaining ground and would soon have their foes surrounded. The Baku officer smiled upon hearing the whistling of northern arrows hurtling toward their southern foes.

The entire right enemy flank had fallen back and cut Hakan off from his exit point. Having fully formed up with archers pelting the Sashramans with arrows, Hakan and his men were forced to a halt.

"Get out of there, you fool!" Pasha shouted after several members of Hakan's kad were torn through by northern arrows.

"He's going to ride straight back into the main force," said Yuwatu anxiously.

Suddenly what Pasha feared would happen indeed happened. Hakan and his men committed to a fight with the enemy's entire right flank, which was growing in size.

"You're exposed, man! Get out of there!" Pasha shouted angrily as the men of the north behind the barricade began to pick off Hakan's men easily with arrows and other missiles.

"The left flank is closing in. They're trying to surround him," said Yuwatu, growing more anxious.

"We can't wait anymore," said Pasha.

"Get 'em lit!" shouted Yuwatu.

Both of their kads lit their arrows while they moved forward.

"Change of plans Yuwatu."

"Yes, Kaudi."

"We both go by the front, and then we go right and drive up the northern scum's rear. I'll go in first," said Pasha as he notched his arrow to his bow and lit it.

He looked to the east. The enemy's entire advancing left flank had suddenly stopped as Naua and Makar archers advanced from the left and center. They fired lit arrows with precision and speed into the barricade. Within moments, the entire southern end of the barricade, which had been caked with dung and the soft rock called *skulifa*, lit up into flame.

Though the enemy's left flank still tried to close in, the Naua and Makar archers stopped them in their tracks, launching volley after volley against them.

King Hanasa and General Ishok looked on the enemy's left flank from the cover of the jungle. In spite of the growing fire, the enemy was trying to use it to cover their advance as they emptied the inside of the barricade of more men in order to reinforce their right and left flanks.

The other end of the barricade had still not been lit. Obviously the enemy still felt it could be used. The king looked to the right. Though archer fire had helped, the Sashramans still were not advancing.

"Hanasa, look!" shouted General Ishok of the Yashani.

From behind the smoldering walls of the barricade, huge northern cavalry being driven by tall men in thick silver-plated armor skewered into the Sashramans on the right with tall lances, while on the left they rode toward the Makar and Naua archers. Behind them marched column after column of infantry.

"Get them out of there!" shouted the king.

The Yashani general signaled a standard bearer, who then put up the sign for retreat.

"They're going to pay for clustering up like that," said the Yashani general eagerly. "We should have the archers form up along the trees and—"

"Incoming!" cried one of the Halor king's men.

From above them came loosely falling fireballs that began to fall toward the jungle. Hanasa leapt from his horse as fire and rock exploded beside him. His shield and sword flew from him when his head smashed into a pile of loose rocks. Fortunately he was still wearing his helmet.

Dozens upon dozens of his men fell in the soft jungle grass, some having been thrown into trees that broke their bodies like twigs. Several feet away from him, Hanasa saw his horse on its side with its entire neck open and bleeding.

"Take cover! They've found our position! Take cover!" shouted General Ishok.

Hanasa, still dazed, ran to Ishok's position.

"Hasn't Nuvahli set fire to the other side of the barricade yet?"

Just as he spoke, a new wave of flame spread about the enemy position, signaling that Pasha had completed his task.

"General!" called out one of Ishok's men. "The enemy cavalry—they're nearly on top of us!"

"Where is Shabaz! He's supposed to be protecting our left! Where are the Sashramans!" shouted General Ishok.

Hanasa looked to his men; more than a quarter had been taken out by the catapult. It was time for the infantry.

"Ishok, forget them! You follow me in!"

The general nodded as the king ran toward the front of the line where his spearmen and the rest of the Halor infantry stood. Taking a place among them, he looked out from the jungle, seeing some of General Marwa's cavalry holding back the advancing northern left flank. Shabaz and his infantry along with his archers were supposed to have been at the left to keep the men of the north at a distance from their position at the jungle, but none of the Mulamar could be seen at that moment.

Still it mattered little to Hanasa. He could see Pasha and the Sashramans along with some Makar cavalry beating back the enemy at the right. They would make their advance from the left it seemed.

"Line ready!" the king shouted, his long, curved sword drawn and ready.

The Halor spearmen went down into a low stance, placing their shields in front of them with the spears ready.

"Forward!"

Filling the jungle and all the earth around them with their war cries, Hanasa and his men charged the enemy's left. The Yashani soon followed.

Already Pasha's sword arm grew sore from cutting down his enemies from Daimon's back. He swung his shield left and right to block lunging northern spears.

Though little by little they were gaining ground, Pasha's thoughts were only worried ones. The plan had not gone like they had thought. Although the Halor were at the left where they were supposed to be, he, Hakan, and Yuwatu were still held at the right.

Makar spearmen and swordsmen punched forward through the northerners while Pasha and the Sashramans stayed at their right and left flanks, with Yuwatu covering the rear. On that night, he found it particularly difficult to focus. All around him he found exploding flames and hundreds of swords and spears swiping at them.

They had crashed into the rear of several kads of Baku spearmen. However, a score of Jakshima and Baku cavalry had charged to their relief. With their long, heavy lances, they had punched huge gaps into Pasha's kad.

It was proving to be to their advantage that the lances were so heavy that their enemy could not carry shields along with them. Whenever he could, Pasha hurled his spears into their line and fired off as many arrows as he could get off before he was cut down.

Without warning, Jakshima spearmen pushed and broke Pasha and his dwindling kads away from the main force of Makar infantry. Soon Pasha was surrounded by hundreds of spears and hands trying to unseat him. Yuwatu came in behind him, cutting into the ones closest to Pasha.

Daimon angrily came to his hind legs and with his hooves crushed the chests of many of their foes, but more soon replaced them. Pasha drove Daimon and what he could of his kad together with Yuwatu's. Together the Sashramans formed a tight circle to combat the enemy while they pressed in closer. Several men's horses were speared out from under them as the enemy deepened in their frustration. Still, the Sashramans stood firm.

"Come on! Let's finish them!" shouted Yuwatu.

Urging his men forward, Yuwatu and his kad plunged head-on into the heaving mass. Seeing little else to do, Pasha followed. They went forward with extreme urgency, bashing with their shields and trampling all that fell beneath them.

At that moment, their luck began to change for the better as Hakan's kad lunged forward and broke the column of enemy infantry that had surrounded them. Together with the Makar spearmen, they routed the enemy infantry and made short work of the rest of their cavalry.

For the first time, Pasha and his men could see inside the barricade, which was full of archers and siege weapons. Inside as well was a sizeable number of Ekoo javelin men and swordsmen. Pasha's thoughts on whether to head straight to the left flank or go through the barricade first were interrupted as he heard the rumble of cavalry from behind him.

Coming from the east was General Shabaz with his cavalry leading the way before his infantry.

"That Mulamar," Pasha swore angrily.

He had still come from the west though they had agreed to stage the Mulamar at the east on the left flank.

Shabaz and his men did not slow down as they approached the Sashramans and the Makar. Some of the Sashramans drove their horses to the side quickly to avoid being clipped by the Mulamar as they raced toward the inside of the barricades.

"On me!" Pasha shouted.

His men wheeled left and pushed hard toward the west. Together they rode around the left flank of the Halor, Yashani and Naua, as they fought, crashing unexpectedly into a tough line of cavalry and spearmen.

Pasha dropped his head as a long lance lunged toward him. Drawing a dagger, he threw it into the lance owner's throat as they passed. Hanasa and his men drew new strength and cut deeper into the enemy lines. The men of the north responded with fury as Ekoo tribesmen cut at their horses with their axes. Still, their efforts would prove worthless.

Soon they came together with the Yashani horsemen who fired many arrows into the enemy from their mounts. The Baku and Jakshima infantry were now faltering. Still the northern cavalry fought on in an attempt to save the battle.

Pasha and his men fired volley after volley into them, dropping dozens at a time. Then to their surprise, the heavily armored northern cavalrymen began to hurl their heavy lances at them. The captain's stomach dropped when he looked forward.

Before him, Yuwatu lifted up his shield, but he did not have one of metal, his being wood and thick leather. The lance gnawed its way through his shield and splintered into Yuwatu's chest. Not even his armor was enough.

Gasping for breath, the Sashraman froze while the shock riveted through every part of his body. Pasha sat stunned upon Daimon's back. It had been awhile since he had lost an officer.

The warrior who had hurled the lance sprang forward upon his mount, his long, straight sword sweeping high into the air. Pasha drove forward but could not reach Yuwatu.

His fellow tribesman's head was torn effortlessly from the rest of his body, sending his body crashing down into the sea of death.

Pasha rode after the warrior who was trying to cut a line through the Yashani infantry. Coming within a good distance, Pasha pushed himself upright onto Daimon's back and sprang into the air toward the warrior. With all of his strength, he knocked him from his horse into the ground.

Arzim tried to get some distance from the black, wild-looking Sashraman chasing after him. Though he didn't understand the southern tongue, he could tell the southerner had a commanding presence among his men. Arzim's plan to steal away into a surging line of fighting troops bore little fruit when his adversary leapt from his mount.

An astonished Arzim felt another body land upon his horse's back and tear him off his mount. Arzim rose quickly as the Sashraman swung his blade toward him.

The warrior proved to be larger and stronger than Pasha. Pasha came down hard with his sword, only to have it stopped by the warrior's muscular arm. Raising his leg and bending his knee, the warrior kicked Pasha's gut with all his strength, sending Pasha flying back into advancing Yashani warriors.

Pasha jumped to his feet before he was trampled. He came at the man of the north at full speed as the warrior drew another sword. Instead of a sweeping cut, he came down in a slashing motion, but Pasha sidestepped and jump-kicked him at the shoulder.

The man stumbled, and Pasha wasted no time. Sidestepping another lunge as the warrior struggled to stand, Pasha punched him in the face. He proceeded to seize the warrior's sword arm and threw him over his shoulder.

Arzim knew he had only seconds before the warrior took off his head. Southerners tended to be a spear-wielding people and slower with swords. The Baku officer took loose earth into his hand and hurled it at the warrior coming for him.

Pasha's eyes were blinded by the northerner's ruse. Before he could catch him, the warrior had disappeared into his own lines just as the other tribes advanced.

With relief, he looked up to find the Yashani and Halor leading the advance, and within moments, the entire northern cavalry line had withered away, with the infantry flying into retreat. As the enemy passed the left flank of the barricade, the entire Mulamar cavalry column barreled into them, splitting them into even smaller groups.

Pretty soon, the fight before the walls of Cafura turned into a cold chase of blood and death. Pasha retrieved Daimon and joined his men as they cut down as many routing Baku as they could.

With the enemy pressing their backs to the city walls, Ivadar could sense his men were losing momentum. Southern arrows rained down upon them from every angle. In spite of their armor and shields, Ivadar saw nothing but northern warriors falling.

"Sir, we can't hold on much longer! Tazharik's line has broken!" shouted Takar, one of his lower officers.

The officer tried to say something else, but a southern arrow drove into the back of his neck.

Ivadar knew he had to act. In the distance, he could already hear some Ekoo officers sounding the retreat. He could no longer deny it. They had not anticipated the arrival of the other tribes; everything had changed.

"Retreat! Retreat!" he shouted to his men before turning north.

CHAPTER 14

A Stranger

To Leyos and Abayomi, it was as if a huge weight had been lifted from their chests that night. Seeing the Baku run had sent a deafening wave of cheering from the warriors of the city. Leyos stepped out from his position along the battered walls to look out upon the city.

Though the city was simple in design, it was one of the largest in the north and the most heavily fortified. Miles upon miles of bedrock stone wall wrapped around the city's outer defenses, with a lesser wooden wall reinforcing the city from the inside.

All of the stone roads and dirt paths wound through the different houses and market places, ending at the alcalde's estate, the city square, the barracks at the eastern part of the city, and finally the temple that stood close to the city square.

Abayomi joined Leyos, looking upon the city as the people came from out of hiding. For the first time in months, there was laughter and dancing in the city of Cafura. It gratified Abayomi as he watched them celebrate. Pretty soon his men joined in. The commander laughed instead of rebuking them. All this time of death and suffering, they had earned that moment.

"I never would have thought the Halor would come, nor any of them," said Leyos.

"Nor I. We should be careful about trusting them," said Abayomi, his tone turning grave.

"Why, brother? It's obvious the malik made a pact with them."

"Pact or no, they'll turn on us in the end, Leyos!"

"It's not like it was before," said Leyos.

"Yes, brother, it is worse!" said Abayomi.

"Sir," called out Takil from above them. "They're coming."

Both men hurried back to the wall to look down upon the army before them.

"They're not all trying to get in, are they?" said Abayomi.

"No, look. They're splitting into a column," said Leyos.

Just as Leyos had said, the main force stayed motionless as groups of all of the tribes came together to make one column.

"Are there any Sashramans?" asked Leyos anxiously.

At first Abayomi found it difficult to tell the different tribes apart. However, he soon distinguished the banners and standards of the different tribes and was able to discern where each tribe fell in the column. He took in a heavy breath upon seeing the blue robes and standards of Sashra. Soon his eyes fell upon Pasha, who rode before none other than the Halor king.

"I don't believe it!" said Abayomi.

"What! What is it, brother?"

"Pasha's here."

"What!" said Leyos.

"There he is, down there," said Abayomi, pointing.

Leyos peered over the wall to look down at the advancing column.

"It is him! And who is that riding beside him?"

"I don't believe it. It's Hanasa, the Halor king," said Abayomi.

"What!" Leyos said, straining his eyes for a better look.

"How do you know it's him?"

"I'd know that man anywhere. I served in Malik Juktan's guard when he went to Halor land to negotiate the borders of the southern territories with them. It is him."

"What about the rest of them?"

"Naua, Yashani, Mulamar, Makar, and Halor, all in one place, on one side. I never would have believed it. Takil!"

"Sir!"

"Open the gates!"

Both Leyos and Abayomi rushed from their position along the wall, descending the many crooked stone steps to the base of the wall. On the ground, they waded through the pressing throng of people swarming the area before the gates.

Everywhere people danced and sang as they pressed closer to the gates, clamoring for the best spots in which to receive their saviors. Never before did Abayomi think it possible that a Sashraman city would receive their brothers to the south with such grace. The scene played out before him like the strangest of all dreams as soon as the gates were opened.

All of Cafura was kindled with light and joy as Pasha passed under the archway of Mijushu and entered the city.

The captain had very little desire to deal with a large crowd, especially when he bore dirt-ridden robes and armor caked in blood. Still, the captain put on a strong face before the people of Cafura as they welcomed him into their city.

Pasha reached out from Daimon's back to the many reaching hands that pressed against him and the men who followed him. It seemed strange to him, their faces. They leapt and sang their praises that night and danced before the moon. In their eyes were written the tales of a long-suffering people.

Sensing that the moment was most appropriate, the captain lifted the standards of Sashra high and was met with roaring cheers.

The way parted as Sashraman warriors advanced upon the gate. A column of spearmen pushed their way through the crowds, led by two officers whom the captain had not seen for many months.

Pasha and the men stopped as Abayomi and Leyos closed in on their position. King Hanasa came alongside Pasha as the two men approached. He dismounted to meet his brothers who came on foot.

The whole of the city came down to a low silence as the defenders of their city met with brothers from afar.

"I swear you must have forgotten where north was to keep us waiting so!" said Abayomi.

Pasha laughed as he opened his arms in embrace. "You always did nothing but complain, you old heifer," said the captain.

Both men embraced, laughing.

"Leyos," said Pasha, turning to the commander.

"Sir."

Pasha embraced him as well. "It does me good to see you."

"And you as well, sir."

"It does us good to see all of you here today," said Abayomi. "For so many months, we thought there was no hope."

"What you thought is of no consequence. What matters is that you held on in spite of the bleakness of your plight!" the captain said in a loud voice for the people, who responded with a massive wave of agreement.

Pasha then turned to King Hanasa who stood behind him.

"My brothers, tonight would not have been possible if it were not for this man and our new ally, King Hanasa of the Halor."

Abayomi and Leyos bowed respectfully as the king stepped up closer.

The king bowed as well to show his respect.

Pasha then turned to the people again.

"People of Cafura and all Sashramans here this night, I am Captain Pasha Nuvahli, sent to you directly from Malik Juktan himself."

The captain paused as the people cheered the king's name.

"Many would have told me it would not be possible. I thought it would not be possible. But in the moment of our most dire need, our old adversaries to the south of us responded with friendship. And now they honor this friendship with a pact that has made them our brothers once more. Honor King Hanasa of the Halor and the generals of the Naua, Yashani, Makar, and Mulamar tribes, our new allies."

The people cheered them with much more warmth than Pasha would have expected. Women tossed flowers to the generals and adorned their horses with wreaths.

King Hanasa waved respectfully as the people cheered on their new friends from the south.

"Tonight marks a new day in Sashra and in the south. For the first time in centuries, all the south has come together to turn back the tide of northern aggression. Tonight is the beginning of the end of the nightmare that descended upon you months before. Tonight we proclaim to our enemies that this city, though it be worn, it is not broken!"

A massive roar of cheering and cries of joy took hold of the city that night as they embraced Pasha's words. Whether or not he believed it all, Pasha did not know. He had never been much about giving speeches, but as a specially appointed officer of the king, he knew it was his duty to reassure the people and give them hope.

Again the city withdrew itself into a frenzy of wild chanting and cheering. Women and children danced in a deepening circle as the men rolled the deep, steady rhythm of the Hebari drum. Pasha knew by the energy that had taken possession over everyone that night that it had been many days since anything good had come from outside the gates of Cafura.

"Captain, how did you manage that?" called Abayomi over the loud cheering and celebration.

"Believe it or not, I didn't ask for it," Pasha answered.

"I'm sure. We should go see the alcalde."

Pasha nodded in agreement. He pushed away gently as people reached out to touch him.

Once he had mounted Daimon again, he, King Hanasa, the rest of the generals, and their trusted men followed the column of Sashraman warriors who cleared the way for them. Pasha looked up to the men who cheered them as they passed the walls.

His men gave him a thunderous round of chants and cheers as he passed by their positions. Pasha's spirits lifted upon seeing so many men who had been in his command.

Standing along the wall as well was a strange woman who immediately captured his attention. She turned from tending to a wounded warrior and looked straight down at Pasha, seeming to see no one but him.

The strange woman was very black and seemed quite tall. Her robes were dark blue and open at the shoulders, revealing the shape of her slender yet muscular frame. From her neck up, her headdress was pulled back, giving the captain full view of her radiant features.

Much time had passed since Pasha had gazed upon such a woman. She had large, dark eyes that seemed to see all, along with a full nose and high cheekbones. From her head fell long, intricately twisted braids that rested lightly upon her chest. The woman lowered her head, seeming embarrassed at how Pasha gazed at her.

Pasha bowed his head toward her and turned back to the streets before them.

Abayomi and his column led them far from the multiplying throng to the city square. They passed through it to the main house that stood just a street over from the city's center.

The alcalde's house though quite elegant did not equal the splendor of other houses Pasha had seen in Kadisha and other cities. But perhaps the alcalde preferred it that way, he thought to himself. His house was of smooth, white limestone and marble, built with only one level, in the cubed manner favored by even the simplest man.

Surrounding the house stood a low wall with an open wooden gate. Though dangerous, Pasha had heard of many alcaldes who threw open the gates of their homes every day for a one-month period to receive the common people and hear their requests, needs, and concerns. Obviously this alcalde bore the mindset that with privilege came responsibility.

The Sashraman column that marched before them stopped. Abayomi and Leyos stepped out from their line and moved toward the house while the other Sashramans spread out into positions all around the house. Pasha and the rest of the generals dismounted and left their horses at a hitching post. Passing through the gates, they went through the small courtyard to the main house. Their way was lit by five bright torches.

Two warriors bearing spears and sheathed swords met them there. Both wore dark purple robes over thick sheets of iron mail, along with amulets bearing black rock and marble strung together with a strand of ox hide. Their unsoiled robes and fine turbans told Pasha that they were obviously members of the city guard. The warriors said nothing as Abayomi led them into the house.

Inside, the men entered into a wide hall of beautiful white rock walls. The floor was formed from clusters of the smooth, black rock found in the sea. The numerous flickering torches revealed four warriors wearing the same robes and armaments as the ones at the door, standing in a row against the left wall. The hall stopped far ahead at a large, open archway that was partially concealed by a curtain of marble beads; most likely, the chambers of the alcalde and his family lay behind it. To the right, the hall opened into a larger, much darker chamber.

Pasha could see very little to the right, causing him to ponder in which part of the house the alcalde wished to receive them.

A rapid gust of light as a torch came to life told Pasha all he needed to know. The darkness receded and left another warrior within their vision. The man seemed different. He was very dark and appeared older than the other warriors. The warrior bore a longer turban along with much finer golden-hemmed purple robes that partially covered the thick armor plating on his chest.

Pasha looked past him farther into the room. Though still dark, he could make out the shapes of other men, sitting upon fine cushions and mats that were formed into a circle.

"Commander Abayomi, Leyos," he said to Pasha's companions.

Both men nodded in acknowledgment.

"Maranhi," said Leyos as he turned to Pasha. "This is him. He brought them with him."

The warrior's eyes passed over Pasha and then moved to King Hanasa and other generals behind him.

"Kaudi," said Leyos. "This is Captain Maranhi of the city guard."

"I am honored," Pasha said, respectfully nodding toward the captain.

Maranhi said nothing but did return the gesture.

"The alcalde will see you now," he said to Leyos.

Pasha noticed Maranhi's eyes shifting anxiously when King Hanasa and the generals of the other tribes passed.

They followed Maranhi and his torchlight deeper into the room until they came upon the group of men and cushions arranged into a circle. At one side of the circle sat an old man dressed in the vestments of a shazhia. The shazhia's fingers twitched nervously about the Ring of Shakana, which he wore upon a long, bronzed necklace. In the center sat none other than the alcalde, a beardless, middle-aged man of a bronzed complexion.

The alcalde wore fine white robes with no turban, letting his hair fall freely upon the nape of his neck. For the longest moment, the alcalde said nothing, the warrior behind him doing the same while the shazhia's eyes were closed in meditation.

King Hanasa and the generals looked to Pasha, but he said nothing. Finally the alcalde spoke. "I guess if you hope for a miracle long enough, the world ought to give you something, even if it is less than what you expected."

"Often times, it must be less or a man would not know a miracle for himself," said King Hanasa.

The alcalde's lips tightened, sending Pasha into a frightened wave of anxiety. His mouth flared into a hurried smile as he spoke.

"King Hanasa of the Halor zealots with the Makar butchers and Mulamar hounds," he said slowly, stressing each word. Pasha's skin tingled as he felt the tension among them rise. Shabaz and General Marwa glared at the alcalde, challenging him to go on.

"Your father honored us with his presence here so many years ago, King Hanasa. I am glad that he lived to a ripe old age. Shame him and his allies could not extend the same courtesy to more Sashramans like my parents and my sisters," he said, directing his words more to the Makar and Mulamar.

The alcalde's attention to them was interrupted by King Hanasa, who attempted to calm the moment before it got out of hand. "Those were unfortunate times, unfortunate for all of us. Still, I would think now would be the time to talk of the future rather than the past."

"It appears your walls have been taking quite a beating for some time," said General Ishok.

"As astute as ever you Yashani are," said the alcalde coldly.

"I have brought some of the best stoneworkers and craftsmen among my tribe. We could help you repair the walls."

"I doubt we'll have much time for that," said the alcalde. "A great victory you have won us today, but you have not seen the full power of the northern army, especially when she is among them."

"Who, Alcalde?" said Pasha.

"Perhaps you had better sit," said the alcalde.

Pasha and King Hanasa sat directly in front of the alcalde. Shabaz and the other generals filled the remaining seats.

"The army you defeated was only one unit of a much larger force led by the red-eyed one's witch woman."

"Who is she?" General Ishok pressed.

The alcalde's face dropped into an almost soundless wave of fright and anger. He leaned closer to Ishok when he spoke. "A whore from hell!" The alcalde paused, drawing a deep breath as he moved back.

"What has been happening?" asked Pasha.

"Bad things, Kaudi," said Leyos.

The room was silent for a long moment until the alcalde spoke again. "Every fifth night, no one sleeps. Our dreams are taken over by that woman; she speaks to us, telling us things no one should hear. No matter what we do, we can't shut her out! On the sixth night, no one comes out of their homes, for that is when the dead walk. And then on the seventh night, everyone goes to the temple. On that night, we see visions of the red-eyed one, and then after the visions, one male child from every family dies."

"They die?" asked General Tayla. "Of what?"

"They just drop dead! No matter how many times we go to the sacred temple, and the shazhia and priests pray over the people. They just die."

They looked over toward the shazhia who had still not opened his eyes from meditation.

"You know why they are celebrating?" said the alcalde to Pasha. "Because today is the third day. They don't believe you can defeat the men of the north. They just think that this madness will stop for at least a week. They're hoping that maybe their children will live a bit longer."

"Alcalde," said King Hansa. "It is important to tell us what you know about the enemy's movements. How many are there, where they are mostly concentrated."

For a moment, the alcalde focused on the pressing issues. "I don't know. My scouts say there are between ten and forty thousand. No one really knows what's going on out there. They're all over the jungle, but the main force, she stays mostly in the mountains. You're only going to get them out by going out to meet them, and I would advise against that. She'd kill all of you."

"All this over a woman!" said Shabaz with a smirk. "She does a few tricks, and she's already got you Sashramans scurrying into your holes."

"If you wish to die by your foolish Mulamar pride, I will not mourn you," said the alcalde, growing increasingly angry.

"It'll keep me alive a lot longer than the timidity of a spineless bushim," Shabaz retorted.

Maranhi leapt to his feet, hands readied upon his sword. Three more of his men jumped into position around him as Shabaz stood, close to drawing his sword.

Pasha came to his feet quickly. "Stop this insanity! Steady yourselves!" he shouted to Maranhi and his men.

At first Maranhi's men did not respond to Pasha's order. But after a tense moment of silence, Maranhi backed away, prompting his men to do the same.

"Let us not forget who the enemy is!" Pasha said. "We are here now, Alcalde. The city defenses will have to be changed and a new strategy set forth."

"Who are you to say what must be done?" said Maranhi, stepping back among them.

"Captain Pasha Nuvahli, special representative of Malik Juktan in this matter. As of this moment, Alcalde, I claim command over all the warriors of Cafura."

"You have no authority!" shouted Maranhi.

"Yes he does, Maranhi," said the alcalde.

"Sir? This is my command! These are my men!" said Maranhi.

"No, Captain," said Pasha. "As a captain with a battlefield commission and a special representative of Malik Juktan himself, I outrank you. As such, I expect you and your men to submit to my authority along with all the Sashraman warriors within this city."

"Alcalde," said Maranhi.

The alcalde ignored him, focusing on Pasha. "Head of our warriors you may be, Captain. But this is my city; no one is above me here, whether they be Sashraman or Halor."

"Understood Alcalde . . . One more thing, Abayomi told me on the way here that it is becoming increasingly difficult to control the city when it is not under attack."

"The people are anxious. Our food and water stores are running low, and sickness is rampant," the alcalde finally said.

"How low?" asked General Ishok.

"It is estimated that we barely have enough for another month, maybe two. And with the rations decreasing each day, people are becoming more belligerent. Tonight is a rarity. Usually the people don't go out at night for any reason. The streets are becoming increasingly littered with thieves and cutthroats. And the only women brave enough to be in the streets after dark are husbandless mothers going whoring to feed their children," said the alcalde.

"And what has your city guard been doing about this?" said General Marwa in a somewhat condescending tone.

The alcalde's anger flared, along with Maranhi's, who responded, "All they can! Protecting the food stores, protecting the water, keeping the people from rioting. I have three hundred and fifty guardsmen, there is only so much they can do."

"Have you not drawn all of the men to defend the city?" asked Pasha. "Why not use some conscripts to keep the streets in order."

"You just don't understand. They are the problem. The only time they do anything is when there is an attack, and they desert or disappear constantly. Once an attack is over, many go to the brothels to rub hashish and indulge their lust," said Maranhi with contempt.

"Abayomi, have you done nothing about these things the alcalde is saying?" said Pasha.

"Sir, when I first came here, I had twenty-five thousand men. Now I have barely eleven thousand. That's including conscripts. At the rate they've been pounding us, I would have been only weakening our defenses if I had let even one kad go patrol the streets."

Pasha took a deep breath as he lowered his head. He expected bad, but he only heard worse in every moment that passed by.

"If we are going to be effective here, a solid command structure with a presence on the streets and the walls must be established," said General Tayla.

"And you think they'll respect Naua patrols and Naua commands under this new command structure," said the alcalde mockingly.

"They'll accept the new command structure of all our tribes, every tribesmen working together and fighting together," said King Hanasa.

"That's cute," said Maranhi. "But no one will respect you unless you can deliver change."

"I will not have this city tear itself apart from within," said Pasha. "There will be no leniency or mercy; the people will respect the city's new leadership."

"Things are tolerable the way they are, Captain. Some people die, some get robbed, others make bastards, but the main defense of the city goes unhindered. If you go around and upset the balance, that could soon change," said Maranhi.

"There is nothing tolerable about a city under siege that is not in control by a central command."

"You think you know Cafura, Captain. You don't know anything yet."

"Maranhi," said the alcalde.

The captain backed away once more, returning to his position behind the alcalde.

"What is the state of your machinery?" asked General Ishok. "I saw no catapults or rock slingers showing any worth during the battle."

"They're few and far between. During a firefight, they're almost impossible to get into position, and all of their operators get killed or they're lost when the Baku blow out a section of our wall," said the alcalde.

"This should be one of our main priorities when it comes to defense," said General Ishok.

"I will have my craftsmen working on it right away. We'll need them when we get on the move."

"On the move?" asked the alcalde.

Then Pasha spoke. "Alcalde, I think I speak for all us when I say that we did not come here to hide behind walls. The main strategy that we shall pursue is finding the enemy and pushing them out of this province."

"Are you fools? The walls are the only place where we have a chance. If you go out there, they will butcher you."

"I think we proved well enough tonight that we're more than able to handle the Baku army," said General Marwa.

"You Makar . . ." The alcalde shook his head. "You know how great the threat is, Captain. Every day at the mountain pass, General Cheokto and his men lose more ground."

"That is why we cannot waste time that could be used to destroy this army and reinforce the northern pass," Pasha said forcefully.

"General Cheokto is fighting thousands upon thousands of northern warriors. How do you propose that we can beat them on open field?" asked the alcalde.

"Malik Juktan sent me word by rider that he shall come with an army from the west," said Pasha.

"It will be too late by the time Malik Juktan gets here," said the alcalde.

"He arrived in the west more than two months ago. By now he's on his way back with the entire western army."

"You dream, Nuvahli," said the alcalde skeptically.

"Malik Juktan will not let us down, Alcalde! When he gets here, we shall purge every northern tribesmen from our land!" said Pasha.

"You must have quite a life, Nuvahli. Making promises you know you can't keep," said the alcalde.

"For the head of a city that rejoices at our coming, you don't seem to have much faith in us. You've heard something. Haven't you, Alcalde?" said Pasha.

The alcalde's face turned graver than before. He had something to say that he wished he did not know. Unable to say anything, he turned away from them, staring into the darkness.

"He's here."

All eyes turned to the old priest. His eyes were now opened, and his mind in tune to the matters being discussed that night.

"Who?" asked Pasha.

"The general. The red-eyed one, the one whose coming was foretold by the oracle."

"Who?" said Shabaz, with a mock tone. "The one you Sashramans believe is the thousand-year-old King Janaha come back to life. It is no wonder you Sashramans have worked yourselves so into such a frenzy," he said, laughing.

The shazhia ignored him, speaking only to Pasha. "I know you've seen him. You know what he is coming for."

Pasha said nothing. The shazhia's words only served to make him more uncomfortable.

"All right," said the alcalde. "I think that is enough for tonight."

Everyone stood when the alcalde got to his feet.

"I am honored to receive you, our new allies," he said while bowing and extending closed fists toward King Hanasa and the generals of the other tribes in the traditional manner. "If Daiyu is willing, may he give us the strength to vanquish our enemies."

King Hanasa returned the same gesture, the other generals following his example.

Abayomi and Leyos stood and began to lead them out of the chamber.

After leaving the alcalde's house, the column of Sashramans and the generals reached the city center, where they found its solemn silence replaced by riotous revelry. From the city gates, the crowd of celebrating Sashramans that greeted them before had now turned into a swarm that filled every corner of the city square.

Before they could take another path, the people had caught sight of the column and engulfed them within an endless sea of bodies, pushing them toward the center. The endless faces passed by Pasha in a flash. Thousands of words spoken at once created an unintelligible noise within his ears that was soon accompanied by even louder Hebari melodies and tunes.

"Kaudi." The captain looked ahead to see Takil and many of the men from his old positing.

"What is all this?" said Abayomi as they came closer to the center of the gathering where all the Sashraman warriors sat.

"A time to forget all troubles, sir," Takil said to Abayomi. "And a time to look ahead," Takil said to Pasha.

"A moment all of you deserve, Takil," said Pasha grasping his forearm in the warrior's way. Takil returned the gesture. Pasha dismounted and moved closer to his men.

"Sir," said Shukimbo, stepping forward.

"Shukimbo," Pasha said in acknowledgment as he grasped his forearm in the traditional greeting.

"We knew you would be back," said Shukimbo.

"Well it gets boring sitting at home anyway," said Pasha, trying to block out the images of Hadassah and Kamili, who were the true reason for his presence in the city.

"Varansi," he said, turning to the young officer he had known in Kadisha. Gone were his boyish looks, having been replaced with a man's beard and a more rugged complexion.

"I hear you made *saji*?" Pasha said.

"Well, I don't see Commander Abayomi as having had much choice. So many of our officers have been killed," said Varansi, with more humility than Pasha was willing to accept.

"Regardless, you deserve it. You've always been one of my best. Do you not think so, Abayomi?" said Pasha.

"Of course, a fine officer," said Abayomi nodding in agreement.

"Thank you, sir. I wouldn't be without your guidance."

"Now the unit is whole once more. It couldn't have come at a better time," said Leyos.

"Your second is growing rusty, Kaudi. I've saved his life more than three times now during this posting. Maybe now you can take charge over him," said Leyos.

"Three times. What!" said Abayomi, half-smiling.

"More like twenty times for you. I swear, Pasha, this sea rat nearly fell off the wall every time we had to climb up during an attack. I'm surprised he survived this long."

"I was trying to put on my sword belt," said Leyos.

"It would be complicated for you," said Abayomi.

"It is during an attack," said Leyos.

Pasha laughed glad to see there was good humor between them.

"Sir, please," said Takil, gesturing Pasha to an empty seat among the Sashramans.

Takil noted his concern as he looked at Daimon. "Don't worry, sir, we'll take care of him."

Though he preferred to lead Daimon to stable himself, Pasha let the reins fall into Takil's hands. Takil turned Daimon over to another warrior, who lead Daimon back through the crowd toward the eastern end of the city where the stables were.

"We have a place for you as well, Your Majesty, Generals. Please come," Takil said, bowing respectfully to King Hanasa and leading him and the generals to a group of several other well-cushioned stools a couple of feet from Pasha and his men. Several women brought them food and drink, which they accepted graciously.

Finding himself among his own men again, Pasha greeted Luma and then spoke with Shukimbo and Varansi before taking a seat among them. Slowly it became disheartening as he noted how many were not present.

The captain occupied his mind by looking out upon the throng about them. Everyone was dancing and singing or eating. A great deal of food was going around that night, Pasha noted. One would expect hardly any food in a city that was supposedly in the middle of a food crisis.

Pasha smiled as three young women brought them large platters of bread, cheese, and a various assortment of fruit. Another served them cool water from a clay pitcher.

"*Hasante yeye,*" said Abayomi.

"*Hasante yeye,*" said Pasha in Hebari to thank them.

The women smiled and bowed in acknowledgment.

"Are you sure the city can afford all this breaking of bread? If there is a food crisis, this should be divvied up more proportionately," said Pasha.

"Relax, Kaudi. We're not starving yet. This bit of indulgence will hardly affect our ration quotas," said Abayomi.

"Even a bit can make the biggest difference in the end, my brother."

"Do not worry about it, Kaudi. We got it all figured out. Besides, right now is usually the only time we can take a meal."

"At night?" Pasha inquired.

"You see, Kaudi, the Baku usually attack us throughout the day and force us to take cover. At night, they slow down for a couple of hours, and this is the only time we can really eat."

Pasha looked around him to his men. He could tell by their ravenous tearing of the bread and cheese that they had not eaten for many hours. Each man savored every bite, taking large bites but chewing slowly as if going too fast would cause them great pain.

"They haven't eaten all day?"

"As the alcalde says, Kaudi, it is a crisis."

"And what of the rest of what the alcalde says about the nights here? Is it true?"

Abayomi cleared his throat. His face became grave as he answered. "Tonight is a happy time, sir. We should not spoil it with talk of such things."

"Happy time or no, I must know what's happening here," Pasha pressed him.

The commander cleared his throat once more, looking toward the dirt-laden stone beneath them.

"It is as the alcalde says. On the fifth night, voices fill every corner of the city, every house, speaking to every person."

"Is it this woman?" Pasha asked.

"Yes," answered Abayomi.

"Have you seen her?" asked Pasha.

"Yes, once before. She is more powerful than any witch doctor or mystic. When she speaks her words, terrible things happen, unholy things."

"What happened?" Pasha asked.

"She spoke, and entire sections of the walls blew apart or sank to the ground."

"No one can have that kind of power," Pasha said hurriedly, not wanting to believe what his friend had said. Nevertheless, Pasha knew Abayomi; he never told lies.

"It exists! I lost almost five hundred men because of it! I almost lost Leyos here," Abayomi said, nodding his head toward Leyos, who remained silent.

"What of the sixth and seventh night?" Pasha asked. Though he prided himself on fearing nothing, none of what his friend told him made him comfortable.

"If there is not an attack, I make the men stay inside barracks. It is as the alcalde says. Every sixth night, the dead walk among us."

"You've seen them?"

"Men I saw fall in battle a day or two before were walking plain as day among us. They tell us that we shall be joining them soon. At least twenty people commit suicide every other week. Many are my men."

Pasha lowered his head; the festivities seemed a far way off as Abayomi lowered him into the pool of realities the city was facing.

"On the seventh night . . . the seventh night is a living hell, Pasha. Men and boys dropping dead everywhere. And what's ironic is that we, the ones who fight every day, we are spared. None of my men die that night. We just watch and collect the bodies. Little boys, some no older than . . ."

It had been a long time since the captain witnessed his friend shed a tear. It had barely escaped Abayomi's eye when he wiped it away furiously.

"The seventh night is the most chaotic overall. There have already been two riots. If you hadn't come, I doubt we could've survived another."

"It's all right, brother," Pasha said in comfort.

Abayomi rebuked him. "No, Pasha. It is not all right. This should not be happening. What have we done that Daiyu would allow dark magic to prevail against us? Why? To allow boys . . ."

"We cannot count upon Daiyu to fix this, brother. It will be our strength in battle that will end this. Things will be different now. I promise you."

Abayomi nodded, saying no more.

Leyos sat silent as well for a moment. He looked at Pasha, unsure of what to say. Finally he cleared his throat and raised his chalice. "May Daiyu receive them and deny entrance to none," he said more as a prayer.

All the other Sashramans save Abayomi and Pasha did the same. He could not place his hope in Daiyu for mercy.

Unexpectedly, the crowd parted to two sides as a group of seven dancing women and three bearing drums and three with pipes came before the Pasha and his men. The mood turned light again as the music filled the air.

"Oh you're really going to enjoy this, Kaudi," said Leyos.

The drummers rolled out sharp beats to a quick rhythm that the pipe players carried. Everyone began to clap to the rhythm as the women's dance became faster. They formed a line and spun several times, sharply thrusting their waists and hips in time with the rhythm of the music. All of them wore blue and white dresses that covered them from the low part of their neck to the knees, leaving their slender arms and shoulders bare. In their hair they wore flowers and gold streaks that gave them the most alluring glow. On their ankles were small gold rings that seemed to keep a rhythm of their own as the women moved to the music. In a circle, they moved their arms in sharp waves and movements over their heads while their waist and hip movement became faster and more pronounced.

Again they made a dancing line, pumping out their chests as they dropped their heads back, letting their long, black hair drop down to their legs. Then, moving with great speed, they went into a running yet dancing circle, twirling into the air and coming down into their position dancing.

Pasha could sense the rising heat of desire among his men. The warriors followed every movement of the young women, not missing one step or position.

"I love victories. They bring out the best in all of us. Don't you think so, sir," said Leyos. Pasha was not surprised. The man of the west had not changed much in spite of many months of fighting.

"They're getting a bit free with it, don't you think?" Though the dance was a welcome diversion for any man, Pasha felt guilty in a small way for indulging in it.

"And that's what we're fighting for, is it not? Freedom!" Leyos shouted it in a loud voice for all to hear. The people responded with louder cheers and more shouts.

"Besides, what is the greater sin, a well-endowed woman hiding her natural gifts that surely come from above or sharing them with her people to lift their spirits?" Leyos said, laughing as he clapped along to the music.

Pasha said nothing to his query. He looked on as Abayomi stood and left them, going over to speak with King Hanasa.

"You had better set up that patrol quickly, Kaudi. The streets are going to be busy tonight!" said Leyos, laughing.

Pasha stood and began to leave the company of his officer. The dance ended at that moment, and the crowd erupted into claps and cheers.

Saying nothing to anyone, Pasha disappeared into the pressing mass of bodies. After passing through much of the city, Pasha found himself before the temple. Inside the temple was dark and full of the smell of death. Even outside of the main worship area, the fine white marble floor was full of litters and beds that bore wounded and dying men. Pasha removed his shoes and sword before entering the sanctuary.

Inside was much the same as the outside. The entire floor of the sanctuary stood covered in mats, beds, and litters for carrying the wounded and dead. As his nose was attacked by the stench of death, Pasha's ears filled with its noise. Men cried out as they writhed in pain that none of the lower priests and older women who cared for them could stop. While he went forward, he stepped carefully over fresh puddles and blood soaked rags that now stained the holy ground beneath them.

At each corner of the temple were three lightly flickering torches. The sharp red flame gave the room an eerie glow, a sense of foreboding that Pasha could feel only too deeply.

On the shazhia's platform were lower priests and temple students singing holy verses while men moaned in pain and soon expired.

"What are you doing here?"

Pasha turned as a woman's voice addressed him. To his surprise, it was not one of the older women, but the woman he saw on the wall earlier that night. She was every bit as lovely to Pasha up close as she had seemed from afar. He noted the wearied expression upon her face. But her words were strong, and in her eyes he saw a woman with an inner strength that undoubtedly enabled her to remain in such a place.

At first Pasha did not know what to say or why he was there. All he wanted to do at that moment was look upon her.

"Well! Did you lose your tongue out there or are you slow to thought?" she said as more of a jest than a sign of impatience.

"Oh. I ah . . . I'm Captain Nuvahli. Pasha Nuvahli."

"I know," she said

"You do?" Pasha asked, immediately realizing it was not a very smart question.

"I saw you speak at the gates. Inspiring . . . but these men here have no more need of your inspiration. No more orders, no more fighting. Their part in this war is over now. Leave what is left of them to Daiyu, Captain."

She seemed irritated with him and went over to a warrior who groaned in pain. Taking a pitcher, she dripped water upon his face while pushing down hard upon his open side with a rag and bandages. The warrior's pain only increased as she did so. Nevertheless, her grip remained firm.

"I can't see! I can't . . . it's so dark! So dark . . . please, please." The warrior who had been taught all of his life of strength under intense pain broke into tears like the most wretched of men.

"Shh. Shhh. It'll be all right," the woman said.

But it soon became clear that it would not be all right. Blood spluttered from the wound in spite of the woman's effort. Within moments, he was bleeding out uncontrollably.

"I don't want to die. I don't."

A debilitating weakness overwhelmed what little strength his body had left. It was a scene Pasha knew too well. For so long, men like them had shown bravery in the most terrible of fights, seeing so much suffering. Yet when it came down to their end, they cried like children in the arms of women as they went to the other side.

"Don't worry, brother. Trust in Daiyu. You'll be all right. You'll be all right."

Slowly the warrior's voice faded, and his eyes became unfocused, like rolling white globes in his head. Within moments, his chest heaved one last time and then fell back never to rise again.

The woman closed his eyes. She pressed his hand to her head as she prayed over him, asking Daiyu to receive him.

Pasha stepped closer, seeing by the warrior's robes and amulets that he was a Yashani. He was quite young, seeming no more than eighteen, close to his cousin Mizram's age.

"Such a waste," said the woman quietly as she went to a table nearby that contained a water basin for her to wash the warrior's blood from her hands. "And you'll be sending in hundreds more in the coming months. Good men who should be raising families. not wasting their lives at war."

"It is no waste, woman. There is nothing more honorable for a man to do than fight for what is his. You should respect that," said Pasha.

She looked at Pasha with eyes that seemed full of rage but an expression upon her face that seemed to bear passion as well as signs of an intense hurt. "You men may try to justify this with fancy words and talk of honor. But it is no comfort to the women who have to bury you and raise your children without their fathers," she said.

Though he was not surprised by her short tone with him, the captain grew increasingly uncomfortable yet drawn to her as he looked upon her.

"You have a man in the army?" asked Pasha.

"No. But if I did, I would not let him go run off to get killed in every war that came about."

"I'm sure any man with you as his bride would fear your wrath more than even the mightiest of hosts."

It pleased Pasha when she laughed. She bore a smile as calming and magnificent as the most tranquil of seas and most beautiful of gems.

"I still don't know your name," he said.

"That is because I did not give it," said the woman.

"What must I do to be worthy of it?" said Pasha.

"I've given it to many men, and none were worthy. What is it you want here, Captain?" she said, her tone becoming serious once more.

"I'm here for my man, Nalar. You know of him?"

"It depends. What does he look like?"

"Very dark, sort of older."

"Right. That tells me so much!" she said with a strong dose of sarcasm Pasha quickly tired of.

"Look, woman, you know of him or not?"

"Try the shazhia's meditation room. That's where the better-off ones should be."

"Right," said Pasha. He began to take his leave. Yet as he looked about him, all he saw were empty walls. In most temples he had visited, the room where the shazhia meditated usually fell behind his platform. Pasha saw nothing but bare wall.

He turned back to the woman. Though he could have figured out where to go himself, he was not in the mood for a long search.

"Um. It's my first time to the temple. Could you . . ."

"Come with me," said the woman, marching off toward the shazhia's platform.

The lower priests and students parted to let them pass as they ascended the platform. At first Pasha did not know what the woman was looking for, but she put his speculations to rest when she reached down in the center of the platform and pulled on a

Nathan Chandler

loose bit of rope. Tugging harder on the rope, a section of the floor gave way, opening into another room below them.

"That's different," said Pasha more to himself.

"Your man's down there," said the woman.

Pasha looked down into the poorly lit room below. He could make out the walls of the chamber, but the darkness made it difficult to tell exactly how deep of a fall it would be.

"How do I get down there?"

"If you're scared of hurting yourself, get a ladder," she said, smiling. "I have things to do. Shout if you need anything."

"And what should I shout in that moment? 'Hey, girl, mysterious woman of the night, my man needs some help?' Come now. There are better things I can call you."

"Mahlinya." With that, she left him and headed back to her other duties.

"Mahlinya," Pasha repeated.

After talking with Nalar for some time, Pasha returned to the Sashraman barracks to get some rest before he collapsed. The day had been long and tiring, yet the captain knew it had barely begun.

174

CHAPTER 15

A City at War

Pasha woke early and went about the walls of the city, making sure patrols were in place and ready to react in an instant. Hakan had developed a new warning system based on horn calls. It had intrigued the captain, who implemented it quickly among his men. Enough of King Hanasa's officers, along with those of the Naua and Yashani, accepted it so that the previously obstinate Mulamar and Makar adopted it as well.

Abayomi joined Pasha to oversee repair efforts on the walls. Most of the work was being done by Yashani craftsmen. Pasha only hoped that their work stood firm under pressure.

They rode out from the northern gate to inspect the roadway leading into the mountains where the other tribes had lodged most of their troops.

"Is this all they've done?" Pasha asked Abayomi. The captain saw very little change in the road from the night before.

"Progress has not been as fast as you expected, Kaudi. Still, they're working as fast as possible." Abayomi referred to a group of about ten, some men, mostly boys. Their charge had been to clear the road, but so far their progress was below what Pasha had expected.

"It's not good enough, Abayomi. Look at this. All of these rocks, trees, and holes. The difference between our defeat and our victory may depend on if this road is clear enough for our allies to ride through without breaking the legs of their horses," said Pasha.

"Perhaps you should talk to our new allies. Some of their commanders have men doing nothing but pointless patrols."

"Then make the case to them," said Pasha.

"They would not listen," said Abayomi.

"You are my second in command. The defense of this city is not your only task, but making sure the other commanders fall in line when orders are given out. I'm counting on you to make this pact work in the lines during battle."

Inside the city, both men were surprised by a bustling crowd that seemed to await them. Men and women cried out his name as they pressed against him and Abayomi. Pasha kicked back defensively from his mount when a man seized his foot and began kissing it, his garbled shouts overwhelmed by the multitude of voices.

All around him, people were touching him and his horse. Some begged him for food, others praised him, and all asked him to save them. The sight of the many ragged and dirt-caked people before him disturbed Pasha. He had never liked large crowds.

The captain could tell some were sick, others half-starved and weary. It angered him to think of his indulgence at the great feast before, now looking upon those who obviously had not shared in the abundance.

Daimon shook his head and legs nervously as strangers continued to press against him. Pasha's mount retained his calm, however. Pasha did not wish to see anyone trampled or battered by Daimon's powerful legs. He looked over heads for a way out, but all he saw were more people coming to join the throng. It seemed that all of Cafura came to the captain.

"Clear the way! Clear the way!" Pasha heard someone shout.

Soon the wall of flesh began to part for a column of warriors closing in on Pasha and Abayomi. At the head of the column was Leyos, who had come on foot along with the rest of his men. And to Pasha's surprise, he saw Rank Master Amran, whom he had served with in the malik's guard, marching alongside of Leyos.

"Come, sir. Let's get you out of here," said Leyos.

Pasha and Abayomi followed Leyos, who led them back to the heart of the city. Abayomi, Pasha, and Leyos went into a small unoccupied house of reeds along a street going into the city center.

"Rank Master Amran, I didn't know you came this far north," Pasha noted.

"I go wherever there is trouble, as is a warrior's way," he replied.

"Well you must be in the right place then, because all I see out there is trouble," Pasha responded. Pasha then looked to Leyos. "What is going on?"

"So many things, sir," said Leyos, drawing in a long breath before speaking again. "You need to address the people, sir, listen to their needs, let them tell you their stories. There are a thousand problems in the city that need to be dealt with."

"What is it they're after?"

"For one thing, the rationing, it's been getting worse. People are getting sick. And women are being kidnapped at night. Many are ending up in pleasure houses or getting killed."

"What about our patrols? Have the new patrols been set up like I ordered?"

"You just got here, sir. This kind of thing has been going on for months."

"Once our patrols start making their presence known on the streets during the night, things will change."

"It's not just that, sir," said Abayomi. "People are scared of 'the night of curses.' What the alcalde talked about before," said Abayomi.

"They want to feel safe, sir. They want to know that you will keep them safe," said Leyos.

"Why isn't the alcalde out there holding their hands?" asked Pasha.

"Because the alcalde was not spoken of by the oracle!" said Abayomi forcefully.

Pasha paused for a moment, drawing the room into silence.

"So they've heard," he finally said.

"All of Sashra has heard by now. They need a leader they can believe in, Pasha," said Abayomi.

"And what would you have me do, Abayomi?" he said angrily.

"Go out and shout, 'Hey, I am the warrior. Believe in me!'" he said in a bitter, mocking tone.

"You are the one the oracle spoke of, sir," said Leyos.

"I suggest you do the supplication rite," said Amran.

"What is that?" Pasha said irritably.

"Bring the people to you. One at a time. Listen to their requests and comfort them if needed. Most important, promise that you'll do all that you can to help them. This will go a long ways toward keeping order, sir," continued Amran.

"I have much more pressing matters than this!" said Pasha.

"Nothing is more important than the people's trust," said Leyos. "Without it, we could not do what we do. Please, sir. Humor them a couple of hours, and they'll go away."

"I suggest we do it in here if we're going to do this," suggested Abayomi out of concern for safety.

Pasha mulled over the prospect of deciding which requests to grant and which not to with great difficulty. Finally he decided. "Bring them in."

For what seemed like days instead of hours, Pasha sat on a low wooden stool and listened to the people. It only served to embarrass him when each new supplicant entered the house with lowered heads and fell to their knees before him.

Most asked about the same thing, the food situation, not getting enough water, and if he felt the army along with the other tribes could defeat the men of the north. It astonished the captain how well he seemed to fit into the role of defender and comforter of the city. He reassured them that though there would be lean days, none would die of starvation or thirst.

Like Leyos had told him, he received many angry and worried fathers whose daughters had been sent to the pleasure houses. The plight of their daughters centered around the issue of debt collection where the father could not pay. For others, it was the old story of the strong preying on the weak. Pretty soon, Pasha got a sense that the alcalde had done little to stop the kidnappings, heartless creditors, and many pleasure houses that had sprung up after the onset of the siege. In spite of siege, corrupt men were keeping themselves fed and still raking up a profit from collecting debts and making subtle investments into pleasure houses. Some spoke in anger of large pools of water in rich men's homes that were untouched and animals that had not been slaughtered.

Armed gangs were also present in the city, robbing people at granaries and markets where most of the city got its food. Halfway through the supplication rite, as Amran had put it, he had to make his first decree. They had gotten a scribe to write his words into official orders.

In his decree, the captain declared debt collection illegal and postponed until the end of the siege. He knew as head of the Sashraman forces during a siege that he had the authority to make decrees.

Still the captain acknowledged that he was walking a thin line between bringing order and supplanting the alcalde's authority. Still, he did not believe it enough for the alcalde to be justified in challenging him.

"Bring in the next one," said Pasha, after finishing up with another man hounded by creditors.

The man with debt problems was followed by a dark, haggard-looking man. His head bore nothing save sweat and dirt, as did much of clothes. Two skinny children, one a boy and the other a girl, followed him closely. The evident weakness in their step showed that they had not eaten well for a while.

He fell to all fours and crawled to Pasha on his hands and knees. "A thousand blessings upon you and your family, Kaudi. I beg that you show me compassion and hear my request for my sake and my family's."

"I would not turn you away, brother. Speak and tell me of your trouble. Be not afraid."

The first exchange was not really their own words but taken from antiquity when people would come before Nateo and beg spiritual guidance. Supplication had been born from those acts of Nateo, and it continued then among Pasha and the people.

"I am Oyadi shem-Harazi," the man said, saying his clan name along with his birth name. "I beg your mercy, Kaudi." The man sat on his knees, staring longingly into Pasha's eyes. "We barely have any food to feed ourselves and no water to bathe or drink. My wife died of sickness, and now I fear my children will as well. I've tried to send my children to physicians, but they all want payment. Kaudi, I have nothing. I am a farmer! But there is nothing to farm while the siege is on! If my children do not see a physician, they will die!" he said as he tightened his arms about his children.

The weakness in their faces and the aimlessness of their eyes told Pasha that they could drop dead at any moment.

"I have already decreed that no credit shall be collected during the siege and no man forced to pay. Tell that to a physician, and they shall take your children."

"The alcalde ordered all physicians to care for the sick months ago, but they still demand payment. If I push myself on them, they may hurt me. Many have private guards."

To Pasha, it seemed incredible that a physician would refuse to heal somebody because they could not pay. It disgusted him. He looked down upon the children and thought of the plague victims they had encountered before. The captain hoped the sickness within the city was not the plague. None of the children bore the gashes and boils. Still, there was no true way to be sure. They could only hope.

"Then I'll tell you this. King Hanasa of the Halor has agreed to share some of his physicians with the temple to treat the war wounded. Go there to them. Do not fear the Halor physicians; they will not refuse you nor harm you. I again make another decree."

Pasha looked beside him to the scribe to make sure he was catching his words onto parchment with his rapidly moving fingers.

"I, Captain Pasha Nuvahli, Kaudi of Cafura and all of its Sashraman forces, decree that no physician shall deny anyone treatment because they cannot pay. No physician shall be allowed to be idle. All must treat the wounded and sick. Furthermore, any physician who does this and keeps a record with the city scribes shall be compensated for his service at a time when it is possible."

Pasha looked again at the scribe. The lightness of his hand and swiftness of his bone pen amazed him. The captain had gotten a smattering of Hebari and Lakina writing instruction as a boy. His mother had been planning to have him study in the temple and become the first of her sons to read and write. The instruction had stopped after her death. Besides having learned a bit of secret symbols in the army, writing in proper Hebari had been a skill that eluded him.

"Rise now, brother."

The man stood, seeming off balance as he did so.

"Do not worry for your children. They shall be seen after. None shall starve as long as I command here. Go now and may a thousand blessings be borne upon you and your family."

"Daiyu bless you, Kaudi."

The man crashed back to his knees and took one of Pasha's hands, kissing it repeatedly. "I know you were sent to us for a reason!"

Leyos moved toward the man, gently prying loose his grip on Pasha's hand.

"It'll be all right, brother," Leyos said softly as he led the man and his children to the door.

A thousand eager faces pressed in closer upon seeing Leyos at the doorway of the house. Leyos turned back inside quickly, saying nothing. The warriors outside pushed them back as some tried to get closer to the house, crying out for Pasha.

"Are you sure it was wise to pledge the malik's gold?" asked Abayomi.

"I did not say the malik directly," Pasha replied.

"Still, they're going to expect payment," said Leyos.

"And they're going to expect it from Malik Juktan," said Abayomi.

"We'll deal with it when we come to that road. I can't have physicians treating no one. And besides, Malik Juktan sent me here to speak in his name."

"I doubt to speak for his purse as well," quipped Abayomi.

"I know what I am doing," Pasha said firmly.

"Yes, sir," said Abayomi, backing down.

"Still, I wouldn't want to be you when the malik sees his yearly ledger."

Leyos and Abayomi exchanged smiles as Pasha called for the next person.

A tall, thin man with closely cropped hair came in next. He was more mature in age yet still seemed to bear the spark of youth in his face. It relieved Pasha to see he was not as dirt-laden and foul-reeking as most of the people he had received.

He longed to end the supplication rite. Still, Leyos urged him to do more. The captain resolved that the man would be his last for that day.

Behind the man came a younger woman in brown dress, her head partially covered by her brightly colored orange headdress with a black barred pattern running through it. She had a pretty face and a good tone to her body.

Pasha could tell by the way the she avoided men's eyes what it was that the man would soon request.

"A thousand blessings upon you and your family, Kaudi. I beg that you show me compassion and hear my request for my sake and my family's," the man said in the traditional way.

"I would not turn you away, brother. Tell me your trouble and do not fear."

"Kaudi, I am Nkwazi shem-Quasi," he said, giving his birth name and then clan name. "I beg of you to avenge the honor of my family and that of my daughter."

"Tell me how your family's honor has been wronged."

Pasha already had an idea of what the man would say. It was a story the captain knew too well.

"I work stone. It is a modest living, but I am beholden to no one. The Boltman clan has put a claim on my life as well as my daughter's. I come to you, Kaudi, begging you for protection."

"Who are the Boltman clan? There is no Boltman clan in Sashra," said Pasha, still unfamiliar with all the facets of life in Cafura under the siege.

"Sir," said Abayomi. "They're a street gang. We have had dealings with them before."

"Dealings? Since when do Sashraman warriors have dealings with dogs and rats!" he said, surprised and angry at his officers.

Abayomi looked hesitantly at Leyos, obviously not wishing to say more.

"Explain!" Pasha demanded.

Leyos stepped forward. "Until you came, we could not spare the extra men to patrol the streets. The alcalde's men were supposed to be doing that."

"Supposed to, but they have done nothing!" the man called Nkwazi shouted. "No place has been safe ever since the siege. The Boltmans, Bomba Wraiths, the Lagombas, they all go wherever they want in this city and the alcalde's men do nothing about it unless you have a big enough purse!"

"What happened to you, Nkwazi, and your daughter?"

"All the street clans are collecting taxes in the zones they control. I live in the zone the Boltman clan controls, so I have to pay. I had nothing, Kaudi. I have nothing! All the work I do is on the wall, and the alcalde won't pay us for it. They came and demanded payment. I told them I had nothing, so they tried to take my wife as payment. They were going to put her on the street like a piece of meat for the dogs to pounce on! I fought them, Kaudi, and they killed her. They came back that night and took my daughter. The Boltmans said that if I resisted, they would kill her too. I've already lost my wife, Kaudi, and my two boys were killed on the wall. My daughter is all I have left."

"What did they do to her?" he asked.

"They did what they tried before. Get payment. To my shame and the shame of my family, they put her in a pleasure house.

And I just let them do it. I let the fear of them make me forget my duty, make me forget that I am her father! I failed, Kaudi! I failed my daughter!"

He paused as a river of tears overwhelmed him. Pasha and his men were silent, angry that such impunity could exist in a Sashraman city.

Eventually he composed himself and continued. "Finally though, by Daiyu's grace, I realized that I could not give up. I found the house my daughter was in. I tried to get the city guard to move against it and take my daughter back, but they ignored me. Finally I did what I knew I had to do all along. I returned to the pleasure house and dropped one of the guards. I took his sword and killed another before I found my daughter and took her from there. And now they call me an enemy and have put word out on the street for my head by the week's end. I am afraid, Kaudi. But I will not let them take her again. The damage is already done. No man would have her as a wife now. She will know no peace for the rest of her days."

"I lament with you, brother, truly. When I came, I promised safety. I shall keep that promise. The ones who did this to your daughter will hang from the walls by week's end. You and your daughter, go stay in the western zone of the city near the barracks; you'll be safe there. I will have a man called Amran look after you. Five of my warriors shall escort you there. Leyos, see to it."

Leyos responded quickly, leaving the house to gather some men.

Again the man fell into a wave of fitful weeping, but his sorrow was now replaced with joy. "Thank you, Kaudi. Thank you."

Pasha felt even more uncomfortable watching him bow his head repeatedly toward him. He did not feel worthy of such praise. Never had he sought it.

The man and his daughter left quietly, whispering words of encouragement to each other. Five warriors met the father and daughter at the doorway and followed them outside. Leyos came back, taking his previous place near Pasha.

"No more," said Pasha once the door had shut.

"But, sir," said Leyos.

"I've had enough for one day. Send them all away!"

"Kaudi, please, just—"

"Leyos," said Abayomi warningly. "Leave him be."

Leyos said nothing. He stepped back as Pasha rose from his stool, stretching his now cramping legs. The captain looked about the walls of the house as if in search for some answer or reasoning behind all of it.

"How bad is it on the streets, Abayomi?"

"It's been better, sir."

Pasha drew in a heavy breath. He had made many assurances to the people and was more unsure than ever whether he could fulfill them.

An abrupt boom pierced their ears with the sound of crashing stone and exploding flames, sending Pasha and his men to the dirt floor. All the people outside of the house scattered in terror as foreign missiles rained down upon their city. Smoke filled every corner of the city's center, erecting a huge barrier of death and confusion for the Sashramans heading to their positions on the city walls. The booms slowly became a repeated stream of fire blasting apart everything in their path.

It was upon the fourth blast that the house of reeds the Sashramans had been meeting in exploded into a shower sticks and jagged edges of wood. The force hammered nearby warriors into walls of neighboring buildings that still stood. Less fortunate ones fell to their knees, gasping for precious breath that had been cut off by splintered pieces of wood.

Pasha saw only darkness. To him, it seemed a dark sleep from which he would never be awoken. He still felt, and he still thought, but where there had once been light, there was now darkness. Never had he expected death to be like that.

But then he heard familiar voices, someone tugging at his arm, someone moving his body.

"Kaudi! Kaudi!" Abayomi shouted. Furiously, he tore away reeds and pieces of wood layered upon himself and the captain. The commander felt trapped and almost defenseless. He had never liked tight spaces that were hard to move in. Though he saw light after pushing away the last piece of wood covering them, it was dull and blurred.

"Kaudi," Abayomi shouted again. He felt the rising of a breath from his captain's chest. He could not give up.

"Pasha!"

Pasha forced his eyes open finally. At first he registered nothing but bright light. The light darkened fast, revealing the smoldering bits of reeds and wood in which he lay. Fire and ash feasted upon the rows of cubed stone and circular reed homes.

To Pasha, everything was passing like a blurred haze that sent sharp pain to his head and coursed all through his body. Though he could not see the rest of his body clearly, his arms and legs cried out in pain while his chest and stomach felt crushed.

"Pasha, look at me! Look at me!" Abayomi persisted.

Finally, the captain's vision focused, and he saw his friend. "Abayomi?" he said softly, finding loud speech too painful. His head felt soft inside, with a torturous buzzing sound impeding swift thought.

"Are you all right?" Pasha asked wearily.

"Forget worrying about me and use some of that worry for yourself. The city's under attack, sir. We need to get out . . ."

Another nearby house exploded behind them. The air filled with the deafening sound of missile as another Sashraman edifice was hit, spraying thousands of pieces of wood and stone around them. Abayomi dived into Pasha and knocked him back onto the ground.

Clouds of dust and stone powder shot into them with great force. Pasha coughed violently to expel the debris from throat.

"Can you walk?" asked Abayomi, raising himself back up to his knees.

Pasha immediately felt sick and weary the moment he came to his feet. The sight his better focused eyes came across did not alleviate this feeling. He had caught sight of the damaged and burning buildings, but now he saw clearly the piles of dead flesh all about the streets and what had once been a house of reeds. The captain discerned the many warriors' bodies half hidden by thick walls of smoke. To the distance in the south he could hear more explosions and the loosening of catapults and other deadly instruments.

Abayomi urged him to move forward, but Pasha stopped. He looked down to the smoldering pile reeds and wood. Somehow he had survived; perhaps there were others.

"Leyos," he tried to say more loudly.

"Sir, there's no time. We've got to move!" Abayomi insisted.

"No!" Pasha said firmly. He was not going to leave his man underneath the rubble to die. "Find him."

"Pasha!"

"Find him!" his voice barked out, reclaiming the volume he thought he had lost.

CHAPTER 16

Those Who Fall

To the men of the south, it seemed they had only made a small dent in the enemy force during the previous battle. Long lines of enemy cavalry, archers, and siege machines snaked around Cafura from the southern end of the city to the eastern end in an extraordinary show of force many of the defenders had not been expecting. Their bright silver armor and tall, thick shields that covered their entire bodies gave them only a more striking appearance as the whole wave of northerners moved forward, glistening in the Sashraman sun.

On the southern end of the city, much of the walls had already been destroyed. Nevertheless, the eight columns of heavy enemy infantry did not advance easily.

Hakan had filled in the void left by Pasha's absence by directing the Sashraman officers at the southern wall. Though he had just learned that Pasha was alive and still in command, he had been left charge over the southern end of the wall's defense while Pasha saw to the east.

Hakan observed the battle from an inner tower only a few hundred feet from the wall. In spite of the damage, his archers rained down death upon the Baku and their allies while they pushed forward into the city. Though there were some swordsmen along the wall with the archers, he saw the enemy moving ladders in place, and he knew they would soon capture the last patch of wall the Sashramans still possessed.

"Pull them back," said Hakan to Amran, who had been appointed his *duma* officer. Amran stepped out on the balcony of the tower to wave signal flags, after which he blew four short bursts with his air horn.

But leading the effort against a siege was not typical of a saji's duties. Hakan did not know how many men were down there in the line fighting, all under his orders. At the most, he had two units, close to two thousand men, but it would not be enough.

The men of the north, along with climbing the walls, had broken through three badly damaged sections in the wall. He had moved the cavalry to form lines to protect their left flank and stop the enemy from surrounding the infantry. But Hakan knew he only slowed them down.

In spite of the seemingly endless hours of fighting, warriors from the other tribes still had not been committed to the fight on the southern end. He heard the horns sound, but they still did not come. Hakan prayed they would get there soon.

Looking down on it all was maddening. Baku spearmen with huge shields and long spears punched into the Sashraman line to break it apart. The Sashramans had positioned themselves in a thick column eight men deep in each row, but they still didn't stand long against the northerners.

Baku spearmen bashed the Sashramans bloody with their shields and gutted them with their spears. They moved like a smooth machine of war. Each kill was exact and quick, no man stepped out of position, and the line stuck together. Coming to their rear were Ekoo and Jakshima swordsmen who would finish up what the spearmen left.

Sashraman warriors dove into the wall of the advancing enemy. They hacked furiously at the enemy's shields while those with spears lunged with rage as they tried to force an opening into the shield wall. In the rear, men with slings and fire bombs hurled them overhead at the men of the north.

Few Baku fell. The northern spearmen cleared the lines of Sashramans with swift sweeps of their large shields, jabbing their guts with their long spears as they came forward. Soon the enemy warriors had advanced far enough into Cafura that their lines opened to unleash endless columns of swordsmen.

The northern spearmen turned over the momentum of the attack to the swordsmen who slashed and hacked at the Sashramans without mercy. Though their shields were round and not tall, the northern swordsmen proved as much a difficult kill as the spearmen.

Hakan watched as his men pushed forward again as hard as they could. But the northern swordsmen were quick and agile. In spite of the close-quarter fighting, they managed terrific leaps and dodges while slashing at the enemy with both their shields and swords. He took note of the way they fought. Most of their swordsmen seemed to prefer to use their shields as an attacking weapon, with the sword being the one that delivered the fatal blow.

A sudden explosion and cloud of dust and ash signaled the arrival of more enemy columns. Without warning, a section of wall on the left flank a couple of hundred feet from the cavalry collapsed, providing an opening for hundreds of Jakshima horse archers, who were followed by heavy Baku cavalry.

The mounted Sashramans fell quickly under Jakshima bows. Despite aid from the archers who came together to concentrate fire on the enemy archers, the Sashraman cavalry was losing ground. Emboldened by their allies, the Baku infantry pushed forward. Enemy horse archers soon targeted the Sashraman archers, cutting a large whole into their line.

In a burst of strength, the Baku cavalry broke through the Sashraman horsemen. Most of the Sashramans were thrown from their horses as spears and heavy lances broke into their bodies. The men were trampled by enemy horses while swords slashed them apart.

The archers broke first. One by one, the line of disciplined warriors disintegrated into a chaotic mob of fleeing men that the enemy cavalry quickly subdued. Instead of trying to break the cavalry, the enemy had only to sweep them into the walls while they advanced upon the Sashraman column to the right.

Having no warning, the Sashraman column nearly buckled under the heavy cavalry charge. Still they stayed together while the officers on the ground repositioned the column into a ring formation to engage the newly combined enemy force. Still, Hakan knew they did not have much time.

"Move the conscripts up the middle to slow them down. Signal all the officers to pull back to the city center."

His officer left him to carry out his order. Hakan looked down upon his scattering men whom the Baku cut down quickly. The right flank spread out its line to stop the left from overwhelming them, but their lines were already too thin. Hakan felt a chilled, nervous sweat spilling down his spine. Within moments, the men would fold on top of one another, and that would be it. He cursed loudly to himself, wondering what was taking the conscripts so long to move up.

Unable to stand and wait anymore, Hakan gathered up his shield and spear. They would have to leave the tower quickly once the men began to move.

Outside on the other outer balcony facing the western end of the city, Hakan searched their rear positions for the conscripts. His eyes immediately came upon two small kads near the western wall, but no others. Where were the conscripts? Had they moved up? He would have seen them.

His duma officer was sprinting back to the tower, shouting, "They're not here! Sir, they're not at the rear!"

"Where are they?" Hakan demanded angrily.

"No man in the kad has seen them, sir. They did not fall in during the attack."

"Daiyu curse them. Curse the lot of them!" he shouted.

The call of a *shokar* horn on the western wall sounded through the city.

"Oh no," said Hakan.

Within seconds, four kads on the western wall fell to their deaths as a section of the wall cracked open under tremendous pressure and then exploded. Scores of Ekoo archers swarmed into the breach along with heavily armored swordsmen. They fired deep into the lines of the two kads near the wall.

Hakan knew that without the conscripts, his small band of kads would not stand a chance defending a breach.

A cloud of arrows rammed into the kads near the wall who had not yet formed a line. Almost half the Sashramans died in the first volley. The rest of them tried to come together, but their defense was pitiful under the northern sword. Instead of sweeping through them like their Baku allies seemed to prefer, the Ekoo swarmed over their enemies, cutting deeper into them. They concentrated on all of the Sashramans before them, unwilling to move on till they had killed them all.

Hakan swore using Pasha's name. The captain knew he had not been ready. Why did he allow him to stay in command? Before, Hakan had been eager for a chance to prove his worth to the captain. But at that moment, all he wanted to do was hide from the world and its wars.

"Sir, what do we do?"

Hakan heard the man, but he stood in a daze. Nervousness seemed to have replaced his blood, for it was all he felt coursing through his body as he stood there.

"Sir! Your orders! Saji!" his officer persisted.

"I don't know," he said softly, wishing at once he had not. One of the first lessons he had learned from Pasha about command was to never let the men see you unsure. He wondered how many other errors he had made that day. From the start, he knew his command was a mistake. They would all soon be dead due to his inadequacies.

"I just don't—I can't . . ." Hakan stammered. He could no longer speak straight. His eyes closed, trying to shield their owner from the chaos about him.

His officer climbed up the tower and seized him by the neck of his tunic. Hakan felt his shield drop when his back hit the wall of the tower.

"Pull it together and lead us! We need to get out of here!"

At first Hakan said nothing, astonished by Amran's sudden change of temperament.

"What? Are you a coward? You want to die a coward's death? I'll kill you right now, you coward! I'll kill you!" Amran unsheathed a dagger and pressed it to Hakan's flesh.

Amran's abrupt fierceness surprised Hakan. At first he had thought his officer a mild-mannered man not given to extreme emotion. However, he saw the emotion in Amran's face, the anger and fear of possibly being dead in a few moments. He had heard of Amran as a man of surprises. Such was evident to him at that moment.

In a swift movement, Hakan seized his knife hand and twisted his hand back to release his grip. Amran fell to the ground immediately and had no defense from Hakan's quick fist.

"Don't you ever call me a coward!" said Hakan.

The saji held out his hand to his duma, which he accepted. Together both men retrieved their shields and weapons and began their descent from the tower. They found their horses and gathered the last kad to them.

Looking back to the west, Hakan noted the swarm of Ekoo warriors had grown. Fewer cries of Sashraman warriors came from that direction. His men were about to die.

"Ride!" he shouted.

Hakan and his men rode behind the rear of the right flank, which was still maintaining a ring formation.

"Fall back! Fall back on me!" he shouted.

Amran followed closely behind him, raising the standards of Cafura for the men to see and follow.

Hakan knew even more of his men would die trying to run away, but he knew by running some would live, and they would stand a chance.

The Sashraman ring pushed forward with newly found strength born of the will of men who sought to survive. For several moments, the Baku charge was halted. Knowing they barely had moments, what was left of the Sashraman column managed to push through the enemy to the main street that led to city center and the rest of Cafura as a whole.

Upon reaching the street, they could no longer hold the formation, and it broke. The Sashramans sprinted down the street with all haste. For a while, the enemy infantry and cavalry halted as the archers engaged in their vicious talent.

Warriors dropped left and right, as they now had their backs to the enemy. Hakan willed them to go faster. Once they had turned at a corner to the left, the archers would have no targets. It pained Hakan that his warriors had no way of defending themselves. Nevertheless, they had to run.

Hakan's feeling of relief faded upon reaching the corner to the left where Ekoo swordsmen lunged at them from the cloud of smoke that now consumed the central part of the city.

The Ekoo sliced through his surprised men, who were growing tired. However, they had not yet grown to the strength necessary to stop the rushing column of Sashramans. The column pushed through them, but many fell with spears in their side.

"They're trying to cut us off!" Hakan shouted to Amran.

"You go I'll slow them down!" his officer shouted.

"Don't be rash, man!" Hakan protested. It would be a suicide task. Though Hakan knew such would be necessary, he had not been ready to have his officer commit to it.

"We don't have time to quarrel. Get them out of here!"

Hakan merely watched while Amran gathered a kad to himself and charged headfirst into the emerging column of Ekoo. Was he a coward? the saji asked himself. Why had he not insisted harder? Why wasn't he the one charging head-on into certain death? Perhaps he was.

Having seen the Ekoo emerge confirmed that they had been moving faster than he had anticipated. The only other option Hakan saw was moving to the right to the marketplace street that ran north and south. The southern end of the street stopped in a wall of stacked cubed houses and stone buildings, while the northern end ran to the wall. Having not considered it before, he realized that the marketplace street nearly cut the city in half. With that many buildings and homes surrounding the street, the area was the most defensible one in Cafura at that moment.

A line of archers stopped to fire upon the Baku who charged behind them. Hakan knew they would all be dead in moments, but their efforts slowed the Baku behind them while Amran held the Ekoo. This was their moment.

By the time King Hanasa and his warriors approached the eastern wall, Jakshima warriors were already moving up the street. While planning the defense strategy for the city, a Mulamar and Sashraman patrol had been put on the eastern wall's defense. But in the distance, the king did not see the standards of Sashra or of the Mulamar. Surely they would have held the Jakshima at the walls until his men arrived, the king thought to himself. Nevertheless, the patrols had not done so.

Captain Nuvahli and a column of Halor warriors from the barracks joined the king just as he came within sight of the eastern wall from the streets. He did not know exactly how many Jakshima came at them, but he knew they numbered close to five thousand. The street gave them inadequate defense from Jakshima bowmen who clambered onto the rooftops and cut into their line with many arrows.

"Form up!" shouted the king to his warriors.

He lifted his shield to block the many arrows hurtling toward him.

"Protect the king!" yelled one of his officers.

Immediately the king's bodyguards tightened into a cluster about him while the other warriors split into two parallel defensive lines. Fortunately the Halor warriors carried shields just as long as the Baku and Jakshima. On both sides, warriors locked their shields together in a rigid wall that deflected most the Jakshima fire.

Pasha immediately jumped from the horse of a Halor officer, who carried him as arrows tore menacingly through the young officer's neck and midsection. The captain rolled and crouched in between Halor warriors who made up the shield wall. For a moment, he was safe beside the Halor warriors, who kept their shields locked together. Still, he knew it would be temporary.

To his relief, he saw Leyos and Abayomi had made it as well. Both men had taken refuge among the Halor in the opposite line, keeping their heads tucked in to avoid the ceaseless storm of arrows.

Some Halor stepped out of the lines to return fire. No matter how many Jakshima the men felled, none of them lived to make it back under the refuge of the shield wall. Pretty soon, groups of two rose, and the archer fired behind a man with a shield. The strategy worked well for some, but the Jakshima still managed to find their targets.

Hearing the booming roar of war cries coming closer let Pasha know that a charge was coming. None of the Halor moved until the last minute when they heard the king give the order. With extreme speed, the ends of both defensive lines swung forward and drew toward the middle to make one line. Enemy archers tried to take advantage of the maneuver now that their backs were to their bows, but Halor horse archers moved forward and began plucking great numbers of the Jakshima from the roofs. King Hanasa's warriors locked shields again and lunged their spears forward as Jakshima swordsmen rammed into them.

Jakshima, like their Baku counterparts, favored attacking with their shields in sweeping blows while their swords they used for the killing blow. Still, the Halor held their shields steady while they punched into Jakshima advance with their long spears that bore curved, jagged heads. However, the Halor horse archers soon became overwhelmed when more enemy archers came onto the rooftops.

There were more arrows flying toward them than the warriors could shoot back. Eventually, being mounted proved a disadvantage. Unable to ride or maneuver their horses very fast, the horse archers ceased firing while they covered themselves with their shields. Such action did not help them.

Jakshima archers had increased to more than a hundred bows firing at once. The horse archers disintegrated into a mass of men while northern arrows seared through the openings in their armor. Without warning, Halor spearmen fell with northern arrows impaling them in their backs. Within seconds, the enemy swordsmen breached the line, and the Halor king and his warriors found themselves in a fight for their lives.

Though they had found Leyos, Pasha saw no sign of his men or many of their Halor allies. All his eyes sighted were swarms of Jakshima coming at him. The captain procured a shield from a dead Halor and blocked with it while lunging forward with his sword. He swung the shield wildly to force back the enemies all around him. A group of three came at him. One jump-kicked and instead of flesh met Pasha's shield. Slashing the man's neck as he lay on the ground, Pasha rammed another with the shield end and kicked him back.

The third came more prepared. Pasha lunged forward with his shield, but the man dodged him and sidestepped. Pasha caught sight of the man when he came at his right side and dropped while rotating his shield arm to the right. In two strokes, he cracked the man in the head and ran him through from under a weak chest plate. Jakshima did not wear as much armor as the Baku, which made a kill slightly easier.

Pasha turned and ducked when a sweeping Jakshima blade came for his neck. His duck turned into a fall, which Pasha made use of by kicking the warrior's sword hand. The Jakshima's blade flew from his hand in an instant. Rolling so as to avoid the warrior's lunging shield, Pasha swept at his legs with his blade. But the Jakshima expected it and jumped. He fell down toward Pasha with his shield out. Pasha could not move in time, so he swung his own shield over his body to avoid being crushed.

Knowing he had only moments, the captain rammed his fist into the Jakshima who lay on top of him. The warrior jerked back from Pasha's blows. Without wasting a moment, the captain bashed into the side of his enemy with his shield. Though the man clambered to get back up, it was already too late for him.

Pasha tore through an opening in the armored plates along his back and stabbed deeply into his flesh. His Jakshima foe gasped as he tried to suck in more air, but all that filled his lungs was his own blood.

Things were not going well for the Halor at that moment. On all sides, King Hanasa's men were exposed to the deadly hail of arrows that completely stopped any chance for his men to advance. A flurry of arrows whizzed by the Halor king's face, prompting him to raise his shield. All of his bodyguards stayed close to him. However, in spite of their skill, they could not protect themselves when a storm of Jakshima arrows dismounted many of them. The enemy was everywhere, and there was nowhere to go.

Wherever the king looked, his eyes burned with the ceaseless images of arrows ripping through his men's bodies, soon to be hacked apart by advancing enemy infantry.

"Dismount!" shouted the king just as more arrows came for him. His horse took them all and crashed to the ground bloodied and dead.

"Come together!" he shouted.

Keeping their shields over them, the Halor column tried to come together as the king said. This time they formed a large cluster, four lines of men standing with their shields locked over their heads while the line facing the advancing infantry locked their shields. It worked only partially. Fewer of his men were being hit by arrows, but the formation was weak, and the Jakshima spearmen easily tore through it. His men pushed them back with all their strength, but the king knew that they would not last.

Hanasa crouched beneath a line of men protecting the cluster with their shields from archers overhead. The king's mind whirled with many thoughts and strategies for how to break the enemy's advantage. There would be no way to advance until they took away the advantage of the enemy's archers. Almost all of his horse archers had been killed, and there was no way for any of his spearmen who also carried bows to take out the archers on the rooftops.

He jumped as a hurled spear flew through the cluster of shields and tore through one of his bodyguard's back. Instinctively, he raised his own shield. The men could not maintain the formation much longer.

The Halor king jumped again when his shield was pushed back suddenly and collapsed against him. King Hanasa's heart began beating faster while fear of having been caught off guard took hold of him. Sword drawn, he moved forward to face his attacker. Instead of a Jakshima, his eyes came upon Captain Nuvahli and his officers.

"Careful, Highness, you might put someone's eye out," said Pasha.

"It'll be a lot more if you do that again," he said angrily.

"Those archers are going to win this whole battle for them if we don't do something," said Pasha.

"Has anyone ever told you that you have a peculiar habit of stating the obvious! They've got us boxed in on this street like a pack of mice!"

"When a man is cornered, he should think like a fox, not a mouse," Pasha replied.

"You got something in mind?" asked the Halor king.

"We're pretty close to one of the houses they're firing from. Can your men maintain this formation while moving?"

"We can barely maintain it standing still!"

"It'll have to do. On my mark, have your men push back to the right until they hit the wall of one of the houses. My men and I will go in and take out the archers."

"And let them surround us? They'll break through the column and split us up. We might as well lie down and let them kill us."

"We cannot give up this position, and we cannot go back! Hanasa! Rule this day!"

King Hanasa looked in the man's face, considering his proposal. The king knew that if they gave up one foot of the street, the enemy would rush through, split up the column, and surround them. That moment was not one of Hanasa's ideal scenarios, but he knew he had no choice.

"You'll need more than two men. I'll go with you. My men will cover you."

Pasha nodded in agreement. In spite of his lack of trust in the king, he knew that in that moment the sentiment would have to be buried.

King Hanasa looked to his bodyguards who were locked in a tight circle about him.

"If I had to decide how to spend my last days, it would be with you, my brothers. You have served me in war and peace since my youth. There are no warriors like you in Halor land or in the south. These Jakshima have long forgotten how fierce we are. I say it is time we teach them again."

His men nodded in agreement, hanging on to their king's words. Hanasa sighed heavily while he looked upon his men. Their deaths would not be meaningless.

Without hesitating, the king and his men jumped to their feet, holding their shields over their heads as they took places in the formation.

"Hard right!" Hanasa shouted.

He knew his men did not wish to do it, for they all knew the slaughter would only increase if the men of the south gave up more ground. Nevertheless, his men knew that none would survive that day if they did nothing. The Halor warriors did not hesitate. In one fluid motion, the entire formation flung itself toward the white cubed houses to the right.

The city rippled with the sound of warriors' bodies crashing into hard stone as their enemies fell on top of them.

Pasha and his men crashed through the door of the white cubed building moments before the entire rear of the formation collapsed on top of itself.

Hanasa and his warriors moved in quickly behind Pasha as he and his men bounded up the white stone steps for the roof. On the second level, they saw only three doors.

"Which one is it?" said Leyos anxiously.

"Quiet!" hissed Abayomi.

"Move to the first one," Pasha ordered.

Hanasa's men took position on one side while Pasha and Leyos stood at the other. Abayomi kicked the door through and stepped inside.

"Oh Daiyu no!"

Pasha and the rest of them rushed in. Instead of enemies, they found a more horrid sight. On the dirt-laden floor beneath them lay a woman and her three children within pools of their own blood.

"Have they no honor?" said King Hanasa in a low voice.

"Not lately," said Abayomi as knelt beside the mother.

"She was with child. But the bastards still cut her! What could make a man do that?"

"No more!" said Leyos angrily.

"No more!"

In fury, he ran out the room and started kicking in the next three doors. Behind each one, the same scene unfolded before him.

"No more!" he shouted again.

"Leyos, man!" Pasha shouted.

Leyos ran to the end of the level where there stood an open doorway to the roof, one they had not seen before. Without hesitating, he went up.

"Leyos, no!"

Pasha and his men chased after him. Their task became more urgent as the clanging of swords filled their ears.

They ascended to the roof to find Leyos hacking into the midst of many Jakshima archers. The archers were ceasing their fire and turning to engage.

Pasha and Hanasa's men charged head on into them. The Halor warriors reached to their waists and hurled throwing knives into the Jakshima before slashing into them with their swords. Many Jakshima fell from the roof when their breaths were cut short by the wicked Halor blades.

The Sashraman captain along with his officer, Abayomi, kicked several Jakshima from the roof into the swirling mass of death below. Pasha and Abayomi attacked together, easily cutting down the Jakshima archers who seemed surprised by their presence. Some Jakshima drew their swords and tried to fight back, but they were no match for the Halor warriors.

Their work nearly became endangered when archers from the opposing roof began to realize what was happening and started firing at them. Pasha crashed to the ground and rolled forward to evade a rushing volley. Four of Hanasa's warriors did not have such luck. The rest raised their shields and continued engaging the remaining archers.

Pasha retrieved one of their bows and fired madly at the other side. Though the Jakshima archers tried to dodge the arrows, the roof from which they stood was flat and had no cover.

Upon dispatching the rest of the Jakshima archers, Hanasa's bodyguards formed a wall of shields about Pasha as he continued his deadly work. Abayomi and Leyos took a bow alongside him while Hanasa stayed behind cover. The work was slow, but eventually the Jakshima realized they were too exposed and withdrew back into the house.

There was no time for celebrating. The enemy below had split the column as Hanasa had predicted, but the Jakshima were having trouble keeping the Halor pinned to the wall, as they were obviously trying to do. King Hanasa's guards retrieved bows and began shooting down into the enemy below.

"We must hold this position!" shouted King Hanasa.

"Now you're stating the obvious," Pasha replied.

Both men looked down. The enemy infantry below had noticed the rooftops had fallen and were pouring more of their own men into the houses again.

"We have visitors. Abayomi, you and Leyos keep them occupied."

His men knew what he meant and ran back toward doorway leading to the roof, bearing bows in hand.

"Ten of your warriors should stay here while the rest go with us," said Pasha.

"Go where?" asked the king.

Pasha looked down.

"What! Are you mad?" said the king.

"We've got to bring the column back again!"

Saying no more, Pasha leapt from the edifice into the bulging mass of sweat-laden, bloodied warriors. On his order, the king and his men followed.

The Halor cheered upon seeing Captain Nuvahli and their king crash down into the Jakshima. Pasha and the king immediately cut down into the warriors they had collapsed onto the hard stone ground. Their actions had taken the Jakshima off balance; Pasha could see it. Possessing a renewed vigor, the Halor pushed back hard against the Jakshima and regrouped with the column.

Chanting vociferously, the Halor pressed back against the Jakshima line, which was starting to weaken. King Hanasa looked upon it anxiously; they were close to breaking the enemy.

But then a shokar horn sounded from the rear, causing Hanasa to turn.

"Coming up the rear!" he heard a man shout.

At first the king could hardly see anything through all of his warriors. But the sound of heavy horse and the cries of northern voices became ever clearer as they closed in on the men of the south.

"Form up! Form up!" King Hanasa shouted as he ran through his men toward the line at the rear.

His rank masters and officers in the rear were already aware of the approaching Ekoo warriors who rode at lightning speed into the Halor. The king's officers and rank masters in the rear tried unsuccessfully to form all the men up in time. Heavy wooden lances with iron tips were lowered and drove right into the heart of the Halor column.

Hakan, Pasha thought to himself. His officer's men had been broken. There was no other way the Ekoo could have driven up their rear so fast without them knowing. Where were the other generals? Pasha asked himself angrily. By that time the forces of the other tribes should have been in the city. Were they in the city at that moment fighting to get to them? Or had they been vanquished just as his officer had been? It angered Pasha that he did not know the answers and that that moment would most likely be his last.

The Halor column split at the seams as a wave of slain warriors gave way to the Ekoo. King Hanasa's men on the wall fired into them, but their efforts were short lived. Ekoo horse archers returned fire much more quickly. Pasha's stomach felt hollow as he saw the ten of King Hanasa's warriors who had stayed on the wall ripped apart by Ekoo archers. From the rear came Jakshima and a handful of Baku warriors who chased Abayomi and Leyos across the roof.

Both men were about to jump to the ground below, but Abayomi stopped himself upon seeing the Ekoo archers below. Unfortunately, Leyos reacted too late.

And then Pasha saw him, the same Baku officer that had killed Yuwatu. His long, straight hair flew in the wind, and his Baku armor shined bright while he looked toward Leyos and Abayomi.

The first Sashraman had ducked upon stopping short his jump. Arzim ignored him and drew back to launch his long spear at the remaining Sashraman as he leapt into the air. Taking a deep breath and making sure of his target, Arzim hurled his spear with all his might.

"No!" shouted Pasha.

He cut fiercely into Ekoo horsemen before him. However, Pasha soon became reckless as he swung his sword wildly before him, not caring or paying attention to what was around him. The captain's only concern was getting to his man. But despite his efforts, Pasha was cut short.

The Baku officer's spear impaled Leyos from the back moments before Ekoo arrows fired from the ground tore through Leyos's body in midair.

As he dove forward to avoid an Ekoo horseman attempting to trample him, an Ekoo ax man slammed into Pasha with his shield and pummeled Pasha back into the ground. The warrior swung his mighty battle ax toward Pasha's exposed neck. The warriors blow was deflected when a jagged Halor spear drove into his chest. While he fell to his right, the flat side of the ax in the warrior's left lunged toward Pasha, striking him in the back of his head.

During his fall, the captain's eyes did not manage to escape the gruesome sight as his falling officer was impaled by the Baku officer's spear and riddled with Ekoo arrows. The body of his officer fell into the swarm of dying men below, his body already gashed and broken.

It appeared as if fate would not be kind to them that day as the Halor line began to break. The fifteen who were all that was left of King Hanasa's bodyguard came into a tight circle about their king. No matter what, they would protect him with their lives.

All seemed dark to Pasha as he came to his knees. His vision was blurred and dark while his head throbbed with pain. The captain did not know if he was dying. It did not feel like it. Little by little, his vision began to clear, and he began to discern forms.

Soon his eyes became filled with a bright light that nearly blinded him. As it cleared, his eyes came upon a warrior in silver armor standing over him. The warrior did not belong to the northern tribes. Though he seemed like most people of the south, his dark face seemed to glow with an aura that no living man could have possessed.

The armor he wore differed from the Baku style. Silver it appeared, but silver it was not. His armor shone bright like the sun, flawless in all aspects. Pasha had never beheld such a man, yet the captain found himself unable to explain the feeling of familiarity he had about the man.

"I know you," he said.

The warrior did not answer, only nodded. Pasha could not tell if that meant he agreed with Pasha's statement or merely acknowledged him.

"Who are you?"

An anxious breath escaped Pasha when the warrior began to bend over toward him. Instead of answering his question, the warrior took him by the arm and lifted him to his feet. In the moment his hands touched him, the captain felt his warrior's vigor return. The pain that had taken possession of his body ceased. Looking around, he saw thousands more warriors all clad in silver standing among them.

For a long moment, the enemy seemed unaware of them. Pasha jumped back in surprise as he saw Ekoo and Jakshima moving through the warriors like they were nothing but air. But the moment the warrior in the flawless armor lifted his arm a bright light engulfed him and all his compatriots.

In the moment the light receded, the warriors' eyes had turned to balls of white, and they stood visible before all. Jakshima and Ekoo warriors paused at the frightening sight. But the warriors did not hesitate. Pasha watched the warrior who had helped him up joining his brothers who had started breaking through the northern swarm.

Everything began to change. The men of the north tried to force them back, but the warriors were like none they had met before. Silver-clad warriors brought down whole lines of Jakshima with the sweep of a sword. Northern warriors tried to cut them down, but the warriors dodged every blow with ease and delivered more lasting ones.

Pasha watched the warrior he had talked to before. Jakshima pounced on him from everywhere, baring their thick spears to his chest. With one sweep of his sword, the warrior broke the heads of all their spears and sent them all flying back when he bashed into all of them with his shield. His brothers leapt into them and stabbed them before their bodies had even hit the ground.

They possessed great speed and agility. Every swipe of every blade aimed toward them was dodged or deflected. Bounding forward at great lengths, a path of silver cut through the Jakshima and Ekoo. Warriors appeared in one place and then reappeared in another to deliver a fatal blow.

Within moments, the entire Jakshima line had been pushed back from the Halor warriors, and soon the fight became a chase as the Jakshima commanders signaled their men to fall back. The Ekoo soon followed suit. Unable to stop them, the men of the north began to break when the silver column of warriors passed through them. Enemy warriors everywhere fell out dead.

After regaining consciousness, Pasha joined his men at the southern gates. Every warrior cheered when they heard the call declaring that the enemy was falling back. Pasha stood with his warriors before the southern gates as an emerging darkness embraced the retreating men of the north.

Through a tiny sliver of remaining sunlight, he spotted a familiar-looking woman riding back in forth before the city. Could she have been the witch Abayomi spoke of before? Pasha wondered. The woman seemed to have seen him looking at her from afar and rode closer toward the city. Accompanying her was a warrior of small stature whose helmet covered his face.

Animosity took hold of Pasha as she rode a bit closer, and he slowly realized who she was. He would never forget her smoothly toned bronzed features, her green eyes, her piercing gaze, and the confidence she had as she rode. She reminded him in almost every way of Hadassah. But where Hadassah had worn a smile, the woman wore an arrogant sneer with her head cocked back like a hawk circling for a kill.

"Helomar," Pasha said angrily.

Having no moment of hesitation, the captain took a bow and bounded toward her afoot. He felt his men's gazes upon him as he made his way toward the woman. It was obvious that they were confused by the sight of their captain trying to continue a battle that had ended.

All of the generals had stopped their men from giving chase. Darkness would soon be upon them, and hunting the enemy down would become very dangerous. Pasha pushed aside such thoughts from his mind. Nothing mattered to him but getting to her and making her pay for the pain she had caused him.

Eventually his men decided to act when they saw the black-robed woman rider galloping to meet Pasha. Pasha had already put a good distance between him and the city. They would not reach their captain before the woman worked one of the wonders of sorcery she had demonstrated to the city before.

Helomar charged toward Pasha with the longing for his blood. Once he had come as close as he dared, the captain stopped and took a knee while he prepared an arrow. He lifted the bow and took the shot.

Helomar dodged the first easily when it flew toward her face. The captain prepared another with haste, seeing that she was almost near. He drew in a deep breath and looked down his sights. Pasha tried to clear his mind like his father had always told him to do on hunts. However, that moment was not like hunting; it would be a conclusion to a terrible chapter of his life, one in which he would finally have control. Pasha let another fly.

Bearing no shield and being so close would make it difficult for her to dodge it. Even if he did not kill, he knew the arrow's flight would knock her from her horse. By his blade, he planned to make an end of her.

Helomar lifted her arm and waved it violently before the arrow's path to her chest. In an instant, the arrow broke into many pieces and fell into the wake of her path.

Pasha jumped forward and rolled when she unsheathed a wicked-looking sword and swiped at him. Coming back to his feet, Pasha lunged at her with his blade and body.

Helomar extended her open palm toward her attacker. From her hand came an amazing force that barreled into Pasha and sent him flying back into the hard ground. He tried to rise, but the moment he did, the blunt end of a blade struck into his back and drove him back to the ground.

"Persistent as ever."

Pasha looked up to see Helomar walking about him, sword in hand. The warrior of small stature remained on his mount, watching with silent interest.

"What did you think, brother? That you could come up here and save them? You were always so noble. I can see why Hadassah took a liking to you."

"It was you, wasn't it, Helomar. You killed her."

She smiled and laughed gleefully like a girl.

"Oh this is so exciting. First the deception, the mystery, and now the revelation. You really are catching on, brother."

"I am not your brother! I knew you had been corrupted, Helomar. But not this. I never would have imagined . . ." Pasha said as he came to his knees. He looked to his side, noting that his sword had already been taken, held in the hands of the small warrior.

"Imagined what, brother? That I would see through your lies, the lies of the priests and shazhias? There is great power to be had in this world, power that your pathetic minds cannot comprehend. A power that we shall use to rid this world of the one false god."

"So now you do the bidding of this Rashtak and live among northern men. You are lower than even the most brazen whore!"

Before Pasha could react, she had struck him again on the side of his face. The captain crashed back into the dirt as a gash on his temple spewed out blood.

"You betrayed us, Helomar. Hadassah loved you, even after what you did to your parents. She never gave up on you."

"She took everything from me. Both of you! You conspired with them and took Jezareel from me. Both of you tried to make me weak. But I have seen through the lies, brother. Oh yes I have."

"The only lies that have been spoken are the ones you utter now. Know this, Helomar. No place on this earth, or sorcery, shall keep you from me. You took something precious from me. I will not rest until I have him back."

Helomar smiled deviously as the sound of Sashraman warriors grew closer. Pasha turned and saw his men were closing on them. As he looked back to face Helomar, her swift foot kicked his chest, sending him reeling onto his back.

His sister-in-law jumped over him and crouched down to speak in his ear.

"Take care, brother, and know this. He's coming for you."

Helomar smiled again, not one of amusement. Her expression said all that Pasha needed to know. Having moved past the vast perplexities of life, she had fallen and been overtaken by the forces of darkness. The woman his wife had known and loved was dead, totally consumed by the sorceress.

She disappeared into nothingness along with the small warrior. Pasha came back to his feet while his men gathered about him.

"Kaudi, are you all right?" asked one of his officers.

"No. None of us are," Pasha said in a low voice.

For so long, he had sought answers and longed to know the truth. After many months, it had found him, placing Pasha in a quandary he had not known before. Kamili was there, he could feel it. But soon the one with the red eyes who had invaded so much of his night sleep would fall upon the city as well. The captain feared what might happen if such a day were to come.

Before, he had not believed Malik Juktan when he spoke about the evil one, a character that had always been a most stressed topic among shazhias and priests. He did not know if this man could truly be him. Though he strongly doubted such a possibility, the captain could not ignore the dark forces that seemed to be vying for him and the soul of Cafura.

CHAPTER 17

Glorious Strife

Night had fallen upon the city, bringing a strong atmosphere of gloom to an already dark moment. Pasha had seen much death in his time. But when he walked through the clusters of corpses that now clogged the southern gates, he felt as he had after his first battle. Weariness, confusion, and shock assaulted all of the captain's senses as he looked upon the many thousands of his dead brothers.

The Halor losses at the eastern wall had been great yet seemed small in comparison to the sea of death at the southern walls. He looked around for Hakan's face or any of his men who had survived. Sashraman warriors from the northern side of the city looked through the bodies, sorting out the Sashraman ones while beginning the long task of stacking the enemy ones.

"Kaudi! Kaudi!"

Pasha looked up to see who called him.

His men Varansi and Shukimbo appeared from among a crowd of Naua warriors seeing to the wounded. Both ran to him quickly. Pasha noted their cracked armor and gashed faces. Varansi's left arm had turned dark purple and hung from the socket aimlessly, most likely broken. Shukimbo looked almost fine to Pasha until he saw his broken sword hand and cracked fingers.

"Daiyu be praised you're still alive," said Varansi.

"And you . . . What has become of Saji Hakan? Were you with him?"

"I don't know, sir. It was madness. One moment we're at the gates holding them back, and then there was an explosion and then Ekoo all over us," said Shukimbo hurriedly.

"Wait. Explain. What happened? Did they get through the western wall?"

"Yes, Kaudi," continued Shukimbo. "We were trying to fall back and reinforce our position. And then out of nowhere, the Ekoo come through the wall and charge right through us."

"Where is Saji Hakan, do you know?" he said, looking at both of them.

"We tried to fall back with him. We made it to the main road, but when we tried to get to the city center, the Ekoo and Baku were all around us."

Shukimbo then spoke. "The men at the rear must have fallen fast because I don't understand how they could have overtaken us so quick. We had no one to cover our retreat, sir. Archers were firing on the run, and our horsemen dropped like flies. When they hit us from the west, it was too much. Saji Hakan tried to push them back, just him and the last of the horsemen. But it was no use; our lines broke."

"Did you see him fall?"

"I don't know what I saw. All I know is when our lines broke, Varansi and I ran toward the east and hid in the nearest house."

A wave of voluminous hoof beats clattered hard upon the city streets and filled the Sashramans' ears as it got closer. More Halor, Yashani, and Mulamar rode up to their position. He soon spotted King Hanasa, who had ridden in spite of his wound. A warrior came quickly to his side to help him dismount.

General Shabaz stopped his horse yards away from Pasha and leapt to the ground. His feet churned the ground with great speed, propelling the general forward with great energy while he unleashed a barrage of blows.

Pasha had not been ready when the general's fists pummeled into his midsection and bashed into his face. The captain crashed to the ground painfully.

Varansi and Shukimbo immediately spurred into action. Varansi rushed toward Shabaz first. In spite of his energy, he did not move fast enough. The General swept his leg from under him and stabbed his foot into the Sashrpahite's stomach. Shukimbo jumped and kicked Shabaz in the chest, making the general stagger back.

"You Sashraman cowards! My men are dead because of you and your cowardly tribe. You beg us to come up here and help your people, and then you betray our trust!"

More Sashramans immediately ran toward them, placing their bodies between the Mulamar and their captain. Varansi came back to his feet, clutching his arm as he drew a long dagger. Acting instinctively, the Mulamar gathering about Shabaz drew their swords, causing the Sashramans to react in the same manner.

"Stop!" shouted King Hanasa as he limped toward them with his men.

"Stop it now, you fools!"

Pasha finally came back to his feet, his eyes unceasingly bearing down upon Shabaz with livid rage.

"Enough have already died this day!" the king said, looking around to the Sashrpahites and Mulamar.

"Have you forgotten why we are here? You want to fight? The enemy is out there!" The king gestured violently toward the northeast.

"Even now you defend the bushim coward when he left two hundred and twenty of my men on the eastern wall alone, without the support his men were supposed to provide. Even now you make excuses for him. My men are dead, and this bushim is responsible!"

"We still do not know all that happened, Shabaz."

"Do we not? I know his men deserted mine when the Jakshima were coming. He does not even deny it. Look at him. Bushim coward!"

"You call me or my men bushim one more time, I will cut your tongue out," said Pasha in a low voice.

He reached for his sword, but the Halor pounced on him and clasped his sword back down into the scabbard.

"Get off of me, you wretch!"

"You want to fight here, captain? You want your men to die?"

"The only one who will die is this *hejukwa* Mulamar son of a catamite," Pasha spat in Shabaz's direction.

By the Mulamar's flared brow and set gaze, he knew the general longed to strike. Pasha no longer cared. The Mulamar general dared insult Sashra among its dead warriors. No longer could he stand such an offense.

Pasha fought back against the king in fury, joined by many of his own men. But in moments, the swift Halor warriors along with Naua and Yashani moved in between the group and began pushing them away from one another.

"Not here, Pasha," the king pleaded. "Not now."

"You left my men to their deaths! I swear I'll kill you, bushim scum."

"You don't want to do this. Just walk away."

Though incensed by the shouts of his rival, he could not help but consider what the king had said.

"And let my men think I fear him? Not a chance."

"Enough of your men are dead, Captain. You want more of them to die? You strike him, the rest of the Mulamar might join too. You are a sensible man, Captain. Be so now."

To his own surprise, he felt his sword grip slacken. Hanasa was right, and he knew it though he would not say it.

The Halor, Naua, and Yashani remained entrenched between the Sashramans and the Mulamar. Fortunately, most of the Makar had remained at the city center. Their presence would have only further enflamed the situation.

Hanasa turned back and stepped through his men toward Shabaz.

"We don't know all that happened. But all that is necessary shall be done. Enough for one day. Stand down!"

Saying no more, the Mulamar general snapped his hand around in a quick gesture, signaling his men to withdraw.

King Hanasa looked to Pasha. "His cousin was on the eastern wall."

The Sashraman began to walk back toward his men. He said nothing, for he did not care about the Mulamar general's cousin. Still, inside, the captain understood his anger.

"You had best take care of this. If they don't feel they can count on your men in combat, this pact will not last."

Pasha stopped and glared back at Hanasa. His blank expression sharpened into a smirk.

"My torturer, my adviser . . ."

Along with his Sashraman tribesmen, the captain aided in gathering up their dead and securing weapons. The Cafura Pasha had entered before had been in a wretched state, but never had it compared to the ominous moment before them. Most of the houses and buildings on the southern end of the city had been destroyed. Very little of the wall the Yashani had been trying to repair stood. Pasha knew that they had been fortunate, but the city would not survive another attack like that one.

He had sent out men to find as many of his officers as possible. Abayomi had survived with several broken ribs and a broken arm, and his men had helped him to the temple to be looked after. Pasha hoped that the woman he had met there before would look after his friend. Though he hardly knew her, she seemed to exude the qualities necessary for trust to be built. The captain had no doubts about her.

After a long while, they had found Hakan barely wounded. In spite of the lack of physical wounds, there were many in his mind. Great shock and confusion had overwhelmed him. The captain hoped his recovery would not take long, for he would have great need of all of his officers in the days to come.

Later that night, Pasha and King Hanasa met at the alcalde's home for a private meeting.

Pasha and the king sat widely apart before the alcalde. Behind him was Maranhi, who stood along the wall in the shadows.

"How many?" was the alcalde's first question for Pasha.

"More than three thousand of our warriors are dead, Alcalde, and another thousand wounded."

The alcalde looked beyond them into the shadows, his mind trying to wrap around the day's events.

"Among all the tribes together, ten thousand were lost," said the king.

"But in spite of that, we still came out victorious," the alcalde said, trying to sound positive.

"This was no victory, Alcalde. This was simply not an immediate defeat. But we are not going to recover from this. The entire southern wall was destroyed, and there is no way its going back up. I have spoken with all of the generals, and the Mulamar, Makar, and Naua are ready to give up and go back home."

"They would go back in shame. They've been calling us cowards, but our men don't have the luxury of running, nor would they indulge it."

"Actually, Alcalde, they might soon have that luxury. We lost greatly in the last fight, but so did the men of the north. Their brothers at the mountain pass are taking longer getting past the Sashraman northern army, and their control over the province has slackened. Now might be the best time to withdraw your men and run south."

"And what of my people? We would be running for our lives; the women and children would hardly keep up. Besides, we barely have enough provisions for such a journey."

"I refer not to your people, Alcalde. Only the army."

"You're crazy!"

King Hanasa shook his head. "Alcalde," he pleaded.

"You are crazy! You must be if you think that I will desert the people. We must wait for Malik Juktan. He will be here soon."

"When, Alcalde? When? How long do we wait for him? He left for the west long before we arrived. Yet ever since we got here, there has been no word. No one knows where he is. We cannot wait on your king; we must act now."

Pasha then spoke. "Alcalde, we cannot do this without help. If the Mulamar, Makar, and Naua left, this city would not stand a chance."

"What is it you are proposing?"

"The last attack took many of ours, but it also took many of theirs. We must strike back at them before we lose our momentum."

"An attack? What good would that do? I doubt Maikael will help you again."

"It just might keep the other generals from leaving and possibly lead to a victory. Our men cannot hide behind the walls any longer and let them pound us with their siege weapons. We must take the fight to them."

"And what would you accomplish? Surprise them you might, but you surely cannot expect to win out there."

"We can win if we have the right field and the right moment."

King Hanasa spoke. "I have discussed it with the generals. They are not going to hide behind walls anymore and be slaughtered. An attack is one of the things that might convince them to stay."

"And what else would?" the alcalde asked.

"The conscripts who deserted their posts must be made examples of."

"Examples!" Maranhi said, stepping out from the shadows.

"The generals are still upset over how our conscripts left the defenses open during the attack and nearly caused us defeat. They won't come back until they're dealt with."

"You mean killed," said the alcalde.

"The men did desert their posts, Alcalde. That is punishable by death in Sashra."

"That is for a regular army. They're common folk who are just as terrified as the rest of us. I will not have them butchered just to appease the Mulamar and Makar!"

"They will not honor the pact unless they see your leadership show that such actions will not be tolerated," said King Hanasa.

"And of course you have no problem watching Sashramans die at the hands of other Sashramans. Such a sight probably amuses you Halor," said Maranhi.

The king did not respond to Maranhi, directing his attention to the alcalde.

"I have come to you in friendship. With friendly counsel. The strength of this pact has kept this city from falling. Twice we have been delivered from defeat. But in my time, I have learned deliverance only lasts for as long as we make it. What you decide is your choice. Just make sure it is one you can live with."

The alcalde descended into a pensive state. Finally he spoke. "We've been through a lot in the last few months. Hard decisions have had to be made along with much sacrifice. For so long, we've been in this darkness. We have got to get out. Do as you must."

"Alcalde, no!" Maranhi moved forward, stopping at the alcalde's right side. "The people do not deserve this! You're just giving into them!" he said, glaring at King Hanasa.

"I have few men left, Alcalde. If we are to be effective in the city and any future battles, I need more, along with competent officers," Pasha said.

Maranhi looked at the alcalde with apprehension, fearing what he would say next. The alcalde did not look at Maranhi but shifted uncomfortably in his direction. He knew what Pasha was about to ask.

"The city guard must fully cooperate with my command in keeping order in the city and must fully absorb into the army during battle."

"I do not take orders from you, Nuvahli. Nor shall any of my men. We will not take up arms against other Sashramans."

"As if you care about the people! Street gangs have run of the streets. Rich merchants are allowed to hoard food. The Baku may have destroyed our walls, but it is your men's laxness and disregard that are destroying us from within."

"You have no right to judge me or my men, Nuvahli. We're the ones who protect the granaries from being ransacked and keep the water in the city guarded so you and your men can have your glorious battles. You don't know the first thing about what I do."

"Let it be done," said the alcalde abruptly, after listening to both men's exchanges.

"Alcalde!" Maranhi said in disbelief.

"It is done, Maranhi."

"Have I not served you in everything? Have I not been faithful? Why do you dishonor me now, Alcalde?"

"The only dishonor I have inflicted is by withholding you from the fight. You kept telling me you were protecting the city's people from the inside, maintaining order. What order? A man cannot go get food without being robbed. Women cannot walk the streets without being harassed and kidnapped. There are whole sections of the city where we have no real control. In spite of your many years of faithfulness, your leadership has only served to disappoint me, Maranhi."

"Will you honor me for anything I have done? All of your properties I have kept safe. The food granaries that I have secured, the protection we have given your family."

"It will be in following Nuvahli's leadership and proving yourself in battle that you shall redeem your honor. That is all."

Maranhi, seeing he had lost, gave up and stormed out of the chamber of the alcalde's home, his men following close behind.

With his hands untied, swift action ensued that night as Pasha and his men tracked down the conscripts. In dark, early hours of morning, heavily armored Sashraman spearmen moved fluidly throughout differing sectors of the city.

Using Varansi and Shukimbo, the captain found the records of all of the men conscripted into duty along the wall since the siege began. It concerned Pasha that they did not know who was dead or wounded and who still lived. Nevertheless, this would be a time of reckoning, reinforcing in the minds of the people that all would do their part or suffer the consequences.

The day soon grew longer as the warriors carried out their work. Each kad went house by house, searching for any young men fitting the descriptions on the rolls and dragging them away. Although each conscript would have a mark on their necks saying they were serving, the captain knew as he dragged young men screaming from their homes that some might be innocent. Nevertheless, an example had to be made.

In the hours before sunset, all of Cafura filled with sounds of wailing women and the prayers of concerned men. The entire eastern half of the city had filled with warriors and condemned men who were marched against the wall. All in all, six hundred had been rounded up and two hundred forty let go.

From the eastern gates, Pasha looked down upon the condemned wretches and the warriors pressed between them and their families. More people had come out than he had originally thought. Nevertheless, it was not the riotous mob King Hanasa had worried about when speaking about how to handle the situation.

The captain was grateful very few of the other tribesmen were present. Except for some Yashani and a few dozen Naua making up the eastern watch, the rest of the tribes had taken up positions elsewhere within the city or withdrawn their men to barracks. On a rooftop in the distance, he knew King Hanasa and a few of his men would be watching. Still, they were not readily visible. This would be a Sashraman affair, and Sashraman judgment would be delivered upon the men.

He looked down into the lines of warriors where Varansi and his group stood ready. Dozens of priests and the shazhia went out toward the men, praying with those who wished it and blessing the rest.

At that moment, the shazhia, brightly adorned in his red robes and black tunic, raised his arms, causing the crowds to hush in silence. In unison, all lowered their heads as he prayed the last prayer the condemned would hear.

"Great father, I do not know where the evil that makes men strife and murder one another comes from. I recognize that we must fight to defend what is yours so that your glory may reign in this land and in our hearts. But we have already given enough in blood as we are commanded. You revealed yourself to us so that together our brothers and sisters might spread your light throughout all the world. Yet this day, a great darkness has come over that light. And now brothers kill brothers for senseless reasons. Save the men who do this from the emptiness of their hearts. Though the light of these men's lives shall soon fade, let not the light of their souls fade from among us. Guide and save our brothers as they go on their journey. Comfort them and let them remember that they are the people of the way and that they shall not be forsaken or forgotten."

To the captain's surprise a small drop of water moistened his face. He looked up searching for rain until he realized that the moisture had fallen from his eyes.

Varansi looked up toward Pasha, eagerly awaiting his order. Before, he had planned on saying something to the men, offering some comfort or a reason for all that had happened. But after the shazhia's oration, he knew all that needed to be said had been said. Staring blankly into the horizon, he lifted his arm.

Behind him, Shukimbo and the forty executioners on the gates and walls readied their ropes. Ascending the walls through the staircase connecting the walls and gates, the condemned joined with their brothers. It all went much faster than Pasha had expected.

In spite of their obvious fear on the ground, the soon to be executed made very few sounds as they were paired with their executioner. Nevertheless, the tense calm of that occasion broke as each man was flung from the wall and cried out before the tight cords about their necks doused their light. This continued until all were dead and the executioners satisfied with their work.

CHAPTER 18

Fifth Night

A heavy rain swept the rocky mud dirt paths while men moved back and forth from their tents. In spite of the rain, the camp bustled with activity. Inside a series of cliffs that surrounded a stony plateau stood rows of erect tents and pavilions of all shapes and colors. Their main identifying features were the red, silver, and orange banners, bearing images of the Baku god of war, blue and gray with red streaks that identified the Ekoo contingent, and green and black bars representing the contrasts between harmony and discord within Jakshima philosophy.

At seven main points on the surrounding cliffs, Baku and Jakshima patrols kept watch. Before, they had felt safe and indulged a reckless sense of complacency while launching their war upon their old southern enemies. But ever since their latest and only true defeat against the Sashramans, increased vigilance had become their code.

Many looked out from their tent flaps as another column of Baku trudged through the camp path, heading toward the tallest pavilion that faced east toward Cafura. It was not the warriors who were of great interest to their brothers and allies, but the woman who rode the great black stallion between them.

The dark woman had drawn much scorn among them, for they knew she was of the south. Nevertheless, a sort of grudging respect and awe had been afforded her upon the manifestation of her powers. And because they knew she held the ear of the leader they knew as Rashtak, whom they had followed onto the path of war.

Some questioned his origins, for he did not look like most Baku, but more like the dark-toned tribes of the south. Nevertheless, few Baku actually believed he was a southerner. In their minds, more than likely he hailed from the Hatakas people on the Baku kingdom's western border. As for all Baku, none doubted his power and command of sorcery.

In the north, only strength and fortitude were afforded any respect, and it was clear to them that King Vladshak had possessed neither when the general led the king's own guard against him. With his growing influence in the north, the general seized former Baku territories from other tribes and brokered many alliances with other powerful kings.

Finally the momentum of his growing influence had turned northern eyes toward Sashra. In the north, it was common knowledge that Baku had once dwelt and thrived in Sashra's Northern provinces until the arrival of the new religion that had united all of the Sashraman clans and southern tribes. That event directed a new kind of animosity toward the people of the north. Eventually during the reign of the newly united South's fourth emperor, all northerners had been purged from Sashra's north in a great bloodletting that no northerner would ever forget. From that day on, no peace had existed between the north and the south.

On her arrival, the woman had been scorned and mocked. Now all feared her. The warriors left the woman at the doorway to the large pavilion where she dismounted and entered.

Inside, darkness greeted her like an old friend while she made her way to the center of the pavilion. She quickly sensed an unknown presence and drew a long dagger.

"You and I are so alike. The dark is a scary place when you don't know what is inside," General Ivadar said as he came from the darkness.

"You're not supposed to be here," said Helomar.

"That's strange because in the beginning I thought this was a partnership. I get what I want, he gets what he wants. Now he keeps me at a distance, doesn't see me when I request it, and only has you in his counsel."

"If you want a man to hold your hand, there's a place for that."

Ivadar slammed his fist into a nearby table. "We were defeated! We were slaughtered! And all for what? So he can sit back and watch us die while he makes strategies without me! He promised me full support!"

"He has not forgotten you, and you need to put your faith in him and the agreement. You'll be a king one day. Don't worry," Helomar said, tickling his face like a child.

The general seized her hand and slapped her across the face before pinning her to the table.

"Listen to me, you southern whore! I will not take this from him or from you!"

Helomar's guards began to rush inside the tent. Before the guards could act, Helomar drove her elbow into the general's gut before reaching back to grab his head and flip him over her back. The general broke the table as he fell.

Ivadar found a cold blade pressed against his neck when he tried to get up.

"There is a plan in place that is bigger than anything your hopelessly pathetic mind could imagine. We're going to win this war and many more. If you stay with us, you'll be rewarded. Do it not and you die! Which do you prefer?"

"All right! All right!" said Ivadar.

Helomar finally released him.

"Leave me!"

Ivadar left with the guards, leaving Helomar alone again in the darkness.

Suddenly a bright orange glow filled all corners of the tent. Once it had dissipated, the one she had expected stood in its wake.

Immediately she fell to her knees under the pressure of Janaha's penetrating gaze. Few had seen him as she had, tall and black with eyes that were like small globes of fire. Along with his stolid gaze, he evoked a strong feeling of fear. He had taught her everything she knew, helped her develop her power. Everything she was she owed to him.

"Why have you called me?" he demanded in a thunderous voice.

"Much of the army has been lost in our last defeat. Will the time of your coming be soon? I fear that without your presence among us, this whole endeavor could fail."

"You fear too much. The south is weak. I have seen what shall come. Cafura and the south will burn. In time, they will regret what they did to our people, how they murdered us, pushed us out."

"You mean for everyone to die then?" Helomar asked, unable to hide her concern.

"After all I have done for you, you still care for them!"

"No. I . . ."

"You cannot hide your feelings from me! Do you remember what you were when I found you? Broken, lost, aimless. I took you in. And what did I do?"

"You gave me a path," Helomar replied.

Moving closer to her, he reached out his hand and took hold of her arm, raising her up to her feet. Her breathing quickened as he bore down upon her with his gaze.

"Do you think they cared about you? They despised you. They did not understand what you were. Even Hadassah hated your gifts."

Helomar breathed in deeply at the sound of her sister's name. Slowly, with his other hand, he reached out to stroke her hair.

"As much as you hated her, you wish she wasn't dead."

"I did as you asked," said Helomar as she tried to turn away her face.

His fingers reached out to caress her face. "In spite of your hatred, you still loved her, didn't you?"

"She was my sister."

"Love is the most powerful of elements and the most dangerous. You must strike away these feelings or they will leave you weak! Only I understand the fire that burns inside your heart! I taught you how to use it. I made you strong. When you asked, I let you have the boy. After all of this, you doubt me?"

"Never," Helomar insisted, shaking her head. In that moment, she looked into his eyes for the first time.

"In being parted from you, my fear can take ahold of me. But I am strong for you. I only desire to be by your side again."

He said nothing, returning deeper into the darkness from whence he came.

"Why wouldn't you let me kill Pasha? I had him under my blade. You saw this."

He turned to face her.

"You think you had him. But there are forces about him that protect. Forces too powerful even for you."

"Yes, I understand."

"Remember what you are supposed to do."

Saying no more, he was engulfed again by a bright orange glow and vanished.

Cafura

In spite of the rain, the flow of the city had returned to a sense of normalcy ever since the executions. Still, Pasha sensed a growing unease within Cafura, which had spread like an infection among the people. Ever since the last battle, life had grown even tenser for the people.

That day, Pasha had been personally overseeing the distribution of Yashani warriors among the newly formed patrols, whose purpose would be to aid the already overstretched city guard. While the patrols along various sections of the walls and gates were made up of men from all of the tribes, none save the Yashani, Naua, and some Halor had shown any interest in helping the Sashramans patrol the streets. In many ways, Pasha preferred it that way; a Yashani and Naua contingent among their patrols was more likely to be better received. Though the people's feelings toward Halor went from lukewarm to hostile, as of yet there had not been many problems.

Although the Sashraman army had few men to spare to patrol the streets, having Maranhi's guard under his command, along with men from other tribes, gave them enough clout to instill a sense of order within the city.

Pasha went along with his men while they passed through the northern end of the city, making way toward the granaries. More and more people were turning to the granaries to receive a ration of bread and old rice while food vendors in the marketplace found their stock quickly running out. Though he had ordered them to sell their foodstuffs for lower prices or simply give them away, many still charged exorbitant prices.

A great throng of people had filled the narrow street before a windowless, cube-shaped edifice of white stone. Maranhi had placed his men carefully before it in a rigid line of shields and drawn swords. Pasha could not see him, but on the steps leading toward the granary doors was a low table around which sat Maranhi and a scribe to take names and record all transactions for the day.

"Take position behind them and to the sides. Be discreet," Pasha said to Varansi and Shukimbo.

Varansi and Shukimbo took two of the three kads he had with him and positioned them at the rear of the crowd and on both sides. Pasha did not expect any trouble that day, but the crowd had been much larger than expected.

The captain looked around at all the people trudging through the dirty streets toward the white building. Many were dirty and bloodied, obviously having suffered greatly after the last attack. In all, he saw the same confused daze he had seen so many times in the aftermath of a battle. However, he also saw something else as he looked at them, expressions of hopelessness. He hoped this would soon pass.

At that moment, Takil, who stood beside him, directed his attention behind him. Coming up the street were another dozen Sashraman warriors. Pasha looked at them with curiosity; he had not ordered more men into that section of the city. And then to his surprise, he saw Hakan at the head of them.

"It does me good to see you, Saji," Pasha said as he approached them.

"And you, sir."

"I trust you are feeling better."

"A bit sore in some places, some dizziness, but I'll be fine."

"Good. Have you seen anything of Nalar?"

"Yes, Kaudi. I spoke to him before."

"How is he?"

"Bored stiff. Itching to get back into the fight, especially after last time."

"I was glad to hear that they had been able to move most of the wounded to the northern gates before the Baku moved in. Before, I had thought him to be lost."

"Not yet, sir. The Halor held their own protecting them. However, the temple is in a bit of disarray since then. Have you seen it?"

"No," Pasha replied.

"The Baku tore the place apart when they went through. They killed two priests who did not make it out in time. I'm glad the shazhia was not harmed though."

"It would not have been possible without you, Hakan. I know you held the main roads so that your men could fall back and the city center evacuate."

"Everything happened so fast, Kaudi."

"Nevertheless. Nalar and many others are alive because of you."

"I didn't hold them the whole time, Kaudi. My duma, Duma Amran. He and a few kads held them back a bit longer so that the rest of my men and I could reposition at the marketplace road in the east. I think we would have been overtaken if he had not stayed behind. Most of the riders that were sent to the city center were from his kads. They wouldn't have had as much time if it hadn't been for him. If anyone is worthy of praise, it is he."

"A good man," Pasha said in reply. "Did that one woman who takes care of the wounded make it out? Mahlinya, I believe her name was."

"Yes, sir, she did."

"Do you know where she is now?"

"I could not say, sir. I saw her in one of the houses where they moved the wounded, but she was gone before I left."

"I see," said Pasha.

Just then, four men came down the road, appearing to be joining the crowd. Suddenly one turned and caught sight of Pasha. He looked upon Pasha and his men, smiling, but it was not welcoming.

"To what do we owe such a great honor? Captain Nuvahli, savior of us all, mingling with the masses!" the man said mockingly. The three men beside him laughed.

"That is, when he's not rounding up innocent men and boys and throwing them off the city gates!"

Takil stepped toward the men, holding out his arms.

"All right. That's enough. Move along now!"

But the man did not stop. "We might be better off living among the Baku. At least they don't put their own people to death like they were animals."

Takil then began to push back against the men as they tried to get closer. "Back!" he shouted.

"You heard the man! Step back!" ordered Hakan.

People in the crowd began looking back in silent apprehension, fearing what would come next. More of the men about Pasha moved forward to confront the men, while the rest of the kads about the crowd looked on with a ready eye.

"Malik Juktan sent you here to protect us, not kill us!"

"Back!" Takil began pushing back harder with his shield as more warriors pressed in behind him.

"You murdered my brother, you wretch! By the blood of the Bumba clan, I will see him avenged!"

Before he could react, the man sidestepped and plunged a previously concealed short sword into the weak part of Takil's armor. Instantly, the rest of his fellows bared their own blades and attacked.

Hakan and the rest of the warriors pressed against Pasha as a terrified crowd ran in all directions. Without warning, a swarm of arrows ripped into the other kads about the crowd who were attempting to join the fight. Pasha drew his sword instantly and looked to the rooftops where dozens of bowmen had taken position.

The four men were soon joined by several dozen more who emerged from the crowd. Together they cut down several of Pasha's men as the rest tried to keep them from getting to their captain. However, their actions soon proved fruitless as they swarmed about Pasha and his kad.

Hakan and his men bashed into them with their spears and shields, hoping to break them up. They were resilient and did not break. The Sashramans pushed back hard to form a line. Little by little, their enemies were pushing them back against a wall.

All was chaos around Varansi and Shukimbo as they ducked and dived to avoid the arrows from overhead. Though both had managed to bring their kads together, they stood immobile in the middle of the street while their men clustered together and held their shields overhead.

Though some of Maranhi's men had bows, they merely stood together at the doorway to the granary.

"Maranhi! Take them out!" shouted Varansi as one of the groups of armed men from the crowd turned back to face them. "Take them out!" Varansi repeated.

"Hold your ground! Hold your ground!" Maranhi shouted.

"You bastard!" Varansi's shouts went unheard over the dozens of dark-robed men crashing into them. "Engage!"

In spite of their precarious position. Varansi and Shukimbo's men stood to engage the enemy. Immediately, dozens fell as merciless arrows tore through them.

Pasha's breath was quickly becoming ragged while he dodged the dozens of swords slashing for him. Hakan punched at every face that came near him and ran them through with his sword. Many hands took hold of Hakan, attempting to throw him down, but his men pushed them back and covered Hakan with a wall of shields. Hakan fell back beside Pasha.

The captain ducked backward and kicked up when a swift blade swiped at his stomach. With a fast kick, he disarmed the attacker and tripped him. Before he could rise, Pasha hurled his sword into the enemy's head. A steady cluster of enemies pressing against them stopped Pasha from retrieving it.

He rolled backward and jumped to his feet, quickly kicking out as an adversary leapt for him. Without hesitating, he fell to his haunches and in a sweeping motion, his leg kicked the man in the face before he could rise.

However, before Pasha could finish him off, another had taken his place. Pasha sidestepped when the man leapt for him, and after several swipes for his chest, which he dodged, he drew his short Lakina sword.

Upon contact with the other blade, sharp vibrations from the impact riveted painfully through Pasha's arm and shoulder. The short sword was lighter and did not absorb the shock of contact with another blade as well as Pasha's other.

Still, he ignored the pain. He sensed another behind him and fell to his feet. Both of his enemies' blades plunged into the other, delivering a fatal surprise to each man. Pasha leapt and kicked both of them back into the oncoming throng of enemies where they were quickly trampled.

Taking a moment to look about him, he looked toward the granary. At the doorway stood Maranhi and his men, doing nothing.

"The bastard is doing nothing but watching!" Pasha said angrily as he lashed out against the enemy.

Though he knew it frightfully foolish, the captain stepped back and jumped forward into their adversaries, slashing in all directions with his blade. Crashing into one, he slit his throat with all haste and rolled toward several more who were lunging toward him. Sparing not a moment, he slashed all of their legs from under them and jumped back to his feet.

Several leapt toward him, but in that moment, they were surprised as Hakan's body slammed into them. In spite of their losses, they still held a sizeable force. The way they were hemmed in to one of the buildings gave the archers overhead less of a target.

But at that moment, his men were beginning to push through, taking advantage of their momentum while the enemy force began to falter. Pasha looked up to the rooftops. Less fire was raining down on them before.

With swelling gratitude, he saw Varansi laying down fire on the archers themselves.

Suddenly the entire group of black-robed men began to break as a roaring column of Sashramans and Halor reinforcements surged forward. Just as the last of the enemy broke and the situation appeared to be improving, a last swarm of arrows pelted the Sashramans below.

Halor archers immediately returned fire and caused the archers to break as Varansi and newly arrived Sashraman warriors pounced upon them.

His men let out waves of cheers while the last of the enemy disappeared. Almost none had gotten away, and the rest would be found and executed before the day had ended.

Pasha looked over to Hakan. The feelings of relief that had swept through the captain immediately dissipated. Hakan's sword fell from his hands as his knees crashed into the ground. In spite of the raspy gasps for air, the arrow that had torn into his chest allowed him none.

"Hakan!"

Unable to say anymore, the saji fell face down into the dirty, blood-laden street never to rise again.

Pasha stared upon the lifeless shell that had once been a man. In spite of the pain it caused, death was one of life's most wondrous mysteries. To Pasha, it seemed so when he looked upon a warrior he had met only months before but at that moment thought of him only as a brother.

The captain cursed himself. No matter how much experience he possessed, all the battles he had been through, he had not been prepared for that day. It had never entered his mind that a street gang would be brazen enough to attack more than one kad of armed warriors.

But then again, the attack had not been like a common street brawl. There was precision and timing, well thought-out strategy behind it. The scattered dozens of dead warriors were clear evidence of the effectiveness of the strike. They had weapons almost as good as theirs. Pasha wondered where they had gotten them.

Finally Maranhi stepped out from among his men. His indifferent expression as he looked upon the dead incensed Pasha. The men quickly picked up on his mood and followed the captain as he sprinted toward Maranhi.

Varansi, who had just returned to the street level from the rooftops, drew his sword and joined them.

Being more than a dozen paces from the main body of his men put Maranhi well within Pasha's reach. Rushing past the few guardsmen with him, Pasha crashed into Maranhi, pummeling him into the ground among a hail of rapidly falling fists.

"You let my men die, you bastard! You just stood and watched! You coward!"

Despite his best efforts to shield his face, Pasha seized his hands and locked them behind his neck, using his right to deliver all manner of abuse to the guard captain's body. He tried to swing his legs to kick Pasha off, but Pasha quickly pinned his legs together with his own.

Maranhi's men who were nearby seized Pasha and tried to pry him off. But they were stopped short when Pasha's men swept through them like an angry wind and pushed them to the ground.

The rest of Maranhi's men surged forward with their swords and spears ready. However, the Halor commander had caught on quickly. and he and his mounted bodyguard rode between them. All of the Halor contingent fell in upon seeing their commander within the fray.

Halor warriors descended upon Pasha and Maranhi and pried them from one another. Pasha did not cease and resisted violently, forcing them to drag him back till Varansi took charge of him.

A warrior offered Maranhi a hand up. The captain of the guard, whose face was now purple and bruised, spat in the warrior's hand. Steady streams of spittle and blood fell from his crushed lips. He came to his feet under his own defiant strength, although by the way he clung to his side, it was clear he remained in immense pain.

"You coward. How can you watch other men be killed?" Pasha continued shouting after coming back to his feet.

Varansi and the Halor warriors stood in front of the captain, allowing him to move no further.

"Did you not think this would happen, Captain?" shouted Maranhi in reply. "I told you not to execute the conscripts, but you did not listen to me!"

"Men are dead because of you!" shouted Pasha.

"No! They are dead because of you!"

Maranhi started moving toward Pasha, causing the Halor to push back harder to keep the two men separate.

"Enough! Enough!" shouted the Halor commander, but none heeded his words.

"They are dead because of your arrogance. Because you don't listen to anyone but yourself. You thought you could come here and turn this city upside down. This isn't your city, Nuvahli. It never was!"

"I swear this is the last of your insolence. Maranhi!"

"What are you going to do about it? Kill me too like you did those men on the wall? All of this is your fault! You brought this on your men, not me! I warned you, Nuvahli. I warned you!"

"That's enough. Move on!" the Halor commander shouted again.

"Kaudi. Maybe we should deal with him another day," Varansi suggested to Pasha, though he knew that was far from both of their minds.

The Halor commander then turned to Pasha. "Sir. This will get bad if you do not move your men back."

Pasha looked up at the Halor officer. He was a young man, but he had the determination of an older one.

Though Pasha did not wish to give Maranhi the satisfaction of seeing his back turn, he could sense the hunger for blood in the air. If he did not act, more Sashramans would start killing one another.

For the rest of the day, his men scoured the city for any remnant of the gang that attacked them. But in spite of their efforts, they found none. Pasha did not know if that meant there were no more or that they were expert at hiding among the people.

While his men gathered up their dead. the captain withdrew himself to a quiet corner on the northern wall. That day, he had expected a small manner of calm within the city. In his pensive moment, Pasha knew that calm would not be returning to the city for quite some time.

CHAPTER 19

Acts of Kindness

Pasha spent most of the next day in strategy meetings with the leaders of the other tribes. King Hanasa and the generals had agreed to meet in an empty house adjoining the temple courtyard.

For most of the day, Pasha met with the Halor king and the other generals. To his surprise, Abayomi had joined them and had proved most helpful in deciding strategy.

Both the news of what had happened to Pasha the previous day and concern about Malik Juktan's arrival played a big role in the meeting. Almost all of the generals had heard of the rebellion in Sashra's west and that the malik had been delayed.

Still Pasha had been granted assurances that the rebellion had been resolved and that Malik Juktan was coming. Pasha greatly hoped so. Complete authority over Cafura's forces and having to deal with the other tribes were charges he would share readily.

After the meeting, the captain was about to head out when he noted a procession of women moving through temple courtyard into the sanctuary.

Most of the women wore long, flowing, purple linen robes with the headdress drawn over their hair. Some of the others wore orange and yellow robes. A familiar orange pattern with bright colored designs stuck out to Pasha. His eyes moved up from the pattern to the face beneath the bright orange headdress. She turned and looked in his direction, almost as if she knew he had been looking at her. Again to his delight, he found himself in a place near the woman he knew as Mahlinya.

Instead of entering the sanctuary, she returned to the center of the courtyard. For a long while, she stood observing the other women while they went inside. Pasha did not know if it was part of her duties or she wanted to be alone.

Neither knowing why nor caring, Pasha walked toward the double doors leading into the courtyards. He stepped into the courtyard just as a last group of three women were coming in. Though he half expected her to quickly follow the last group of women, she did not. Instead she remained in the courtyard, and then to Pasha's surprise, she drew back her bright orange veil to reveal her rich black hair.

"Captain Nuvahli," she said, bowing her head.

Pasha returned the gesture.

"I've never thanked you for all you have done for my men, tending to the wounded and helping them heal. I would like to do something for you."

"Nothing is necessary. You are not beholden to me, Kaudi."

"But what if I want to be?"

Pasha could clearly see the question had surprised when she turned her head uncomfortably to escape his gaze. But Pasha did not stop his inquiry. He wanted to know everything about her.

"Surely there is something you want that I can give you," he said.

"I don't live my life chasing after my wants and desires. Whatever my needs, they are provided for," she replied with a smile.

"By Daiyu?" Pasha asked, unable to hide a small twinge of disappointment.

"Yes," she answered.

"Do you let no man do the same for you?" Pasha asked.

"A man can always disappoint," she replied, shifting her eyes away from him.

His eyes lowered to the ground as if in search of the next thing to say.

"I must be going now, Kaudi," she said as she reached back to pull her headdress back over her hair.

"Do you spend all of your time at the temple?" Pasha asked as she turned to leave.

Mahlinya stopped and turned back toward him. "There is much to pray about, Kaudi." With that, she left him and entered the sanctuary.

Seeing that he was alone, Pasha turned back toward the house adjoining the courtyard, where Shukimbo and Varansi waited for him. The moment he rejoined them, he stopped and gazed back at the empty courtyard. "I think I'll stay awhile at the temple."

His men exchanged quizzical looks, but they said nothing more than expressing their agreement.

"As you wish, Kaudi," said Varansi.

His men took up places in the courtyard just outside of the temple while Pasha went on inside.

The captain went through the marble hall to the doorway leading into the sanctuary. Pasha watched as some of the women burned incense while the rest sat on their mats in solemn meditation. Soon the silence was broken as the women sang a slow ancient melody. It was unlike any song he had ever heard.

While he observed, the captain learned many tales of suffering and shame among the women gathered. Mahlinya and those with her comforted them and seemed to give them hope as they embraced them, listened to their stories, and gave instruction. They drew a strange ring on their faces with marks Pasha did not recognize.

Soon it had ended, and Pasha realized that he and Mahlinya were for the most part alone.

"I did not expect you would come in," she said.

"Why is that?" Pasha asked.

"War is not usually a time many warriors make time for the temple and prayer."

"Some may not come to the temple. But you would have us wrong by saying a warrior's mind is not focused on spiritual things."

Mahlinya smiled but said nothing. Pasha moved closer to her. "Those women seemed comforted by what you did for them," said Pasha.

"All we did was show them love and support, something the women of this city need a lot of."

"It may not be any of my business, but did something happen to them?" Pasha asked.

"Some have lost family, some children, all of them are struggling to find food and protect themselves."

"Protect themselves?" Pasha asked.

"None of them have any family to look after them. It's made their lives much harder."

"And who looks after you?"

"I look after myself."

"Where do you stay?"

"Here and there. No real place in particular."

She turned and began walking toward the shazhia's platform.

"Where are you going?" Pasha called after her.

"Come and see."

Pasha followed her as she turned right at the shazhia's platform and went through another arched doorway leading to some stairs.

By the spiraling staircase, Pasha ascended the temple tower. Though the journey up wore at his knees, he did not show discomfort, as Mahlinya did not.

Once they had reached the top, Mahlinya spread her arms wide while she moved to the center of tower's upper level.

"I love coming up here and looking out on the city and people."

Catching Pasha's gaze, she turned and twirled several times as if in a dance.

She laughed when she caught sight of Pasha's confused look. She went toward the edge of the tower and leaned against the waist-level wall that wrapped about it.

"Sometimes I think if I come up here, my problems down there won't be able to find me," she said, nodding toward the city streets below. One of her hands reached up to pull back her headdress. A light breeze blew through her hair, slightly waving her long, black locks.

"Do they find you?" Pasha asked.

"What?" she said, seeming surprised by the question.

"Your problems. Do they ever find you up here?" Pasha asked again.

"Not usually. Most of the time, Daiyu is merciful," she answered.

"It's a shame not much of that mercy goes to the warriors on the ground."

"Do you talk only of war and despair?"

Pasha cursed himself for upsetting her. "These days, those are the only subjects in abundance."

"They tell your story in the marketplace and here in the temple. Of how you were sent by Daiyu to vanquish this evil that has been set upon us. At first, many did not believe in you or the other tribes, but the last battle has many convinced that better days are coming."

"That is what we hope," Pasha said, looking out at the city.

"For someone who is supposed to be a holy warrior, you're not often seen in the holy places," Mahlinya said as she turned to face him.

"I leave the holiness to others more practiced in it," Pasha answered.

Silence came between them once more. Mahlinya began walking around the line of the wall, running her hand along the smooth stone.

"Those markings you drew on that woman's face. What do they mean?" asked Pasha.

"The Ring of Shakana is a symbol of love and renewal in Daiyu. The seven marks on the forehead are for the seven truths revealed to the Oracle during her seven months in the mountains of Tabor. We reminded those women who have been hurt and whose faith troubled that they are still loved by the father. A lot of people in this city have forgotten that."

"You like helping people," Pasha said.

"It brings me joy," she said, smiling as she circled the inside of the tower.

"I see. Is that why you tend to the wounded and sick? For joy?"

"Joy and satisfaction come in many forms. For me, it is when I am helping people. What brings you joy, Kaudi?"

Tremendous waves of sudden shock riveted through Pasha's body at the question. Long before, he would have had a ready answer. In that moment, he could find none.

Mahlinya stopped walking and moved toward him.

"Is it when you look at me?" she said half-teasing.

"What!" Pasha knew what she had said, but the suddenness of her inquiry only further caught him off guard. Though he had felt apprehension and worry, it had been a long time since the words and looks of a woman could make him feel as self-conscious as he did at that moment.

"Is that why you followed me here?" she continued, pressing him for an answer.

"No . . . I mean . . . it's so much more than that. I came here to talk to you and learn about you. To see if there was anything I could do for you. To thank you for taking care of my men," said Pasha, cursing himself when his tongue stumbled.

"I understand," said Mahlinya, smiling.

She turned to the horizon. Much time had passed. The sun fell in the west while darkness crept over much of the city.

"It's getting dark," said Mahlinya, her tone becoming grave. "They'll be coming anytime now."

"Who?" asked Pasha.

"It's the sixth night."

Pasha nodded in understanding. He had almost forgotten.

"Are you afraid?" Pasha asked.

"No. Daiyu will keep us," she said with conviction.

Pasha joined her as she went to look over the wall, down into the streets where people moved about in hurried fright. The darker it grew, hurried steps became full sprints. Mothers called out to their sons and daughters frantically while others swept them up from the streets.

At that moment, a column of Halor and Naua warriors on patrol marched down the quickly emptying streets. The warriors helped clear the city center and neighboring streets of beggars and the old. They also assisted mothers in finding lost children. Eventually they spread out into three groups while one took up positions in the city center directly in front of the temple.

A terrified group of women and children tore across the street to make their way toward the temple.

"It makes them feel safe to be here when they come," said Mahlinya.

"Do these spirits do anything in particular to people when they pass through?" asked Pasha.

"When they passed through three weeks ago, five hundred people disappeared, mostly children."

"Disappeared?"

"Vanished. In spite of our searches, they were never found. We have no idea what happened to them. That is why the mothers fear this day more than any. It's frightening enough when your child dies, but having them disappear is even more painful. There!"

Pasha looked down as shouts and cries filled their air. A bright silver mist appeared from nowhere and began to fill the streets below. A thunderous song of shouting, crying, and high shrieking laughter began to fill the city along with the midst.

Pasha saw hundreds of people in silver fill the streets and surge forward against the Halor group, which had stayed. Their appearance was haggard, dazed, and rotting. Many wore thin frames and faces, seeming to possess nothing of who they were when they lived.

The Halor warriors came together with shields raised and swords drawn as they were overwhelmed by the dead.

"Daiyu no!"

The sight was horrendous. Swinging Halor swords touched only air while dozens of hands seized them and dragged them to the ground, biting them at their necks and faces. Screaming and bloodied Halor warriors tried to escape but were quickly caught and dragged back into the fray. Dead hands took hold of the warriors and hurled them dozens of feet in the air.

In only moments, the Halor were broken. They had no retreat, as the spirits surrounded them in a thick wall of dead flesh. Their screams only became louder as the howling, shrieking spirits tore at their flesh. Pasha did not know if they were trying to kill them or merely cause them pain. All he knew was that paralyzing fear now swept over the Halor, many of whom barely resisted, being too frightened to do anything.

"Stay here," Pasha said to Mahlinya as he turned toward the arched doorway leading to the descending stairs.

"No!" Mahlinya said as she ran in front of him. "They will kill you! We're safe here!"

"Get out of the way." Pasha pushed her back.

On his descent, his sword hand retrieved his blade from its locked scabbard. The captain did not know what he was going to do; all he knew was that he had to act.

The moment he came to the ground level of the temple, leading out to the streets, his eyes beheld a terrible sight. Dozens of the spirits were now ascending back into the night sky, carrying terrified warriors in their grasp.

Pasha sprinted toward the warriors in all haste. He stopped just a couple of feet from the outside of the group of spirits. At first they continued to feast on the warriors without taking notice of him.

"Let them go!" he shouted.

To his surprise, they stopped and became silent. All of them turned to look at Pasha, gazing at him with contempt but a bit of fear.

A large man whose skin had been brightened with the blood of Halor warriors pushed through them toward Pasha. He stopped only a few feet away from him.

"Do not come between us and those we have claimed if you value your life," he shouted in a deep, raspy voice that echoed in the night air. "They are ours now!"

"They belong to no one. Release them now!"

"Before, you may have ruled over us. But your time is over. You escaped us many times, but you shall join us soon."

"Release them now and leave!"

"Or what? What can you do to the dead?"

As the spirit's eyes bore down into Pasha's own, the captain felt no fear. In that moment, Pasha felt nothing only purpose.

The captain rushed toward the laughing spirit, with his sword hand hanging ready at his right side.

In one swift motion, the blade arched upward into the spirit's chest. The man continued to laugh hysterically until he looked down. Starting out in an almost unnoticeable stream, dark blood began to soak through his raiment.

"How di . . ." His voice faltered as he lost strength. Before Pasha could react, he had fallen.

For the first time, he saw fear when he looked upon the spirits. In an instant, they released the warriors and began rushing down the street.

Pasha pursued them, cutting down as many as he could. Dozens fell beneath his sword, and others tried to resist. But none triumphed as Pasha passed through them.

Several spirits turned back and pounced. He dropped his shoulder as they fell into him and knocked them back. His sword had moved among all of them before they could rise back up completely.

Once he had reached the Halor warriors, most of the spirits were in full flight and returning to the sky from where they had come.

"Help! I need help!" shouted Pasha as he tended to the warriors.

Most were bloodied and bruised with bits of flesh missing from their faces and necks. Pasha began turning them onto their backs while trying to bind their wounds with bits of his robes.

"I need help!"

Shukimbo and Varansi rushed out of the temple grounds, swords drawn.

"Kaudi. Are you all right?" asked Varansi once they had reached him.

"See to them! They're bleeding out! Shukimbo, gather some physicians!"

Shukimbo hesitated as he looked back and forth between the injured warriors and the streets around them.

"Shukimbo!" Pasha shouted

"Right away, sir!" he said. Shukimbo rushed off toward the buildings on the other side of the city center.

Together, he and Varansi tore apart parts of their robes and those of the warriors to make bandages to bind their wounds.

"What on earth did they do to them!" shouted Varansi over some of the warriors' moans and cries of pain.

Pasha did not answer. He too was having trouble understanding everything that had happened.

And then when he looked up, he saw the stranger in silver armor who had appeared before.

"Who are you?" said Pasha.

The stranger stared with great intent upon Pasha, as if trying to give him a message. However, the warrior said nothing.

"Sir?" asked Varansi.

But the moment Varansi turned to look, the stranger had vanished.

The captain looked up to the tower where he saw Mahlinya gazing down. She did not seem to be looking at Pasha but the place where the stranger had appeared.

After a few moments, her gaze seemed to shift directly toward Pasha. She could see him too. Pasha could feel it.

CHAPTER 20

A Time of Confession

The day started out as a somber occasion for all in the city. Although many of the bodies from the previous battle had already been gathered and burned, there were still a great many that had lain in the field uncovered. The delay had also been a result of most of the executed conscripts' bodies being burned days before to make sure none would be placed with the honored dead.

None of the warriors who gathered just outside the southern gates failed to miss the stark contrast between the bright, cool, sunny day and the sad event they took part in. While the people watched near the gates and what was left of the walls, the warriors gathered in four tight columns before eight massive body pits. In between each column stood four men with burning torches.

Pasha stood at the head of them while the alcalde and shazhia looked on. Abayomi and Nalar, who had recovered his strength, stood among the men.

The captain stepped forward to look down into the first pit; in it were most of the men from his old unit. Now only a few dozen remained.

His eyes burned red at the sight of Leyos in the middle of them all, his flesh in the beginning stages of rotting.

A quick prayer was said and torches lit, telling Pasha it was time. He took a torch from one of the men as the rest of the torchbearers spread out among the pits. The captain looked upon

Leyos and his men once more. Without looking back upon them, he threw the torch into the pit, and within moments, the heavy flames feasted upon the flesh of his men.

Pasha walked back toward the city. His men remained with clenched fists raised to the sky, silent as women came from the city and mourned and ululated over the dead warriors.

In the center of the city, dozens of people crowded the doors leading into the temple courtyard. Most of the people who waited were marked with the signs of sickness and wearied by the pangs of hunger.

Inside, the sick were seen by physicians and women of the city while the lower priests passed out food. The shazhia, who was more than conspicuous in his red robes, white tunic, and red turban, went out among the hungry and sick, offering words of comfort and blessing.

On the right side of the courtyard, which was the furthest away from the doors, the women of the city looked to the sick.

Mahlinya cradled the head of a small boy who was barely conscious as the Yashani physician, Sajal, looked over his body. Behind the physician was the boy's anxious mother whose tear-stained face had yet to dry. One of the other women there stood with the mother, comforting her while Sajal did his work.

"You see how his stomach is swollen," said Mahlinya to Sajal. "It's hard like a stone. Nearly half the children we've seen today have been like that."

"Yes, I see it," responded Sajal.

"And he gets a bad fever too. Every night, he burns so bad!" said the mother frantically as tears overcame her again.

Sajal looked at the boy's emaciated face and into his eyes, which were blood red.

"How often does he eat?" said Sajal to Mahlinya, who repeated the message to the boy's mother.

"Once a day at the most," she said.

"When was the last time he ate?" said Sajal.

Mahlinya repeated the question.

"It's been three days since. My man could not get us any food from the granary. They said they wouldn't be giving any more out until tomorrow. Oh please, is he going to be all right?" she wailed.

"Don't worry. He'll be fine," said Sajal in an unconvincing tone.

"Majirah. Would you?" he said to the woman next to the mother.

Majirah gently moved the woman to a distance away from her son, wrapping her arms about her in comfort as she did so.

"Is he starving like the others?" asked Mahlinya.

"That's part of it," said Sajal. "It's harder on children to go without food. But three days wouldn't have left him like this. There's something else. I'm thinking these sores down here on his thighs . . . this may be what we're looking for."

"What could it be?"

"I don't know. It might be something in the water, something bit him. I just don't know. I'm going to have to bleed him."

"He's just a boy," Mahlinya protested. She looked down on him as his head tossed and turned wearily. Small moans escaped his mouth as he did so. Mahlinya continued wiping his face, which was continually inundated with sweat.

"I have no choice. Whatever this is, it is killing him. I doubt he has another three days left. Bring the frame and see to the mother."

Mahlinya removed her loosely kept turban and placed it under the boy's head as she rose to leave. With another woman's help, Mahlinya retrieved the tall, open wooden frame from the temple steps and placed it before Sajal and the boy. Moments later, a long thick mantle was spread over the open frame, blocking Sajal and the boy from the sight of his mother.

"What are you doing?" shouted the mother in fright. "Saiyeri! Saiyeri! What are you doing to my boy!" Majirah came behind and started to tug her back.

"It's all right," said Mahlinya, blocking the woman's path.

"What are you doing to my boy! Let me see him! Saiyeri!"

"Listen. He'll be all right," said Mahlinya as she gently held the woman back.

Her tongue stammered, and her breath tightened as she pleaded with them.

"Please, he's all we have left. Please just make him feel all right! Please save my boy! Just . . ." The woman collapsed in a fit of tears in Mahlinya's arms, worried and frightened by what would happen next.

The yelps and screams of a child rippled through the temple courtyard.

"Amah! Amah!" wailed a child for his mother.

"Saiyeri!" The woman pushed violently against both women, but they held her firm.

"My boy! What are you doing to my boy! Let me go! He needs me!"

In spite of how much Mahlinya wanted to let her go, she knew she couldn't. All eyes in the courtyard turned on her and Majirah as they tried to calm the woman down.

Soon the boy's cries died down, and all was silent.

"Saiyeri!" wailed the mother. She finally stopped resisting, and their grip slackened.

The shazhia came behind them and reached out to the crying mother. "Why don't you come sit with me, my daughter," he said quietly as he wrapped his arm around the woman's shoulders. The shazhia led her toward a canopy beside the temple steps where they both sat on two high wooden stools.

Mahlinya looked at Majirah and then toward the covered frame. A small stream of tears soiled her face as she looked around toward the hungry people filling the courtyard and the sick who were being tended to beside the courtyard walls. Mahlinya prayed silently, hoping for only good to come out of that day's labor.

Sajal finally stepped out from behind the frame. The sight was not promising, as he was covered in blood from his hands to his forearms.

Mahlinya stared at the Yashani physician as if in a daze. Seeing blood had always affected her, but seeing the blood of a child caused a sickening pain to overwhelm her.

"Have his mother see me when she's ready. He's going to need to rest awhile."

Sajal said no more. Not looking back, he made his way toward the gates leading outside of the courtyard.

Mahlinya left Majirah in charge of the other women looking to the sick while she went and sought solitude.

Inside the dark marble hall just outside of the sanctuary, she sat on the edge of the small pool, gazing aimlessly into the water.

The water seemed to sparkle in the room of darkness, receiving its light from an open window directly above it. Mahlinya observed how clear and peaceful it seemed, nothing like the lives they lived.

Mahlinya turned when she heard approaching steps.

"I see you like solitude as well," Pasha said as he stepped out of the darkness.

"At times," she said.

"A lot of people here today."

"The rationing is getting worse. Some days I barely recognize this city."

"You grew up here?"

"I was born in Haretii village, but my father brought us here when I was eight."

"Us?"

"My mother, my two sisters, and my brother. I remember when caravans would come from all corners of Sashra. Riverland traders would bring teas and fish, Ashuli merchants brought fine linen and silk, and Kirarani traders brought salt. Some months we even got traders from Kadisha who brought all sorts of things—cloth, gold, beautiful stones, all sorts of meat and seed. My sisters and I would go to southern gates every day to see the different caravans come in. We always got excited when merchants would give us a bit of fruit from the central provinces or let us taste real Riverland tea.

"I remember once when this Ashuli trader gave us some *daishi* cloth. It made us so happy, especially my sister Jakira. She always liked fine things and could make the most beautiful dresses. Shamai could be like that too, but usually she was a bit more reserved like me. Jakira could talk to anybody and make friends easily. She was so pretty too."

"What about your brother?"

"Oh, Qawole. My sisters and I were the jokers, Jakira even more than Shamai and me. But Qawole was serious like an old man, even as a boy," she said laughing.

"Not very talkative?"

"Silent as a rock. Still, he was the youngest. I suppose being born in a family of girls made him like that. Qawole loved us though, and he always looked out for us. And he'd fight any man or boy he thought was bothering us, no matter their size."

"You were happy here?"

"Oh very. My father was just a common laborer and farmer when he brought us here, but he and my mother made us feel as rich as the wealthiest merchant. He would clean the streets and worked as an apprentice for an iron worker until he learned enough to do it himself. My mother was very proper. She'd let us enjoy ourselves, but she wouldn't let us go wild like some children in the city. There was always enough food, and we always had clothes. When we came here from Haretii, every day in this city was like an adventure for us. We thought it would never end. Never," she said, staring into the water.

"I saw you with the mother and the boy."

Mahlinya looked up at him but said nothing. Pasha walked around the pool to the side she was sitting on. He sat down beside her. "It hurts you to see so many people in pain. I know what it's like."

She looked at Pasha. His gaze had not wavered for a moment.

Mahlinya's face swelled with tears. "I barely recognize this city anymore, and I can't stand it! You men! You make war in an instant. But it is the women and children who pay for it!" Mahlinya turned her head away from the sparkling pool and from him. She loved and hated the way he hung onto her every word and gave her utterances such great importance, as if they were more sayings of Nateo to be copied down.

"Your family, they're gone, aren't they?"

Heaviness came over her, but she said nothing.

Although hesitant, Pasha reached out his hand and grasped hers while it rested on the pool edge's marble stone.

"I've been there," he said softly.

Her head turned quickly. She looked down at Pasha's hand as it wrapped around hers. Contrary to what her common sensibilities told her, she did not resist his touch. To her surprise, her desire for more only increased. The feel of his palm was rough yet surprisingly warm and pleasant. For the first time, Mahlinya met his gaze.

"What do you want from me?"

"I want you to let me heal the hurt so you can hope again."

Mahlinya gazed long and hard at the captain. The captain's deep brown eyes seemed mournful yet caring. When she looked at his wearied face, she discovered the same warmth and longing that she hid deep within her. In each moment she looked at the captain, she felt her control slipping away.

"I must go," she said, abruptly rising from the edge of the pool and making her way back to the courtyard.

Pasha sighed. Where emptiness had once reigned over him, a longing for her had begun to firmly take hold. The captain thought that he would never again find himself so drawn to a woman. But once again, the fates had caught him off guard.

For a long while, Pasha remained there thinking of what he had said to her and what he should have said. Nagging feelings of foreboding needled at the captain as he thought on the future. War was no time for pursuing a woman, but then again, for some it was the only time.

Never before had he imagined his life as it was at that moment. Living without Hadassah, not knowing what had become of his son. The cruelty of existence had thrown a high number against him; all he could do was learn to live with it.

After a long while, the captain's mind returned to his purpose in coming to the temple that day. The last vision had left him deeply unnerved. For such a long time, he thought he could live with the constant invasions of his thoughts, but the last time had convinced him that he could no longer ignore what was happening to him.

Pasha found the shazhia had returned from the courtyard and was in the sanctuary alone. When he entered, he found Cafura's chief holy man lighting a line of candles placed in a long row before his platform.

"Though we have so many questions, often times we don't understand the answers. That is what my mentor called the irony of man. We can ask so many questions yet have so little understanding."

Pasha was not sure whom the shazhia addressed. Nevertheless, he steadily moved closer.

"I think that's why we come here. We come seeking answers to light our paths just as these candles give light to this room."

"Shazhia," said Pasha in acknowledgment.

The shazhia continued his labor with the candles. "This is the last place I would have expected someone whose faith turned its back on him to be."

"Things are changing, Shazhia."

"As they must, my son."

"I have been troubled with visions of things I don't understand. Terrible things."

"You see things that have happened, but you don't remember. People that you know but have never met."

"What do you know of this?" asked Pasha.

"I know that the warrior with the red eyes has invaded your thoughts more than once. I know of the connection between you and him that you have only recently realized."

"You know something of him?"

"I know that this warrior in the visions is no stranger. And that he and the red-eyed general to the north are one and the same."

"They say you have the gift of sight, Shazhia. You know what this is that plagues me, don't you?"

"Visions are a window into the heart and the soul. When Daiyu gives them, he gives them with a purpose. Sometimes it is to warn, other times to remember."

"And what is it that I must be warned of or remember? How do you know these things about me that I have told no one?"

The shazhia paused from his labor, turning his head toward an image on the right side of the wall behind his platform.

Pasha looked at the image. Though he had seen it during his last visit to the sanctuary, he had never truly realized what it was. The image was a mural of a heavily cloaked figure holding a Ring of Shakana in two outstretched palms. The figure stood between two warriors with drawn swords in their left hands, their right reaching out to grasp the Ring of Shakana.

"When I was younger, my father told me of that image and what it meant. It is of the Forgotten War and the two warriors."

"What is that?"

"They don't call it forgotten for no reason. There were two warriors. One kind and gentle, the other passionate and worldly. The purpose of their birth was to be guardians of the people. As youths, both shared close bonds of friendship. But when they grew into men, one of the warrior's passions overwhelmed him. He became proud and lusted for power. Eventually he fell into the way of dark magic and became a great sorcerer while the other warrior continued his duty to protect the people of Daiyu. Finally the proud warrior raised an army of sorcerers and pagans and made war on his gentler friend."

"And what happened?" Pasha asked when the shazhia stopped speaking.

"There is only one who can give you the answers you seek, Kaudi. Go to the temple tower this night, and you will know all."

The shazhia turned back toward the doors leading out of the sanctuary.

Pasha followed him as he went.

"Know what, Shazhia? What will I know? Tell me!" Pasha said, seizing the holy man by his arm. The shazhia stopped, looking down at Pasha's hand clasped around his arm and then at Pasha.

"The way leads to all understanding, Pasha. In the coming days, you're going to need to remember that."

Having nothing to say in response, Pasha removed his hand from the shazhia's arm and let him pass.

As the day went on, the captain joined his men in a clearing just two miles from the eastern gates of the city. They used it for a temporary training ground when they could, and given the upcoming expedition, more training would be needed. Much of the training was in the form of spear combat drills and archery, with some moments of sword work. There would need to be extra mounted drills as well, Pasha thought to himself. He hoped the horses would serve their masters well in the coming days; finding extra food for the horses and other necessary animals was becoming a problem. When they met the enemy, things would move quickly. They had to be prepared.

Dusk came quickly, reminding him of his pending engagement. After returning with Abayomi and his men back to the barracks, the captain made his way to the temple.

After returning to the temple grounds, he followed the path he had previously trekked with Mahlinya to the temple tower. By then, darkness completely engulfed the city.

He had passed the sanctuary unnoticed, but through an open arched doorway, he saw what the alcalde had spoken of before. Rows and rows of women and some men fearfully held their sons as the shazhia and lower priests said prayers and blessings over them.

The captain stopped when he arrived at the base of the steps leading up into the spiraling tower. A twinge of apprehension needled into his consciousness, but he quickly plucked it out. Now was the time for answers, not fear.

Pasha stepped onto the tower steps, climbing higher and higher toward the unknown. Though he bore a torch to light his way, the darkness before him seemed impenetrable. His journey ended faster than he expected. Raising his foot once more, Pasha reached the last step and pushed himself up into the top of the tower.

His eyes immediately discerned a figure in black robes looking out on the city near the edge of the tower.

"Are you the one who has the answers I need?" said Pasha, moving closer.

The stranger in black turned. Pasha looked intently upon the person whose face was covered in a headdress.

"You have never needed to go far to find them, Pasha. They've always been inside of you, in your dreams and your visions."

The voice seemed familiar.

"What do you know of that?" Pasha demanded. "Who are you? If you're responsible, I want this to stop!" To his surprise, the captain found himself shouting. He wanted someone to be angry at, and the mysterious stranger seemed the perfect choice.

The stranger reached for the headdress and unraveled a small knot on the left side that held it together. Slowly the left hand pulled the headdress down.

Pasha stopped breathing as the headdress touched the stone beneath.

The moon's light struck the tower to reveal a young woman with smooth brown skin and luscious black hair. Her features were sharp and distinct with full lips, finely cut cheekbones, and perfectly positioned eyes. Pasha remained transfixed on her eyes. They were the same green globes of light that had gazed into his eyes with unwavering love and devotion. Pasha had never thought he would ever again feel the warmth of her gaze. In that moment, she looked at him in the same way.

"Mother?" said Pasha.

"Yes, my son. Do not be afraid."

Pasha circled her a couple of times as he studied her. The woman who stood before him was indeed Larea. Not one part of her bore any blemish. She was as young as the day that Pasha had last seen her and radiant like the sun.

Many tears swelled in Pasha's eyes. "I saw you . . . I saw you in the field. I saw where the blade . . . tore through your bosom," he said tearfully.

She reached out and took Pasha's hands. The warmth of her flesh shocked Pasha as she took his hands and placed them on her bosom, over the place where the wound had been. "I'm here, Pasha. I've always been here."

Anger gripped the captain, and he tore his hands away from her. He stepped back hurriedly.

"What are you?"

"Pasha, it's me. Your mother."

"I don't know you!" he shouted.

"Pasha, please," she said, moving toward him.

"I don't know you!" Pasha backed into the wall of the tower.

"Please, son, it is me, you must believe it. You know it is me!"

"I saw them put you into the ground beside Asdalaya. I saw them lay Zailo in your arms as they buried both of you. The shazhia said the prayer of the dead for you. How does a ghost have the warmth of summer in her hands?"

"You have always had the answers inside of you, Pasha. You have only to search for them. I know this is difficult, but it is me, son. Your mother. You have now come to a crucial part of your path, and I wish to make sure you see it through. It's time for you to remember, son, remember who you are!"

"And who is that?" said Pasha in challenge.

"To understand that, you have to understand who I am. When I was seventeen, voices like the ones you hear and visions invaded my thoughts. The voices told me to do things I did not understand. As for the visions, they were always of a warrior . . . a warrior . . ."

"In silver armor," said Pasha, finishing her thought.

"Tall, black, and beaming of moonlight. He would always appear in my dreams. Telling me to go somewhere. For a while, the visions and voices stopped, and so I thought they had left me. But then one day I was at the well, and the warrior appeared to me, plain as day. He told me to follow him, and I did. I followed the warrior to a mountain. Once there, he told me what was wanted of me.

"I stayed in the mountains for many years as Maikael taught me. When I left the mountains, forty years had passed, but I had only aged five years. After that, I would not age at all. I said good-bye to my parents who were dying and then later on to my brothers and my sisters. Soon, all of my family had gone, and that was when my task started.

"Nateo had died when I was thirteen, and by the time I left the mountains, it had been many years since his passing. The people's faith was weakening, and some turned toward the old ways. However, through prophecy and speaking the will of Daiyu, I helped revive their dying faith. So they called me Truthful One. One who spoke the truth of Daiyu in a world of darkness. They called me another name as well, Pasha, one that you know. They called me Oracle."

She placed both hands on his face.

"Now you must remember, Pasha. Remember!"

It was as it had been before. His mother disappeared as thousands of images of places and people flashed before him.

Larea continued, "After many years, I met a man."

Suddenly Pasha was in the green field with a solitary house. He saw his child self and another boy running toward a man who greeted them with open arms. It was a man in priestly garments, features black and soft as those of the boys he held, and a long, wavy mess of hair falling onto his shoulders.

Suddenly the boys disappeared, and there he was in the field again, this time with Lareah, Pasha's mother. Both held each other with great affection as the man layered his mother with kisses of passion.

"He was you father. His name was Yalari. I loved him dearly. Your older brother, Janaha, and you. My first children."

His body was yanked from the scene once more as a flurry of images rushed past him. He watched as the boys grew from boys into men in seconds. Each year seemed more distant, and soon they were fighting.

The captain's feet landed in the midst of an unfamiliar jungle where the other boy sat around a fire with two women. On the other side stood Pasha.

"This way of yours is filled with lies and trickery, brother. You only fool yourself by pretending otherwise."

"And you have all the answers, no? Slaughtering a temple full of women and priests who do not see your way! Murdering our father!" The other Pasha shouted angrily.

"The only way to kill a lie is to cut out its tongue, take out its head, and tear out its heart."

"That is your way! Not mine! I will no longer be silent and do nothing while you let your hatred consume you and everyone around you."

"We could do great things together, Pasha. We have a great power, you and I. It comes not from some god but from within us."

"That power was given to our mother, who gave it to us when we were born. But you have corrupted it, Janaha. You shame our mother and our family!"

"You shame yourselves by continuing to believe in these lies and by resisting me when I try to free you with the truth. I'm warning you, Pasha. Brother or no, if you stand against me, what happened to father will happen to you."

"I regret that I am your brother and that I have to do this."

The other Pasha reached for the sash about his robes. His hands withdrew three knives, which he quickly launched at the other brother.

The blades missed Janaha as he fell back, but nothing could be done to save the women as the knives cut into their necks.

"You bastard!" shouted Janaha.

He came to his feet and crossed his arms with his palms outstretched. Within seconds, a reddening flame was born into his hands and launched toward Pasha.

Pasha crossed his arms in the manner of his brother, and the flame suddenly bounced off his flesh and to the side. Janaha repeated this movement as he said many curses toward his brother. More and more flames escaped from his hands and hurtled toward Pasha. Soon the whole jungle became engulfed into a huge ball of fire.

His mother's voiced continued. "He grew distant and left us. Your brother fell into the company of two witches who taught him all manner of dark magic. He became consumed with power, and his hatred for you and us grew. Your brother raised a mighty army to crush you and all the people who followed the way."

Images of burning homes and armies marching under strange banners filled Pasha's head. He saw the duel again where he and his brother battled before each of their armies.

"But he could never overcome you because the both of you were too close."

In an instant, he was there with the two brothers as they dueled. Strange hissings and whisperings filled his head; within moments, he realized he was hearing each of the brothers' thoughts.

"Get out of my head!" he shouted.

Something began to happen in Pasha at that moment. When he looked out at the sparse, dusty field they were in, familiarity began to return. That day seemed familiar; he remembered the stale air, the crows circling above. Around the other Pasha's neck was an amulet of blue beaded stones his father had made for him as a child. With each passing moment, the other Pasha's world seemed real and his false.

"Enough!" Pasha shouted. "Enough of this!"

In a sudden jolt, he was snatched from that place and hurled into the stone floor of the temple tower.

"Pasha!" said his mother, falling down beside him to help him steady himself. "You remember now. You know, don't you? These days would not have happened if it had not been for me. If I had seen when I did not, so much of this evil would not have visited you, my son."

"Did you know before they killed my brothers?"

"What?"

Pasha turned his head to face her. Angry words left his lips as he spoke. "Your sons! Zailo, Asdalaya, Malakim . . ."

"I know their names, Pasha."

"Do you? Do you really?" Pasha shouted, pushing her away as he stood back up. "Do you remember the color of Zailo's eyes? Do you remember how Malakim used to work so hard though his left leg was deformed? Do you remember how Zailo could sing! How noble and loyal Asdalaya was and how we looked up to him? Do you remember that! Because I swear with all your riddles and stories of a past life and visions and sorcery, I think you've forgotten!"

"I have not forgotten my children, Pasha. I have not forgotten one of you!" she said as tears trickled down her face.

"Then tell me. Why have I survived all this time and not them? If you are the Oracle, why didn't you stop that from happening? Why did you pretend to be killed along with them? If you are the Oracle, then what am I? How is it that a man who lived centuries ago can be my brother as well as men who lived only years ago?"

"Pasha, I . . ."

"Tell me that, Mother! Tell me why I was so special and Zailo wasn't! Why do I have memories of two lives?"

"Like I said. All of this comes back to me and Yalari. For more than one hundred years, I had been alone, and my desire for companionship grew. That's when I met Yalari. I did not think of the consequences when I married him, the consequence of coming together with a mortal."

"That's what we are, Janaha and I. Hajjaram."

"You and your brother are the result of something that shouldn't have been, coming together. Hajjaram in the old tongue means two who are one, two who are bound. When a mortal and one who is not mortal come together, the essence of the child that is conceived cannot be contained in one body.

"Therefore, two children are born. One is born kind and gentle with a peaceful nature. The other is born kind as well, but also passionate, at times brazen, with a hunger for authority. What connects the two children are strong bonds of love that can keep them unified, peaceful. But when the other child fights those bonds, rage and out-of-control passions can overwhelm him. That is what happened to your brother.

"The farther away from you he drew, the more power hungry and out of control he became. I realized that this singular nature between the two of you could be a problem. But I also believed that it could be harnessed for good. Your father, Yalari, believed it most of all.

"But I realize the truth now. The both of you are a blessing and a curse. Janaha destroys cities and men while you are destroyed from within. That is the nature of the dual nature. You are two opposites who are one. But one part of you is trying to destroy the other."

"I died before, didn't I? In the city of Muzha?"

"On that day, you defeated your brother but only temporarily. Janaha escaped the battle and fled to the coast. From there, he opened up the heart of the Mulamash Sea and descended into Getzumbo."

"What is Getzumbo?" asked Pasha.

"An abominable place. It is where those who are between mortality and immortality go to escape death and return to the land of the living when a bridge is made. Janaha had wounded you fatally in the battle, just as you had done the same to him."

"Why am I still alive then?" asked Pasha.

"The nature of the Hajjaram is that they are constantly reborn after they die."

"Reborn?"

"When Miori and I conceived our last child, your essence came into that child, and you were reborn. I felt Janaha's presence growing stronger, and I knew that it was time."

"Why did you have more children with Miori after what had happened with me and Janaha? Weren't my brothers Hajjaram as well?"

"No, they weren't. I was cursed with the weakness of mortality after what I did."

"So what are you now? A spirit?" asked Pasha.

"I have come back to let you know the truth. The truth about who you are."

"With all that foresight, you seem to not see the most important things."

"I loved your brothers, Pasha. I loved all my sons, but what was important was making sure you were born again and that someone capable of defeating Janaha would be around when he rose again!"

"What about Hadassah? What about my son, Mother? Why weren't their lives important enough to save?"

"Hadassah's death is what spurred you to go to war and put you on the path toward Janaha."

"So you knew!" he shouted. "You knew and you just let her die! You knew and just watched my son be taken away!"

His mother turned her head to look out upon the city. "There's a lesson I've finally learned after so long. Only one thing is as important as how you live your life. It's what you leave behind. I didn't think of that before. I only thought of myself, and now look. Again a war has begun and people killed because of something I brought into this world that should not have been. That is the nature of Hajjaram, Pasha, a blessing and a curse to mankind."

His mother turned back to face him, her eyes heavy with lament and worry.

"That is your story, Pasha. You know everything now."

Pasha watched as his mother put her headdress back on and edged back toward the edge of the tower. As she did so, a sudden gust of wind swept through the tower, and she disappeared.

When the captain descended the steps of the tower and returned to the temple grounds, his ears caught the distinct sound of shrieking women and frightened children. He drew his blade and followed the sound to the temple sanctuary.

Inside, everything was dark and murky. He managed to discern the silhouettes of dozens of people shrouded in darkness at the opposite side of the temple, directly in front of the shazhia's platform.

At that moment, the moon shone on the quivering mass of people who were keeping their distance from something on the other side of the temple. Pasha looked to his left and saw what it was.

A hazy green midst sat at the back of the sanctuary near the doors. From inside of the midst, Pasha saw dozens of shadowy figures moving about. They seemed to be trying to move forward to get at the people cowering before them, but an invisible force seemed to be holding them back.

The captain knew immediately what it was, and he immediately stepped in front of it.

"Release us now, Pasha, and give us the blood that we are due!" said numerous raspy voices speaking as one.

"You will have no blood tonight. Not of a child, man, woman, or anyone."

"Do not come before us and our due, Captain! You will regret it dearly!"

"And you will regret it dearly if you cross me!" Pasha said without fear in his speech. He no longer feared spirits, no matter how deadly they could be. "Leave this city now or you will be destroyed!"

The voices all cursed to one another but said nothing to Pasha. They rose and flew out of the open window into the night air. The captain watched as they left.

It took the people many moments to realize what had happened. Mothers checked their boys to make sure they were not harmed while others gathered around Pasha shouting praises.

"Our sons are safe! Nuvahli has driven the spirits away! The spirits have fled before Kaudi Nuvahli."

In spite of his wish for no celebration and a great wish for solitude, they shouted and cheered his name throughout the night as the men hoisted him on their shoulders and took him out into the city. A thunderous celebration was beginning to take place in the streets.

CHAPTER 21

A Time of Action

A bewitching calm had taken hold of the city ever since the events at the temple on the seventh night. Seeing the forces that had terrorized them since the beginning of the siege turn back was a healing salve for every man, woman, and child that dwelt within Cafura's walls. For eight days, a bit of normalcy and tranquility returned to the battered city. For eight nights, dreams had returned to the people.

On the rooftop of a white cubed house in the eastern part of the city, Pasha sat with Mahlinya while two older women who were her aunts sat quietly on one side. He watched as Mahlinya tended a pot containing a strange treelike plant he had never seen before.

"What is it about that plant that makes you labor over it so?" said Pasha.

"When you've been in a prison of stone and clay for as long as us, you'll do anything to remember what the outside is like."

"Well you'll be seeing more of the outside soon enough. Soon, people will be able to wander outside of the city for a bit."

"That would be a good thing."

Mahlinya ended her task over the plant and came back to the low rooftop wall that Pasha sat against. Her hands and body pressed against it as she looked out into the horizon. The captain rose to stand beside her.

"Lately I've been missing herding. My brother, my sisters, and I would drive sheep all the way from Haretii to the city. We'd move them over those hills," she said, motioning to the hills in the east. Pasha remembered the part in their journey where they had to pass over them.

"Shamai would sing and . . . She'd always take careful count of all of them. Jakira really didn't care for them. She'd always complain about their wool getting in her hair and getting her clothes soiled. It didn't matter that we were farmer's daughters, the way Jakira would carry on was as if she thought of herself as some grand lady, a princess even. But to Shamai, they were her children. She'd sing to them and always go back if one was missing."

"What was it you liked most about herding?"

"It just being us and the sheep. I suppose just being free. What about your life in Nuva province? Was preparing to be a warrior all you ever did?"

Pasha hesitated to answer, but her reassuring gaze strengthened his confidence.

"Nuva hasn't always been my home. Along the Aliso River where I grew up with my brothers, we farmed, we farmed hard. But as for me, to tell you the truth, I used to be scrawny and delicate."

Mahlinya looked at him for a moment, laughing.

"What?" he asked.

"Nothing. It's just I can't believe that you were delicate. Go on."

"My father had gone to war many times before, as had some of my brothers. My mother had different plans. Whenever the older boys would go race horses and make spears, my mother would keep me with her."

"You poor boy. That must have been so embarrassing being with your mother all day," Mahlinya said jokingly.

"It was for a while. But I loved her, and I liked being with her. She taught me songs her mother taught her and all of the sayings of the prophet she knew."

"You can sing? Well another secret of the kaudi revealed. What songs did she teach you?" Mahlinya asked.

"Mostly songs about family and love."

"Never about war and dying?"

"No. I knew nothing of war when I was with her."

"Sing me a song then, Kaudi."

"No. No, those days are over."

"Please, Kaudi."

Heat rose in all of Pasha's body as she took hold of his hand.

"I'm sorry. I can't," he said with a mournful face.

Though he wanted to please her, in light of all that had happened, it just felt strange for him to do so.

"Is it because you saw her again?" she asked, becoming serious again.

"When I was younger, they came to me easily. But then we left the river after what happened and went to Kadesh province, and then Nuva province. There with my father and uncle, my life took a whole different path. As I grew, I stopped singing my mother's songs. I did backbreaking farm work with my father, and then I learned of hatred and violence. Seeing my wife die and losing my son only took me farther away from the path my mother wanted. Since then, my hands have always prepared themselves for war. Every time I look back on my life, I can never make sense of how I got here and what tomorrow will bring."

"There's a proverb in Haretii land. *The road changes, but the way is constant.*"

Mahlinya paused, hesitant to say anything else, but Pasha remained silent. "That's why you hurt so much, isn't it, Kaudi. What they did to your family and now these visions and seeing your mother have you wondering, what now?"

"I've always felt like the sheep. On a road but not knowing where it will end."

"Daiyu never said you had to wander alone, Kaudi," said Mahlinya, squeezing his hand tightly. She greeted his gaze with the warmth of her smile, which washed over Pasha like the most potent of potions.

Three Weeks Later

For Pasha, the time leading up to their departure went mercifully slow. For more than ten days, the forces of all the tribes had ridden west to set up a defensive line of outposts and barricades, manned by warriors eager for a new test. Heavy enemy movement in their mountain base signaled that the time of battle would come soon.

In the mountain outpost to the north of Cafura, the Halor contingent prepared to move. Inside his pitched tent along a rocky slope, King Hanasa stood as his servants helped with his armor.

The flap of his tent was pushed back to allow General Mashilo to enter. Hanasa looked back as the general came forward. He was a middle-aged man with a few graying hairs in his mostly bald scalp. Mashilo entered, armor from head to foot but with his helmet tucked under his arm.

Hanasa was grateful that Mashilo came with him. The general was a man the king had known all his life. He had served his father and had been a mentor to young Hanasa when he was a boy. Everything he knew about war had been taught to him by Mashilo. There was no one he trusted more.

The king adjusted as they fastened his chain shirt.

"Good day for a fight, no, Mashilo?"

"Any day is good if you have the determination and the strategy," answered the general.

"And how are we looking on those things."

"Promising."

Both men smiled.

"How are we looking on provisions and water?"

"In a place like this, water is easy. Food is where we may have trouble. We've put together enough for barely two weeks. But the men are ready and refreshed."

"Do you think it was a mistake, Mashilo, coming here?"

"I always taught you to do what you thought was right. That applies here more than any other place."

"You know I've been in more than a dozen battles. But today for the first time, I can't clear my head and immerse myself in strategy. I can only think of my wives and then my sons. Zhanaro most of all. I haven't been all I should have been, Mashilo."

"There's no use crying about it. You should just settle for who you are. Hanasa our king."

"Even that's not easy. Is there . . . is there any news from home, from Zhanaro?"

"No, I'm sorry, sire. I'll keep trying."

"That's all right. I know they're all right," said the king, breathing deeply.

"Why don't you have a wife and a home, Mashilo? You're rich enough. I could get you a whole palace of wives."

"I've had my fill of women, and they of me."

"Come now, Mashilo. A man wasn't meant to be alone. You may be old, but I can muster quite a few shy village maidens you can take your pick from. It'll be good to have a young body warming your old bones again. When we get home, you'll have the pick of them all."

"I've got my share of pleasures and treasures, sire."

"Of that I know much indeed, Mashilo."

"You seem on edge, Hanasa."

"Well, my friend. Like I say. Things are different today. I used to think all of this . . . coming here was such a bad idea. I fought against it so much. But now I realize that this is the point in my life that my birth was centered toward."

"Like destiny?"

"Yes, like destiny."

And so the last piece of his armored plate was fitted on, and the king went from his tent accompanied by Mashilo, going to the horses and on to battle.

CHAPTER 22

The Joys of War

By twilight of the next day, all the forces of the south had gathered in a massive defensive line spanning the distance between the impregnable northern mountains and the treacherous jungles to the south.

For most of the night, Pasha had ridden its length instead of seeking sleep. The mountains of the north had been still for more than three days. Though he knew not the man, Pasha knew for sure what the enemy general was doing. His mind did not linger on whether to attack the southern forces, but when.

If the enemy saw the many barricades and pikes they were building, their coming would be soon. Along every part of the line there were barricades to slow a cavalry charge and protect against a barrage of arrows.

Pasha and Abayomi returned to the Sashraman part of the camp. Daylight would be coming soon, and both men had not yet slept. Inside of the officers' tent, Abayomi crashed into the soft mats while Pasha and Nalar stayed up.

"It's hard to sleep, knowing you have so much to do," said Nalar.

Pasha nodded. "How are your officers shaping up?" he asked.

"They're fine warriors, though I do wish they had a bit more experience."

"Well this place will give them plenty of that."

"Do you really think they're going to come after us on open ground?"

"They have no choice. They won't stay holed up in the rocks forever."

"Just like us now, aren't they. Backed into a corner with only two choices, fight or die."

"Well, when they come, they won't easily acquire the triumphs they're used to."

"There hasn't been word from General Cheokto in weeks. It's got some of my officers worried.

"Tell them that lapses in communication are normal. All that matters is that the general and his men are holding on, as shall we."

"You know I've had dreams of this moment. I feel like we're on the verge of something big here. Either that or something terrible."

"After all we've been through, I'd say we're way overdue for some good fortune."

"What's next after this, sir?"

"Hopefully we push them back north and end the war by the year's end," said Pasha.

"I'd like that," said Nalar.

"You know, I don't know where you're from, Nalar, or much about your life there. You never talk about it much."

"There isn't much to say. The army has been my life. I joined at sixteen."

"What did your parents have to say about that?" Pasha asked.

"I wouldn't know. I never knew them."

"They died?" Pasha asked.

"No. I never knew them," Nalar repeated. He paused to draw in a heavy breath. "My mother was a whore."

Pasha said nothing, ashamed that he had even started the conversation.

"And my father, more than likely a late-night customer looking for something sweet. After I was born, she just went to the walls surrounding the temple and left me in one of the cracks. A priest saw her do it and tracked her down, tried to get her to take me back. But she refused and left. Never been able to find her since."

"I'm sorry," Pasha finally said.

"I'm not sorry. I have nothing to be ashamed of. I'm not responsible for the nature of my birth, only the way I live my life. But I keep a picture of her in my mind. The priest who raised me told me what she looks like. And sometimes I see her face in my dreams. I wonder if she knows what I am and what I do. Does she know I'm in the army? Does she sense something when I'm in danger? Yet I always fool myself by ignoring the other question. Does she even care? More than twenty-seven years later, I'm still waiting for the answer."

"Wherever she is, I'm sure she regrets what she did," Pasha said, trying to be reassuring.

"I'll never know. In the end, I'll never know," he said.

"What about a family of your own? Have you a wife, children?"

"I've had many loves but nothing proper and acceptable like a wife and a home. The army is my home, I suppose."

"And after this is over, what will you do?"

"Probably go someplace south and raise horses. And you, sir?

"You know. I've never thought about a life after all of this. I thought I would never enjoy life again or love its mysteries and dangers. But being at Cafura has changed me. I've learned to reach out to life again."

"When you find a good woman, that tends to happen."

"Abayomi has been talking to you, hasn't he?"

"Abayomi does not have to explain what a clear eye can see. I'm glad for you, sir."

"Thank you."

King Hanasa wandered through the Halor encampment, greeting his men and reviewing defenses. Though daylight was still a couple of hours away, many of the men did not sleep. They saluted their king appreciatively as he went past.

The king went to the outskirts of the camp near the barricades where small groups of archers kept watch.

"Sire," greeted one of the men.

"Captain Kanda," said the king.

"How are things here?"

"Quiet, sire. All night."

"Well, we didn't come here for quiet. Did we, Captain?"

"No we didn't, sire," the captain responded.

"They're out there somewhere. Waiting."

"And we'll be ready for them, sire," said Kanda.

"What do you think of all this. This campaign, Captain?"

"I am a Halor warrior. My duty is to live and die for you, sire."

The king smiled as he nodded. "That's what I thought you would say."

Without warning, the calm of the night air was broken by the sharp hiss of an arrow as it dug deep into an unwary warrior's chest. Suddenly dozens of lit arrows tore through the calmness of the night and ripped through the uncovered flesh of unsuspecting warriors.

Hanasa ducked down as Kanda ran behind his men shouting. "Eyes out! Eyes out!"

"Fall out! We're under attack. Fall out!" shouted the rank masters back toward the camp.

The whole of the Halor encampment was roused from its sleep and scrambled for their positions.

As the cries rung out, the Halor archers fired back blindly into the darkness. Their multiple volleys did little to stem the tide of enemy fire.

"I don't see them. Where are they?" shouted one of the men.

The same man cried out as an arrow tip punched through his exposed neck.

"Sire, fall back!" Kanda ordered the king.

But before he could react, massive figures began emerging from the darkness. Halor archers fired at them, but they were overwhelmed as the enemy returned fire in a hail of arrows and spears.

The line of horsemen was suddenly illuminated when they came within the gaze of the flames.

"Spears!" shouted Kanda. "Fall into position!"

Hanasa looked back at the camp where the first group of spearmen was just beginning to head their way. The rest of the men seemed confused about where the attack was coming from.

Hanasa drew his sword along with the rest of the archers as the massive northern horsemen bore down their spears and rode towards them. Dozens upon dozens of northern horsemen were impaled by the pikes and barricades as they went through. For a moment their charge slowed when southern pikes seared into their fellows. Nevertheless, not even the men of the south's barricades could halt the sheer force of the northern charge.

The northern horses trampled many of the archers while their masters' spears made short work of many others. Hanasa jumped onto a barricade just as a wave of horses leapt toward them.

Once they had passed, the king charged from behind them. His blade slashed the hind legs of their horses as he went forward. Having no shield, the king dodged and ducked carefully when dozens of spears lunged toward him.

He saw Kanda gathering what was left of his archers into a line. Though massive, the northern horsemen were slowed down as the first kads of spearmen arrived to reinforce them.

The spearmen pushed forward while the archers fell back to carefully choose targets.

"Protect the king!" shouted Kanda, joining the spearmen as they pressed against the northern horsemen.

Hanasa seized one of the heavy northern lances lunging toward him and flung the rider from his seat. Blocking dozens of blows, the king ascended the horse and began to furiously attack the northerners.

At that moment dozens of the enemy horsemen began to drop as Halor archers regained their momentum. Suddenly an even greater surge of arrows flung the enemy horsemen from their seats as Halor horse archers joined the fight.

The spearmen eventually reached Hanasa while they went forward punching their spears into the northern horses, causing their riders to fall onto their spear points. Horsemen were soon impaled on the long, curved Halor points while those with swords hacked them down.

Just then the king's heavy cavalry lancers circled the northern horsemen and drove into them. Before they knew it, the enemy horsemen were fleeing. However, Captain Nezhu, who led them, did not give chase. Instead, the king's men fell back to the king's position among the spearmen.

"Sire. We've been looking for you."

"Well now I'm found, Captain."

"Here," he said, gesturing to one of his men who led out the king's horse.

Hanasa let the Baku horse loose and climbed onto his own mount.

"You see any more?"

"Not yet. They were a scouting force, but the rest of them are gathering in the north east and south."

"Have any of the other tribes made contact?"

"Not yet, sir. It seems this was the only force. But they're gathering. We have to move."

Nezhu stopped and looked to the north. A brightly lit flame was flashing toward them. A similar fire soon lit in the east and the south, signaling the same message.

"They're coming now, sire."

"All right . . . get into position!" the king shouted to his men. "Get into position!"

His men hurried and formed tight columns as the king rode back toward the encampments. He shouted the orders again as men hurried to put out the last of the fire.

Soon the sound of horses filled his ears as the rest of his generals approached with their captains.

Mashilo rode at the head of the other two generals and the captains who rode under them.

"Sire," said Mashilo. "A wave is moving toward the left flank in the north, and the Mulamar are about to engage in the south. The east will be hit next."

"Who is in the north?" asked the king.

"Only Captain Jeshumbo," answered General Kimana. "General Tayla and General Marwa are pushing their forces south while General Ishok and the Sashramans are pushing north from the south."

"What are we up against?"

"It's their whole army, sire," said General Kwaba. "They're attacking mostly with heavy cavalry and archers. They're trying to breach a hole in the line."

"Right. Azota and Shiri," said the king to two of the captains there. "Take your men north and link up with Jeshumbo."

The two captains rode off immediately, and within moments, their whole kads had broken off and fallen in behind them.

"Mashilo, you go north but have your captains spread their kads along my left flank."

Mashilo immediately parted.

"Kimana, you stay on my right. Kwaba, you and your captains spread your men on Kimana's right to the south to stick with the Sashramans. All right, let's go."

Saying no more, the generals and the captains made haste to their positions.

Daylight was slowly creeping along the horizon as Hanasa sat on his mount at the head of all of his men. In his group were four kads of horse archers and a dozen units of spearmen. His mounted lancer bodyguards clustered about the king like a protective sheath, determined to not lose sight of him again.

Lines of Mashilo's spearmen stood linked up to Hanasa's while General Kimana's lancers stood ready. Kimana's lancers stood behind his captain Kanda's archers while swordsmen waited at the rear position.

Kimana's captain, Akari, had spread his kads of archers before the lines of Mashilo's spearmen on the left flank while the swordsmen stood behind the spearmen.

In the distance, the king could only capture a small glimpse of Kwaba's numerous lines of spearmen, whose standard became more visible in the increasing light.

King Hanasa looked to the right, where he saw General Kimana looking back. The general bowed his head toward the king. Hanasa returned the gesture.

The calm silence quickly ended as a blaring chorus of horns sounded across the plain.

Immediately after, a bright light fired at them as the sun came up and reflected off of the silver and bronze armor off the enemy coming into position.

Hanasa squinted his eyes. The glaring light seemed disarming to his men, who could barely look at their enemies. Still, this did not worry the king because once they had bloodied the enemy, their armor would not shine as it did at that moment.

Instead of charging, the men of the north began to pound their shields and armored chests while they cheered and lobbed curses at the men of the Halor.

He turned to Nezhu. "Show the men that we don't fear them."

His captain nodded.

Nezhu rode to the front of the line and dismounted. Reaching down, he pulled up some earth and threw it into the air before him. He repeated this action several times while shouting out to the enemy.

The rest of the men took heart and began to do the same thing while they rhythmically stomped the ground. Some ululated while others released the war cry of the Halor, which was like a high shrill ended with clicking noises.

And then they continued clicking their tongues as their feet stomped the ground in unison. Men leaped high in the air, brandishing their spears in threatening ways, others shot wads of spittle in the northerners' direction.

His men had not lost heart. The courage they would need was propagated throughout the lines.

Again the horns of the north sounded, but the men of the north had ended their taunts and now readied to fight.

Nezhu broke off from his taunting and rode back to the king's position.

A massive column of horsemen broke out from the northern lines, charging head on toward the men of the south. While the barricades they had set up would slow them, they would not undo the incoming wave of horsemen.

Soon, enemy spearmen fell in and charged, followed quickly by swords and pike men.

"Eyes out!" shouted the king.

"Eyes out!" the archer rank masters repeated.

In one calm, smooth motion, the archers drew their arrows and took aim.

All were consumed by the spirit of fearlessness and determination as they waited for the order.

Hanasa watched anxiously as the larger, thickly muscled northern horses broke up the ground beneath them in their charge toward the men of the south.

The spearmen bared their spears and locked shields as the enemy came within range.

"Fire!" Hanasa shouted.

The rank masters quickly relayed the order.

Hanasa and his men drew swords and spears as a heavy barrage of southern missiles hurtled toward the charging northern warriors.

Dozens upon dozens were flung from their seats upon impact. Scores of horses crashed into the loosened earth, their bodies stuck with arrow tips. Many who rode behind collapsed, and their horses tripped on the accruing corpses. But the charge did not stop.

Hanasa's archers fired again, this time at the spearmen. The arrows zipped through cracks in their armor and bloodied their faces. More than a hundred fell into the dirt, trampled by their fellows as they moved forward. Swirling dust and blood soon dirtied their once brightly polished armor, reducing the sun's glare.

Halor archers and horse archers picked off northern horses and spearmen that found themselves caught in the barricades while Halor spearmen went forward.

Hanasa and the lancers hit the enemy cavalry with powerful speed. Yet engaging the enemy cavalry soon became difficult. Their massive northern lances seemed to make the Halor ones useless as they bashed and tore into Halor warriors before their weapons could even come close to inflicting a blow.

Soon the men became rattled as the northern horsemen began pushing through them. Halor shields were punched through by northern lancers, knocking many warriors from their mounts to be trampled and hacked to death by northern spearmen.

Captain Akari's swordsmen were beginning to pour in from the left flank while spearmen from Kwaba's kad pushed north from the right flank.

To their surprise, northern horsemen came together and fanned into a seemingly unbreakable crescent formation. The enemy spearmen quickly fell in behind, spreading out to push Captain Akari's men back.

The lancers were merciless as they flung Hanasa's riders from their seats. Nezhu and his men clustered tightly about the king, raising their shields as the northern lances came toward them.

Their weak wooden and bronze shields seemed to explode underneath the pressure of the northern lances, and dozens of Hanasa's riders flew out of their mounts. However, the enemy advance slowed as spearmen from Kwaba's kad broke through to the king's men.

Hanasa pushed forward with his men. Northern horsemen began to wane under the pressure from hundreds of southern spearmen. The men threw themselves into the enemy horsemen and spearmen, bashing their shields into them while lunging toward exposed horse flesh.

More enemy horses and swordsmen charged. Hanasa slashed down hard at the hundreds of bodies beneath him. His head and neck swiveled from right to left to avoid rapidly moving spear points. The king's sword cut into wooden spears northern spearmen lunged toward him. With careful blows, he slashed their throats and bashed their faces with his shield.

As an enemy lancer moved toward him, the king bared his shield and lifted his sword high. The lance struck his shield with paralyzing force. Hanasa's shield cracked, and the lance point seared into his shoulder. King Hanasa was pushed back, his sword falling from his hands.

Not hesitating, the king reached to the side of his mount and retrieved a spear tucked into the belt about his saddle. Gathering all of his strength, the king swung the spear around and cracked his attacker's helmeted head.

Letting his shield and the impaled lance fall, Hanasa pulled himself back up and plunged his spear into his attacker's throat.

In a smooth, quick action, he withdrew the spear point and pushed the rider from his mount.

The number of enemies around him was becoming smaller as his men continued pushing them back.

"Sire!" shouted Nezhu. "To the north!"

Hanasa snapped his head quickly.

In the north, he could see the standards of Shiri and Azota's kads. They had been far to the north, but now they were being pushed south into Captain Benyari and Akai's spear kads. General Mashilo's captain, Akai, led cavalry lancers into a charge against the enemy, but they too were pushed back.

Shiri's men waved the black and red banners, calling for reinforcements. Hundreds of enemy cavalry were riding them down while horse archers easily downed their targets.

"Shiri's in trouble," said King Hanasa. "Forward on me!" he shouted. "Forward on me!"

The spearmen immediately began turning north instead of east while pushing the enemy back. Hanasa and his lancers went ahead of them, trampling all under their path to reach Shiri and Mashilo's captains, who were almost surrounded.

Suddenly a heavy force slammed into them as the columns of horses and swordsmen they had overlooked charged into them. Hanasa's men found themselves completely cut off as their enemies widened the gap between them, and their fellows and the enemies to their rear regained their confidence.

In the south, Pasha could see General Shabaz's men flying red and black banners, signaling they needed help. But the problem facing General Kwaba was more urgent. He had ordered his men forward upon seeing the Halor general overwhelmed by northern forces. Pasha knew that they would break soon if they did not act.

"Signal Maranhi to go south," he said to Nalar.

Shabaz would be annoyed that Pasha had not ordered all three of his kads to help him, but Pasha cared not what angered the general. Maranhi would have to do.

"Abayomi, you take them from the left. Nalar, from the right. I'll go up the middle. Drive them back with your archers and drive into them with your spearmen."

His men left immediately to get into position.

Pasha looked toward the enemy and raised his spear, urging Daimon forward to start the charge. His lancer kads all fell in behind him, bearing their lances down as they went forward.

The Sashramans struck deep into the heart of the northern spearmen. Enemy horsemen moved against them. Dozens of lances lunged toward them. Many Sashraman lancers fell as the northern lances plucked them from their mounts.

Pasha and his men fell back a ways as Varansi lead the horse archers forward and unleashed volley after volley. The enemy advance was halted. General Kwaba' men, becoming more reassured, began pushing back against the northern forces.

Soon Abayomi was circling the enemy from the north while Nalar came from the south. A few ragged lines of spearmen tried to come together to push back the advancing Sashraman lancers.

However, their lines crumbled as Sashraman horse archers fired into them.

Pasha drove forward, driving the shaft of his spear deep into the enemies beneath him. He fell right as a hard, whistling noise rang into his ears, just in time to avoid an arrow.

As many spears lunged toward Pasha and Daimon, the captain began swinging his spear to deflect their blows and strike their heads. Daimon kicked them back and trampled many as they went.

Suddenly as Pasha looked to the south, he saw rigid lines of enemy swordsmen and spearmen advancing toward them. The standards of Maranhi were nowhere to be seen.

"Where is Captain Maranhi?" he shouted.

"He's still at the rear," answered Varansi.

"What!"

In the northwest, Pasha could see Maranhi's men just starting to advance. But instead of going south, Maranhi's men advanced east, ignoring Pasha as his men waved red and black flags.

"I swear I am going to kill him!" shouted Pasha.

Having no choice, Abayomi, Pasha, and the Halor general fell back to form a line to meet the advancing enemy troops from the south. Meanwhile, Nalar pushed against the enemy to the north, trying to keep them from surrounding the Sashramans.

General Ishok and his men charged with great haste as the enemy pushed hard against the Sashramans and Halor general. Ishok moved up twelve kads of Captain Rukari's spearmen as Captain Nkuru's horse archers opened fire.

The lancers who rode with Ishok bore down their lances and drove into the enemy. Sashraman spearmen parted to give them room as they trampled and crushed the northern spearmen.

Northern cavalry were made obsolete by the Yashani horse archers as they took careful aim.

Ishok punched his lance through many of the spearmen before it got stuck in one's gut. The general immediately retrieved his bow from his back and took aim. His rapid fire tore into the many northerners before him. Though many tried to dodge it, there was little room to maneuver.

Soon the horse archers and lancers had come together in one force. In one rapid pulse, they pushed into the enemy line just as Abayomi's forces circled them and drove up their middle. This maneuver sent shockwaves circulating through the men of the north, and within moments their lines had broken.

The wave spread quickly across the line, and soon the entire enemy army was in flight.

Ishok and his horse archers joined Nalar as they gave chase, eager to drive the enemy from the field.

In the south, the Naua forces had pushed back most of the enemy force, forcing them to fall back along with the rest of their retreating forces.

Pasha and his men tore across the earth in pursuit of the enemy as they made for the mountains in the north.

By that hour, the sun had fully risen, shooting down powerful rays of heat upon the men of the south. However, the heat molested none. All that mattered was getting to the enemy and ending the battle.

Captain Jeshumbo was the furthest ahead, with Nalar trailing him. They would catch up to the enemy within moments.

Jeshumbo caught up with straggling enemy spearmen and quickly rode them down. Nalar soon caught up with him and started to work on what they could of the infantry.

About five kads of northern horsemen broke off from the northern force and charged back toward Jeshumbo and Nalar. They managed to push them back while the rest of the army retreated.

Pasha could see them in the distance reaching the beginning slopes of their mountain camps. To his surprise, they did not ascend to lose themselves in the rocky wilderness. Instead, the northern forces stopped and began to form up again.

"Half pace!" Pasha shouted.

Soon the commanders of the tribes began repeating the same order. It took a long while to slow the men down, but they eventually got the infantry to slow to a jog while the galloping horsemen went into a trot.

Eventually their speed became a brisk march as units came back together and reformed columns.

Pasha and Abayomi's forces formed up alongside one another while Maranhi's men came up from the rear.

The Halor and Mulamar slowed down enough for their units to come together and form columns, but they did not stop. Once together, King Hanasa led his men toward the center of the enemy line along with Pasha while Shabaz and his men headed north to the left flank. General Ishok, Marwa, and Tayla all fell in together to charge the enemy's right.

The air was filled with sounds of metal and flesh crashing together as Jeshumbo became the first to hit the enemy's left flank in the north. His horse archers rained down a fearsome barrage of arrows before the lancers tore into the enemy line. The captain's spearmen then quickly moved in as the enemy tried to push them back.

Within moments, Nalar's lancers had charged up the middle of the enemy line while his spearmen drew in from behind.

Pasha drew his spear as his men came near the enemy lines. Long rows of enemy spearmen bearing tall shields waited steadily for them while archers in the rear opened fire.

Dozens of Pasha's men fell out when they were struck. The captain ducked his head down as arrows whizzed by his head. Varansi and the horse archers responded with an even greater torrent of fire, aiming slightly over the heads of the spearmen before them and striking into the heart of the archers' lines as their arrows fell.

Pasha rode alongside Shukimbo and the lancers who bared their spears and steadied them as they rode into the enemy line. Abayomi's archers released short bursts of fire as his swordsmen and spearmen made contact with the enemy.

Enemy spears made little contact with them, as the men who bore them were repeatedly filled with arrows while lances tore into their flesh. Pasha managed to look back to see Maranhi remaining in the rear, although his archers were doing a good job firing upon the enemy. It annoyed Pasha that Maranhi had not followed his orders, but he did not think of it much as he went forward with his men.

Though they fought hard, the enemy spearmen were showing increasing weariness and fright. As Pasha and the men pressed them, the captain was sure that they would break soon. But then in the distance, a fresh column of enemy lancers and swordsmen rushed out from the mountain path and joined the fight. At their head rode the same Baku officer with the long, straight hair.

Pasha grinded his teeth as he thought of Yuwatu and Leyos. The warrior caught sight of him as well and began to charge toward him along with dozens of spearmen.

Arzim went quickly toward the wild-looking Sashraman. He desperately wanted to kill him and knew the battle would go easier once he did. Arzim's fixation upon the Sashraman did him harm as a southern blade cut into his exposed thigh.

Pasha drew in a deep breath while getting the Baku in his sight. Thinking of Yuwatu and his friend Leyos, he hurled the spear with all his strength.

He knew he was not good at throwing spears from horseback, but Pasha's heart rejoiced when the pole impaled the Baku officer's shoulder.

The Baku flung back on his mount but stayed on. It mattered little. The moment Arzim rose back up, a long, thin Sashraman blade came to meet his neck. Though he saw death coming, he could not escape. Pasha took his head in a clean stroke, and his headless body rode on into the fray.

Riders in black and green robes, worn over armored plates, began driving into the middle where the Sashramans were advancing. Abayomi's men met them first. In one sudden stoke, the one who rode at the head of them raised both hands, and massive fireballs erupted to consume the Sashramans beneath them.

"What the . . ." said Pasha as he lifted his arm to cover his face.

All that had been accomplished seemed to be undoing itself as the rider in black broadsided them with heavy torrents of flame. The rider seemed to sense Pasha's gaze and lifted the helmet visor covering her face. Beneath the helmet, the face of Hadassah's sister gazed back at the Sashraman captain. Though it was Helomar, she did not look at Pasha with the same arrogant contempt. For the first time, she seemed fearful and concerned as she looked at him. As Pasha looked at her, he too felt a profound change. The hatred that often consumed him when he saw her face had left him.

The small warrior who Pasha had seen before rode beside her, hacking into the burning warriors beneath him. Enemy swordsmen moved forward as bowmen began picking off the flaming Sashramans. Many of Abayomi's men were falling back as Helomar shot flame after flame into them.

King Hanasa's warriors began pushing toward the Sashramans but were cut off by the newly strengthened force. Northern horsemen broke through Abayomi's columns and began pushing Pasha's men back while swordsmen fell in.

Their dark masks that were formed into various facial expressions caused great fear among his men. Pasha's lancer kad became overwhelmed when the enemy warriors began cutting their horses down from under them. More arrows pounded into Pasha's men, knocking many from their mounts. Horses began running amok, being speared by the enemy as they pressed forward.

Suddenly a rider-less horse charged into Daimon, sending Pasha to the ground as another round of fireballs consumed his lancers and horse archers.

The captain landed painfully on bloodied corpses. Just as he rose, several spear shafts lunged toward his side. Pasha dodged most, but his quick eye missed one stray shaft as it tore through his weakened shoulder blades and lodged into his flesh. He jumped back as far as he could and drew his sword. Moving as fast he could, Pasha tore the shaft from his shoulder as enemy swordsmen jumped at him from all sides, doing their best to push him into his burning fellows behind him.

Pasha ducked and swept his blade low, slashing their legs from under them. His shoulder cried out painfully as he raised his blade to block more incoming blows. A heavy foot kicked him in his stomach, causing him to stagger back. But the captain recovered his balance and plunged his blade into the man's side as he swiped his blade toward Pasha's neck.

Only a few dozen paces away, Pasha could see Varansi and his men pushing forward to get to him while Shukimbo continued waving the red and black banner, signaling for reinforcements. However, Maranhi and his men did not move, staying in the rear and watching as fire and numerous enemies overwhelmed their fellows.

Varansi had recovered Daimon, and Pasha mounted his back once more. Once on, Pasha reached down, drew his bow, and aimed toward Helomar, who continued sending hails of flames into the warriors. His men were on the verge of routing; it had to be done.

The captain drew back and let the arrow fly. It flew fast and not as noisily as northern arrows. Though Helomar seemed unaware of the arrow hurtling toward her chest, the smaller warrior did and reached out toward her. He pulled her toward the right, barely saving her from a fatal blow. However, he did not save her from the arrow shaft entirely. The arrow glanced off of her shoulder, breaking off its point deep within her flesh.

Shock and terror swept over Helomar's face as she realized what had just happened. Pasha could see and feel her gazing back at him. She looked at him as if in wonder and confusion, not understanding what he had done or why he had done it.

Overhead, thunder roared from behind the newly formed clouds, and within moments, a hail of rain fell down upon them. Flames were doused, and cheers went through the line as

Jeshumbo and Hanasa's men broke through and began pushing the enemy back. At that moment, Maranhi finally moved in and joined them as they began to pursue the enemy.

In the south, the enemy was breaking as General Tayla and Nalar's spearmen swept through them, and the archers and quickly moving lancers thinned their lines even more.

Helomar and her warriors turned back and fled toward the mountains. Pasha tore after her, with Varansi and Shukimbo following him closely.

The horse archers lobbed volley after volley at the warriors. Many fell, but the shafts came short of hitting Helomar and the small warrior with her.

Pasha and his men followed Helomar up the rocky path leading into the mountains. Soon their mounts began to trip and stumble as they came upon rockier and steeper parts of the path.

In the distance, they could see Helomar and her followers veer off toward a cliff in the west. As they approached the rock face, they dismounted and ran, doing their best to avoid the mounds of jagged rocks and numerous boulders.

Pasha and his men did the same as they came upon the cliff. Though unwise, Pasha leapt from Daimon and sprinted as Helomar and her followers climbed up a rock formation leading to a cave opening in the cliff.

The captain's ears warned him as two quick blades lunged for him and another lay back waiting to strike. Just as he entered the cave opening, Pasha sidestepped and struck back when Helomar's followers tried to make a quick end of him. In spite of the dark, Pasha could feel the heat of their breath and hear their weariness as they panted and sweat. One fell, and Pasha blocked another's blow and kicked his stomach. While the man staggered back, he cuffed him with a free hand and drove his sword into the enemy warrior's throat.

Finally his men began climbing in from the cave opening. Though Pasha wished to continue quickly, he knew that he would need their help. With Varansi, Shukimbo, and ten other men close to him, Pasha continued through the dark cavern. By the little light that came from openings in the cave ceiling, their path was partially illuminated.

The noise of pattering feet in the distance let them know they were close. Still the men of the south proceeded at a careful pace, not knowing what surprises might lurk in the dark.

Suddenly a rapid flurry of shafts tore into them. Six of Pasha's men fell in an instant as more than nine spears came at them from the dark. Pasha and his officers along with two other men came together in a tight circle. Almost in unison, they struck back and blocked the spear shafts as they searched for open targets.

Varansi spun his head in all directions as the spear heads tried to impale him. Using his shield, he blocked a shaft and kicked it out of the hands of its owner. He ducked at once as another came for him.

Shukimbo moved quickly in between his fellow officer and hurled his blade at the warrior attacking Varansi. The sound of metal ripping through flesh filled their ears as the blade struck its target. Being without a shield, Shukimbo stood seemingly defenseless as two more spears lunged for him. Varansi jumped back to his feet and blocked one with his shield while Shukimbo sidestepped and seized the lunging shaft with his hands.

Obviously bearing greater strength than his adversary, he ripped the spear from his enemy's hands and drove it into his gut.

Pasha fell back as the two other warriors with them were struck down and five more northern warriors joined the fight. Shukimbo and Varansi were eventually pushed back and formed up with Pasha as almost fifteen warriors came towards them. The captain cursed himself for not bringing enough men. His move had been rash at best.

All let out a fearsome cry as they charged them. They came behind Varansi as he pushed back against the enemy with his shield. Shukimbo swung his spear in all directions to keep the enemy warriors at a distance.

Pasha's shoulder cried out in terrible pain, and the more he swung his blade, it felt like he held a massive boulder in one hand. Nevertheless, he made his arm work in spite of the pain. He seized a spear as it lunged toward him and slashed the neck of the Baku who held it. The captain crashed to the ground just as more spears lunged toward him. Moving quickly, he seized the enemy warrior's shield and put it to good use when he rose again.

The Sashramans managed to put down five enemy warriors to their rear, allowing them to slip off to the side of the dark cavern. Unable to see what lay behind them, the Sashramans shouted when the ground beneath them disappeared and they dropped into open air.

Their descent was brief. Pasha and his men crashed into a shallow cave stream that ran underground. In an instant, their attackers were leaping down on them. They had only one point to advance from, due to the thick mountain walls surrounding most of the opening to the cave stream. Suddenly the Sashramans had an advantage since their enemy could not surround them.

Varansi and Pasha pushed the enemy back with their shields and swords while Shukimbo took their spears and hurled them at the enemy. Two fell as he did so, but then five crashed into the water behind them, compromising their position.

Varansi and Pasha hugged the walls with their shields out while dozens of enemy warriors fell into the crevice to attack them. Water sprayed all over them when enemy boots crashed into the cave stream and began pressing against them.

The captain watched in horror as a shield-less Shukimbo tried to defend himself against five warriors with spears. Just then, a shaft tore into his thigh, causing him to stagger back. While he did so, another drove into his arm.

"No!" Pasha cried as the rest of the enemy warriors drew back their spears, preparing to lunge.

Shukimbo merely stared at them while he sat on his knees. Yet they were cut off as their spears went toward Shukimbo's flesh. A cascade of arrows rained down and punched into them, collapsing them into mounds of flesh.

Pasha and Varansi raised their shields on instinct as dozens of shafts flew down around them. When it had stopped, the men lowered their shields to gaze upon all the warriors of the north dead beneath their feet.

Pasha looked up to see more than fifty of his men looking down with drawn bows, as well as his good friend as he stepped into the light.

"I don't think now is the time for a bath, Kaudi. We've got a witch woman to chase," said Abayomi, smiling.

They accepted the help of their fellows appreciatively as they climbed back to the upper level of the cave. Shukimbo's wounds were bound quickly as the bleeding worsened.

"See that he gets to a physician."

Abayomi repeated the orders, leaving four men with Shukimbo while the rest of them continued on their path.

In the distance, they could still hear running feet and various movement as daylight began to reappear. No longer being hesitant, Pasha and his men sprinted toward the opening at the end of the cave.

When they exited, they came onto a rocky hill leading toward a flat plateau that went to the northwest. Near the end of the hill were Helomar and her men, who were making their way down toward fresh horses below. The plateau sat between parallel rows of hills that would hide any rider going north from the southern forces outside the mountain camps.

Abayomi's men fired their bows quickly, scattering the nearly three dozen northern warriors who were heading toward the plateau.

Helomar dodged the arrows and ran quickly toward the plateau while her men charged the Sashramans. The small warrior led them.

Abayomi and his men made a hole in the enemy line, which Pasha ran through quickly while the enemy closed in on the Sashramans. Some gave chase but were immediately struck down by arrows.

Pasha sprinted down toward the plateau just as Helomar was galloping away on one of the horses. The captain mounted as well and gave chase.

Harsh wind ran through his hair, freeing his locks while he rode. The gap proved difficult to close. Helomar's mare proved faster due to its lighter load. Nevertheless, Pasha urged his stallion onward, determined to catch her. Helomar's horse came to an abrupt halt as it tripped over a loose stone. Helomar was hurled into the air and landed on her back.

For a moment, she did not get up. However, in the moment Pasha's feet touched the ground, a sudden force took over her and pulled her into the air. To Pasha's surprise, his wife's sister stared back at him in midair, seeming to dare him to attack.

The captain ran back to the Baku horse he had procured and retrieved a spear, which he promptly hurled at Helomar. Helomar drifted slightly to the right and avoided it. And then to Pasha's surprise, she launched toward him like a flying arrow. The captain readied his sword to cut her neck the moment she passed.

Instead, Helomar stopped short of his blade and kicked Pasha's face as she fell back to ground. Pasha staggered back while several dozen rocks lifted into the air. Without warning, they all shot toward him. Using his shield, the captain blocked many, but several stones cracked into his legs and caused him to collapse.

Suddenly the force increased and pushed him onto his back. He rose up quickly as Helomar came toward him. Helomar circled him repeatedly like an animal stalking prey.

Pasha swiped his sword at her side and touched nothing. Helomar sidestepped and drove her knee into the weakened plates surrounding Pasha's gut. The force of her blow seemed more like a man's than a woman's, causing Pasha to double over.

But as Helomar raised her foot to kick him again, Pasha reached out and caught it. With all his strength, he twisted her foot. Helomar jumped and spun with the twisting motion in order to prevent her bones from being broken. A stray rock pummeled into Pasha's head, forcing his grip to slacken.

"You feel anger, brother? You feel hate? Surely you can avenge her better than that!"

She dodged his lunge and jumped back as he swiped toward her stomach.

"I can see what she found in you. You're a man of passion."

"Do not speak of her!" Pasha shouted.

He lunged, and she leapt into the air. Before Pasha knew it, she had landed behind him and reached out to pin his arms to his side. She then pulled him back into her chest as she spoke into his ear.

"Men of passion have always driven the women of our family mad with desire! I think I feel it too!"

The kiss she placed on his neck burned Pasha like the worst of poisons. In a sudden jolt, the captain bent forward and pushed up with his shoulders, tossing Helomar over his back. A carefully placed kick went into Helomar's side, making her cry out for the first time.

She rolled away before Pasha could place another one and finally drew her sword. Without warning, mounds of dirt exploded before Pasha's eyes. He drew his shield in front of him as the dirt blinded him. A heavy rock crashed into his shield, pushing him back. Pasha staggered back but did not fall as Helomar came toward him.

The captain blocked her wild blows as she swung toward him. She used the full strength of her arms as she attacked him, trying to trip him as she pressed toward him, but Pasha kept moving his feet.

His blade lunged toward her, but she sidestepped and punched his face. The captain swept his blade toward her, but she dodged it and moved back. Pasha moved forward, but she disappeared as a mound of dirt exploded in his face.

The captain's back suddenly caved in as it was kicked from behind. Pasha could not stop himself as he fell forward. Helomar pounced once he was on the ground.

Pasha turned onto his back and rolled away, Helomar's blade skewered the tender ground beneath as he did so. Blow after blow came toward Pasha. He could see the fear and desire to kill him written over Helomar's face. His wife's sister had expected to kill him sooner. Instead, they fought on.

Pasha blocked another move and seized Helomar's hand. Without warning, he spun into her and slashed down with his blade. Helomar quickly seized his sword hand with her only free one and struggled against him as he attempted to end it. In spite of her impressive strength, Pasha could see she was weakening as he gazed into her eyes.

Just then another mound of dirt exploded between them, sending Pasha hurtling backward while Helomar disappeared. Suddenly she was behind him when he came to his feet. Her blade slashed toward Pasha's back. The captain swung his blade completely behind him and blocked it. Pasha pushed backward against her and turned, slashing toward her neck. She sidestepped and rammed into his shield, causing the captain to drop it.

Again she spun and slashed down toward Pasha's neck. But Pasha turned quickly and blocked her blade with his own and kicked her knee down with all his strength. As she staggered, he seized her by the back of her head while resting the tip of his sword right at her bosom.

Helomar dropped her sword. Her eyes lit up with terror as Pasha gazed at her, wondering what to do next.

"I always knew this was how it would end," Helomar said in a quivering voice.

"You and me. Here in this place."

"You . . . you have caused me so much pain!" Pasha said through grinding teeth.

"Pain is always what comes when you fall for a lie as I did. You think the world has turned against you, and you feel like your life does not mean anything anymore. Then you meet someone. He pulls you up, takes care of you. And then when you're well again, he expects things of you."

"He made you do it, didn't he?"

"It was so he could get to you. There is none in this world he hates more than you. He finds people like me, helps us when we are low. Promises us things. Promises us food . . . power . . . love. He makes it look so good, but to get them, he wraps you so tightly to his will that you do things you never thought you would. He took my anger toward Hadassah, turned it into hate. Before I knew it, my sister was dead beneath my feet!" Tears began to rain down her face. Slowly Pasha lowered his blade. "I only realized when she was dying that I had made a mistake."

"You only realized when she was dying? She was your sister!" Pasha shouted.

"I fell for a lie, Pasha, and it consumed me. He let me believe that I hated her. Yet I only felt love when I watched her dying, love like we had known as girls, and then remorse. It was never about me. It's always been about you and him."

"Is that why he started the Forgotten War?"

"You know that too, Pasha. He can't have all the power if he has to share it with you. He promised to share it with me once. He blinded me with the possibilities. That's why he hates you so much, Pasha, because you're the only one standing between him and the power he craves."

"You knew all this, yet you served him!"

"I've been living in a web of deceit and lies ever since he came to me. Ever since Hadassah. I once knew the way. But the roads I took turned me into this wretched creature."

"Do you have my son?"

"He's been precious to me. Much like his mother."

"Where is he?"

"Have you ever loved me, Pasha?"

"What!" Pasha shouted.

"As I thought. The wretch always dies unloved, not forgiven."

Helomar began to chant. Pasha's blade flew from his hand and drove through Helomar's chest. Bearing an expressionless face, Helomar gasped for her last breath and fell onto her back.

The captain was unsure of how to feel as he looked over her body in amazement and shock. He had hated her with a passion before. Now when he looked at her, he could only think of Hadassah and the great love she had for her sister. When he looked down at Helomar, he felt no sense of relief or closure. All he felt was weariness and remorse.

"Amah! Amah!" screamed a voice from behind.

Pasha turned and nearly dropped. Before him, he stood with his mother's hair, her eyes and features.

"What did you do to her!" yelled Kamili. "What did you do to my mother!"

"Kamili, listen to me—"

"What did you do!"

"Listen! I am your father, son. She is not your mother."

"Tell me any more lies and you'll regret them." His son skillfully drew back the thick Baku bow sitting comfortably in his outstretched arms.

"You know the truth, son. Don't you remember?"

"You are my enemy. You killed my mother. That is all I need to know." He raised the bow and pointed it straight at Pasha's chest. Suddenly another shaft tore through the air and lodged into Kamili's shoulder.

"No!" shouted Pasha as Abayomi and his men were closing in. "Stop firing! Stop firing!" he shouted, growing more fearful.

More arrows sung their song of death through the air as young Kamili sprinted away from Pasha and remounted and fled.

Finally Abayomi and his men arrived.

"Did you not hear me saying no fire!" shouted Pasha.

"Yes, sir, we did," responded Abayomi. "But it takes time to get the word up the line. We'll go and get him for you."

"No."

"What?"

"I said no."

"But, Pasha," Abayomi protested.

"It's my son, Abayomi! It's Kamili!"

"Kamili?" asked Abayomi, confused.

"Just let him go!" said Pasha.

The captain stared off in the distance as all that remained of him and Hadassah rode away from him. Pasha wondered what he was thinking, where he would be that night. The way his son had stared at Helomar's body, so lovingly, and the anger he had shown toward Pasha reminded the captain a lot of himself in times past.

Much damage had been done between them, more than Pasha could imagine. He hoped that the future would see it undone.

CHAPTER 23

Two Who Are One

Not knowing what else to do, the captain dug a shallow grave for his wife's sister as the fighting outside the mountains subsided. Most of the northern forces had broken and fled north and west. Though they knew that the enemy would eventually come across poorly defended Sashraman towns and probably sack them, the generals decided to not give chase. Too many men had been lost that day. For Cafura to survive, they would need all the warriors they could muster.

By three hours after midday, Pasha had recovered Daimon and rejoined his men. The Sashramans and their allies gathered before the mountains, recovering the bodies of fallen friends and gathering weapons.

"Kaudi!" a voice called out to Pasha.

"Nalar," said Pasha as he turned.

"How many of your men are accounted for?"

"So far only fourteen hundred."

"That's not even half your force."

"So many are dead and wounded, and then others are missing. It's mad right now, Kaudi. Mad."

"Are you all right?"

"Yes, Kaudi, I'm fine. What about you?" he said, gesturing to Pasha's shoulder, which was now wrapped in bandages.

"It will heal."

Nalar nodded in agreement.

"Nalar."

"Sir."

"Did Maranhi and his men make it?"

"Yes, sir."

"Bring him to me."

Nalar nodded once more and departed. Pasha turned to look about him. All throughout the field, he could see the different tribes gathering weapons, looking for dead, and tending wounded. In spite of the battles he had been in, the sight of a field after the battle was always the most haunting. Though it would be at least a day before they knew how many had died, Pasha could see it with his own eyes as he looked about him. There were more men lying in the dirt than those who stood and drew breath.

Pasha turned as he felt someone drawing near him. The captain nodded when he saw it was Abayomi. His officer returned the gesture.

"I knew we could do it, Pasha. But I did not think it would be this costly."

"Everything has a price, brother. In this life and the next."

"Are you all right?" Abayomi asked, looking at his shoulder.

"I'll be fine," Pasha said.

The captain looked forward as Maranhi and some of his men came before him. Nalar took his place by Pasha. Maranhi came within five paces of the captain and then stopped. Any closer would have been seen as a challenge.

"I heard you've been looking for me," he said with a strong dose of sarcasm.

"I heard that the city guard of Cafura were some of the most skillful warriors of the north, not a band of terrified children."

"There you go again, giving ear to ideas that must surely come from the brothels."

"I'm sure your mother gave you a thorough teaching."

Anger flashed across Maranhi's face as his hand twitched anxiously on his spear. His fellows drew in closer, reaching their hands toward their weapons.

"Be respectful, brother," said Abayomi.

"Men don't grow old here."

Glancing at Abayomi and Nalar's half-drawn swords within inches of his gut was enough to make the captain of the guard back down. His men immediately followed his example.

The city guard captain glared back at Pasha, who had not moved once or flinched a muscle.

"I'm only going to tell you this once. Don't let me see you holding back when I tell you to move forward. Now I don't care if you don't like me. I don't care if you hate me. But if I ever see you putting the lives of men in danger by your inaction and cowardice, there will be consequences. I have charge over this army, and you will obey my authority. Do you understand?"

"Understand this, Kaudi," he said, coming with three paces of Pasha. Abayomi and Nalar pressed in closer with their sword hands loose and ready. "We make up a large part of the Sashraman forces now. My men do. And my men follow only me. I think you'll do good remembering that."

For a lingering second, Pasha thought they would come to blows and then weapons. Still, Maranhi did not move his spear. After a long moment, the captain of the city guard turned away from Pasha and moved away.

"Pasha. Right now is not the time for testing him," said Nalar. "We don't need anyone else against us."

"Shut your hole, Nalar!" Abayomi said in rebuke. "It's time you set the bastard in place," Abayomi said to Pasha.

"The problem is that he doesn't know his place," said Pasha.

Pasha and his officer went to the middle of the field where the generals and King Hanasa had gathered.

They dismounted and walked toward them as they stood looking over maps and staring into the distance.

"Kaudi," said General Ishok in acknowledgment.

"General Ishok. Generals."

"Pasha, it is good that you made it through this mess," said King Hanasa.

"I don't think we could have prepared for this. Nevertheless, all has ended well."

"So what's the final count?"

"We don't have one yet," answered General Tayla.

"But overall it's reached more than seven thousand dead and a thousand wounded. Still the number keeps rising."

"And it will rise even more if we do not give chase," said General Shabaz.

"We've been through that, Shabaz. Chase is too risky," said King Hanasa.

"Risky. We've broken their will, and they're running like rabbits. What can be risky about that?"

"They've run toward over twenty miles of forest and jungles. It'll take us weeks to get at all of them and in doing so we'll divide our forces."

"What worse thing can happen? More than half of my men are gone. I want to get every one of those bastards!"

"Shabaz, we understand, but we have to be practical," said General Ishok.

"What? What is that? The Yashani understands what the Mulamar is saying. Daiyu have mercy. What could happen next?" the Mulamar said in a mocking tone.

"What I don't understand is why we came here. Why we came to sacrifice ourselves for cowards who stay in the rear instead of fight their own war," he said, directing his words toward Pasha.

"Shabaz. My men have given a lot as well."

"Have they now! Were they cut to bits while those who were supposed to be their allies sat and watched?"

"We did not sit and watch. We've given everything you have and ten times more. Because this is our land and our blood, we will never stop defending it."

Pasha knew he was referring to Maranhi, but he couldn't let a man like Shabaz know that he did not have full control over his men.

"I see more Mulamar on the ground than Sashramans!"

"Please! Brothers, please!" said King Hanasa, stepping between them as Shabaz came closer to Pasha.

"You are not my brother! And neither is he!"

Without hesitating, the Mulamar general shot a wad of spittle at the king's feet. He did not bat an eye as the king's warriors twitched their sword hands anxiously. Saying nothing, he turned to return to his horse and his men.

"Trying times these are," said the king.

"We should gather our dead and head back for the city then," said General Ishok.

"But leave a unit here and an outpost to make sure we keep control of this area from now on," said General Marwa.

"Agreed then," said the king.

"Right now, I think—"

The king's words were cut off by the heavy sound of horns and moving feet. They turned around, seeing their men running in all directions to form up.

And then they saw it. In the northwest, dozens of rows of enemy warriors were spilling over the horizon.

"Form up! Form up!" shouted King Hanasa.

They parted ways quickly as the generals sprinted toward their horses.

"Captain Nuvahli," said the king as he went for his horse. "Form up on me. We'll go this one together."

"Fine," Pasha said as he climbed onto Daimon's back.

When the captain returned to his men, they moved toward the center of the line and merged with the Halor troops. Pasha, his officers, and the king watched from the rear as the events unfolded before them.

Pasha could not even begin to fathom their number as dozens upon dozens of endless columns poured onto the field. The rain was beginning to cease while the enemy began falling into a massive line. Silver-armored Baku horsemen fell in first along with several columns of chariots, driven by massive black warriors from some of the darker northern tribes.

The sight of chariots shot torrents of fear throughout Pasha's body. He had seen chariots only once before, in the west fighting against Sadras clans. And their thin wooden vehicles had been extremely deadly for the men he had commanded.

Seeing those thick, bronze war machines coming toward them only made Pasha perspire even more. From each of the spokes of their wheels ran thick spikes for tearing warriors' flesh as they fell.

And still more came. Hundreds upon hundreds of horse archers and then endless columns of spearmen and then swordsmen.

Within moments, they were in position, and the line had been formed. Pasha did not have to look to sense his men's fear when some of them began inching back.

"Are you men of Sashra or little girls!" Abayomi chided.

"Take heart and send these dogs to hell like you did their brothers!"

Those who were backing down quickly fell back into position. Abayomi's words immediately shamed them for their fear and doubt.

Pasha tried to give Abayomi an appreciative look, but he felt what all of his men were feeling when they looked out before them.

"What do you think?" asked King Hanasa.

"I think we should ask them to send up more men. That little rabble will barely last us through the dinner," said Abayomi, joking.

None responded to his humor with warmth.

"We should probably fall back," said Pasha.

"To where, my friend? Those horses alone could ride us down if we ran. And those chariots . . ." The king stopped short, like Pasha, not wishing to speak any more of them.

"Kaudi, the mountains," said Nalar.

"It would take hours to reposition there," said the king.

"And they'll be on us long before then. Archers to the front, I guess, and spears to the middle," the king said as more of question to Pasha than a suggestion.

"Archers to the front. Spears to the middle," Pasha said more to himself than to Abayomi. The commander followed the orders through.

Down the line, the other generals did the same. Archers and horse archers repositioned themselves in the front while the spearmen fell in the middle. The lancers and Halor horsemen took positions on the flanks.

Heavy drumming filled the air, and thunderous chants erupted within the enemy ranks. Without warning, the center of the ranks parted to make a path as men on horses rode down the line.

Though Pasha could not clearly make him out, he knew the profile of the red-eyed warrior, his brother, anywhere.

"He's here!" a man in the ranks quivered. "The one who sees into us and destroys our souls. The one who breathes fire and ash. He's here to kill us!"

"Quiet, man!"

"He's going to kill us all!"

"I said quiet!" Abayomi shouted again.

"Flee from him before it's too late to flee from him!" he began to rant.

Two of the rank masters moved forward and grabbed the man, dragging him to the rear.

"I guess we know what happened to General Cheokto," said King Hanasa.

Pasha said nothing. The man had been a mentor to him for a long time. Accepting his death would be difficult, just as accepting Leyos's had been.

The drumming resumed. This time, loud cheers and cries followed the rhythm while it got faster.

"This is it," said Pasha.

He looked far down to the right at Maranhi, whose men had formed up between Nalar's and Captain Jeshumbo's. Maranhi saw Pasha looking at him but did not look back. Pasha hoped all would go well.

With a loud roar, the enemy horses rushed down the field with the chariots close behind them. While they did so, the archers stayed behind, firing repeated volleys toward the men of the south.

"Incoming!" voices shouted as a barrage of arrows rained down on them.

Pasha pulled his shield over him as three shafts fell toward him. The captain repeated this action two more times before the archers stopped their fire. By then the enemy was within a few hundred feet of them.

"Are you ready?" he said to the king.

"Yes."

"Signal the charge," he said to Varansi.

Varansi immediately drew a blue and white banner and waved it furiously. All throughout the line, the other commanders and generals responded in acknowledgment.

Both men drew their swords and raised them high.

"Rule this day!" Pasha shouted, urging his men forward.

A thunderous explosion of bodies and machines colliding filled the air as both forces met. Pasha stayed back with his lancers and Varansi while Abayomi, Nalar, and Maranhi advanced.

Abayomi's archers fired rapid bursts as they drove toward the enemy's left flank. Enemy chariots suddenly ran through them, putting the archers down with hundreds of shafts while their wheel spikes tore into the southern warriors. Abayomi's horsemen tried to push them back while the spearmen fell in. Enemy horse archers and archers on chariots continued firing shaft after shaft into Abayomi's lancers. In spite of their shields, the lancers found themselves quickly surrounded. Soon arrows tore through them all and sent them hurtling to the earth beneath them.

Seeing them weakened, chariots rode through them, slashing their horses' bodies as they went. Abayomi looked about him, ordering his archers to fire while the spearmen pressed forward. Chariot archers immediately responded to the volleys with larger ones of their own. Before Abayomi could react, enemy horsemen tore into his archers. Within moments, they were routing. Enemies closed in all around Abayomi. Seeing hardly any of his lancers, the commander rode back and fell in behind his spearmen.

It seemed as if their supply of arrows was limitless. Having broken the lancers and archers, they fired repeatedly into the advancing line of spearmen. The spearmen were heavily armored and, having shields, few of them fell. But then the archers charged head on and rammed into them while enemy spearmen and swordsmen pushed forward.

Nalar's lancers charged alongside of Maranhi's. In the blink of an eye, men flew like leaves in a gusting wind while arrows tore through their bodies. Some were thrown off by the force of the volleys in spite of their shields. Giving the signal, Nalar and his men hurled their lances into the enemy horsemen, catching their foes off guard while their lance tips dug into them.

Nalar took his sword in hand and slashed sideways, lobbing off several heads in the process. Men rammed his horse with their own, causing his mount to rear up onto its hind legs and furiously kick the attackers. Nalar trampled them as they fell.

He lost his shield as a massive pike impaled itself on his bronze shield and tore it away. The pike returned, and Nalar blocked it with his sword. Suddenly a chariot rammed into him, crushing his leg as it dug into his horse's flesh. Nalar cried out in pain as he felt the bone in his leg snap.

Fortunately, his mount recovered its balance and proceeded to charge the attacking chariot. Nalar retrieved a spear and dug it into the chariot driver while his horse commenced to kick the machine over while biting at the horses that pulled it.

He looked to see his spearmen holding the enemy spearmen back while the chariots were failing to break them. His men would let an advancing chariot into their line while swordsmen prepared to pounce onto the war machines and their drivers.

Captain Jeshumbo's spearmen seemed to be holding their own against the enemy while Maranhi's men pushed forward alongside them. But then everything changed when a rapid burst of arrows pounded the city guard captain's lancers. Though few of them fell, they slowly began to lose their momentum as Maranhi began ordering them back. His cries to fall back soon extended to the spearmen, and before Nalar knew it, the city guard spearmen were falling back.

"No retreat! They're faltering! Keep moving, you coward!" he shouted at Maranhi.

Soon all of Maranhi's men were in full flight while enemy chariots shot through Captain Jeshumbo's men. Enemy chariots ran down the Halor while spearmen tried to dodge the advancing machines. Halor lancers tried to push back, but the enemy horsemen cut them off.

Nalar looked forward to see a heavy force throwing dozens of his own spearmen into the air as it advanced. Within moments, the general with the red eyes was before Nalar and his men. Nalar's spearmen and swordsmen pounced on him, but it was no use. Mounds of dirt exploded before his men, blinding them while rapid fireballs were launched forward and consumed them.

To Nalar's horror, many of his spearmen became a long line of flame while the general came behind them and hacked them down. Nalar retrieved another spear and hurled it at him. For a moment, it seemed the weapon would reach its target. The general did not see the rapidly moving shaft inching toward the back of his neck. But then it stopped in midair.

Pasha cursed heavily as he saw Maranhi run from the rear of his advancing spear column. Jeshumbo's forces were quickly overwhelmed as the enemy took advantage of Maranhi's flight.

"That's the last time, you coward!" shouted Pasha as he drew his bow.

"No, sir," Varansi said as he grabbed Pasha by the hand. "His men will turn against us."

"Let go of me!" Pasha said.

But he never raised his bow. For the moment he turned to face Maranhi, a stray arrow sailed through the rows of fighting men and struck Maranhi in the back of his head.

The moment proved intensely shocking for Pasha as he considered what had happened and what he was about to do. Still, the captain moved his mind to other things as he saw Nalar was in trouble.

Lancers and spearmen followed him as he drove toward his men. Suddenly enemy spearmen cut off their advance, driving their spears and stakes into their mounts and the advancing spearmen. Daimon reared up and crushed many as they drove spears toward him. Pasha hurled two of the six spears he carried on his mount while blocking blows with his sword.

Halor spearmen began to gain momentum and pushed hard against the enemy line. King Hanasa and his lancers hurled their lances into the enemy line and hacked down the northern tribesmen with their swords. But it would not be enough as the chariots moved in.

By then they were closer to Nalar but unable to reach him. Suddenly dozens of men were launched into the air while a massive force tore through the line. The earth exploded before Nalar's spearmen's eyes while massive fireballs consumed them. Pasha watched in horror as the red-eyed general stormed through Nalar's men. Just then Nalar reared back and released a spear shaft toward the enemy general. For a moment, relief came to Pasha as the quietly moving spear shot toward the unaware foe.

But then it stopped in midair and fell to the ground. Suddenly the general turned and glared at Nalar. The fiery globes that were his eyes reflected the flames licking the flesh off of Sashraman and Halor warriors. His mouth curved into a crooked smile as he witnessed fear consuming Nalar.

The commander hurled another spear with all of his strength. However, it too stopped in midair and fell within a couple of feet of the general.

"Run, you fool!" Pasha said as if Nalar could hear him.

Instead Nalar drew his sword and charged toward the general. Janaha continued smiling while he waited for Nalar. Coming within several feet, Nalar lifted his sword high to strike down at Janaha. All of a sudden, the fallen shafts reanimated before the general and took flight. Before Nalar could react, both had punched through his weakened armor plates and seared through his flesh.

"No!" shouted Pasha.

The captain reached for his bow and fired repeated volleys at the enemy chariots while King Hanasa's men kept driving into the enemy spearmen. All Pasha could do was watch while Nalar gasped while the air began to escape his lungs. However, the general had not finished with him. Taking a long pike, the general swung up high. Nalar's head shot off while his body fell limply to the ground.

Many of Nalar's men panicked and began to retreat. Chariots mercilessly rode them down while archers filled them with torrents of arrows.

Upon King Hanasa's signal, Pasha and what was left of Nalar's men pulled back to merge with the Yashani, whose archers covered their retreat. General Ishok formed up the infantry in five columns while his horse archers continued firing away at the enemy chariots. It felt like they were having no effect as enemy spearmen snaked around to surround them while Baku horsemen led a head-on charge. The spearmen braced themselves and held their spears firmly as the enemy horsemen crashed into them.

Pasha charged with General Ishok and his lancers while King Hanasa urged his spearmen forward. To Pasha, it seemed they were only delaying the inevitable as enemy swordsmen hacked into their spearmen with ease.

Every shaft thrown or fired was outnumbered by enemy horse archers and chariot archers. Enemy spearmen tore into the Yashani lancers, panicking many of the horses while Yashani tried to push the enemy back.

Pasha's shield rang like the most ominous bell as enemy spears and pikes bashed into it. Daimon kicked many attackers as they tried to spear him. Using his bow once more, Pasha fired into the enemy as quickly as possible.

An unknown blow suddenly struck his head, spinning his helmet in the opposite direction. Pasha put his shield before his body while he peeled off his helmet. A quick blow glanced off one of his chest plates; the pressure sent him reeling into the ground.

His helmet had barely come off when a dozen blades lunged toward him. For a moment, the captain thought it was over. Then to his relief, Daimon leapt into the depths of the attackers and trampled many into the ground.

Chariots began rushing toward Pasha, their metal spikes spinning with deadly speed. Pasha ran back toward the Yashani columns as the chariots approached him. The machines tore down many men that stood before them, slicing through their bodies like cleavers.

"Here. Here!" Pasha looked as General Ishok rode toward him.

Without hesitating, Pasha climbed onto the back of the general's mount.

"Make yourself useful!" shouted Ishok as he gestured to several spears attached to his saddle.

Pasha unstrapped them and began hurling the shafts into the chariot drivers and their riders. General Ishok seemed unstoppable as he went forward. Spearmen fell beneath him while his sword slashed at the enemy in all directions.

But it all changed. Coming at them on a massive chariot was Janaha. Pasha then looked to the south where an enormous roar erupted, with Makar and Naua forces fleeing before enemy spearmen. Northern horsemen rode them down while the Mulamar struggled to hold on.

Ishok had seen Janaha by then and tried to ride away from him. Several flying spears struck his mount and dug into its flesh. Pasha and Ishok crashed into the ground while Janaha advanced.

Just when he seemed ready to strike, King Hanasa and Abayomi suddenly came from nowhere, their men following behind into the enemy lines. Their progress was halted as more enemy chariots and horsemen moved up and crashed into them.

King Hanasa rode furiously toward Janaha along with his lancers. The king hurled shaft after shaft at the enemy general. To their horror, each shaft melted when it came within a couple of feet of the general.

Janaha waited for Hanasa as he rode toward him. Moving quickly, the general swung his long pike toward King Hanasa's mount. In a massive feat of strength, Janaha's blow flung Hanasa from his mount while the Halor warhorse's head fell off.

King Hanasa struck another rapidly moving chariot. The impact slumped the king onto the ground, gripping his shoulder.

Janaha ran up behind him, preparing to use his pike once more. Pasha hurled a spear at the enemy general. A sudden force struck the shaft as it flew, but the flesh on Janaha's shoulder was not saved as the spear tip slashed into it. Somehow the general knew where to look when he turned and put his gaze upon Pasha.

King Hanasa rolled away with haste, shooting Pasha an appreciative look as he fell back toward his men.

Suddenly the earth exploded before them, and Pasha fell into a hail of flying dirt and grass. Just when he recovered and stood, a sudden blunt force struck his back and dropped him back to the ground. Pasha rolled but could not escape when gruff hands seized the back of his armor and tunic and flung him into the air.

Pasha had lost his shield when he managed to stand once more and face Janaha. The captain sidestepped as a quickly moving pike slashed toward him. Janaha turned and lunged, nearly catching Pasha off guard. But the captain dodged it and jumped back. His sword reached his hands just in time to block the pike as it came for his neck.

Janaha pushed down hard while Pasha blocked the blow. The captain began to lose his balance as his body seemed to buckle under the pressure of Janaha's strength.

"You won't survive this time!" he said, his red eyes flickering with hatred.

Pasha jumped and kicked out. Janaha stepped back and caught his foot and flipped him back. Pasha rolled again when he hit the ground and got back up quickly when Janaha came for him. Violent vibrations shook painfully through all of Pasha's body each time he blocked a blow from the pike. His shoulder cried out for relief.

He jumped when Janaha tried to slash his legs. With a free foot, he kicked at Janaha's face. But the general lifted his opposite hand and blocked the kick with his open palm.

Pasha reared back and leapt toward the enemy general. But then Janaha's quickly moving pike stopped when Varansi leapt onto his back. Earth exploded before Pasha again, sending him hurtling back. When he rose, he witnessed Janaha seizing Varansi by the throat and throwing him over his shoulder

When Varansi came back to his knees, the general's pike swept behind him and took him at the neck. Varansi slumped over as his head fell to the opposite side.

By then, the entire southern end of the line was in full retreat as enemy spearmen and horse archers tore into their retreating foes. Pasha ran back as more and more of the Yashani spearmen began to fall.

To his surprise, Daimon found him while he ran toward the rear. Pasha mounted him quickly.

Within moments, the Sashraman and Yashani lines broke. Pasha and Abayomi fled together with King Hanasa and the rest of the men while General Kwaba and Kimana brought their forces together to cover their retreat.

The deadly enemy horse archers and chariots were slowed as the two Halor generals tried to hold their ground. But they all knew the day would end in defeat, not victory.

CHAPTER 24

The Compassionate One

The men of the north scattered the southern tribes like beaten dogs all through the east. Mulamar and Naua had been driven north toward the mountains. Among the Sashramans, not much was known of the other tribes. Halor along with some Yashani had fled with Pasha's men. For more than three days they fought back pursuing northern horsemen.

Though the number of casualties among all the tribes had been difficult to ascertain, Pasha knew that they were great among his men. Nalar and Varansi were dead, two good officers who could not be replaced. Overall, they had come into the fight with almost eleven thousand men, but at that moment barely fifty-five hundred warriors could be accounted for.

Pasha merely had to look at the grim faces of King Hanasa and General Ishok to know that the casualties for their armies had been great. King Hanasa had heard no word from his generals, or General Ishok from his captains.

For more than three days, the enemy had driven them deep into the jungle. But when their forces had reached the main road toward Cafura, the pursuit had ended.

By midday, Pasha and King Hanasa rode at the head of the men as they finally broke the tree line and had Cafura within sight. While they rode, Sashraman and Halor warriors looked to the east and west, expecting an ambush as they went onto open ground.

General Ishok had remained in the jungle with archers ready in case the enemy tried to rush them.

Still Pasha saw nothing while he made his way to the city. However, when he looked toward Cafura, it was clear that something was amiss. Her gates were flung open, and he could not see any guards or people.

The captain and King Hanasa rode faster. Suddenly a heavy crash and sound of rumbling filled their ears as riders came from the gates. The faces of the Mulamar were unmistakable. There were more than two hundred of them, but they did not stop upon seeing the Sashramans and Halor closing in. Instead they made a quick dash for the east.

Something was clearly wrong. Pasha sent riders to intercept them. But the men of the Mulamar were already disappearing behind the rolling eastern hills before the Sashramans turned to pursue them.

Inside of the city, only an eerie silence greeted them. King Hanasa looked about the walls, but there were no guards.

"What is this?" the king said.

"Keep your eyes out!" Pasha said to Takil.

They moved cautiously through the southern end of the city. King Hanasa's horsemen kept their bows ready, not knowing what to anticipate. Pasha and the king led their men along the main street toward the city center.

Pasha looked at the houses as they passed. Most of them were closed off. The doorways and windows were blocked, showing no sign of life behind them.

"Look to the houses!" Pasha ordered.

Takil and several dozen men broke from the column and began to search the houses. Just then, their horses cried out and reared back as a strange odor filled the air. It was like the sweetness of honey and milk mixed with the rancid odor of decaying flesh.

"Nuvahli, look!" said King Hanasa to Pasha.

They had just passed a smith's shop, and hanging out of the open doorway was a hand filled with cuts and gashes.

Pasha dismounted and started toward the door. Ten of his men came forward with him. The captain approached the shop from the side and held his spear readily as he turned the corner and looked into the house. Inside, all the windows had been covered, giving no light to illuminate the body.

"Get him out of there," Pasha said, turning to his men.

Unlike him, most of them were wearing thick gauntlets.

"Kaudi! Kaudi! Come quick!" Takil called out from behind them.

"Hold on, Takil!" Pasha shouted back.

"Kaudi!"

Just then, the body of a man riddled with scars, gashes, and boils collapsed onto the ground before them. The sweet, rancid smell they all knew struck them hard. Pasha's stomach did somersaults when he looked at the man's side. Whole patches of skin and muscle had been cut off, while other parts had been gnawed by teeth. Their horses cried out even louder as the Halor and Sashraman warriors jumped back in fear.

"Get back, get back, get back!" Pasha shouted.

King Hanasa repeated his cry.

Takil appeared behind them. "Kaudi. They have plague!"

"I know, man!"

"But, sir!"

"I know!"

Without warning, several dozen men appeared down the street. All were bearing clubs and knives as they approached them.

"Archers, ready!" said King Hanasa as they got closer.

Soon Pasha could discern the highly visible boils and open cuts on their faces.

"Look up! Look up!" called out one of Pasha's rank masters.

Large black shapes jumped down toward them from the roofs of the surrounding houses. Their hands clutched clubs and knives as they crashed into Halor and Sashraman warriors. None could miss the scars and bright boils of their attackers.

"Eyes in!" shouted Pasha as he ran back toward the middle of the column.

The plague carriers attacked them like wild animals, jumping and howling madly while they drove their blades into the warriors.

Pasha and the men beat them with the blunt ends of their spears while Halor bashed them with the spears. But their hopes to kill few of them were dashed as more appeared down the street.

"Eyes out!" shouted King Hanasa.

His archers looked out to the carriers approaching them. With careful aim, they fired into them. It pained King Hanasa to watch while the scarred and bleeding men seemed to burst into a pile of blood and flesh when the shafts tore through them.

Pasha drove his spear into a carrier wielding two knives while the rest of his men had drawn their swords and began hacking them down. Another leapt onto the captain's back and began to clamp his teeth on his shoulder. Pasha swung his elbow back and struck the man's head before his teeth went through the fabric of his tunic.

The man landed behind Pasha on all fours like a cornered animal. Suddenly a knife lunged toward Pasha's side. He sidestepped and slashed the attacker's throat. The cornered animal leapt and pounced onto Pasha. However, the man soon expired after Pasha drove his blade into his gut multiple times.

Several Sashramans and Halor fell to the quickly moving carriers. Many were pounced upon and bitten while knives were driven into their backs. Nevertheless, short work was soon made of them by Sashraman and Halor spears.

After many moments, the Halor archers were beginning to drive back the carriers gathering on the streets before them. Having seen many of their fellows torn by arrow tips, the plague carriers retreated.

It did not take long for the column to end the remaining attackers. Pasha and King Hanasa ordered their men to fall back.

"In Daiyu's name, what was that!" shouted King Hanasa when they had fallen back to the southern gates.

"They're mad with the plague. I've seen it before, but not like this," Pasha answered, remembering their earlier encounter with plague victims.

"But this is not like before. The people the men have found. Some of them have been cut apart, gnawed on. I don't think it's wild dogs. These people have fallen into the most hideous kind of darkness."

"He's right, Kaudi!" Takil said fearfully. "Daiyu has cursed this place. Let us burn the city and destroy them."

"No! This does not come from Daiyu! And we will not kill any more of our own!"

"We have to do something, Nuvahli. Either we kill them or we leave. We can't let it spread among the men."

"I won't leave the city!" said Pasha. "We can camp around the city for the night. But we're going to take the streets back, with or without you."

Though he wished to argue, Hanasa halted his words. When he looked at Pasha, he saw something he had not seen for a while, conviction. The man was determined; he could not be refused.

"All right, Nuvahli. I am with you."

Most of the army waited anxiously for the five hundred Sashraman and four hundred Halor that had gone back to take the city. By late afternoon, Pasha and Hanasa's warriors had taken the city back after hours of fighting.

The horrors of what lay on Cafura's once glistening streets sickened Pasha like the most potent poison. In every house they had gone through, every inhabitant was either sick or starving. Many terrified families were barricaded in their homes against the plague carriers, starving while trying to evade the terrible disease.

The evidence of cannibalism was overwhelming. Bones and carved flesh were strewn throughout the streets, bearing the marks of human teeth.

He and his men approached the courtyard of the temple, wearing heavy tunics beneath the armor, along with turbans, scarves, and long gauntlets. Nothing scared them more than the thought that they might have the plague. Still, they had a thorough washing before the assault and covered themselves head to foot so that no skin was exposed. Though it would save many of them, Pasha knew it would not be enough for some.

Pasha entered the courtyard with Takil and some of the Halor warriors. Suddenly the hundreds of stricken Sashramans rose from their beds and began to cry out, mainly to Pasha. They begged for food, others for healing, bearing in mind the encounter in the temple with the spirit.

"Please, Nuvahli! Save us, Nuvahli! Food! Our children are dying!"

Men came to him bowing and clutching his robes while women crawled and reached out to him.

His name became the song on their lips as they cried out for him. Pasha flinched and became startled. Their suffering confused and terrified him as much as their cries. What could he do? How could he protect them and feed them when such darkness had laid claim to their bodies and souls?

Pasha and his men batted away their hands and pushed them back gently while they passed through them. Inside, it was no different. Bodies of the starving and those dying of plague filled every corner of the sanctuary.

Many looked at them and called out to them, but they were too weak to move.

"Kaudi!" a man called out to him.

Pasha looked to the front of the sanctuary where a man layered in a thick red hood and cloak approached him. Though a thick turban covered his head and a headscarf his face, Pasha recognized the voice and gait of the shazhia.

"I never thought I'd be seeing you again."

"I can see why," Pasha said, looking around. "What has happened?"

"The city is dying, Pasha. The plague came two days after you left, and just now the Mulamar came and stole what was left of our food. We barely had enough for a day, and the Mulamar took it! Twenty guardsmen were killed trying to stop them."

"What about the food stores? I thought there was enough to last several more weeks. And what about the foraging?"

"There has not been enough to feed this city for weeks. The alcalde has been trying to sustain us with hunting and slaughtering his animals. What could have gotten us through another day the Mulamar took, and they killed our people to get it. Now we have nothing. People are dying every day, Kaudi. There's nothing we can do to stop it."

"Curse you, Shabaz!" Pasha said angrily. "Gather a kad and track them! Kill them all!" said Pasha to Takil.

Takil went quickly along with a dozen men.

"But we have you here now," said the shazhia. "Now that you are here, there is hope."

Pasha was silent. He looked at the man. Although unable to see his face, he imagined the pain that must be etched in it. It pained his heart to return to the city to only give more burdens to an already burden-heavy people. Finally he spoke. "Shazhia, there is someone I need to find."

Pasha found Mahlinya's aunts weeping when he entered the house. His men waited outside while he went about in search of her. He passed the weeping women and went toward the other room. Inside he found Mahlinya, her beautiful figure laid out on a goatskin mat.

She wore a light white dress, which was now dirty and laden with the stains of perspiration and blood. The captain's breath nearly stopped upon seeing her arms and legs. Heavy gashes and boils violated her once smooth, beautiful skin. Though drenched in sweat, her face and graceful neck still remained the same. Her eyes were closed and hands crossed over her bosom in the manner the dead were prepared for burial.

Pasha fell to her side and took hold of her hands. Anger flared up inside of him as he looked at his hands, sheathed in the heavy gauntlets, unable to feel her warmth.

After long moments, she began to stir.

At first she did not know who was there beside her. Pasha's headscarf covered most of his face.

"It's me," he said finally.

Though her eyes were weak, they glanced back with warmth at Pasha. "I hoped I'd see you again."

"And I came. I should never have left your side," said Pasha.

"You had to do what you had to do. How did it all go?"

"That does not matter. All that matters to me right now is you."

Mahlinya groaned softly as a cough escaped her. Pasha could tell that her strength had nearly gone.

"It's been getting dark lately . . . so dark. I've been afraid that the light would leave me, and I would not see you again."

"I'm here now, and I'm not going anywhere."

"Do you remember when you first came . . . to Cafura, and you saw . . . me on the wall? When I saw you . . . I knew things would be different. I'm glad I got to know you . . . even if it was for a few moments . . . I've always thought of death, and I thought I was ready for it. It may be Daiyu's will, but I wish I could have had more moments with you."

"No . . . no. I'm not letting go. Do you hear me? We're not through yet. I will not have us part."

"I like the sound of your voice," she said, smiling.

Pasha stopped. Those words had completely disarmed him of his arsenal of angry words and flooded him with emotion.

"I think you still owe me something. I don't want to leave here without it."

"This is not the time," Pasha said as his eyes became red and full of tears.

"The time to die is certain. The time to live is now."

His scarf became wet as the water from his eyes began to cascade down his face.

And to his surprise, when Pasha opened his mouth, his words came out in song.

> *Through the tall trees and little light I went, carefully*
> *trying to find my way,*
> *And as I went, before my eyes I saw the light of day,*
> *The black angel of light in the heavy night there to show*
> *me my way.*
> *Do I go and turn at an angle on to my life along the way,*
> *Or do I linger with the black angel who turns my night*
> *into day?*
> *Her neck is long and graceful as the swan,*
> *And in the sparkle of her eyes I see the coming dawn.*
> *Shall I go and follow her path, risking the danger of the*
> *night's wrath?*
> *By day shall I follow, and in her bosom at night shall I*
> *lay?*
> *Will she let me give her honor and teach me the nature*
> *of beauty?*
> *Will she give me charge of her and let me have her as my*
> *duty?*
> *Will she teach me of love, of the joys, rewards, and pain*
> *it brings?*
> *Twas in the arms of the black angel of light in the heavy*
> *night I learned all of those things.*

Pasha looked down at Mahlinya as tears swelled and fell. "Like an angel," she said to Pasha.

Over the next seven days, the rest of the scattered southern forces found their way back to the city of Cafura. Instead of lodging their men within her walls, the generals made camp in the mountain caves to the north and along the outskirts of the city.

When all the tribes had gathered again, the losses from the last battle became increasingly evident. More than ten thousand men were dead.

Upon learning of the flight of General Shabaz, General Marwa and his men made their own quiet exit. King Hanasa and the remaining generals knew that with such losses there was no way they could repel the enemy forces.

Yet, as of that moment, the enemy had not moved against the city. Most of the tribes had been chased into the jungle and on until they reached the main road. Instead of continuing the pursuit, the enemy forces had fallen back to reassemble ten miles away to the city's west. There they remained in wait, as if expecting the men of the south to assemble and challenge them. Such things weighed heavily on the Halor king's mind but did not concern Pasha, whose focus was on more personal things.

For the entire eight days since they had returned, Pasha did not leave Mahlinya's side. Abayomi took charge over the men without question. The commander resolved to keep things proceeding smoothly so that his friend could stay with the one he cared for. In this manner, Abayomi wished to honor their friendship.

Pasha looked at Mahlinya while he sat by her side. Though the rising and falling of her chest told Pasha she could still breathe, her eyes had not opened for three days. In spite of his efforts, all of his attempts to wake her had failed.

The heaviness of twilight was quickly broken by the coming of the dawn, yet it mattered not to Pasha. For him, life could not go on until she could take part in it again.

". . . And when I was young, Zailo called me little chicken. He called me that because I was always chasing after him and my other brothers when they went to do something. And because my legs and neck were skinny, skinny like a chicken. One time my brothers told me that if I kissed a bird every day and flapped my arms real hard, I would fly. It took a month before I realized they were playing a trick on me . . . Another time. Zailo and my brother Malakim told me that if I saw a crow in the daylight, they would come at night and eat my feet, because they love the taste of little boy's feet. The skies around the Aliso River were always full of them. Then Zailo told me that the only way to protect them was to wrap them in cloth dipped into cow dung. For weeks, my mother could not figure out why I smelled so bad. But Asdalaya would always find out and put an end to my brothers' games. He was always there to sort me out and speak for me. Were your sisters ever like that? Or your brother?"

Pasha paused for her to answer. It surprised him how long he waited for an answer that would never come.

"You always sleep through my stories. They can't be so bad. I try to liven them up for you."

Pasha paused.

"You can't be tired. The day just started. What do you want to do today? We can go riding. Oh wait no. Right now it's too dangerous. We could go walking . . . What's that . . . No walking. Well then let's go make a meal. Oh, not hungry. I have it! Why don't we just stay here and rest . . . Sound good to you? I knew you'd think so . . . Why don't you wait for me here while I go to the roof? No, I won't be long, just need to figure out some things . . . Save my place."

Pasha stood and turned to leave the room. He said nothing to her aunts who were waiting outside. The captain went up to the roof, stumbling to his knees as he made his way to the center of the highest level. His head lifted up toward the sky.

"In the beginning, I would have refused the path you have set for me. But I know who I am now and what my duty must be. But I am only a man! A man you have tested so harshly since childhood! The people tell me that the way is mercy. Where was the mercy for my brothers and my wife? Where was it for me? I know who I am now. But know this. No more! No more of my family or friends shall you take . . ."

Pasha exploded into a fit of tears and emotions he had kept guarded for days.

"I am only a man. If you strike me down once more, I will not rise again! Bring my son back to me. Save the woman I love, and I promise I shall never part from the way again."

CHAPTER 25

Take the Day

For the next few days, the continuing food crisis in the city worsened. People began to drop dead daily, children making up a large portion of their numbers. Sorrow and despair permeated every level of the city. Along with the food crisis, many worried about the men of the north who could come at any moment and burn the city to the ground. Others did not care; living had lost its value for them. They gathered outside of the temple under the sound of the shazhia's voice, who stood on a high platform outside of the doors to the sanctuary.

The shazhia spoke in a clear but mournful tone to the weary people before him.

"And so Nateo told us that the master would never leave us. Nor would he forget his people. He cares for the wounded, the dying, and the sick. Maikael will deliver them into his arms, and he will embrace them into the glory of the heavens. For every darkness there is a dawn. Even in these times, we must remember that Daiyu is still with us."

"Where is he when our children are dying? Where was he when my wife died?" shouted a man in a dirty brown tunic, his head adorned with a dingy white turban.

Several dozen nodded as they voiced their approval.

"Brothers and sisters, now is not the time to be discouraged. Daiyu does not leave us when the darkness comes. He knows your pain, he knows your sorrow. Entrust him with it; trust that he will bring healing."

"We are tired of hearing these lies! Daiyu does not care for us! Daiyu does not care for us! Do not tell me to believe when I am forced to burn my wife's body and when I'll do the same for my children," shouted the man again.

The shazhia was weary. Though he had every right to strongly rebuke the man, he hesitated. He understood his anger. The way led one to serve Daiyu, but that path did not come without trials.

Just then a dissenting voice arose from the crowd. "And of what good are your children's lives? Of what good was that of your wife if you do not believe?"

The man turned around to see who spoke to him. Shock and surprise sprung into his face upon seeing Captain Nuvahli making his way to the center of the crowd where the man stood. All eyes turned to him.

"Daiyu gives us life and gives us others to share in that life so that we may know his beauty and love through the people we share our lives with. It is our intimate knowledge of these things that bring us closer to him. I am like you, all of you, a man who has been dealt a great many blows in life. I lost most of my family as a boy, and as a man, my family was taken from me once more. I fought against Daiyu for a long time and hated him, driving my path further into darkness. But then I realized that through our sorrow and pain he renews us and makes us stronger. It is by the finality of life that we can realize the beauty of his creation. He will not leave us, and he does care for us. That is something we must remember at all costs. We must gather strength from it and carry on as our people have before."

Pasha tore off his turban and let his cloak fall. Many gasped upon seeing the seven thick lines painted on his forehead. The captain fell onto his knees and raised his open palms. In both palms were images of the Ring of Shakana painted onto his hands.

The captain said his prayer in the old way, but the people understood.

"Into your hands, Daiyu, most merciful one, I put the burden of my people. Let them carry it no longer. Let them be renewed as you have renewed me."

Suddenly the skies became overcast. Wind sped through in all directions, bringing with it previously unseen clouds. Pasha did not move while the others grew agitated and fearful. And then in the sky, black shapes began to dive down from the clouds. Soon they were a swarm and coming in fast.

In moments, they began to realize that it was a massive flock of birds. The birds flew until they were completely over the Sashraman city. Then they stopped and fell dead into the crowds below.

Many of the women screamed as they ran with the men for cover. But Pasha did not move. He stayed in place while the birds fell all about him. Within an instant, the last bird had fallen. It took awhile for the people to register what had just happened. Once they had, a ferocious roar of cheering and laughter exploded within the city that day.

Men, women, and children dove and seized as many of the birds as they could. The cheering intensified as formerly starving people hoisted the fowl over their heads.

As Pasha stood, his name became a song upon their lips. The captain looked about the crowd of people in search of something.

And then he found it when he looked toward the doors of the temple. Standing beside the wall leading into the temple was Mahlinya. She wore a light orange spring dress with her arms and shoulders bare. Neither her arms nor neck bore any blemish. And in her eyes Pasha saw new strength as she smiled at him and waved.

That night the mood was light and empty of fear for much of the city. It was so for Pasha and Mahlinya that night as well as they sat on the roof of her house, inseparable in their embrace.

Pasha watched as Mahlinya stared up to the star-filled night.

"Do you think much of the future?" he asked her.

Mahlinya turned to look at him. "Haretii people aren't really brought up worrying about the future. My mother used to say that for everything in life Daiyu has a purpose that shall be realized. Until it is, all that matters is the moment and who you share it with."

Impulse suddenly seized Pasha, and he took hold of her neck and the back of her head as he came down to kiss her. As his lips touched hers, she did not resist. Instead she drew him closer as they drew life from each other.

"I would not have one more moment without you," said Pasha.

"Nor I without you," she said.

The next five weeks were like a miracle for the people. All of the plague had disappeared from the city, and all that were sick recovered. The number of fowl that had fallen had been so large that the city was with enough food for another month. In the absence of the enemy, farmers went out to harvest while foragers and hunters sought fresh game and wild fruit.

During this time, Pasha's love for Mahlinya only grew. Each day they were inseparable, and Pasha thought only of her. Every moment together he spent studying her, the light in her eyes, the way her hair looked, what pleased her and made her happy. For a long while, it had scared him, the thought he could feel for someone like he had felt for Hadassah. Nevertheless, the fear he had carried disappeared.

But it did not take away the many other fears the captain carried in his heart. No day passed when he did not think of his son. After so long, he had seen him, a boy more than ten years older than he should have been, bearing hatred in his eyes. He prayed that Daiyu would let him find Kamili again and break whatever evil his sister-in-law had put upon his son.

At times Pasha thought of Hadassah, wondering if he loved Mahlinya as much as he had her. Hadassah had been more than beautiful; she had been a part of his body and the center of his heart. He felt the same about Mahlinya, but was it as strong? Perhaps the matter was not whether he loved Mahlinya as much as he had loved her. Long ago, Miori had taught his son that people come together in different ways; therefore they love in different ways, but love's strength never fails to see them through. Pasha hoped it would be so for them.

After taking his leave of her, Pasha went to the temple to seek out the shazhia. He found him in the sanctuary at a low table before his platform, writing on parchment.

"Shazhia, I would speak to you," said Pasha.

"Kaudi," he said, bowing his head toward Pasha.

"I have need of your services later on this night," said Pasha.

"Are you mourning someone?"

"No. I'm celebrating life and a new purpose."

"Such are the blessings of Daiyu. Have I ever told you about the Vati?"

"The Vati?" asked Pasha.

"You don't know of them. Well I'm not surprised. Not a common story anymore in the south. Few people still know it."

"You're trying to tell me something?"

"On Malik Juktan's throne, have you not seen the engravings of the great winged horses?"

Pasha thought back. He remembered the image from the last time he had been in the king's presence.

"The Vati have always been seen as great sources of strength. Guardians who once kept watch over the entrance to the sanctuary of the great temple in the holy city of Muzha. Daiyu sent them to man to serve as guardians and protectors. Some of them mated with other horses and conceived the Miza, greatest of all the horses in the land today. But it did not last. They were such pure creatures that their blood could heal the sick and dying and even revive the dead.

"But people forgot the way and forgot Daiyu. They lost sight and started to slaughter the Vati, cursing themselves for generations. Only those that seek out purity can take the blood.

"It is said that they fly in and out of the eye of the sun when it rises and when it sets. And when one who has the voice of conviction calls, they will fly down from the heavens and come to him."

"Can they break the bonds of the hajjaram and end this once and for all?" asked Pasha.

"In the Vati many answers lie," said the shazhia, smiling.

Saying no more, the old man left the captain alone while he pondered his words.

In the early hours of evening, Pasha returned to Mahlinya's home in the city, finding her on the rooftop. When he stepped onto the roof, he found her looking out as the sun was beginning to set.

"You asked me about the future before. The reason I don't think of it is because I know that this, this is only a dream. Like all dreams, it has to end, never to return. That is what I fear when I think of the future, when I think of you."

Pasha marched to the center of the roof where she stood and took her in his arms.

"I will be more than a dream. I swear it."

Mahlinya reached up with her hand, taking hold of one of Pasha's twisted black locks. "What do you think of, Kaudi Nuvahli?"

"A simpler time, when kindness and laughter ruled over us. I wish I was brave like you."

"How am I brave? Do I lead men into battles they may not survive? Am I the first to go into danger when I know I may not live through it?"

"You and I are the same in many ways. We don't fear death. But unlike me, you don't fear life either. I'm still trying to be like that again. You said your mother told you that what matters is every moment and who you share it with."

"Yes," she said, looking into his eyes.

"Do you love me?"

"Yes," she said, kissing his neck.

"Come with me into the city. There is someone waiting for us."

In spite of their love, Pasha knew their time would be short. The drums of war were calling once more, and the captain knew he could not escape his fate. The generals and King Hanasa knew they couldn't defend the city anymore. Instead of waiting, Pasha and the leaders of the remaining tribes had agreed; the only way to keep the men of the north from Cafura would be to take the fight to the enemy themselves. In the mountains and the jungles, they could keep the men of the north occupied for weeks if not months. It pained the Sashraman warriors to leave their city, but all of them knew that the people would live longer if they took the fight to the enemy and held them back for as long as possible.

CHAPTER 26

Final Hour

During their flight, they had gone through the jungles surrounding Cafura and drove deep toward the southwest. Though the enemy followed, they did not try to engage them. Upon leaving the jungles, they had split their numbers as they went through the tall grassy plains of the west.

After passing through Viali village and warning its residents to leave, they crossed the only shallow crossing of the Usoni River and went into the passes of Mount Tabah. The mountain's slopes were surrounded by more mountains to the north and the Usoni River to the east and southwest. Behind the slopes to the northwest were the Mahara fields that spanned for miles.

To the Sashramans, it would be the perfect place to defend. With the harsh terrain and limited access, they would make the men of the north pay dearly for following them inside. Such had been Pasha's oath when they crossed the river.

The Sashraman captain slept among a small grove of trees at the base of the mountains. Sensing something, Pasha awoke from his sleep and looked to the trees. He could not explain it, but there was something there he had to find. Pasha rose to leave the camp and headed down the path. He quickly left the grove of trees and stepped onto uneven ground while passing through mounds of rocks and dirt.

Looking above to the heavy moon, the captain remembered his task.

He seized handfuls of sand and began to make a circle. Inside he placed three black rocks. He placed the rocks at three points while drawing the image of the Ring of Shakana between them. Once he had finished, the captain stepped inside of the circle, looking once more to the heavy moon above.

"I call unto you, old guardians, protectors of the way. Old friends, being of virtue and strength. The pure ones whose way is honor and whose heart is of mercy. Come back to me, your brother, one who has need of you again. Fill me with guidance, teach me wisdom. Hear the one who calls out to you. Your brother, seeker of the way."

Dark clouds began to shroud the moon as a gusting wind tore through the night air. Its strength grew and lifted Pasha from his feet and threw him back more than twenty paces. As quickly as it had come, it vanished when Pasha came back to his feet.

Though the clouds about the moon had dissipated, Pasha could see dark shapes flying out from beneath the moon. At first they flew east but quickly turned west and began flying down toward Pasha.

When they landed, the moon cast a bright light over them. Seven tall, muscled horses walked the ground before him. Not one bore a blemish. They were perfect in all ways, with strong legs, graceful necks, and arched backs. Four were a flawless bronze color while two others wore a majestic white mane, and the last was of a royal black tone. And most notably, from their shoulders came long and powerful wings that were quickly tucked to their sides as they moved toward Pasha.

Pasha's heartbeat quickened as they all looked at him. Thousands of whispering voices filled his head. After several moments, they slowed and became clear.

Though their mouths did not move, Pasha could feel and hear their every thought rippling through him. They spoke as one, yet they didn't all say the same thing. The black one stood before them all, bearing his gaze down on Pasha.

"Come to me, brother. Teach me of your ways. Help me in this time," the captain said to the creature.

Pasha knew he understood as he came forward. Soon the creature stood directly in front of Pasha and leaned out its neck to him. Pasha's hands twitched fearfully as he remembered his task.

The men of the south woke to the sounds of horns. They reacted on instinct, rushing through the grove down to the rocky slopes below. It was not long before all of the warriors of the remaining tribes were rushing to their positions while rapid blasts from the horns warned them of the enemy advance.

Once they crossed the river, the enemy would run into a set of parallel cliffs and rock faces that made up the base of the mountain slopes. From there, the Sashramans and their remaining allies would be waiting.

Pasha looked out from the top of the second rock face, directly across from the first one where the Halor waited. On the ground below, infantry and cavalry units clung tightly to the rocky walls in anticipation of an attack.

Many command changes were made in the aftermath of the previous battle, including Shukimbo's advancement from duma to saji. Pasha had divided the army into three units between him, Abayomi, and Shukimbo to lead the remaining Sashraman warriors in the next fight.

Archers from all three of their units had been placed along the remaining two cliffs while some infantry units remained on the cliffs. They would charge down the cliff behind the enemy once the men of the north had made their advance, in the hope of surrounding them and cutting them off.

Pasha and some of his men on the cliff sat on rocks and watched while Takil and others labored over clay bowls.

Abayomi came and sat among them. "All the men are in place, Kaudi."

"And the enemy?"

"They're still waiting at the river. More than likely, they still don't know whether to advance or not."

"They're going to. You can rest assured of that."

Takil and his fellows finished and began to pass the bowls among the men. To Abayomi's surprise, the bowls contained brightly colored paints that Takil and his men began smearing on the other warriors faces.

Soon Takil came to Pasha. Working quickly, he smeared bright blue streaks onto both sides of Pasha's face. Using another hand, he dipped into some yellow paint and began to form the image of the Ring of Shakana onto his captain's forehead.

"I thought it was forbidden for warriors to put any mark upon their skin," said Abayomi.

"Do you really think marks on the skin decide your fate in eternity?" said Pasha.

"Here," he said, handing the bowl to Abayomi.

Though reluctant at first, Abayomi reached down and dipped his hands into the paint.

Blaring horns filled their ears. Pasha and his men looked east toward the opposite cliff where Halor warriors were madly waving their warning banners.

"The Yashani and Naua have engaged!" said Pasha.

"All right, boys, into position! Everyone get down!"

"Into position!" Abayomi repeated.

Just as they ordered, the men of Sashra fell to their backs with their bows ready.

Before they knew it, they heard the steady roll of the northern drum. The sound rattled their eardrums as the enemy banners came within sight. Pasha and Abayomi crawled toward the edge of the rock face, looking down at the continuing battle.

Yashani and Naua horse archers covered their retreat as a steady column of northern pike and ax men in thick armored plates surge forward. Dozens of kads of enemy archers fired on them while cavalry units charged forward.

Yashani and Naua archers began to fall as enemy volleys began to overwhelm them. Many of the fleeing spearmen and lancers were stuck in the back while they made way into the cliffs.

Halor archers suddenly came to their feet and began firing down into the enemy.

Pasha took his bundle of spears and readied them for swift action. "Now!" he shouted.

"Eyes down!"

In unison, the Sashramans came together and launched their volley into the enemy forces. Pasha hurled spear after spear into their foes below.

To the northerners' surprise, their advance slowed as arrows and spears nailed their cavalry and archers. Their line of spearmen turned right and raised their shields while archers on the ground tried to move into position.

The Sashramans scattered hundreds of enemy archers as they took fire from two sides.

"Abayomi, you'd better get down there!" Pasha shouted.

His officer began to rush in the opposite direction toward the level pass that led to the ground below.

Northern horsemen cried out as their bodies were mangled by Sashraman arrows. In spite of their mobility, the northern horse archers were easy targets between the constricting walls. With their archers being overwhelmed on open ground, the entire northern column began to press back. The pike and ax men locked their shields into a wall while the remaining archers formed up behind them.

Pasha heard the familiar Halor horns and looked east. On the opposite cliff, Halor warriors now had their attention directed to the more than a hundred northern swordsmen climbing up the cliff wall and moving up the open pass that connected the cliff to the ground.

"Takil!" shouted Pasha.

His man looked over toward him, awaiting an order. "Sir!" he responded.

"Move them in!"

"Yes, sir."

Takil understood without asking. He went and retrieved one of the warning banners and ran to the opposite end of the cliff. Upon seeing the waving banner overhead, Abayomi began to move the ground forces forward as the enemy came closer.

Below, the enemy was beginning to push forward again while archers fired at the Sashramans from behind the heavily armored and shield-wielding pike men. Soon more enemy archers moved up and began to overwhelm the Halor archers just as enemy swordsmen reached the summit of the cliff.

Pasha ducked when a torrent of enemy missiles soared toward them. The speedy shafts impaled many Sashramans and sent their bodies hurtling toward the ground below. His men rose back up and fired off quick volleys and ducked down once more. Dozens more fell as the enemy archers increasingly began to hit their targets.

To their horror, the archers formed a line behind the advancing enemy pike men and began to fire into the sky above the cliffs where the Sashramans and Halor were. Swarms of enemy shafts hailed down on the barely prepared men of the south. Those with shields flipped them over their backs as they curled into tight balls.

Like the rest of them, Pasha curled into a tight ball and flipped his shield on top of him. Most of the spearmen and swordsmen had shields, but they were not so numerous among the archers. They fell in, curled up beside shield-wielding men, but many were not saved as rapidly moving shafts tore into their backs and pinned them to the rocks beneath them.

A loud roar filled their ears, signaling the charge of the ground forces. With General Ishok beside him, Abayomi and the Sashramans crashed into the advancing northern forces, sending ripples in the wave of advancing northern troops.

The Yashani and Sashraman lancers pressed the attack while the spearmen went on behind them. Yashani horse archers peppered the enemy with hundreds of rapidly flying shafts. The enemy responded in kind with hundreds more arrows. The

Yashani archers were driven back while many fell with arrows stuck in their flesh.

In the east at the opposite cliff, the unit pressing against the Halor was pushed back as King Hanasa and his generals joined the fight.

As Pasha watched it all from the top of the cliff, he knew it was time to move.

"Let's go!" he said to his men.

The Sashramans rose once more and fired off a volley into the men of the north before breaking into a run toward one of the passes leading to the ground.

Pasha found the spearmen and swordsmen ready once they arrived at one of the passes. The captain quickly retrieved his awaiting horse and mounted while the brush and stones partially hiding the pass were removed.

The archers rushed down first and began letting shafts fly while Pasha and the lancers surged forward. Spearmen came in behind Pasha just as his lancers drove their shafts into the enemy. The cries of war tore through the mountain walls as the Sashramans advanced.

Enemy ax men chopped into the Sashraman horses, keen to make short work of their riders. The captain carefully directed Daimon's strength against the northerners. His mount kicked his legs into them and stomped them into the ground while Pasha finished them off with his larger spear.

Dozens of arrows and spear tips glanced off of Pasha's shield and armor as he went forward. He slid his shield down to block when an enemy ax lunged toward his leg. With his other hand, he drove his spear into the enemy warrior's neck.

To his surprise the warrior snapped his neck back, taking Pasha's spear with him. Pasha drew his sword as the enraged Baku swung his ax one last time. Pasha blocked it and slit the man's throat.

In the distance, Pasha could see Abayomi. Separated by a vast sea of struggling men, they could do little for each other. Initially they had scored many enemy casualties by dividing their forces and attacking on multiple sides, but being divided, they could not gather their little remaining strength to make much of a difference.

Already Abayomi's advance had been halted. While enemy spearmen and archers bled his men, Abayomi and General Ishok held their ground, at least for the moment.

In the east was one sign of hope as General Mashilo and King Hanasa blazed a path toward Abayomi and General Ishok in the center. Pasha resolved to get there as well.

Shukimbo, who led the other unit, had nearly pushed forward toward Pasha. The captain regrouped his spearmen into a crescent as enemy cavalry were driving his spearmen apart. Several times the line nearly broke, but his men hung on.

Having only two kads of archers left, Pasha centered them behind his spear formation as it pressed forward. The archers fired short volleys into the enemy ahead of them while the spearmen drove their spears into an enemy, swarming them in all directions.

The sight horrified Pasha as dozens of spearmen fell out of the line to their deaths with each step forward. Heavy feet quickly trampled their bodies.

Shukimbo's spearmen and swordsmen soon broke through to them. Pasha and the men then tried to circle back around the main northern force to the center by moving against the cliff walls.

Suddenly ripples went through the sea of men again as another northern column advanced. Feelings of foreboding took hold of Pasha when he saw the standards of Janaha and what looked like his black riders in the distance.

Without warning, massive fireballs barreled into the advancing Halor warriors and consumed them. Their advance halted while the column of black riders rode into them and hacked them down.

Heavy columns of smoke shot up into the sky. The only ones seen coming from them were the black riders; no Halor warriors followed.

Moving swiftly, the enemy column broke off in two. One continued driving into the left flank while the other and much larger one drove up the middle. Soon Janaha became clearly visible as he led his men down the middle.

His fiery red helmet and armor were like a blaze of red lightning as his men tore into the Yashani and Sashraman spearmen.

Pasha and Shukimbo's units pushed hard toward Abayomi while his archers tried to slow the advancing riders. Fear took hold of them as another unstoppable torrent of flame slammed into them. The Yashani and Sashraman spearmen began to crumble.

As their units came closer, Pasha searched around for Abayomi, but the billowing smoke blocked his view.

Pasha and Shukimbo linked up with a line of General Ishok's spearmen as the Sashramans and the rest of the Yashani fell back. However, Pasha knew that they had lost the momentum and that there would be no stopping the men of the north in between the cliffs.

The moment the Yashani and Sashraman spear line had crumbled; the men of the north punched through the gaps in the line and began spearing down the men of the south.

Janaha quickly caught sight of Pasha as he urged his men forward. But the massive tide of northern warriors only grew as Janaha went forward. Northern archers punched deeper holes in their remaining line while the ax men hacked into the southern spearmen. Pasha could see that the men were faltering; they needed to fall back. No Halor warriors could be seen in the distance; it was obvious that they were alone.

Suddenly Janaha came within Pasha's view as his mighty pike swept through dozens of Yashani and Sashramans. Shukimbo moved his remaining spearmen against Janaha while the ranksmasters led the swordsmen.

Daimon reared back as hundreds of spears lunged toward him. Pasha blocked most of them while Daimon kicked the rest.

Seeing Janaha rushing forward, Pasha joined most of his men as they followed General Ishok's call to retreat.

However, as Pasha went, he was followed by a massive line of fire as Janaha shot flames at him and his men. Pain stabbed at Pasha's insides as he saw the flames consume Shukimbo and many of his men.

The rushing of wind filled his ears. When Pasha looked back, his eyes were filled with the sight of orange flames. But then he felt a force wrapping around him, and he was thrown from Daimon's back hundreds of paces forward.

Pasha's body crashed into the rocky ground while hundreds of warriors around him fled. He rose back up, seeing that he was far off from Daimon and the pursuing men of the north. Another heavy column of smoke filled the air, and the captain gazed in horror as red and orange flames licked the flesh off of his mount.

Daimon's cries of fury quickly faded as the flames consumed him.

"No! Daimon!" shouted Pasha.

His friend of so many years went in the way of his noble ancestors and was no more. Pasha stared back in dazed disbelief, trying to understand what he had just seen.

From the billowing smoke, Janaha and his riders surged forward.

Pasha stared long and hard at him while his hand reached down for his blade. But his plans for vengeance were interrupted as General Ishok rode to him.

"What are you doing? Come!" he shouted.

He quickly hoisted Pasha onto the back of his mount and fled the pursuing men of the north.

The Sashramans and Yashani fled to the base of the mountain in between two narrow rock faces where the Naua had formed up their lines. General Ishok dismounted, and Pasha ran alongside him and fell in behind the line of archers as they readied for the coming Baku and Jakshima spearmen. Naua spearmen and swordsmen stood ready as the remaining Yashani and Sashramans formed up behind them.

As the enemy came within sight, General Tayla ordered his men to fire. The volley slowed the enemy for a moment as hundreds of spearmen fell to their deaths. Naua archers followed the volley with another as the black riders rushed forward.

Firing off once more, the archers rushed to the right and left flanks and fell in behind the spearmen as they moved forward.

Pasha stood with General Ishok and his warriors as the black riders crashed into the awaiting Naua spearmen. The Sashramans and Yashani immediately charged.

Northern spears quickly tore holes into their line, but the Naua held on. Naua archers in the caves above hailed down arrows on the enemy. The northerners howled in anger as their archers were unable to reach them.

The heavy masses of men broke spears into one another as they tried to break the spirit of the other. Moving in unison, the Yashani and Sashramans joined the Naua and pushed hard into the enemy with their shields while stabbing with their spears.

What little ground was gained was soon lost to the wild northern ax men who battered the Naua line. Archer fire slowed them down, but it did not stop them.

An even greater roar filled their ears as dozens of men were hurled into the air by a powerful force. They soon knew the force to be Janaha's pike as he pressed forward. Though he proceeded on foot, the northern general proved more deadly than ever.

Once more, his eyes made contact with Pasha's, and so the captain rushed forward to meet him. Janaha swept away five Yashani and hacked down two Naua before lunging toward Pasha.

The captain ducked and swung his blade at Janaha's legs. Already anticipating that move, the enemy general leapt and kicked Pasha's side. Pasha rolled away, clutching his side. Janaha bounded forward and rose in the air like a mighty cat. He came down with his pike, slashing down toward Pasha's neck.

Pasha sidestepped and drove his sword at his foe's side. Janaha blocked the blow and stepped toward Pasha, but the captain jumped away as he drove his pike toward Pasha's chest.

Pasha leapt and jumped back toward him, but Janaha swung up to block his sword. The blow caught Pasha off guard as the blunt side of Janaha's pike drove his sword back and struck him down at the neck and shoulder.

Pasha collapsed into the ground, and pain riveted through his body. On the ground, Pasha saw Janaha coming to drive his pike into him. Pasha rolled quickly and came to his feet.

Janaha's pike struck only rock and dirt. Pasha wasted no time and ran back into the pressing ranks of Naua and Yashani.

Seeing the hundreds of warriors standing before him, Janaha stretched out his hands and began a low chant. Mounds of earth exploded from beneath the feet of the warriors. A gusting wind tore through the ranks of the men of the south, soon to be followed by a massive column of fire. The center of the southern ranks was completely consumed with fire as the rest of them struggled to hold the line, and the men of the north swarmed over them.

Janaha rushed forward in pursuit of Pasha as he entered one of the many mountain caves. Pasha stopped at the doorway of the dimly lit cavern and turned back. His eyes beheld his struggling allies as their lines were breaking and many men retreated.

When he looked back, it was Janaha's image that filled his eyes.

"Going somewhere?" he said, laughing. He stretched out his hand toward Pasha, and an invisible force seized the captain and threw him deeper into the cave.

"Look at you! So brave and noble!"

His hand raised again and jerked suddenly. The force seized Pasha once more and hurled him into the cavern walls. Pasha collapsed onto the cavern floor.

As he lay there, the same whispering voices he had heard before filled his ears. He felt a rising strength gathering inside of him.

"Running like a whipped dog! You may wish me to be quick, but I'm going to work on you very slowly, my brother! Like last time," he said, laughing.

Janaha raised his hands toward Pasha, and flames appeared within them.

"I would have it no other way!" Pasha said.

The rising strength took over Pasha just as Janaha hurled the flames. His body flew to its feet and jumped away as the fire came closer.

Grinding his teeth angrily, Janaha threw another fireball at his enemy. Pasha dodged it again as he stepped back deeper into the cavern. Suddenly five balls of fire erupted into Janaha's hands, and he hurled them at the Sashraman.

The captain stood ready. Moving almost on their own, his arms crossed themselves, and his palms reached out as the fire came his way. The flame extinguished itself as it touched his skin. No part of the captain's body burned or was singed. Janaha glared at Pasha.

Not wasting a moment, Pasha came down into a low posture as he stretched out his palms toward Janaha. Pasha felt something warm surging from all parts of his body before it made its way to his hands. Suddenly the captain's hands erupted into fire and light. Flame shot from Pasha's hands toward Janaha. The enemy general barely managed to duck the flame that shot toward his hand.

"You're remembering!" he said in anger.

Soon the entire cavern became filled with light and flames as both men shot fire and stone at the other. Pasha quickly learned of his dormant abilities while defending against his foe. Flames no longer burned or singed his skin. He quickly learned to make the flame pass through him.

With each glance at Janaha, he sensed his next action. Pasha jumped and ran back right before Janaha tore down patches of the rocky ceiling. Janaha leapt over the fallen rocks and boulders and continued to push forward. Pasha launched more fire at him while he fell back.

The strength in Pasha's body shot through his legs, giving the captain speed like he had never known. In spite of the darkness and sparse light, Pasha's head felt light and clear, and he saw and sensed everything about him.

The walls beside him suddenly exploded, and hundreds of rocks slammed into Pasha. Though he was slammed to the ground, he felt little pain as he was pelted with the sharp cavern rocks. When he rose, the rocks shot off of his body. Without warning, Janaha's feet slammed into his chest. The captain flew back a dozen paces as his adversary bounded toward him.

Pasha rolled away, narrowly missing the swinging pike. Throwing his hands out in a pushing motion, Janaha was seized by an invisible force and slammed into the wall.

Seeing light at the end of the cavern, Pasha ran toward it. When he emerged, he found himself in the Mahara fields. In the distance, he saw many Naua and Yashani along with some of his own men fleeing.

The captain began to run after them. In spite of his exhaustion, Pasha sprinted without stopping. Some of the Sashraman and Yashani warriors stopped and looked back as they saw Pasha coming toward them.

Pasha was halfway to them when he saw a group of thirty black riders riding toward them. He stopped and readied himself as the riders came closer. Most of them bore bows and started firing on the Sashramans and Yashani while the Naua who were ahead began running back to help.

The riders picked off the men of the south with ease while the rest who bore swords started to ride them down. Five of them came toward Pasha. The captain raised his hands, and words came from his lips that he had never heard. Mounds of earth exploded beneath them. The black riders were thrown from their mounts as dirt and rock slammed into them. Many of the horses fell headfirst and broke their necks as the earth was ripped from under them.

Pasha made short work of the five and turned his attention to the rest who were riding down his men. His hands were raised once more, and strange words again came from his lips. Mounds of earth lifted into the air and hurtled toward the remaining black riders. The earth exploded into them upon impact, and the Sashramans and their allies quickly subdued the rest.

Just as Pasha thought it was over, a sudden force barreled into him, sending him flying back several dozen paces. When he rose back up, he saw one of the black riders coming at him on foot. He was smaller in height and build than the rest of them, but he worked the same sorcery as Janaha.

His hands ignited into fire, and he hurled the flames at Pasha. Pasha dodged them and looked back as the flames began to consume the ground beneath. Another ball of fire came toward Pasha, but he lifted his hands and sent a gusting wind toward it. The wind forced the flame back toward his attacker, who quickly dodged it.

The warrior leapt high into the air like Janaha and landed beside Pasha. He immediately drew his sword and began to slash at Pasha's side. Air took hold of Pasha's feet and pulled him back. The captain drew his own blade and ran toward the enemy warrior. He sidestepped as the warrior lunged and swung toward his back. In a spectacular duck, the warrior bent backward at the waist and spun around to face Pasha.

He came at the captain, swinging his blade wildly toward Pasha's chest. Pasha blocked two of his blows and spun into him. Without hesitating, Pasha punched into his stomach, but instead of driving his blade into him, the captain seized his neck and ripped off his helmet.

"No!" said the captain. Shock pulsated through his body when he beheld Kamili's face. So great was the shock that Pasha let his guard fall. Kamili seized the opportunity and lunged toward Pasha's stomach. Pasha barely deflected the blow, but the blade slid down and slashed his leg.

Pasha seized his son by the neck and wrestled his sword from his hand.

"Kamili, it's me!" he said.

"You are not my father! You killed my mother!"

"You have it all wrong, Kamili. I am your father. That woman was not your mother. She used you, tricked you, and turned you into this. You know you are my son! Don't fight it!"

"Never!"

A mounting force was suddenly triggered between them. Pasha and Kamili were immediately thrown away from each other in opposite directions.

When Pasha looked up, he saw Janaha flying in the air above them. The general came down just as Pasha's men were closing in. He stretched out his hand and burned a ring of fire around all three of them.

"Do not let him poison your mind, boy! All his tongue speaks are lies!"

"The only lies are what you have put into his head. What have you done to him!"

"I have made him strong! Stronger than he ever would have been!"

"End this, brother! I beg you! Must the whole world burn before you're satisfied?"

"Man's way is clouded. I will bring clarity and direction as only those of our kind can bring. You were my brother once, Pasha, long ago. I still offer you my love and my mercy. Do not go down the path of a fool! We were meant for this!"

"I called you brother once. Never again! Now give me my son!"

"Shame," said Janaha as he threw his pike to Kamili.

Reaching down to his side, Janaha drew his long, curved sword.

"Let's end this the way we did last time."

Janaha pounced toward Pasha, swinging wildly. Pasha sidestepped and blocked as Janaha came toward him. Suddenly Janaha's lips parted, and spittle sprayed into Pasha's face. Pasha was blinded as two blows struck him in the stomach and back, sending him to the ground.

"You used to be so strong. Now look at you!" said Janaha. He kicked Pasha in the side once more and stabbed toward him.

But Pasha rolled away and came quickly to his feet. The captain wiped his eyes as Janaha came toward him.

Each blow felt liked twenty when Janaha struck. Pasha blocked the best he could as the explosive force within his foe's arms struck against him. Janaha struck once more, sending the blade flying from Pasha's hands. Kamili quickly retrieved it as Janaha punched Pasha's face, sending the captain's helmet flying from his head.

Captain Pasha fell to his knees before Janaha. His foe kicked him repeatedly in the gut. The Sashraman gasped for air as his insides cried out in pain.

"Did you really think your mortal body could defeat me! Did you! Even after all of these years, you still don't understand."

As his brother lifted his blade to deliver the final blow, Pasha drew a dagger hidden on his leg. The moment Janaha come close, Pasha rolled into him and plunged the dagger into his stomach twice.

Though he tried to stand, Pasha found the strength within him waning.

Janaha looked down at the dagger within him, but within moments he was laughing. He slid the dagger out of his gut. "Weak mortal fool," he said.

He stepped over Pasha once more, aiming his blade directly at his throat. Pasha looked not at him but at Kamili who stood holding his sword.

To his surprise, his son did not wear a glad expression as Janaha prepared to make an end of him. Instead, Pasha saw the same worry and concern he had seen so many times in Hadassah's face.

Pasha turned his head and looked up to the sky. The captain breathed in deeply.

"That's right, brother. Draw that last breath! Savor it!" Janaha started to plunge his blade into Pasha's chest. But in a sudden jolt of energy Pasha felt his sword as an extension of his body; his mind centered on the blade and increased his power over it. Pasha's blade shot from Kamili's hands and buried itself into Janaha's back.

Janaha stopped, looking back at the blade sticking into his shoulder blades.

He began laughing again. "Amazing how you tr . . ." His words were cut off as his breath became ragged.

Finding strength, Pasha stood as Janaha began to stumble back. His breathing began to shorten, and his body trembled.

To his horror, the once proud Janaha fell to his knees.

"What! What did you do to me!"

"It's an old story, brother. One that you should know. One that tells of what happens when something pure and righteous comes near something so evil and corrupt."

Pasha circled around Janaha and pulled the blade from his back. Janaha let out a heavy gasp as the trembling worsened.

"The Vati!" he said.

"Yes," Pasha said as he brandished his sword before him.

The blade was a smooth red as if it had been painted.

"When you slay a Vati, the blood never goes away. Eventually it starts eating away at the blade, and at you. You can't stand it, can you? The pureness of their blood inside of you, eating away at your hardened heart!"

Janaha's face twisted from fear into hatred as he looked at Pasha. "You . . . you . . ."

"I know . . . I know, brother," said Pasha.

He plunged the blade once more into Janaha's chest. His enemy's cries rung out through the air. In one final stroke, Pasha swung the blade down at his neck. The cries finally stopped as the head of Janaha rolled off his shoulders. What was left of Janaha disappeared.

A frantic Kamili, unsure of what to do in the present moment, gave off a yell as he charged toward Pasha.

Pasha lifted his hand, sending Kamili crashing into the ground. Pasha came over him as his son lashed out with fists. The captain seized his son's hands and pinned them behind him.

"Why did you kill him!" he cried.

"I didn't want to. Your mother and I didn't want any of this for you."

Pasha took hold of his son and embraced him in spite of his attempts to fight him off. Eventually, Kamili gave up and surrendered to his father's embrace.

"I failed your mother, Kamili, and I failed you. I can't change the past, but I promise your future will be different."

The Sashramans and their allies approached slowly, their weapons ready.

"Sir," called out one of Pasha's men. "We'll deal with him."

"No! Put your weapons down. This is not the enemy!"

Though it took a long while to convince them, the Sashramans and their allies eventually did as he asked.

"Look there! Its Malik Juktan's banner!"

Pasha looked back to the mountains in the distance. Sashraman warriors were now pouring over the cliffs, led by the standards of the malik's house in Kadisha.

Riding ahead of them, Pasha saw Abayomi and his men approaching.

"Abayomi," Pasha said, standing. "See to him," he said to one of his men, gesturing toward Kamili.

The captain walked toward the approaching horsemen, relief washing over him many times. But he stopped when he saw a woman in black robes approaching him from the right. His mother removed her veil as she greeted him with a smile.

"Is it time?" Pasha said, breathing heavily as he looked back toward Kamili.

"Yes, my son. What you have done here will never be forgotten. Peace will come to people of the south once more. There was never a mother more proud."

"What of him? I thought there would be more time."

"Do not worry. His path will become clear again. He shall be as great as his father."

Abayomi rushed forward to greet Pasha, who stood waiting for them. He longed to tell Pasha of Malik Juktan's miraculous arrival and the defeat of the northern tribes. But then Pasha's body began to sway back and forth, and he collapsed to the ground.

"No!" Abayomi yelled.

When they came close, he leapt from his mount and fell beside Pasha as the rest of the men closed in.

"Pasha! Pasha!"

Pasha's breathing grew ragged, and his eyes unfocused.

"Can you hear me?"

"Abayomi. Are the men safe?"

"Yes, Kaudi. Malik Juktan has come," he said. "Get a physician. Get somebody!" he yelled to one of the men.

"Abayomi." Pasha's voice became softer as his breathing slowed.

"No, no, no, no, Pasha. It doesn't end like this. Pasha!"

The captain's head turned to the other side, no longer aware of his friend.

"Mahlinya," Pasha said softly.

CHAPTER 27

Warrior of the Way

The streets of Cafura were silent that day, bare except for a long procession of Sashraman warriors who were of the malik's guard. Juktan walked in the middle of the procession behind Rakimo and his men while they made their way through the streets from the Sashraman barracks. Having shed his battle armor, the Sashraman king walked the city streets in his blue robes and turban under the golden band that marked him as the malik.

Malik Juktan looked up; it was a beautiful summer day. It seemed a bitter irony that on such a day he would have to perform such a saddening duty.

He thought of the time he spent in the west during the Sadras campaign and the strengthening of his friendship with Pasha. Though he had seen the body, it did not seem real that his friend and brother in arms was dead.

The malik knew it would be Nuvahli's fate to face Janaha, but the price for Janaha's defeat had been too high. All in all, more than fifteen thousand Sashraman warriors had been slain during the entire length of the siege. As for the people of Cafura, the numbers of their deaths was still being tallied.

In spite of their horrific trials, the Sashraman king knew that through every challenge, Daiyu had a purpose that would make them stronger. The malik hoped the purpose would be realized in the days to come.

Just then when the malik looked up, he saw a woman in black robes staring down upon them from the roof of a house. Juktan stopped when he quickly recognized her face. His men stopped with him.

"Maliki. What is it?" asked Rakimo.

Malik Juktan turned to answer, but when he looked back, the woman had vanished.

"Nothing. It's nothing," he said.

Every corner of the city center leading into the temple was immersed in an endless wave of people waiting to pay their respects to the Kaudi.

In the temple courtyard, the people of Cafura pressed together tightly while they looked to the shazhia. Men and boys sat on the temple walls looking down on the ceremony.

At the head of them all before the doors leading to the sanctuary stood the shazhia alongside Malik Juktan and Abayomi.

In recognition of Juktan, the shazhia stood back as the malik came forward to speak.

On a wooden litter before them all lay the body of Pasha Miori Okala Nuvahli, adorned in the blue robes of Sashra with his hands gripped firmly about his sword. A long turban wrapped about his head. And on his forehead was the image of the Ring of Shakana. Halor, Yashani, and Naua warriors stood among their Sashraman brethren before Captain Nuvahli's body. And in the front of them stood King Hanasa, General Tayla, and General Ishok.

"We all have a purpose. There is a reason we are all born. But so many times the purpose can seem hidden to us. Other times it is something that seems impossible or that we do not wish to do. Our brother Kaudi Nuvahli saw much suffering as a boy when all of his brothers and his mother were murdered before his eyes. Sorrow visited him again as a man when his wife was killed and his son taken from him. Such things tear men apart, and few rise again.

"Nevertheless, he was sent to us for a purpose! And the emperor's grandson did not let us down when this purpose called out to him. No one believed that Janaha, the red-eyed menace of our legends, would return. And when he did, no one believed Daiyu would save us from him. How little faith we had. Some would ask why would a man Daiyu had struck down so many times rise up to do his will. Because he had a purpose; there was a purpose behind all that happened to him. And if you knew Kaudi Nuvahli . . . If you knew Pasha as I did, you would know that he would never walk away when his people called.

"He came to this city and wasted not one moment in keeping the people safe and fighting back their enemies.

"I commend the people of this city for holding on when all looked bleak and for believing in this man even when the way was not clear.

"He was more than just a warrior. He was a husband, a father, and a friend. He was always faithful to his family, his men, and to his tribe.

"Despite the deep sorrow that wrestled inside of him, he loved, he danced, he laughed and enjoyed life's pleasures as the rest of us. He moved past his own mistrust and anxieties and made other men do the same. And so he made pacts among tribes we once called our enemies and now call our friends."

The malik nodded appreciatively toward King Hanasa and the Naua and Yashani generals.

"Pasha looked past himself to something greater. Such was not just his or the Sashraman way. But it has been the Hebari way ever since the beginning. May we never forget the great lesson his life has taught us."

Malik Juktan breathed in heavily when he had finished and stepped back as the shazhia came forward. The old man looked down upon the captain's body and bowed his head. All the people followed his action.

"Daiyu, lord of us all. You promised us you would forever be faithful to your people, and we can see the evidence of this in the warrior you sent to us, the man who lays before us this day. As we received him on earth, receive your warrior back into the bosom of your glory. The way is truth, and the way is life. May your people never stray from it. May we never be lost from your sight. *Amindei*."

Once the shazhia had finished his prayer, Abayomi stepped forward toward Pasha's body. "I guess we won't be old men together. It probably would not have suited you anyway. We will never forget, brother! May your example rule over us in the days to come." Abayomi looked out to his fellows in the crowd and drew his sword. With a loud voice, he shouted final words for his friend. "*Yana Haradi!*"

"*Yana Haradi!*" the men responded, lifting their swords and spears into the air.

Soon the cry was taken up by the Yashani, Naua, and Halor warriors as they drew their spears and swords to the chant of *Yana Haradi*, which is to say, "Rule this day!"

And so for hours the people circled about the body for a chance to lay their hands on the captain's heart, as was southern tradition after a death. Finally, Rakimo and the malik's guard came forward and draped the body in the banner of Sashra. They were about to lift the body to carry it off to be prepared for burial when they were stopped by Abayomi and many of Pasha's men.

"We will carry him," Abayomi said, looking Rakimo squarely in the eye.

The captain of the guard was tempted to become indignant at his challenge; nevertheless, he quelled any irritation because he understood. Malik Juktan's guard moved aside as Abayomi and others fell in to lift the litter.

Having no other choice since Sashraman rites required the body to be buried within seven days, a grave site was made within the slopes near the mountains to the north. In a small reed hut along the road leading into the mountains, Pasha's body was readied for burial.

Malik Juktan and his men passed Abayomi's men who stood guard and entered the hut. When the Sashraman king entered, he was surprised as he beheld a woman in orange robes with intricate braids, weeping over the captain's body.

Pasha's body had been washed seven more times and oiled, as was Sashraman custom. His sword was too valuable to be buried and had been removed to be passed on to his family. In its place, he clutched a short Sashraman spear.

Juktan came forward, ever curious about the woman that wept over him. She was very dark and lovely in spite of the sadness in her face.

"Maliki," said Abayomi as he bowed.

"Maliki," said the man who stood alongside him.

By his face and robes, the malik saw he was not Sashramans. Malik Juktan nodded in acknowledgment.

"And this is how it ends," said the malik.

"Yes, sire," said Abayomi.

The malik looked to the other man. "Who are you?"

"Sajal of the Yashani, Maliki. I am a physician."

"Did you know him?"

"I bandaged a few of the kaudi's wounds."

He looked back at Abayomi.

"And the woman?"

"She was precious to him."

Abayomi went forward and knelt beside her, placing his hand on her shoulder.

"I'll be outside," he whispered to her. "Excuse me, Maliki," he said as he moved past the malik.

Juktan watched as he went out trying to hide his tear-stained face.

"Is he ready?" he said to Sajal.

"Yes, he is ready. I'll leave you."

Sajal then turned to leave.

Juktan moved closer to the woman. Her weeping had paused as she kissed Pasha's face and whispered into his ear.

"What do you say to him?" he could not help asking.

"He left something with me. I'm letting him know what it is," she said, not turning her gaze from Pasha. The woman touched her stomach with both hands as she said this and then returned to caress his face.

"What is your name?" Malik Juktan asked.

"I am Mahlinya."

"What was he to you?"

"My protector, friend . . . lover. He was my husband, and I his wife. I carry the life that he left me. But now he shall not share in it."

She then spoke only to Pasha, still not looking back at the king. "You broke your promise. I was such a fool to listen to your sweet lies. But I'd play the fool for a lifetime just to hear them once more!" She buried her head into his chest as grief overwhelmed her.

Malik Juktan gazed upon her for a long moment, and in his heart he mourned with her.

Outside, the king and the rest of the men waited. Finally Sajal and Abayomi returned to lead Mahlinya out of the hut. The darkening skies told them they would have to bury him soon.

Just then a young boy appeared in the distance. As he approached, Juktan saw Pasha in his gait. The boy was dark like Pasha, but when he came closer, in his face the king saw the unmistakable trace of his mother, Hadassah.

He stopped a dozen paces from the warriors surrounding the hut.

Malik Juktan rushed toward him. The king stared at him almost in disbelief. He had the same skinny frame of his father at that age. His neck was slender, and his features smooth like his mother's. And his eyes were green globes of light as hers had been.

"Kamili?" he said.

"Is he in there?" asked the boy, looking straight ahead.

"It's really you," said the king, studying every part of him.

"Is he in there?" he said again more strongly.

"Yes. He is," said Mahlinya, coming closer.

Kamili looked straight at her and came forward as if drawn to her.

"I remember now. I remember everything."

"Good. Kamili. Good. He . . . he would have been happy to hear that," she said, smiling through her tears.

"But he never will. What am I supposed to do? He left me alone," he said as a tear streaked down his cheek.

Mahlinya wrapped her arms around him. Kamili fell into her embrace as his voice became muffled in sobs.

"He's gone, Kamili. But you are not alone, I promise you."

They slowly released from each other's embrace, and Kamili went to Abayomi. Abayomi placed both hands on the boy as he looked deep into his eyes.

"Your father was my friend. I shall watch over you as I did him. Do not fret. Your path is not lost. I will help you find it again."

The boy then turned back to Malik Juktan. "You are the malik of this land, but you called my father friend."

"Your father was unlike any other man. I was honored to call him so. I know you shall be every bit as great as he was."

"Kamili," Mahlinya called out to him.

"Yes," he said, turning toward her.

Mahlinya smiled as she held out her hand. "Come. He's waiting for you."

With that, Kamili took hold of her hand and went with her into the hut where his father lay.

So it was that peace came to Sashra for a time. Old men told stories of Kaudi Nuvahli, most of them fantastic lies, others the truth. And when warriors in Kadisha left the city to go to war, they touched his image along the Wall of Heroes so that his strength might live among them. His road had changed, his way had been constant, and his memory eternal.

. . . The End . . .

*In Loving Memory of Frances and Joseph
Chandler, and Haywood Cox Sr.*

Printed in the United States
By Bookmasters